Praise for If I Don't Have You

Sareeta Domingo's If I Don't Have You makes you fall in love with love all over again. A beautifully intricate tale of flawed, real people and the way they navigate the delicate avenues of the heart. I devoured this book. Pick it up and savour every word until the last delicious line.

—Dorothy Koomson
author of Tell Me Your Secret and
The Ice Cream Girls

Another extraordinary novel from one of the UK's leading romance writers, Sareeta Domingo. Filled with drama, suspense and of course, Domingo's now signature passionate page turning narrative. If I Don't Have You is sexy, raw, honest and intense. Once again Domingo gives us the revolutionary gift of exploring the life of a Black woman in love whilst being loved. Phenomenal.

—Melissa Cummings-Quarry,
Black Girls Book Club

If I Don't Have You

Sareeta Domingo

JACARANDA

TWENTY
in 2020

Black Writers, British Voices

This edition first published in Great Britain 2020
Jacaranda Books Art Music Ltd
27 Old Gloucester Street,
London WC1N 3AX
www.jacarandabooksartmusic.co.uk

A CIP catalogue record for this book is available from the British
Library

ISBN: 9781913090210
eISBN: 9781913090418

Cover Design: Rodney Dive
Typeset by: Kamillah Brandes

Printed and bound by CPI Group (UK) Ltd, Croydon, CR0 4YY

This book is dedicated to You. Hold tight to your dreams, embrace love when it comes to you, and never hesitate to look in the mirror and say you're proud of yourself.

"And indeed there will be time
To wonder, 'Do I dare?' and, 'Do I dare?'"

—T.S. Eliot, *The Love Song J. Alfred Prufrock*

𝓟rologue

(No Subject)
October 7 2016 6:13 AM (EDT)

To: **Ren Morgan** <ren@edenstreetproductions.com>
From: **Kayla Joseph** <kaykay@murdercreation.com>

You still won't answer your phone, so this is all I've got.

The thing I can't help thinking is—if this *was* real, if you really understood me or wanted to try, then you'd at least listen to me. You'd let me explain properly. Honestly, it really hurts me that you won't. So maybe you were wrong about this thing between us meaning anything at all.

I don't want to believe that.

You're hurt too, I understand that, but you said we'd have time and that's obviously not true either. Maybe regret is all we'll really have. Is it wrong to hope we'll share that, at least?

I didn't tell you the whole story because I didn't want this to end, and now it's way past that.
I know I've been calling all night, but I promise I'll leave

you alone now. It probably is better if we just draw a line under it all. You left without a goodbye and to be honest, I'm not sure if I'd be able to cope with you actually saying it.

I'm sorry, Ren.

X

Caution to the Wind

10th - 11th August 2016

One

Ren.

I've been staring into light so much today it's inevitable that darkness is starting to crowd the edges of my vision. The blaze of the sun outside has long since given way to hard slices of rain, pounding against the windows. I let my eyes crumple closed for a moment, sighing at the glare of orange behind my eyelids. I've been daydreaming about sleep for the last three hours. Night's beginning to fall and it feels like I've been in this hotel room half my lifetime, talking endlessly into camera lenses and without any real meaning.

Ione walks over to me, tossing her hair over one shoulder as she glances at her tablet with a burgundy-lipped smile, and that look in her eyes that's always there now—a certain knowing. She reaches over and squeezes my shoulder, kneading for a moment, then she releases. It did kind of feel good, but her smile says she's got me figured out: that she's certain I wouldn't be able to resist if she ever decided to stake a claim on me again. She's probably right, even if it would be less about sex than having a warm body next to me afterwards. I've only recently begun to admit I'm such a sap.

'How many more?' I ask.

'Almost done, just one more. And to be honest, she's some new online-print, so I can just blow her off if you want? I think she's already been in with Jeff and Elena.'

I shrug and tuck my hair behind my ears. It's in-between, getting long enough to brush my collar. I'm never sure which suits me better, short or long. I'll just let it grow until it's distracting. 'No, it's cool. What's one more, huh?'

'Spoken like a true pro. Hit all the angles—right, Mr Director?' She winks at me, making her false lashes flap like a crow's wing. I smile back even though I barely found the quip funny. Did she mean it seductively, an ego stroke? Or sarcasm? Hope not. 'Like I said, her site is pretty new, but it's consistently top ten amongst eighteen to thirties. All publicity is good publicity, and other clichés,' Ione adds. Striding around me, the points of her heels sinking into the deep pile of the carpet, she adjusts the poster on its easel behind me.

Good publicity? I'm not sure our leading man booking a stay in a holding cell really counts, but so far people seem to be buying the "man-flu" excuse the studio put out today. And there is, of course, that other story, which everyone wants to bring up with me even all these months down the line. God, if only it *was* just a story, not actual and painful and way too embarrassingly real. I torture myself with another flash of memory, but manage to push it away to the dull ache in the back of my mind. Later, when I'm alone again, I know it will all force its way back to the surface anyway.

'Just a words site, right? No filming?' I ask, and Ione nods, smirking a little at my phraseology probably. 'Then can we...?' I shield my eyes dramatically, and gesture to the lights and reflectors set up for the TV and YouTube channels, still casting their semi-flattering illumination on the tired crevices of my face, my three-day beard. If all the on-camera interviews are done then surely they can be switched off.

'Oh right, sure. Let me get, uh, was his name Pete? I'll be right back. Shall I send her in?'

I shrug again, but then draw in a long breath and straighten up in the armchair. 'Yup, send her in.'

Ione holds up two manicured fingers to indicate she'll be back shortly, then hustles out of the suite. I hear her voice in the hallway, fast and clipped, talking to the final journalist. Then there's a muffled knock, and the door slowly begins to open.

'Hello... Mr Morgan?'

A bare shoulder appears, smooth and deep brown as mahogany. A face follows—eyebrows arched and curious; wide eyes not only dark in colour but like they're holding a weight of intelligence; high, sharp cheekbones; lips full and expressive, only a fraction paler than that gorgeous skin which looks like it's lit from within.

Is this that sappy part of my brain again, or is she one of the most beautiful women I've ever seen?

She nudges the door the rest of the way open with her shoulder, and I see why—her hands are laden. A leather backpack hangs off the other shoulder, and she's clutching

17

a notepad, a cell phone and the strap of what looks like a Polaroid camera case in one hand, and an over-filled, half-eaten salmon and cream cheese bagel in the other. A bottle of the "artisanal" water the hotel insists on is clamped underneath one armpit. I should help her, but I've become immobile.

'Sorry, I, uh, I seem to have overburdened myself…' she murmurs, trying to look past the lighting set-up to see me. Her voice sounds like it's floating on a cushion of smoke, light but husky. I still sit, mute. She makes her way over to the skinny-legged designer chair set opposite me and dumps most of her stuff on the floor beside it. She exhales and flips back her tangle of long, skinny dreadlocks, licks her lips and wipes cautiously around her mouth with her free fingers. She puts the half-eaten bagel down in its napkin on a nearby side table, then she smoothes her hand slowly down her thigh, which is clad in tight black denim, before holding it out to me. I swallow.

'To murder and create,' she says, looking at me expectantly.

'What?'

'Kayla Joseph, To Murder and Create?' She sounds more hesitant now. 'Sorry, it's my website—did that publicity woman—?'

'Oh. Yes! I'm… I'm pathetically behind the times. I should know that. Have a seat, Kayla, good to meet you. I'm Ren Morgan.'

'Ren. Right.' She smiles slowly at me like I'd answered an

unasked question and shakes my hand, the myriad rings on her fingers clacking softly together. It's rare I feel the implied insecurity of not using my given name in everyday life, but what do you know? It's sneaking up on me now. As she sits down, the lights prevent me from being able to see her properly any more, and I frown at the door, hoping Ione finds the guy soon.

'Wow, those are seriously bright, aren't they?' she says, her voice disembodied now as she sits in the shadows. I think she sounds British?

'Yeah, someone's coming to deal with them. Can I get you— You already have some refreshments, I guess?' I laugh self-consciously, hearing myself sounding like a Grade A moron.

'Oh… Err, yeah I raided that snack table out there. Hope that's OK? I've been saving myself for all the free press junket food I've heard so much about.' There's a moment of silence as she opens the bottle of water and takes a long drink. She pulls the bottle away and wipes her mouth again. 'I particularly enjoyed the *Detonate* branded cupcakes. Pleasingly ironic.' Humour dances between her words, and a short chuckle slips from my throat.

'Makes them all the sweeter,' I retort, and she laughs too. Her laugh is as beautiful as she is. I can't help feeling emboldened. She's a reporter, though; I need to remember that.

We both turn toward the suite door as Ione busies back into the room with the Pete guy in tow. 'We can take all this down now, thank you. Just move it to the side while

19

Ren finishes up with, um…' She consults her tablet. 'Ms Joseph.' Ione scans Kayla, almost unnoticeably, and then her eyes flick over to me. 'I'll just hang back here.' She nods to the couch in one corner of the vast room, like I'd need notifying—it's been her perch all day. Babysitting, making sure they don't ask me things I don't want to hear. Making sure I stay on-brief too, I guess. I've let my feelings be known about the finished film in private strongly enough that maybe she's a little nervous of what might fall out of my mouth if she's not there to catch it. But I'd say mainly her announcement is for Kayla's benefit.

Kayla. Her name feels settled right into my mind already.

'Thanks, man,' I say, blinking as the lights click off and Pete clears them away with a nod. It's a relief, the heat of them disappearing like a blanket kicked off on a hot night. The radio on his waist crackles, and he excuses himself with a wave at Ione. I finally get a better view of the woman in front of me. Toned arms emerge from the loose-fitting white sleeveless shirt she's wearing, adorned with a black and white photograph of a sad looking man holding a cat. I think it's Jean-Michel Basquiat. There's all that smooth, glowing brown skin against her shirt's starkness, its neckline cut a little jaggedly like she took scissors to it, but it looks deliberate and artistic and… I think I'm staring. Jesus. I need this interview to get going before I wind up ceding any appearance of professionalism. Kayla's eyes flick up from her notebook like she read my mind.

'OK… Oh, let me just…' She taps at her phone until

a red "recording" button comes up on whatever app she's using. 'Attempt to be professional,' she finishes, the curve of her smile betraying a hint of fluster as she places her phone on the table between us and looks up at me. Getting any kind of reaction that implies attraction feels like a victory. 'So. Right. *Detonate*! Bit of a departure, isn't it?' she begins, and I shift in my seat. Somehow, I don't know why, but I thought her questions might be different. I'm projecting again, obviously. 'Not a typical João Ren Morgan film,' she concludes, raising her eyebrows slightly but still making it seem like a statement of fact.

I feel the words I've said a thousand times today begin to trip from my lips automatically. 'Well, it's definitely different from my first projects, but I think any versatile film-maker has to be ready to try something new, push themselves outside of their comfort—'

But I stop, because she gestures with her hand as if she'd intended to say something else before I interrupted. She looks down a little bashfully, then crosses one leg over the other. I notice her black ankle boots, tightly laced, with high, chunky heels. She's not tall, but the line of them makes her legs seem to stretch on endlessly.

'Who are we to say what's typical anyway, though?' she asks. 'Maybe they forced you into doing those first two. I mean, you could have been all "art-house, schmart-house, bring me the guns".' She smiles at me, a glimmering spirit of rebellion emanating from her. I lean forward in my chair, drawn to it. To her.

21

'Maybe you're right, maybe this is the real me,' I say, unable to hide my own amusement—but a thought echoes in my brain, just faintly. *A sell-out?* I remember Yann arguing against that back when he was my so-called friend and producing partner, telling me how I should try this type of picture, just once, like he knew something I didn't. I guess that was true, just not about the movie... I push the thought away and cock an eyebrow at her. 'Schmart-house?'

Kayla laughs self-consciously—endearingly—and messes with her notebook, running a fingernail up and down the ring binding like a washboard. 'No, but honestly, I thought it was just the right level of ludicrous,' she says. 'It was great. I mean, on its own merits. I really, *really* liked your first films, don't get me wrong—'

'Oh, so *you* were one of the five people that saw them? I thought someone was unaccounted for...'

'Yeah, that was me,' she replies with a grin. 'But what I mean is, sometimes you just want to blow the cobwebs away with a good old-fashioned, sexy fucking shoot 'em up, right? It was like you'd unlocked something, stylistically. In terms of content... I don't know. I thought the whole thing was actually quite a brave move.'

Huh. The smile hasn't left my face yet. It feels like using some dormant muscle. But I'm not totally sure if she's just being kind, or if she's trying to get something out of me. Could she really mean all that, or is this a journalism trick? Did I have any *real* intentions when I got behind the camera on this turkey, other than to cash a cheque and distance myself from the past? 'Brave,' I repeat. 'Yeah.'

'Sorry, I should probably ask something specific about the movie, shouldn't I? I'm not really… Um, press junket-au fait.'

'Junkets not your scene?'

She chuckles. 'Is there a scene? Maybe I'm not cool enough for it.' I highly doubt she's not cool enough for anything. She undoes the water bottle lid again, then redoes it absently without taking a drink. 'Actually, someone just proposed this in our features meeting and I drew the short straw.' She realises what she's said. 'I mean… Err, no offence…'

I smile again. 'Well, some taken.'

She looks at me and bites her lower lip. I stare at it, clamped for a split second under her row of even, white teeth. 'It's actually been quite fun,' she back-pedals. 'The snacks, the free movie—'

'That was just the right level of ludicrous,' I finish for her, faking a frown.

'I'm doing well here, aren't I? That really *was* a compliment, you know,' she says, and I feel bad. Disproportionately bad.

'Oh, yeah, totally. I think I might put it as a puff quote on the one-sheet here,' I tell her, gesturing to the top of the poster, above the garish image of Terrence Bolt's gun-toting general and the bullet-ridden graphic of the word "Detonate". I look back over at Kayla, focussing my most wry-charming grin on her and, thank God, it works. Her lips curve into another slow smile, its warmth washing over me again.

'I'm not sure my opinion will hold much sway with the cinema-going public,' she says. 'Anyway.' She glances down at her notes again. 'It's a bit random, but I did really want to ask you about the dog in the film. I thought it was quite interesting the way you didn't go the obvious route and use him to soften up... What was his name? Mr Bolt, in the movie?'

'General Hammer,' I mutter reluctantly, cringing at the reminder.

'Right.' She hides a tiny smirk. 'I'm slightly gutted I didn't get to speak to Terrence Bolt today actually, seeing as he was... indisposed.' She pauses, glancing over at Ione. Shit, do the press all know about the arrest? It's probably all over the blogs, but he must be out by now anyway. A bar fight is hardly going to test the gears of his PR machine. 'He would have been interesting to interview,' Kayla's saying. I sense irony. 'So, usually there'd be some aching bullshit with the hero rescuing the mutt to show that even though he's a hard-nut, he's, like, a sweet-natured loveable softie too, do you know what I mean?' She looks at me and clears her throat a little. 'But... you let the dog be a way for us to get to know Elena Wright's character instead, and we don't usually get to know the women in these movies, do we? They're normally just fodder or, I don't know, some *tits* to look at as far as most filmmakers are concerned. I mean, she does use her sexuality, but as a means of manipulation—there's a feminine power there, a rejection of the pure objectification that turns up in so many films. So... Was that a conscious decision?' Her eyes punctuate the end of her sentence, locking emphatically onto mine, eyebrows raised again, like she's kind of relieved she remembered to tack a question on to the end of her analysis. I attempt and fail to look away from her.

'Well, yeah. Her sexuality is only one facet of her character, but it's a powerful one. A weapon's only really useful if you know how to use it, right?' I'm only looking in Kayla's eyes, but I'm very aware of her body. Of my own. She rubs her bottom lip briefly with one long, elegant finger and it's my turn to clear my throat. 'And yeah, her interaction with the dog was useful for broadening her character out a little for the audience. I guess the dog's actually kind of a substitute for me,' I say, before I have a chance to think it through. I can feel Ione concentrating on the back of my head, willing me to stay on-topic.

'The dog is you?' Kayla repeats, squinting a little at me like she's analysing how serious I am.

'Well, he's a mongrel, like I am. And I like to get to know women— People, I mean.' *Shit.* I run my hand through my hair, pulling it back behind my ears again, feeling the tips of them heat.

'You're a *dog* who likes to *get to know* women,' she summarises slowly, and I think I've definitely fucked up, until I hear that teasing back in her tone.

'Play me at my own pedantry. OK, I deserve it.'

Kayla chuckles and shakes her head, her dreadlocks shuffling around those beautiful bare shoulders. 'No, sorry. That's… That's bad interview etiquette on my part. Go on.

I really want to know this.' She looks up through dense eyelashes, expectant and inquisitive.

'What I mean is, the dog was a conduit, I guess, like I am as a director. He's a way in to her character for us, a way for her to verbalise what it's like to find herself in this crazy situation. You know, to at least bring a subtler human element to the story somewhere. Ironically. Since he's, you know—'

'A dog,' Kayla finishes, smiling a little, but nodding. She uncrosses her legs and leans her forearms lightly on her thighs, moving closer to me. 'I really like that, though. That idea of finding the humanity, I mean.'

I breathe in faint wisps of her warm amber scent, blinking quickly so as not to miss too much of the interrogation her eyes are still giving mine. Should I have told her that? It's weirdly personal. I didn't even explain it to Tommy, when he was confused about why I was so adamant that I wanted to keep that mutt in during the edit. Not that I got my way on much of the final cut once the studio got involved.

'So you say you're a mongrel?'

I shrug. 'Well, my mom's Brazilian, and she has some Chinese-Brazilian thrown in there for good measure on her dad's side. I'm named for my great-grandfather, Renshu. And, uh, my father's African-American.' The tension creeps into my jaw a little again, and I clench my teeth. Why am I even bringing them up? This woman is a magician. 'Racial ambiguity on lock, I guess.'

Kayla chuckles. 'Yeah. Turns out that's a good combination.' She seems to catch herself, and scans her notes intently for a moment. 'Um… I sort of reckoned you might have some mixed heritage from your name, obviously.'

I wait until she looks up at me again. I'm greedy for those eyes. 'Yeah, it's a bit of a hotchpotch. Ren's easier to go by. I just keep the João up front for work because three names sounded director-ly.' I laugh, but it's true. 'I was impressed with your pronunciation, though.'

She breaks into another wide smile. I feel rich off them. 'I Googled it,' she confesses.

'What else came up under my name?' I ask, challenging her, and her face settles into something more serious and equally as enchanting. I want it out in the open, whatever else she wants to ask. About Yann, Eve, the whole mess. I can feel it coming in most interviews, and for some reason I want to head this one off at the pass, even though right now, more than in any other interview, I don't want to think about any of that, feel any of it.

Kayla's eyes connect with mine again. 'That you ended a relationship with a collaborator,' she says quietly. 'A friend.' We stay looking at one another for a long moment, silent, until I hear Ione clear her throat.

'We should probably be wrapping things up here, Ren,' she says. 'Your car's due in ten.'

'I'm good for a few more questions,' I say, too quickly, still watching Kayla.

'One more,' Ione counters.

Kayla bites her lip again, and I feel a jolt low in my gut when she catches me looking at it.

'Gosh, pressure. One more question,' she says, with a trace of sarcasm. 'Actually, if you're short on time, is there any way I could take a couple of pictures instead? I'm doing a project with my trusty old Polaroid camera here.'

I feel Ione stand and loom behind us. 'Is it for the site?' she asks dubiously. I cut my eyes toward her.

'To be honest, it's a personal project at the moment,' Kayla says, 'but it probably would be included on M&C, yeah. I try and squeeze in the full spectrum of my, uh, creativity—if I can, that is.' Her tone is self-deprecating, but with an undertow of determination. 'And we'll probably need a picture for the article, so I'm sure I can tie it in. Actually, if it helps, I think I have a…'

She tails off and rummages in her backpack, pulling something out. She leans over to wave the flyer under Ione's nose, then moves it toward my outstretched hand, and I take it from her. The flyer features a stunning, semi-abstract black-and-white sketch of a young girl, and Kayla's name in bold print underneath it. An exhibition, here in New York? 'I think I know this gallery,' I say, unable to hide the impressed note in my voice. 'You showed there?' The date was a few weeks ago. Regret sinks in my stomach, even though I'm leaving the city tonight so it wouldn't have mattered. Another reason I hate living in L.A. now.

Kayla nods. 'It was only small to be fair, and it wasn't a solo—there were a couple of other artists. It was the first thing I did since my post-grad exhibit, but… Well, it was cool to show, anyway.' Her eyes dim a little momentarily.

'Sorry I missed it,' I tell her. 'I feel like I'm lacking strings to my bow—you've got artist, journalist, photographer…?'

She *pshhes* and arches an eyebrow. 'I reckon I've got a way to go to get to all this,' she says, gesturing in the air around me and the suite, then shrugs. 'I mean, I've always tried to work in different media and stuff, but it's a bit of a juggle doing the visual art, and getting the site absolutely right…' She frowns. 'It's just a question of making the time,' she adds, almost talking to herself, and then seems to remember her train of thought, nodding down at her camera. 'Anyway, it's more just that someone was giving this away a while ago, and I couldn't resist it. Thought I'd give myself a new little side project.'

I get the feeling she's being modest. 'Really.' There's not even a question in my voice.

'Um, yeah, because I'm a masochist, apparently.' She smiles, and I can see ambition radiating off her. I want to soak it in. 'Photography's actually quite new for me, and I suppose I'm a bit of a fake with this camera and everything—' she holds the case between her hands reverently '—but I like the instant nature of it. And I'm customising the Polaroids afterwards so that—' She glances over at Ione, who is obviously making her impatience clear. 'Well, it's a bit long-winded, but yeah, hopefully it's going to be portrait studies for a book. I mean, it's not sold yet, but I showed a friend of mine some ideas, and he's interested in putting it out. He has an independent press. Just a little one,' she adds quickly when I clearly look even more impressed. 'The idea is, when

I can, I get my subjects to answer six set questions that I've devised to go alongside their pictures.'

I can tell she's really invested in this. The suppressed excitement in her voice sounds distantly familiar. I used to hear it in my own. 'Set questions?' I ask, too eager, but I'm intrigued. I've long ago given up any conscious attempt at flirting.

'Mmhmm.' She glances away, and I realize I'm staring again. 'As in, the same six. Don't get me wrong, I'm no Proust or anything. I'm just... really into questionnaires. You naturally anticipate the other person's answer, and you're immediately thinking about your own. But I think actually hearing someone else's response helps you understand more about them *and* yourself,' she says softly, then takes a breath. 'That probably doesn't make much sense, and I'm sure you're finding the whole idea ironic, given my apparent lack of ability as an interviewer. I usually just do reviews, op-ed columns, that sort of thing.'

My eyebrows flatten into a real frown. 'You're not bad at all,' I say, my voice lowered too. 'Uh, what are they? The six questions?'

Ione coughs again pointedly, and Kayla opens her camera case in response. She pops open the camera so that the flash is ready, and waits for it to charge up. I can't stop my grin— the sound is so reminiscent of a moment of my childhood, of some forgotten feeling of genuinely oblivious happiness. Before I'm ready, the bulb pops and the film whirrs and spits out its picture, taking me by surprise. Kayla extracts it, pleased with herself.

'Sorry,' she says, unapologetically. She stands and moves around me, finding an angle. 'They are…' She pauses. 'Don't answer though—we don't have enough time.'

My gut clenches at her words, because they're way too true. Kayla exhales a little. Maybe she feels it as well.

'They are: Do your dreams feel real?' Another flash. 'What is it you most admire about the person you admire most?' She pulls out the picture and rests it face-down on the table next to the other. She moves closer, reaching out a hand towards me, but I stupidly notice it's because my collar's sticking up and fix it myself before she gets a chance to touch me. But… then she re-adjusts it anyway, the very edge of her thumb grazing my jawline as she does. I cease to breathe just for an instant as her eyes examine mine closely. She pulls back and looks into the viewfinder, leaning down, and I can see her chest rise and fall in the dark space that opens at the neck of her shirt, beyond a tangle of thin gold necklaces. 'How often do you look up?' she says suddenly. I stifle a red-handed smile as I cast my eyes heavenward quickly, and she snaps another shot. Whirr. Spit.

She smirks faintly and straightens up, gesturing for me to stand as well. Ione hovers by the suite door, tapping rapidly into her phone and watching us. Now that I'm standing, I really feel how small Kayla is—but strong. Petite and soft, but solid somehow… She tilts her face up toward mine, and takes a slow step backwards. Then she holds up a finger, and I immediately still. Kayla nods. It feels weird to be on the

31

receiving end of directions for once, but I think I like it. 'Why is that song your favourite?' She looks into the view-finder. *Flash.* 'When did you last get goose bumps?' She pulls her gaze up for a moment to let it linger directly on me. The picture hangs out of the front of the camera. She eventually pulls it out and rests it beside the others to develop.

Her voice drops lower. 'And…' I turn and face her, looking right down the lens as she bends to check the framing through the finder. Then she raises her head and looks straight at me again, and my eyes follow. Her finger hits the button and the flash goes off one last time. 'And… Why do we create?' Whirr. Spit. Pull.

She exhales loudly, and goes over to examine the first pictures as they slowly start to reveal their secrets. She nods again, satisfied. I don't even want to look at them. I'm scared of what they show on my face.

'Thank you,' she says to me, her voice almost a whisper now.

I take a step toward her, not sure what to say. "You're welcome" doesn't seem right.

'Ren, it's here. The car,' Ione says, looking over at me expectantly.

I hold out my hand, and Kayla slips hers into it. I tighten my grip, and she regards me with an expression I can't describe, but that makes me want to throw away my plans and stay right where I am.

But instead, I simply say: 'It was great to meet you.'

Two

Kayla.

I gaze out of the window for a while as the cab inches forwards onto the Williamsburg Bridge, watching the occasional cyclist whip past us on their way up onto their own path, battling the wind. The driving rain doesn't even seem to bother them, and I almost envy it. It's too clammy everywhere at the moment, even with the air-con valiantly trying to crisp the air inside the car. I pull at my seatbelt, shifting around in the back seat trying to catch a better angle on it. Thunder rumbles resolutely in the distance, and I'm anxious, uncomfortable, like I forgot something back at the Vincent Hotel.

Ren Morgan keeps drifting back into my mind.

Yeah, I already loved his films and I massively admire what he's achieved so far as a filmmaker. And yeah, I knew he was attractive; I'd seen pictures, I'm not blind. But that actual experience was something else entirely. *He* was something else entirely. The acute awareness of him I felt in his presence has stayed with me, and it's unsettling and exciting and... Guilt grinds me to a halt. How am I already having thoughts that could derail this whole plan with Cole? Or at the very least make it even more awkward. Maybe it's just because I'm leaving the city tonight and I don't really want to be.

I don't have much choice, though, and every day takes Cole and me further down the line to really committing to it all. *To each other.* I close my eyes, trying to not to let a bubble of panic rise up as my fingers twist Cole's engagement ring—a vintage, ornately moulded black-diamond studded gold band, so painfully, perfectly to my taste—around my finger. It sits next to all my other rings, blending in but standing out. Given the way my so-called love life has panned out so far, it's only today that it even occurred to me that there could be another reason why being engaged—getting *married*—like this might be a bad idea.

What if I meet someone else?

Because my thoughts are still stuck hard on Ren. But it's fine—thoughts aren't reality, and there's pretty much zero chance I'll be anywhere near him again anyway. Why is that so disappointing? I don't get *crushes*, if that's what this even is?

God knows it would be so much more unambiguous if I actually had deeper feelings for Cole, but friendship is all I feel, as special as that is. Except now, of course, here I am getting random pants-feels and palpitations for a virtual bloody stranger. And on a work assignment, no less—one that Cole proposed and I got handed. The universe is truly a joker.

But...

I wish I'd asked Ren more. Maybe I should have asked if I could email him or something? No. But I'd love to have known his answers to the Questions. Honestly, I'd love to know just about *anything* more about him. Well, more than what it says on the internet. And let's face it, the dedicated Tumblr pages full of thirst over his dark, dishevelled-male-model good looks are now embarrassingly bookmarked in my phone's browser. I scroll through the images, feeling like I already know him. I can conjure up in my memory the way he juggled his words with his hands, his long, slim fingers, his skin the colour of sand where it meets the sea. The way he listened. His faint undercurrent of melancholy…

Ugh. I lock my phone screen and stifle a self-berating groan in my throat so that the cab driver doesn't think I'm a lunatic, but I look down at the Polaroids again, shuffling through all of them. That first one, unguarded. The last one, when Ren's eyes were fixed on mine. I stare at that one a bit too long. I want to start working on them already. Maybe on the plane? I make a mental note to check that my pencils and pad are in my hand luggage, then I glance at my phone again as another alert comes through. *Possible flight delays.* I reckon at this point they're being ambitious to say "possible", but I'll head to the airport anyway. I want to get going so I can be done, start the journey towards that elusive Green Card and—

I startle as my phone begins to vibrate in my hand, emitting pulses of electronic beeps. It's my mother. Since discovering the ability to ring me over the internet, my previous excuses to minimise family communication while I'm over here have been thwarted.

'Hiya, sweetheart.'

I prepare myself. 'Hi, Mum.' I'd ask why she's up, but one in the morning is hardly late for her and my Dad—they're both night people, so this is their witching hour.

'Kay, listen, have you heard all this about the storm over there?'

I look out of the window at the water lashing sideways against the glass. 'I have heard, yes.' I roll my eyes, and then I'm glad she can't see me. 'It'll be fine, don't worry.'

'Well, I hope your flight will be all right? And I still don't know why you won't just come and stay at the house, you know.'

I sigh. 'It will just be too hectic over there, Mum. Sami's got a massive flat and a whole spare room, she's only a couple of stops away from you guys on the bus.'

I hear her clattering a spoon against the side of a saucepan, even though my grandma would tell her that was bad luck. I can picture Mum right now: tall and slim and gorgeous even in a house dress, head wrap and slippers. She was near enough an actual, legit supermodel back in the day before she switched tracks. A make-up artist who doesn't need a lick of make-up—it still baffles me how her clients aren't galled.

I also know Mum will be stirring at least three pots' worth of food in their cramped kitchen, filling the freezer to the gills in catering pre-prep, because there's another reason I need to head home, regardless of all the visa stuff. My mum and dad would never forgive me if I missed their 30th anniversary and renewal-of-vows next week. They'd made a promise to recommit to each other every ten years. They don't even know yet that I'll be taking vows of my own soon, without anything approaching that level of romance.

I hear Mum *mmhmmm* in the merest of concessions to my argument. 'So you're gonna rent with this Sami 'til you find something?'

Shit shit shit. I've been avoiding this conversation at all costs, and now is definitely not the time. They're all expecting me to restart my life at home now that my one year of visa grace after finishing at Columbia is coming to an end, not to be planning "I dos" back across the pond. My mother hints at my 'settling down' practically every time we speak now. I'm surprised she hasn't—

'…time to settle down, you know, Kay? Maybe a place of your own might be better, anyway. I told you, if you can get that PGCE sorted, you could…' I tune out again. Spoke too soon. *Teaching art is still creative…* Ugh. I get it. I do. My parents chose to pursue art for their livelihoods, and they've been lucky to scrape by. They know how rough this path is. But I'm not going to give up on what feels right.

Bloody hell, though—I'll only have ninety days from getting my new Visa to re-enter the US and marry Cole, or it's all for nothing. In fact, our immigration guy says it's best to do it within a month. The very thought makes me swallow tightly. *Jesus. Am I really going to go through with this?* But it genuinely is my only option if I want to stay in the States—believe me, I've explored them all. Can't do another degree to stay as a student—don't earn enough, or have enough independent wealth, to get another type of Visa—and I can't find a job good enough to get me perma-nent status, especially if I want to keep building the website business with Cole...

'Listen, Mum, I'd better go, OK? We'll talk about it later. I'll let you know when my flight gets in. They said it might be a bit delayed coz of the weather, but you should be able to just keep an eye on it online or whatever.'

'All right, sweetheart. Well, fly safe, yeah?'

'Thanks, Mum. See you soon, all right?'

'All right, darling. Love you.'

I end the call, more guilt piling on me, but I know I'm almost touching it—the missing part, the missing piece of my puzzle. I can't let go of it now that I'm so close to achieving it. My eyes drift down to the pictures of Ren Morgan held between my fingers. Is *his* success part of why I find him so attractive? Probably. Not that he'd need any additional help in that department...

'Wooah,' the cab driver says suddenly, his voice riding out on an anxious laugh. 'You see that?'

'Yeah!' I reply, even though I'd only vaguely perceived the flash of lightning as my gaze lingered on Ren. He has such a fascinating face: that soft, wide mouth with ten different smiles, those deep brown eyes that are sort of innocent-looking, but the wrinkle between his brows offsets them, like he's constantly trying to work something out.

And there's those tired bags under his eyes, and the dark, wispy scruff of a beard that I wanted to feel tickle against my cheek… Or inside my thigh…

Christ. *Calm down, Kayla. This is just jitters. Right?*

Another huge burst of lightning finally does distract me, and I turn back to my phone, checking the driver's name next to his picture on the app. Mustafa. If we're going to be electrocuted, I should at least know whom I'm going to die with. The idea of attempting to get another cab to JFK makes me want to stab myself in the eye. It took twenty minutes and an insane price surge to get this one. I think for a moment. Fuck it, it's going to cost a bomb anyway.

'Listen, I actually just need to grab some luggage and then I'm heading straight out to the airport. Is it OK if when we get to my building, I nip in to get it and you just hover outside for a minute? I mean, you can complete this job or whatever, and then I'll just re-book straight away on here?' I hold up my phone and look at the cabbie hopefully via the rear-view mirror. Mustafa seems a bit dubious, like he'd rather just call it a day and head home, but he shrugs.

'Yah. OK, OK,' he says, then smiles a little. 'Where you flying?'

'Oh… London.'

I see the back of his head move up and down. 'Ah, yes. London is good. My cousin lives there. Very nice.'

'Best city in the world,' I reply with a grin.

It's true, but I'm still anxious to be leaving just as New York is finally starting to feel like my home. I mean, it's *not* the same as London—it never will be—but after all this time and effort it really feels right. I suppose it better had.

The idea of some breathing room between Cole and me is a relief, though. In the last few weeks we've had a weird adjustment period where we have to get used to this new thing we are to one another. The word *fiancé* still freaks me out, and I haven't had the guts to change my online status, especially not before I've had a chance to explain it to my family. We've decided to keep the engagement quiet until I have. Then it'll all have to get a bit more public, to help with the "authenticity" element of this whole escapade…

Mustafa glances at me in the rear-view, and I give him a stiff, guilty smile before looking down at my phone again. Shit, is that the time? I should probably message Cole, I'm running later than I thought. He wanted to hang back at the flat to say goodbye.

Goodbye. It hits me again how mental it is that I'm leaving—leaving all my mates here, Cole, my work, our poky little *M&C* offices. That I'm stepping off the path I've set myself. Even if it's only for a moment, it makes me anxious.

I sigh and tap out a quick message to Cole.

KAYLA:
Traffic's a madness, sorry. Hope I'll catch u x

I hit send and peer ahead into the driving rain, a general anxiety hovering over me like a cloud.

'You have family there?' Mustafa asks, and I nod at him as he glances at me again in the rear-view.

'Hmm? Oh. Yeah. My parents...' I sigh. 'And my sister.' Christy.

My heart feels like it's sliding down into my stomach at the idea of how *she'll* take the news about Cole and me when she eventually finds out what we're planning to do. I bet she's dying to pull out her old favourite Big Sister words: *I told you so*. All primed for me to be back in London with my wannabe-artist tail between my legs. I don't know though; she'd have an inkling that I'd do whatever it takes to pursue this, because she would have done, too—only she never had to try so hard. Her final-year show at Central St Martins was stupidly well received, the list of ateliers lining up to hire her practically made me choke, and she was all set to move to Milan. Things only screeched to a halt because of her dickhead ex–boyfriend, and a tough decision or two later she's now just a few short weeks away from single motherhood. Her career is on hold.

And what did I do? Gloated, like the idiot I am. Made cheap shots about her getting up the duff—a reaction to the jealousy I'd always felt for her. Last time I was home, we were bitching back and forth. I didn't hold back, and Christy didn't either: her barbs were sharper than the pine needles on the Christmas tree. I can still hear her rounding off with, *'You're spoilt, your goals are... well, spurious at best,'*—she's always with the big words, and—*'You need to face facts and consider if you really have what it takes to be a* successful *artist.'*

The way she emphasised that penultimate word stung most of all. Of course, as far as my parents are concerned, the sun continues to radiate from my sister's arse. The irony of her thinking *I'm* the spoiled baby of the family...

It's going to be fucking weird to see her eight months pregnant. I honestly can't believe she's going through all this and we're not really even speaking. Well, it's her choice. Mainly.

Wow, my good Ren-Morgan-induced mood is well and truly gone. Serves me right I suppose.

'Ah hah,' Mustafa says, then mutters something under his breath, looking relieved as we finally pull off the bridge and he can follow his sat-nav towards the apartment. I tap at my phone quickly as he pulls up.

'Cool, all done. I'll just be five minutes.' Maybe I've missed Cole, I never got a message back. Is it awful to think maybe it's easier if I have? But the idea of not seeing him before I go feels so wrong at the same time. *Not complicated* is starting to seem like a bit of a pipe dream.

I rush up to the apartment, then jump as the door opens on me as I'm slipping the key into the door.

'Oh shit, Kay. You made it!' Cole exclaims, exhaling as he takes a step back. I scoot past him as he lets the door drift shut again. 'I was worried I'd miss you.'

'I know, sorry—the traffic's a bloody nightmare. I messaged you.'

He looks at his phone, and I try to ignore the picture of me on his screen saver. *It's all just part of the plan, right?* 'My bad,' he says. 'I didn't see it. You gonna be able to get a cab in this weather?'

I nod rapidly, dropping my sodden leather backpack by the door. 'Yeah it's cool, I've got one waiting. I'd better get a move on.'

'Yeah, yeah.' He eyes me with an expression that I know means he's feeling awkward too but he's trying to mask it. 'I should hustle if I'm gonna get to this book launch anyhow.'

'Are you walking? I'm surprised it's still on, to be honest.'

'You kidding me? Rain won't stop these Brooklynite verse fiends.' We both chuckle, and it feels a bit better. 'My buddy's been trying to convince me this chick is the new Claudia Rankine or whatever anyway, so I guess I better check it out for the site.'

'Yeah, so I hear,' I call from down the hallway, grabbing the last of my stuff from the bathroom and then pulling my suitcase over to the door, careful to avoid some of my work that I had framed, still leaning against the walls because I haven't had time to hang it. More of it is pressed flat in large black portfolios in one corner. I'm leaving so much work behind. What if this all falls apart and I never get to come back and finish it all? I suddenly feel a sinking sense of being untethered and in limbo.

'You want some help with your bags?' Cole asks gently, and I nod gratefully. He takes the handle of my case, but as he does, I wordlessly reach up and give him a hug, wanting to do it while we're not out in the deluge. He wraps his free arm around me.

'It'll be all right, Kay,' he murmurs knowingly. 'We got this.'

I pull back and nod once, resolutely, hoping he's right.

God. This shouldn't be awkward. The handful of years we've shared had felt like a lifetime up until now; the moment I met Cole on the first day at Graduate Studio, me fresh off the plane, him fresh off the subway from Jamaica, Queens, our friendship was instant. We just understood each other—our ideas, the way each other's mind worked. We felt like kindred semi-outsider spirits. We'd been on-off room-mates for the better part of the last two years as leases and partners (on his part) came and went, so when he asked me to meet him at the Highline at dusk that Sunday a couple of months ago, I was only a little bit puzzled. I could feel the energy fizzling off him, the way he gets when he's had *the best idea* in the world. And to be honest, I was already primed and vulnerable. If I never again heard the words "visa cap" or "overstay" or any combination of letter-and-number that could be the key to letting me live this life I've only just started, I would have been forever grateful.

Cole's afro was freshly lined up, and he had on a dark green button-down shirt rather than his usual expensively minimal t-shirt—that should have been my first tip-off. There was fine sheen of sweat on the skin of his forehead that I realise in hindsight was more to do with nerves than the late-Spring warmth. He'd handed me a stout, cold glass bottle of Martinelli's apple juice as soon as I sat down at the huge observation window looking out over 10th Avenue. 'Kay, you know what this is?' I took a sip and as I suspected, he'd put a nip of dark rum in it. His favourite covert concoction.

I chuckled. 'It's your "beverage", Cole.'

'It's our *future*. It starts right now. You belong here in New York, and I can help you stay. It's simple.' He'd clinked his bottle with mine, followed by a long sip.

I can't say it hadn't occurred to me that it could *maybe possibly* be a way out as an absolute last resort, but it just seemed so far-fetched. I was still half-dreaming that there'd be some other miracle cure for my Visa crisis. I was not prepared for Cole to put down his drink and sink down onto one knee then and there.

'*Marry me*, Kayla. We need you. The website, the city, all of us.' He'd looked up at me with so much love and vulnerability in his eyes, it shot right to my heart. 'We need you to stay. *I* need you stay. You're... you're my homie, you know? My best friend. And I really... More than anything, I don't want to stop everything we've started. I can't do the website without you, make it what it needs to be. This is it, Kayla, *this is the idea*, I can feel it. We can't let it go. We can't let *you* go. It would be my honour to help you stay.' Then he'd reached into his back pocket and *actually pulled out that box*, the snap of its catch making me jump as a I stared down at him, struck dumb, the condensation from the Martinelli's bottle threatening to make it slip from my hand.

'Oh my God!' But it hadn't come from my mouth. A late-middle-aged woman with a frazzled blonde dye job and an all-denim ensemble had paused near us, hand over mouth. 'You guys want me to take a picture? Oh my God, that's so *adorable!*'

Cole was already pulling his phone out from his other pocket and nodding, grinning up at me. 'Capture the moment, huh?' he murmured. 'We've got to make it look real if this is all gonna work. Might as well start now.' His eyes seemed to see it as kind of real already.

That's what worried me, just a bit; the way he'd made it so full of meaning, romantic almost. The Highline was our spot. It was where we'd usually go to bitch and tourist-watch and throw out ideas. Where I'd listen to Cole complain about the latest undergrad girl he'd dumped, inevitably while the sheets were still warm. Where I'd sound out my dilemmas about paying for art materials, or jealously dissect the last novel I read, or recount my most recent bad date. It had been right at that very spot we'd first decided on the idea for *To Murder and Create* a year and a half earlier, and it still blows my mind how far it's come. So I pretended not to remember those nights when a group of us would all have been out and had two or three too many, when I'd rest my head on Cole's shoulder absently, and he'd mumble something subtle—something I could brush aside… *"It's you, Kay. None of those other ones matter."*

I said Yes. Just like that.

So here we are.

We lock up the apartment and head downstairs, where Mustafa is happily reading a newspaper while my cab ticks up in cost. Cole and I dash over and chuck my stuff in the

Prius' boot, battling the gales.

'Let me know when you land, OK?' he shouts quickly over the wind. He wants to get out of this gathering storm, and I don't blame him.

'I will. I'll see you in a few weeks.' I feel my jaw tighten.

Cole looks at me for a moment, bouncing on the balls of his feet. 'Yeah.' He stills, picking up my left hand and looking at the ring on my finger. 'Then it's *on*, Mrs Bennett,' he says with a grin.

'Fuck off.' I snatch my hand away with a tight laugh as the nerves churn in my stomach. 'Listen, don't mess up the site without me.'

'Hah. You'll be kicking my ass on Skype and FaceTime every second.'

'Damn right.'

We look at one another a second more before Cole leans down and pecks my cheek then straightens up, salutes, and turns to jog off down the street in the opposite direction, flipping up his hood and jamming his hands into his pockets. He knows I can't deal with anything too drawn-out and emotional.

I jump into the cab and watch my friend recede through the rain-drenched window, wondering if we're going to make it to the other side of this thing.

Well—there's only one way to find out.

*

The traffic is starting to gridlock as the storm gets worse, and I get a bit obsessive checking the airline's app on my phone as we edge our way to the airport. So far, flights seem to be taking off though. As Mustafa peels away from the kerb after dropping me at JFK, I dash to the check-in with my over-stuffed case and feel the usual anxiety as I haul it onto the scale.

'Just so you know, ma'am, flights are starting to be delayed due to the extreme weather, and there is currently a three hour delay on this one, so you'll need to go ahead and keep checking the departure boards for more details as they become available,' says the desk clerk, too-perkily. Great.

I'm suddenly feeling exhausted. Getting up early to finish packing this morning before the screening and junket has taken it out of me, and I remember that I never finished my bagel. A couple of branded cupcakes are all I managed other than that, so I might as well round things off with a burger. After I make it through security, I reassemble all my shit—my appearance always seems to single me out for special treat-ment—and head to the nearest fast food outlet. I order and then find a seat at an awkward side counter, clamping my bag under one foot in the crowded restaurant and irritably eyeing a group of ketchup-smeared kids darting between the tables. I only manage a few bites of the dry burger and linger over the fries, thinking about this afternoon again. I grab my phone and plug in my headphones, vaguely considering starting to put together the *Detonate* junket piece for the website while it's fresh, get it over and done with. I hate hearing myself speak, but listening back the interviews with Jeff Ford and Elena Wright aren't bad, and I'm pleased that I also got a couple of great pictures of her as well as her answers to the Questions. I pull out my notepad and jot down some half-hearted notes, but I put down my pen after a while and scroll past Jeff and Elena, unable to delay it any longer.

I want to hear Ren's voice.

It's strange, listening back to our conversation; like hearing fresh memories replayed to me. Even though it was only a few hours ago, my whole body responds to hearing his deep, soft voice again in my ears. It's as if I become more aware of myself, just like I felt in that room with him. Or perhaps just more *myself*. Connected.

Even though this is where I've decided to stay, I do often feel a step removed here in the States. My history isn't what people immediately assume. I open my mouth and they're confused. That's probably what I like about being here too, though; subverting expectations. That's one of the reasons why I found *The Balancing Act*, Ren's first film, so affecting—it seemed like he understood that strange interplay between wanting to connect with people and completely rejecting conformity. *I wish I'd told him that...*

Then again, since his work's changed so dramatically now, could be just as well that I didn't. I'm guessing what happened earlier this year might have something to do with it... I stop my recording and open up the video I've book-marked on my phone, re-watching the clip. It was endlessly recycled on the blogs at the time, and while it wasn't quite

Bey, Jay and Solange on an elevator, for a minute there it was certainly the punch that rang round the industry. Yannick Roy, Ren's producer on both his first films, is sitting there with him and the cast at a press conference for *Touch/Taste*, Ren's sophomore feature. One second they're all calmly fielding questions—even if, admittedly, Ren is conspicuously monosyllabic—and the next he's launching himself at Yannick, laying into him until the others manage to pull him off. Rumour is that Yannick had just told Ren he was shagging his girlfriend. The whole thing doesn't seem like something the man I met would do, but watching it again, all I can focus on are the tears balanced in Ren's eyes. The hurt...

I close the screen.

Jesus. I thought *my* life was complicated. The reasons for the change in the films Ren's making now are probably very personal. I'm amazed he could go straight into another project at all. If that happened to me, I doubt I'd be able to make any kind of art, or get on with any work. The thing is I *can't* actually imagine anything like that ever happening to me. I've never been caught up in anything near that emotional or overwhelming.

I'm almost jealous that he has.

I'm too ready with my opinions most of the time anyway. I can't help wondering what Ren really made of me. Just another nosy journalist, with a pretentious photography shtick to boot? I exhale, dropping a cold French fry back on the pile. Looking at them removes the last of my appetite. I genuinely want to know the answer, but I don't see how I will. It's like an itch I can't scratch.

I take a few quick gulps of my Coke, then clear my tray and abandon my seat to the next traveller, heading to the loos to wash my hands and splash a bit of water on my face. The last thing I need is to miss my flight departure time because I've fallen asleep. Despite the oppressive air outside, I'm starting to feel a chill, so I pull the embroidered black denim jacket out of my carry-on and slip into it, tensing my jaw when I catch a glimpse of myself in the mirror. Christy got it for me at some vintage place years ago, saying it was just so "me" she couldn't resist. She was right, of course, but that was then. Back when.

I head out of the Ladies and check the departure boards just as my flight time ticks on another hour. Some of the other flights are already starting to show CANCELLED in final, block letters next to their destinations. I look around at the dejected people slumped in plastic chairs, and decide I'd better hunker down for a long night. I actually don't mind— there's something about airports that makes me feel oddly secure.

The only thing that's missing is that comforting feeling of heading home. I just hope my family will understand why I'm doing this whole marriage thing. I wish I could think my way out of my doubts, the way I can convince myself about most things. Up to now I've been right, but suddenly I'm starting to question everything and it's driving me mad.

I distract myself by scanning the seating area for somewhere to plot, and I spot a free chair amongst a few stretched-out student types in a prime position near a charging outlet—but first I'd better get some supplies in. Coffee and shit gossip rags, maybe some gum… The line at the nearest coffee shop is mental, so I start with the magazines. I head into the newsagent and pick up all the most cringe-worthy titles, and then go to browse the art, fashion and film section. The selection is extensive, but my eyes immediately fall on a name on the matte cover of one chunky art-house cinema tome. *João Ren Morgan*. I pick it up hastily and scan the line underneath, feeling a jolt of unexpected anger: "Has Cinema Lost Another Auteur to the Hauteur of the Dollar?"

'They really know how to hurt a guy's feelings, don't they?' I hear a deep voice say, and the frown is still on my face as I whip around. *Oh. My. God.* I look at him, then past him, to either side, as if I might be seeing an apparition or something.

'Um…'

Ren smiles at me, a smile that's at once embarrassed and charming. I add it to the list. 'You know, I thought that guy was cool. We chatted, I introduced him to my goldfish,' he says. 'Next I know, this thing comes out and it's judgment central. You're not going to do me like that, are you?' His eyes stay fixed on me, and I'm still trying to gather a coherent sentence.

'What are you doing here?' is the first thing I manage. Shit.

He chuckles a little and moves aside to let a willowy brunette get past us. She browses the limited selection of paperbacks nearby, unsubtly checking Ren out. Who can blame her? He seems even taller now he's back in front of me, and the sleeves of the navy blue shirt he has on are rolled up to reveal the sinew and muscle of his brown forearms, warm veins standing to attention. His wavy, dark hair is all messy like he's been ruffling his fingers through it.

'I'm guessing same reason you're here—to catch a flight. You don't live in New York?' He's carrying a leather holdall, which he drops between his feet, folding his arms like he's settling in.

'No,' I reply slowly, still a bit flustered. 'I mean, yes, I do—Brooklyn. But I'm heading back to London for a month or so. Well, if the flight ever takes off.'

'Right. It's not looking too good, huh? I'm supposed to be headed to Toronto, but so far no go.' He reaches up to tuck a stray strand of hair behind his ear. 'Is London home?'

'Well… Yeah, it's where I'm from…' He raises his eyebrows, but doesn't question my uncertainty. 'But I'm only heading back for a while to, um, sort out a few bits and pieces. And for some family stuff, you know.' I'm barged closer to Ren by a retirement-age couple sporting "fanny-packs", who clearly *have* to examine the fishing magazines. He moves a hand to my shoulder and guides me into an open space on the shop floor, turning with me. His hand lingers for a moment before drifting down again. Is it… is it possible he's sort of interested in me? The idea makes spikes of adrenaline dance in my stomach. 'I should probably pay for this stuff, it's getting a bit crowded in here,' I say. Ren follows me over to the till, and I dump my magazines and gum on the counter. 'I can get that if you like?' I point to the nearly-out-of-date New York Times he's just picked up. He starts to shake his head, but I grab it from his hands and add it to my pile.

'Thanks,' he says.

'They don't have newspapers in whatever lounge you're surely camped out in?' I ask.

Ren gives me Wry Smile. 'Some asshole had already done the crossword in the only one I could get my hands on. It's getting kind of busy in there, too, you know.'

'The struggle is real,' I retort, and he rolls his eyes. I smile at him. 'No, actually I'm jealous.' I hand him his paper, and we stroll slowly out of the store, not sure if we're about to say goodbye again. 'Look at the bloody queue for coffee.'

He looks down at me, one eyebrow quirked. 'You want to come into the lounge? They've got the shit on tap. No waiting.'

'Can I get in?'

He grins at me. 'Hey, I know people.' He hoists his bag onto his shoulder, eyeing me expectantly.

I look at him for a moment, wondering what would happen if I declined.

Wondering how there would be *any* way I'd say no.

I nod my head. 'OK. Cheers.'

He gestures towards the escalators that lead to the business and first class lounges, and I walk over and step on, feeling him standing just one step behind me, close enough to feel his warmth, smell his delicious, clean smell. The juddering mechanics of the escalator shake through my body in subtle jolts, and I grip the handrail harder. The crowds thin out as we dismount, and Ren leads the way to the podium outside his airline's lounge. He flashes a proprietary-yet-charming smile at the be-suited man scanning a screen like he's a maître'd.

'Mr Morgan,' he says with a nod as Ren shows his boarding pass, but the guy eyes me suspiciously.

'It's OK if my friend comes in, right?' Ren says, stepping aside to let me through without waiting for the response, even though I hear a vague *of course, sir* as we drift into the carpeted space. I smile a little to myself, even though I want to pretend not to be impressed—or intimidated. Piano music tinkles low in the background under a dull melee of men in shirtsleeves talking loudly into their mobile phones and well-heeled couples clinking glasses of champagne together.

'Relaxing,' I quip, but who am I trying to fool? The chairs look far more comfortable than they did in the waiting area outside, and I see the departure board in the corner has my flight currently delayed by four and a half hours.

But mainly, of course, there's Ren here. It almost seems too good to be true.

He's studying me closely with a half-smile. 'Over there?' he suggests, pointing to two armchairs facing each other across a small table in a quieter corner.

I nod, and we make our way through the Vuitton hand luggage littering the floor. I sink into the chair gratefully, feeling the ache in my muscles again. Almost immediately, a woman is standing attentively beside Ren's chair with a tray in her hand, her long ponytail still swinging as though she'd moved at record speed.

'What can I get you, sir?'

Ren gestures to me, and she turns expectantly. 'Oh, could I just get a large black coffee?'

'Certainly, ma'am. We have a Kenyan roast, or an excellent Argentinian blend, cold drip or—'

'Err… the Kenyan one?'

'Of course. Anything else?' She turns back to Ren eagerly.

'That sounds good,' he says, glancing at me with amusement in his eyes. 'Thank you.'

The woman nods once, then bustles away again to get our order. To be fair, I could get used to this. But now that we're alone, I feel like I've woken up in the middle of a dream and I'm not sure how to make sense of it. I think maybe Ren feels it too. Not that it's awkward—just not knowing quite where to begin.

'So what's up in Toronto?' I ask. I would really rather ask how long his flight delay is—how long we have before this ends again, and whether I should dispense with small talk and ask questions I really want the answers to. I try to work out which flight might be his, glancing surreptitiously at the departures board again.

'More press for *Detonate*,' he replies wearily. 'The others went on ahead but I decided to get a later flight, try and, uh, see my dad while I'm in the city.' His eyes drift to the floor for a moment. 'We shot some of the movie up there, actually. Hollywood North, they call it. Downtown Toronto standing in for Manhattan?' He lets out a derisive breath and shakes his head. 'But I guess I'm lucky it's only Canada tonight—we're going straight into principal photography on the next project in a couple weeks, and that's shooting in New Zealand.'

I raise my eyebrows. 'Wow.'

'Yeah. My stupid idea, the studio's crazy budget, even though the producers seemed to sell it as a tax break. I thought I'd try for some kind of juxtaposition, you know? Green and lush and open versus... feverish action and explosions.' His chuckle is part self-deprecation, part *almost*-excitement, and it does something strange to my insides.

'Sounds great. Another blockbuster?'

He fixes me with a look, and then shrugs. 'Well, we don't know how well this one will do yet.' The muscles in his jaw tighten a bit. 'But either way, I'm just chasing that dollar, right?' He nods to my pile of magazines.

'Oh, of course,' I say, though I hope my sarcasm comes across. I don't want him to think I genuinely agree. I pull out the offending magazine and flip through to his article. 'So many bloody ads in these things,' I mutter. 'Ah, here. Well, at least you look sexy in the pictures,' I say, then immediately regret going straight for that word. 'I mean I like the, um, the aesthetic they've gone for.' I look up, trying to hide my embarrassment, and turn the spread around to show him.

He does look sexy. Very. But not in the same way he is in real life.

'Oh yeah?' he asks, the corner of his mouth tilting up.

'Yes,' I affirm. I try not to, but I can't help casting my gaze down for a second coyly before lifting it again to meet his. 'But I also think you shouldn't pay too much mind to this type of shit.'

Ren's expression turns more curious. 'True. Looks fade, right?'

I laugh. 'So they say.' I glance back down at the article, scanning, but it really does piss me off, so I slap the pages shut and return to Ren, thinking for a minute. 'I don't know, maybe it's since I've started doing more of this sort of thing… Interviews with people, I mean, rather than op-ed and stuff? I've noticed the conventions in magazines more. Doing a profile like this, it's like they're writing a bad short story. The journalist establishes a character—their subject—and they base the whole thing around that. But mostly, that character is *actually* based on their own assumptions, made within a very short period of time and influenced, no matter how much they think it's not, by their previous knowledge of the public image of that person. Then it's mixed in nicely with what they think their *reader* will expect.' Ren nods, listening, so I go on even though I know I'm mounting my trusty steed, the high horse. 'You know, they'll start the piece with, like, the person doing something immediate. "So-and-So is doing X-Y-Z"—look at one of these profiles next time you're reading your Times weekend magazine, I *guarantee* it. It will be all *"Polly Pocket is eating pomegranates, with a concerned look on her plastic-y face".'* He laughs. 'Then they'll throw in some dialogue that allegedly took place during the interview, followed by a précis of that person's career, along with some judgemental but supposedly journalistic asides and misquotes. And... and the end result is a pile of nonsense snap-judgement about someone they don't even *know*.'

I finally come to a halt, reigning in my gesticulating hands, but still shaking my head in exasperation. Ren is quiet for a while. I roll the end of one of my locs between my fingers, starting to get that sense I hate—that I've been too forthright. Most of the time I follow it up with the thought "so what?", but with him it matters—his opinion of me.

'Wow. OK, maybe you're right,' he says at last, regarding me with a bemused furrow between his brows. His voice drifts close in the space between us, quieter now. 'That actually makes me feel better, Kayla.'

The way he says my name feels like he's running his hand down the back of my neck. A surge of pleasure wells up inside me at the idea of comforting him, and I start to feel hot, almost embarrassed. I'm not sure what to say next, and Ren's words hang in the air as the waitress returns with our coffees. She sets them down on the table with a smile, and then turns away with a quick 'Enjoy'. Apparently they really are complimentary. I reach for mine quickly and inhale the rich, warm vapours before taking a sip.

Ren leans forward in his chair and pours a sachet of brown sugar into his coffee. He stirs slowly, but doesn't lean back when he picks it up. I can smell his fresh-soap scent mingling with the earthiness of our drinks, and my temperature rises further. 'So is that why you came up with those...' He pauses for a split second as I put down my cup and peel off my jacket. 'Is that why you came up with your six questions? They've been playing on my mind, I've got to tell you.'

'Yeah... Well I reckon if people are answering the same set of questions, it's more democratic, isn't it? Maybe I should have skipped my attempts to interview you about *Detonate* and gone straight to those instead?'

Ren smiles into his cup of coffee. 'It's true, given your *clear* issues with traditional journalistic interrogation.'

I suck in my lip, self-conscious again even though he's obviously teasing.

'Why *did* your site choose to cover our junket, anyway? I'm intrigued to know. I checked it out, it doesn't seem like your vibe.'

I shrug. 'Well, I suppose the idea was to focus more on the experience itself—what that type of promotion is like, the business of selling an artistic endeavour of a certain sort...'

'So, mocking us, basically?' Ren interjects, raising his eyebrows good-naturedly, but he does sound like he's a bit pissed off at the notion.

'Not at all,' I say quickly. 'It was Cole's idea anyway— my, uh, my... co-founder of the site.' Ren studies me as I stumble on my words, and he leans back in his chair again. 'He's more interested in those sorts of angles on things,' I continue, feeling unasked questions about Cole floating up between us. Guilt prods at my conscience. '*I* mainly just wanted to see if I could meet some subjects for my Polaroid project that I might not otherwise have access to. And I did get to meet someone really interesting out of it,' I add, looking up emphatically to meet his gaze. Ren's eyes dance with thoughts, and his mouth twitches, like he's not sure whether to make a joke or take the compliment. I'm glad when he doesn't push it away. We fall silent, and I finish off the last of my coffee, putting the cup down on its saucer with a clatter. I look over at the departure board, wondering if I should thank him for the drink and go and wait back outside alone again.

'Would you like another coffee, Kayla?' Ren asks.

My name again… 'I probably shouldn't,' I begin, and that little wrinkle between his brow deepens. 'I mean, I might need to pace myself. Maybe in a little while?'

His lips lift, and he pushes a hand into his hair. 'Sure.' He takes in a breath. 'You know, I had wanted to ask you about the name of your site, too. To Murder and Create? T.S. Eliot, right? Prufrock?'

'Yeah, that's right. "*There will be time to murder and create.*"

He nods, leaning towards me again. 'I actually don't know why I'm asking like I don't know—it's one of my favourites.' He hesitates for a moment. 'Did you name it that, or, uh… your co-founder?'

It's obvious he can sense it—some kind of story there. But then, maybe *he* has someone I know nothing about, someone he's going back to. I want to convince myself I wouldn't care if he did.

'I named it,' I reply, a bit defiantly maybe. 'There's just something about that phrase I could never get out of my head.'

Ren folds one leg up so his ankle rests on his knee, and begins to jog his foot up and down absently. 'Yeah? It's funny, I guess the reason I love that poem so much is because it sums up how it feels to be so eternally wracked with doubt.' He chuckles self-deprecatingly. 'I can relate.'

I look at him quizzically, almost annoyed at him for suggesting he'd doubt himself. Doesn't he see how much he's already achieved? 'Hmm...' I begin, trying for once to consider my response, but Ren continues.

'I thought it was kind of interesting that you found a line in there that could be read so... confidently, I guess? There's so much agency in that phrase, on its own.' He shakes his head. 'Maybe I shouldn't be surprised.'

I watch his long fingers picking at a stray hem on his jeans. 'What do you mean?' I ask cautiously.

His eyes flick up to mine while two men in dress shirts and slacks pass us, arguing loudly in a way that makes me think they've been a couple for a while. Ren laughs as I raise my eyebrows at him, waiting.

'I mean, you seem confident,' he answers simply, watching for my response. 'You don't seem like the type of woman to agonize over much?' His voice holds a question, as though *he* wouldn't want to make a sweeping assumption.

'Hah.' *Seem like* being the operative. 'Well, I suppose that's fair. I try not to *overthink* it—my level of confidence, I mean. But it is something I've had to build for myself, as a woman.' I look at him. 'A Black woman, especially.'

'Yeah.'

He nods several times, and I smile. 'And to be fair, I *am* bad at keeping my opinions to myself...' My voice dwindles a bit as memories of my argument with my sister push unexpectedly into my mind. Ren tilts his head and examines me for a moment.

'That's not a bad thing,' he asserts, waiting as though he wants to make sure I take in his words. Then he drains his coffee, smiling faintly. 'See, if *I* was going to take a quote from that poem that resonated the most, it would be "*Do I dare disturb the universe?*" he tells me, looking back down at his leg.

I frown. 'But... Come on, Edie in *Balancing Act*? I don't reckon you could have written her like that and portrayed her on the screen like that without understanding what it is to challenge the world around you. And, like, the *whole* of the last part of *Touch/Taste* is just so unexpected and vivid and— Nah. No way, I don't buy it. You must think about how your films are connecting with their audience, what questions they might be provoking in the people who see them, right? Why would you even *tell* a story if you don't? I just... If nothing else, I'm a firm believer that it's a waste of time to doubt the merit of your own creativity. I mean—' I press my lips together, coming to a sudden halt. 'God, I'm doing it again, aren't I? Shit. Sorry!' I laugh self-consciously.

Ren's eyes roam over my face, and it heats up with each passing second that he doesn't speak. He does that a lot, I've noticed—thinks before he speaks. Maybe I should take some lessons.

'No, don't apologize. You're right. I'm glad you really did like my movies though,' he adds. After a while he reaches up and scratches the scruff of his beard and then gestures towards me. 'It's a question in the poem anyway, right? Prufrock's asking *if* he dares, not necessarily saying he hasn't, or won't.'

I shift in my seat. 'True.'

'But that's why I've been thinking so much about the final question of your set. "Why do we create?" That's what it comes down to, right?'

I nod, finally able to stave off humiliation enough to return his gaze properly. When our eyes meet, I feel that connection all over again. 'Exactly.' My voice is hoarse, and I clear my throat.

Ren draws in a long breath, and I urgently try to think of a way to change the shift in mood. But a loud announcement over the Tannoy does it for me.

'*Ladies and gentlemen, can we have your attention please? The Aviation Authority have just informed us that the severity of the storm this evening will prevent any more flights from being authorised to depart for at least the next three to four hours. Due to the backlog of flights, we urge you to speak to your airline regarding cancellations and arrangements for new flights. We thank you for your co-operation at this time. Again, please contact your airline's ground staff for further information. Thank you.'*

My heart quickens into a panicked rhythm, and not from the prospect of having to spend the night in JFK, or trying to get a room in an over-priced, over-subscribed airport hotel. Ren's expression is a picture of disappointment, too.

'Shit,' he says.

'Yeah,' I whisper.

Three

Ren.

It's impossible in this sea of people all lined up at the airline desks, but I scan the crowd anyway, as if there would be a beacon signalling where Kayla is—like I might be able to sense her. It worked earlier, right? I mean, shit, it was almost like I was thinking about her... and thinking about her... and then *boom*: I manifested her into being right there in front of me. Fate, I guess.

Turns out fate is a tease.

I shuffle forward in the line, not even slightly pissed about delaying the trip up to Toronto. My phone rings, and I hear Nick's deceptively languid voice on the other end.

'OK, Mr Morgan, that's all arranged. They still had a couple of the suites at the Vincent from the junket, and yours is still under your name.'

'Really? Fantastic. Thank you, Nick.'

'I'm having a little trouble with the car service right now though, sir. I'll call you back as soon as I have something.'

I smile to myself. It's nuts to have all this shit just magically arranged for me now, like I've been handed a key to a brand new kingdom. 'I understand, it's pretty chaotic here.

Thank you, man. Sorry for interrupting your evening. I really appreciate it.'

The call ends, and I feel bad for letting him continue to "Mister" and "sir" me. Hopefully he'll loosen up a bit when it's been more than a month. I finally reach the front of the line, and the clerk pulls at the knot of his tie like he can't wait until the second he can take it off.

'Can I take a look at your boarding pass please, sir?' he says wearily.

I hand it over, and he explains the flight cancellation and rebooking arrangements, and then where to go and re-claim my luggage. I nod, distracted, but then have a thought. 'Uh, is the baggage reclaim information for all the cancelled flights on the boards?'

'Yes sir, if you need more information, you can check there. I'll write your collection point right here on your pass, though…'

I nod my thanks and head off to get my suitcase, scanning the board eagerly for the departures to London. I think I saw the airline on Kayla's boarding card when we parted ways outside the lounge, vague with suggestions of trying to find each other before we leave the airport. Fuck, why didn't I get her number at least? If I'm right, then her collection point is the complete opposite end to mine—what if she's already grabbed her bag and disappeared? Well, at least it doesn't seem likely she'll get a cab easily… *Is* she even going to leave? She murmured something about thinking it might be better to stay in the airport rather than heading back to

Brooklyn tonight. My stupid ass was trying to play it cool, so I managed not to ask her to meet me or wait or make any real plans.

I see my case come through and grab it quickly, then head back over to do my best to deduce where Kayla might be waiting for her luggage. But I don't have to break out the deerstalker for long, because suddenly she's standing right in front of me, flipping back her dreadlocks and staring up at the boards looking frustrated as people jostle around her. I break into an unrestrained grin of relief, but wrestle back some dignity before she notices me. She's looking down again now, busily typing out a message or email or something on her phone as I walk up beside her, and my hand reaches out to the small of her back before I have time to wonder if it's too familiar. She spins toward me, indignation on her face at first, but then it smoothes away into that incomparable smile. It takes me a second too long to stop touching her.

'Hi,' she breathes, and I think she sounds as relieved as I feel.

'Hey. How's it going?'

Kayla gives me a half-laugh. 'I'm still trying to figure out my collection—' She looks back up at the board as she speaks. 'Oh there—seventeen C.' She turns back to me and takes in my suitcase. 'Looks like you're all ready to go?' Her voice tries to convey perkiness, but sinks around the edges.

I look along the ranks of carousels and gesture in the direction of the one she needs. 'I think it's down there, right? I'll come with you.'

We walk in silence, staying close as the crowds of arguing families and harassed businessmen swirl around us. She looks over at me, as unsure as I am about what step comes next in this dance, I think. But we get to the carousel and wait, still quiet, as the bags trundle past.

'There!' she says suddenly, already breaking away toward an incredibly huge orange case. I go to help, but she hauls it off with surprising strength and grins at me. I bug my eyes out exaggeratedly.

'Piss off—it's *a whole month*. This is admirably light packing, my friend.'

I hold up my hands, laughing. I want to be her friend. I want to be her—

'So, what are you doing now, then?' she begins slowly as we start to move away from the people all brimming with focussed intent to retrieve their bags and head back out through customs.

'Well, I need to wait for my assistant to get back to me about the car service...' I begin.

Kayla rolls her eyes. 'Oh yeah, me too.'

She pulls another smile out of me, and I shrug. 'Be as snarky as you want, but I'm betting you won't be so sarcastic if I offer you a ride.'

My last phrase rings in my ears, the maybe-unintentional double entendre invading my thoughts distractingly. She regards me for a moment before looking down, a slow grin spreading on her face. If she's even vaguely thinking something dirty right now too, I'm a goner. 'Maybe not,' is all she says.

I take a breath. 'Do you know if you're going to stay here at the airport, or…?'

She reaches up and rubs her forehead. 'Well, they're saying there's no chance of re-booking onto a flight until at least tomorrow night, and I don't think I can take staying here that whole time. I don't want to…' She presses her lips together, not finishing her thought out loud. 'I suppose a hotel anywhere close would be a bit expensive. I could call a mate, but—' She checks her watch, possibly running through who she'd call at pushing-midnight for a place to crash. I'm thrilled that whomever she comes up with is giving her pause. Maybe that guy, the business partner, co-founder or whatever—if that's all he really is to her? Kayla glances through some nearby sliding doors as they open and close, letting in bursts of angry weather. 'Jesus,' she mutters. 'Um, yeah, I suppose I should start sorting something out.'

She feels it—I do to. The real world encroaching, pressing down on the delicate shoots of what we were starting to plant. I don't want to go back to being in another anonymous hotel room alone, trying to sleep, haunted by all the crap I can't shake. My phone buzzes with a message. 'My assistant,' I tell her. 'Car service is on its way.'

Kayla nods slowly. 'OK. Well—'

'Listen, there were a couple of suites at the Vincent still booked out by the studio from the junket. I'm pretty sure I can nab you one of those, and that's where I'm headed anyway.'

She messes with the handle of her suitcase. 'Really? I mean, if you think that would be all right, maybe…' She seems to think for a moment, then her shoulders relax and she flicks her dark eyes up to mine. 'I think that would be OK… Yes. Thank you, Ren.'

The rush I get when she says my name takes me by surprise, even if it's almost drowned out by the chorus of Handel's Messiah playing in my mind. *Yes. Yes. She fucking said yes.* I cover by looking back down at my phone screen as it illuminates again. 'Cool—perfect timing. The car's just pulling up now. We better get going, I'm guessing it's kind of crazy out there.' I search around for the signs to the pick-up area, and we wind through the crowds with a renewed sense of purpose. When we reach the doors, we both pull our jackets over our heads and drag our cases along, our laughter whipped away on the speed of wind and damped down with the driving rain. I just about make out my name written on the card propped in the windshield of a waiting SUV, and I guide Kayla toward it. The driver jumps out to help us, and I shout for Kayla to get in while he and I wrestle the cases into the back. I finally get into the rear passenger seat next to her, pull the car door shut and exhale loudly, pushing back my wet hair. I turn to Kayla and we both laugh again, drenched and shivering despite the relatively warm night.

'They say the worst of the storm should pass in the next little while,' calls our driver, jumping into the front seat and pulling off the rain mac he'd put on to help us out.

'Oh yeah, definitely. Barely a hint of precipitation out

71

there,' Kayla says with a grin.

The driver laughs good-naturedly. 'To the Vincent Hotel, right, Mr Morgan?' he says. 'Let me get that heat up for you guys.'

I turn to Kayla, feeling smug. 'See, sometimes selling out to the Man has its perks,' I whisper, but she presses her lips together.

'Oi, I didn't write that article. I'd never dream of calling you a sell-out,' she says part-joking, part-earnestly. I'm slowly becoming aware that we're so close in the confined space of the car—especially as she lifts her damp Basquiat shirt away from her skin, pulling a face, and then lets it fall back down, clinging to her chest. She catches me watching her again, and her lips twitch for a moment before parting to allow a slight exhale. I ease my gaze forward to the wipers flinging rain-water away from the windshield in a mesmerising rhythm that's about half that of my heartbeat.

It takes forever to get out of the airport, but once we do, the roads are surprisingly clear. Or maybe not so surprising, considering the storm means we have to drive twenty below the speed limit. Kayla shuffles a little in her seat, and I turn back to see her looking at me. She checks her seatbelt, and nods to mine. I do it up with a click.

'Do you ever think about how you might die?' she asks suddenly, and I let out an incredulous laugh.

'Is that one of the reject questions from your set?'

She chuckles. 'No. Well, maybe. But I mean, think about it—this is prime aquaplane-into-the-Hudson weather. If they find us, there'll be some write-up about how award-winning director João Ren Morgan tragically died when his car service crashed in inclement weather on a stormy Thursday night. And then there would be this mystery, at least for a while, about who the hell I was and why I was in the car with you.'

'It would hardly be Chappaquiddick,' I retort. 'And I also think you overestimate quite how much an Independent Spirit award counts for in this business.'

She laughs, and then we fall quiet again for a while. It feels like an indulgence, just being silent in this space with her with only the sound of the wipers and the rain against the windows around us. And yet it feels so right, I almost want to reach over and take her hand. How is that possible? I close my eyes for a moment, and when I look back out the window, I'm surprised to see the lights of midtown loom into view. I watch water whip along the wide streets, infinite long thin threads stretching down from the sky relentlessly, illuminated by the street lamps.

We pull up outside the Vincent a short while later, and a porter rushes out from under the protection of the awning to help us in with our bags. I thank our driver, then make sure I have some bills ready before rushing inside with Kayla under the umbrella another porter is extending, just barely able to hold it up against the wind. I tip the guys, but as we head into the warm dark wooden cave of the lobby, I hear Kayla explaining a little awkwardly to the guy loading our stuff onto one trolley that the luggage will be going to two separate rooms. It's crazy that I'd almost forgotten. Is it a bad sign that she hadn't? Anyhow, I best prepare my attempt to charm the neat-looking blonde clerk watching me expectantly from behind the lobby desk.

'Mr Morgan, welcome back to the Vincent. We're checking you back in to a Master suite, is that correct?' Nice—Nick must have called ahead. Of course. The guy needs a raise.

'That's right. Thanks so much for having me back,' I reply, widening my grin and wishing I'd had the foresight to get Nick to prime the hotel for Kayla staying in one of the other suites, too. I maintain steady eye contact and the desk clerk lady smiles, her cheeks flushing a little. 'Listen,' I continue, 'I was wondering—my friend here needs a room as well. I know that Galaxy Studios had booked out a whole bunch of them for our press day earlier, and my assistant said there were still some that hadn't been cleared tonight?'

She nods, but then a frown crosses her smooth forehead as she taps something into her screen. 'Oh. You know what, I'm very sorry, sir, but those suites were released to other clients by the studio. We're fully booked with the storm. I can see if one of our sister hotels might be able to accommodate your guest?'

Shit shit shit. I look over at Kayla, who can obviously see something's up. I turn back to the lady at the desk. 'That's OK. Give me a couple minutes, I'll be right back,' I say to her, already trying to think of how to phrase what I'm going to ask Kayla. Will she see right through me? I don't even intend it like that.

Not entirely.

Kayla unfolds her arms as I walk over to her and looks up at me expectantly. 'No go?' she asks, visibly deflated at the prospect—but her reaction has the opposite effect on me. She *wants* to stay... But then she pulls out her cell phone and glances at the screen. Damn. She might have already called someone else.

'Not exactly,' I begin cautiously. 'All the other suites are booked up—the studio got to them already I guess. But listen, I'm in a Master. It has a separate bedroom and a fucking huge couch. I could crash on that and you take the room?'

She regards me for what feels like hours, thoughts dancing through her mind, assessing. I'm about to open my mouth again to try and fix it somehow, but she stops me.

'Well... I'm not sure if I like the idea of going back out there trying to drum up some alternative shelter,' she begins. 'And I suppose you're not demonstrably a crazy person, so far.'

I shrug one shoulder equivocally. She gives me an amused look, but I search for any further hesitation in her eyes. It's gone. I think I actually see a flicker of *desire*. If I'm not imagining it—

'It's just one night, right?' she says finally, almost to herself. Then, 'If you don't mind?'

'I don't mind,' I say, my voice coming out more emphatically than I intended. Kayla turns and catches the eye of the porter waiting patiently with our stuff.

'Sorry, it looks like it will be one room after all,' she says, turning back to me as she finishes.

'All right,' I say. *Very all right.* I return to the desk and let the lady know we've made an arrangement regarding the rooms so I won't need her help. Her gaze flicks over to Kayla momentarily, and I expect some kind of conclusion to be jumping in her eyes when she looks back at me, but she's clearly a professional. She nods once, neutral.

'Great. Please call down if you need anything, Mr Morgan. You have a good night.'

I grab the key cards for the room and turn to head back across the lobby, which is still bustling with night owls confined by the storm. Kayla's standing off to one side, leaning against one of the carved wood columns that punctuate the space. A beautiful woman—*this* beautiful, fascinating woman—is waiting for me. I'm suddenly hit by the fact that this is temporary, like she said. *Just one night.* As I walk over to her, I almost want to grab her hand and lead her away to somewhere our separate lives don't exist. Maybe we're already there, though. For now, anyway.

'Ready?' My voice sounds sort of alien.

'Lead the way,' she says to me, that smoke swirling in her speech, and I start over to the elevators with Kayla and the porter following close behind.

'Which room, sir?' he enquires, reaching up to smooth the beginnings of a moustache that seems out of place on his youthful face.

'Oh—it's a Master suite…' I check the key card. 'Uh, The Michelangelo?'

He nods. 'Great. Seventh floor. I'll meet you guys there, these elevators can get a little cramped.' He moves over to what must be a service elevator just as the doors in front of us open, and I see what he means. Kayla steps into the small glass box and I follow, watching our reflections surround us. I press the button for our floor and we begin to rise, an electronic bell signalling our slow ascent toward the unknown. I sense her looking at my image in the mirrors, and then her eyes sweep away and fall on the real me. Her striking features are serious, her gaze intense as her lips part ever so slightly. But just then the bells stop and the doors open. I gesture wordlessly for Kayla to step off the elevator and follow behind her.

She notices the porter already waiting outside the suite door and makes her way down the hall, turning to look over her shoulder at me, flipping her long dreadlocks. Her strides are languid and I can't help staring at the roll of her hips, the tight curves swaying left to right. She stays looking at me for a moment longer, and one corner of her lip curls knowingly, again like she sees right through me. Does that mean I'm not here, or that what she sees is something inside me… something hidden?

Kayla moves aside so I can get to the door, and I pull out the key card to let us into the suite. The moustached porter heads inside with us, arranges our luggage on the stands and points out where all the amenities are. I slip a bill into his hand as he bids us goodnight, *almost* scared for him to leave, but desperate for him to go. As the door clumps shut, I turn to Kayla. She's standing in the middle of the huge suite, looking around, anywhere but at me. I worry that she thinks she's made a mistake, but finally she looks at me, taking in my expression, and as she does the warmth of her smile—the heat of it—almost feels like an embrace.

She exhales loudly and goes over to drop her bag onto the couch.

'I did not expect this to be how my night would pan out, I have to say.'

I nod, returning her smile—reflecting it. *Expect*, no. Hope...?

'Yeah.' I pause for a moment, rubbing the back of my neck, thinking. I need something to stop me feeling so fucking aware of every millimeter of her in this space with me. 'Are you hungry? I'm starving, I've just realized.'

She clutches her stomach. I watch her hand. 'Yeah, actually, me too. I had some pathetic attempt at a burger earlier in the airport, but I didn't manage much of it. I could definitely eat. What were you thinking?' She takes in the plush furnishings in the suite, and the small round dining table set up with the expensive designer chairs. 'Room service might be a bit... intense?' She chuckles, and I get a slight glimpse of nerves. I feel them too, but looking at her makes it easier to push them to one side.

'Room service is pretty damn intense, you're right.'

She smiles wryly and gives me the finger, then goes over

to her suitcase, pulling it off the elasticated rack and heading toward the darkened bedroom with it and her other bag. 'OK, smart arse. I'm going to change into less soggy clothes, you sort out where we want to go and eat, assuming something's still open. Otherwise it's bar food in the lobby.'

The door closes, and I stare around the empty room, then back toward the bedroom, thinking of her peeling off her clothes in there, her skin cool with the damp of the evaporating rainwater... To distract myself, I scan my brain for decent places to eat in midtown after midnight. I come up with the 24-hour diner I used to go to with a high-school girlfriend after we'd hit up some dive that didn't card on weekdays. In fact, the coffee in the diner was so good I went back a few times when I was home last month, seeing as it was near to the hospital. I felt bad that I remembered the restaurant, but not that girlfriend's last name. I was glad it was still going though—I've gotten sick of memorising Latin names for frothed up milk with a pipette-full of coffee in it from the chains, or complex cold-drip from the new places. I even snuck Dad a carry-out cup of half-caff when the nurses weren't looking. I probably should have felt bad at that too, but at least it made him smile at something I'd done for once. The minute they gave him the all-clear to leave hospital, it was back to the status quo. I felt it this afternoon—each of us too scared to admit we're afraid of time threatening to part us. Him barely hiding his disappointment that he ended up raising an artist not an academic. If I can even call myself that now...

Jesus. Enough with the self-pity.

I clear my throat. 'I know somewhere we can go,' I call toward the bedroom door, then stride over to open my own case, unbuttoning my shirt. 'It's pretty decent as long as you don't mind a breakfast menu at one in the morning,' I add, just as the door opens. Kayla stands in the doorway, stopping short as she watches me pull my button-down off and throw it on top of the stuff in my suitcase. It takes me a minute to find another shirt in there, and I feel her eyes on me all the while. I think I like it… And I think I'm really fucking glad for one thing about being in Los Angeles now: it made me join a gym.

'Sorry,' she says, still staring, sounding like she did when she ambushed me with her first photograph—not sorry at all. Her eyes journey slowly back toward mine, and she bites her lip. Eventually I grab out a T-shirt and slip it on.

Goddamn. I'm not sure I want to leave any more.

She's changed into tight dark blue jeans and a denim button-down in almost the same shade of blue, open at the neck to show her tangle of necklaces and a long V of smooth brown skin beneath. Somehow, in spite of the fact she's wearing a hipster version of a Canadian tuxedo, she looks effortlessly sexy-cool. And the way she's twisted her hair into a knot on top of her head pulls her features into relief in a way that has me staring too.

'Is it far?' Kayla asks.

'Huh?'

'The restaurant?'

'Oh… no.'

She heads out of the bedroom, carrying a smaller purse and a red nylon mass in her other hand. 'Still,' she says, 'I have this bad boy, so I'm ready for the onslaught.' She opens out what she's carrying, which turns out to be some kind of all-weather poncho. She grins triumphantly.

'Wow, and here I was thinking you had taste,' I say, laughing. 'I guess, yeah, it'll do the job.'

But she pulls it on, and of course it transforms into a hooded couture dream coat. It's actually almost annoying how good everything looks on her. Almost.

She swirls around, giggling with a child-like abandon as the material fans out around her. 'This is possibly the ugliest thing I've ever seen, but it spoke to me so deeply, I had to buy it. Have you ever had that?' she asks.

'Are you kidding me? I own about five things, just in variations of color,' I reply. 'No item of clothing has ever attempted to converse with me.'

She stops swirling, breathless and still smiling. 'I like your style,' she says. 'It's not too distracting.'

'Uh… thanks?'

I pull out a black hooded sweatshirt and zip it up over my T-shirt, then throw on my jacket over it, pretending to GQ-pose in the mirror by the door. Kayla walks over and stands beside me, linking our arms spontaneously and examining our reflections with an assessing tilt of her head.

But the smiles melt away from our faces as our eyes meet in the glass, and I stand dead still, absorbing the sensation of our limbs interlocking. She opens her mouth to say something, but seems to stop herself. After a while, she slowly unfurls her arm from mine, still standing close as she looks up at me.

'Let's go,' she says softly.

Four

Kayla.

As we step out into the darkness, the rain has eased to a manageable but insistent sizzle. The wind pulls our clothes tight around us as we walk into it, and the energy in the air is still heavy with electric portent. The pavements are wide and mostly free of people, but Ren walks close beside me and I edge towards him, our faces concealed by the hoods that we struggle to keep on our heads.

'Just a couple more blocks this way,' he says, raising his voice over the gusts, and I nod. We wait for a taxi to pass before we jog across the road, and then Ren steers me in the right direction with one hand at my elbow momentarily, turning his head to look at me with a smile. For a second, I think about all the other options I could have taken tonight. I think about Cole, about our plan and what it should mean. If there were a possibility of this lasting more than a handful of hours, I wouldn't be here. I want to believe that. But I feel hidden somehow, like the world has stopped, like this isn't my real life—like none of this counts, just for tonight. I don't know what's going to happen, but I couldn't ignore my frankly embarrassing elation when Ren suggested we could stay together. Is this completely crazy? It doesn't *feel* crazy. That could be the only bit that's giving me pause.

The rain begins to pick up momentum again, and we quicken our pace.

'So it could be a little further than I thought,' Ren shouts over to me with a sheepish grin, and I mock-frown at him under my hood.

'Excellent. No, I mean, an evening of perpetual dampness is what I was after, anyway.'

He ignores me, but beautiful little crinkles form around his eyes as he turns away from me chuckling, and I repeat the words *one night* three times in my mind like a protective incantation.

'There it is!' Ren says suddenly, audibly relieved as we finally see a diner up ahead, illuminated and bustling. We speed-walk the final steps towards it, both of us laughing again lightly, and Ren holds the door open for me to go through, pushing his hood back off his head and tucking stray strands of hair behind his ear. I really want to repeat the gesture for him, to get the ones he missed and feel the heat of his skin under my fingertips as they skim his neck… I curl my fingers into the palm of my hand as the hostess grabs two laminated menus, starting towards us with a tired smile.

'How you guys doing tonight?' she says, not wanting an answer. 'Right here OK, hon?' She shows us to a table by the window, and I nod.

'Perfect.'

As I look across at Ren taking off his jacket and enjoying

the rigmarole involved in me taking off my poncho, I realise it *is* sort of perfect: being here right now, with him. An unfamiliar warmth unfurls inside me, but for the first time since bumping into Ren again, I'm also worried that I might be relying too much on my usual attitude of only dealing with the immediate. I *want* to avoid thinking about what happens tomorrow, but tiny pebbles of concern are casting ripples in my thoughts. I mean, this has literally never happened to me before—feeling so weirdly intoxicated by a complete stranger. What if one night isn't enough?

It doesn't matter. You can't mess up the plan. And besides—

'Your server will be over in just a minute,' the hostess tells us briskly. The restaurant is surprisingly full, and noisy with words shouted in excitement or mumbled in lethargy, punctuated with familiar musical stabs of Springsteen and Motown from the jukebox. I glance outside at the shine of the wet pavement under the street lamps, bubbling now with another downpour.

'It's nice to be inside, looking out,' I murmur, almost unaware the words have slipped from my mouth until I hear Ren hum in agreement. The low sound resonates within me unexpectedly and I cross my legs underneath the table, observing his profile as he leans towards the window and watches the rain fall, his breath fanning faintly against the cool glass. His beard grows in dark, sparse wisps on his golden-brown cheeks, only a little bit denser on his chin and around his lips, but his jaw is strong. And that frown, and his long eyelashes, the wrinkles folding on his forehead like

James Dean when he looks up through them. His features seem both delicate and intensely masculine. I want to take another picture of him, right now, and I'm really pissed off that I didn't bring my camera.

But somehow I don't think the image will fade from my mind.

Ren turns to me slowly, like he's been allowing me to study him. 'So what you're saying is, I was *right* to make us walk through a storm. It was, like, a service in appreciation of contrast.' His eyes sparkle with mirth, and those crinkles appear again.

I smile. 'All I know is, I'm starving.'

As I speak, the waitress arrives to take our drinks order. Her cleavage wobbles intimidatingly as she clutches up a few stray glasses from the now-empty neighbouring table with one hand.

'What can I get you to drink, sis?'

I glance down at the menu. 'The hot chocolate sounds nice, actually. I'll get one of those, extra marshmallows.'

She looks at me over the rim of her glasses, like she doesn't have time for someone messing around with gibberish. 'A what now, hun?'

'Hot chocolate,' I repeat calmly, but refusing defiantly to adjust my accent.

She glances at Ren, who barely stifles a laugh as he repeats my order in a manner she can understand, then asks for coffee for himself. She nods once and then turns away shaking her head a little, and he lets it burst forth. My nostrils flare as I try not to join him.

'Happen a lot?' he asks.

'More than you'd imagine,' I retort drily. 'Certain words really throw people. I think it's that expectation thing.'

He raises his eyebrows briefly, nodding, then leans back from the table and unzips his hoodie, pulling it off. I inhale his scent as it drifts towards me on the faint humidity, and as he extracts his arms from the sleeves I remember the slim, defined brown muscles of his stomach and chest as he changed into his T-shirt in the hotel room. My skin starts to prickle embarrassingly with heat. I really need to get a hold of myself.

Ren leans his elbows on the table and knits his fingers together interrogatively. 'So... How long have you lived in Brooklyn?' he asks.

I cast my eyes up, calculating. 'It'll be three years in September.' I pull one of my necklaces up around my chin, zipping the charm back and forth absent-mindedly before remembering Cole saying once that it's a tell for when I'm about to lie. Am I? I let it drop down again, trying to stick to the relatively mundane. 'I was actually living on the Upper East Side when I first moved here, staying with my Aunty for a couple of months while I got settled. She married into money and divorced into more, so she was my sponsor for grad school at Columbia.' I fiddle with my napkin, wondering if it might be a bad idea to bring all that up.

'Yeah? So you're done with school now, or...?'

'Mmmhmm,' I begin cautiously. 'Yeah, it's been nearly a

year since I finished there.'

He must catch some air of wistfulness in my voice, because he nods in understanding. 'I miss getting to study filmmaking. That feeling of possibility, you know? Before it all becomes a reality.'

I smile wryly. 'Oh, the crushing weight of expectation when you've become the director of multi-million-dollar movies, eh?'

Ren, thankfully, chuckles at my sarcasm. 'So what you're saying is I should be grateful, right?'

'Well, what percentage of the eager young filmmakers you graduated with do you think have actually become directors or producers or writers or whatever they were hoping for?'

Ren holds up his hands, conciliatory, and I'm momentarily distracted by their size, by his long, slim fingers... 'You're right, you're right. I'm an unappreciative bastard,' he says with a smile. 'It's a luxury to even be able to study any art form, though, right? Like, an indulgence.'

He's right. I think about my sister, and the fact that Aunty Bimi had sent Christy a fat cheque when I'd moved to New York to do whatever *she* wanted with it, too. She'd already finished at Central, and of course she'd sailed into a post-graduate scholarship there anyway, so half of her fee had been paid. But now Bimi's cheque will be going towards paying off the rest of Chris' debts, her rent, and looking after a baby on her own, rather than allowing my sister to pursue *her* artistic dreams—of which she also has many. The unfairness hits me like an unexpected gust of wind, and guilt swamps me. And now I'm doing something potentially stupid to keep going with what that luxury started…

No. This is what I'm meant to do. I have to believe this will all be worth it, and will all work out. I ask myself every day how much pursuing this really means to me, and my answer is still: *everything*. I swallow, looking back up at Ren.

'So what have you been doing since you finished grad school? What are your plans?' he asks, picking up the menu and scanning it absently as he speaks. 'I know you have some,' he adds with a smile. It seems like he's consciously trying to keep the conversation light. Of course, I could tell him why this is an awkward subject, but apparently I really am selfish. I don't want him to see me as off limits.

Just one night…

'Um…' I clear my throat. 'In a nutshell? After I graduated I got a job in a bar downtown and carried on working on my art. I met a broker at our final shows who was really into some of my stuff, so I've managed a few sales, and that show you saw the flyer for. But I'd been doing some blogging and stuff as well while I was at Columbia, and a friend of mine had got me to write a couple of features for an online magazine she was editing. And… Well, Cole and I had met at grad school—' I watch for Ren's reaction, and he's suddenly studying the menu like it's got the secrets of the universe written on it. '—And anyway, it all sort of came together when we decided to start *To Murder and Create*. It was just one of those flukey things, right place right time. It's snow-balled in the last year or so, which is great, but it's also kind of a lot. It's funny, you mentioned having dedicated time to focus on art? Sometimes I worry about finding the headspace to focus on all the different bits and pieces I want to do. Like, the creative energy?' I blow out a breath as my back muscles tense. *Let alone the actual possibility of continuing to do it here at all...* 'I don't know. Maybe that show a couple of weeks ago sort of cemented it.'

Ren finally looks up from the menu, frowning. 'Didn't it go well?'

'Not really. It wasn't what I hoped, anyway. I wanted it to be the thing that proved I'm...' I hear my voice drop lower. 'I'm really an *artist*.' Why am I telling him this? For some reason I feel like he'd understand. It's weird having someone to express it to. With everyone else in my life, even Cole, admitting something like that feels like it would call everything they know about me into question. 'But it didn't feel right, and not a lot sold, and I wasn't massively happy with the pieces anyway. I know I can do better. It's hard, trying to hone in on the way you really want to express yourself... Having the time, and space. Not letting go until you do.' I can't help another sigh of frustration. 'Do you know what I mean?'

Ren smiles wryly at me. 'Think I have some idea, yeah.' He exhales hard, too. 'I thought that doing *Detonate* would be some kind of creative palate cleanser, that it would free me up so I could finally make something that... connected, I guess. And instead I'm going straight into another BSU flick.' He shakes his head. 'There's only so many cobwebs that can possibly need blowing away, right?'

I look at him quizzically. 'BSU?'

'Blow Shit Up.' He fiddles with one corner of his menu, bending it back and forth. 'That's what Yann—A… a friend of mine used to call them.' He looks down. 'He was always trying to convince me to bring my—' He throws air quotes up with one hand '—"sensibilities" to something on a bigger scale like this.' He stops bending and presses the menu's corner down hard.

'Well, you decided for yourself eventually, then,' I venture. He doesn't look up.

'Classic needs-must,' he retorts, a bit more sharply than I expected. Then, 'But yeah… Maybe he had a point.' Light flickers faintly in the gloom that's grown in Ren's gaze, and I try to chase it.

'It's pretty annoying when your mates are right, isn't it?' I suddenly realise that obviously it's doubtful he and Yann even *are* still friends, but I smile at Ren anyway and I think he feels it because he finally looks at me. 'I mean, Cole had all the belief when it came to M&C,' I continue, then instantly regret this whole thread of conversation, but it's too late to back out. 'I can't pretend part of me didn't think it was a waste of time when we first started fucking about with it.' Ren nods, but his eyes darken again. Shit. 'But it worked out pretty well, so…' I trail off, eyes trained on the menu myself now, even though I've already decided I'll have the banana walnut pancakes.

Ren's hand moves up to rub the little crease between his

brows, and he gives a barely noticeable nasal sigh as our wait-ress returns with the drinks.

'Your *hoh choc-leh*,' she says to me, her expression dour but her eyes flecked with good humour as she mimics my accent. I smile half-heartedly. 'Free refills on the coffee, hon, you just ask,' she adds as she puts a mug in front of Ren and pours from the jug in her other hand. 'What can I get you to eat?'

I order my pancakes, and Ren mumbles a request for eggs over-easy. He reaches for the sugar container as our waitress heads off to place our order, still silent.

I decide I have to say something.

'Ask me,' I say quietly, leaning on the table and dipping my head to catch his eye. Is this another bad idea? *Probably, Kayla. Jesus.* Does he already know? I'm not sure how much honesty to allow for here. How much it might really affect what's happening. Maybe he won't care.

Maybe he will.

One night one night one night…

'Ask you what?'

I stare at him, raising an eyebrow, and he stirs the sugar in his coffee, then taps his teaspoon loudly against the rim of his cup.

'I… This is crazy,' he says in a low voice. 'It's none of my business if—'

'Ask me anything you want to know.' Sweat prickles my palms.

He waits, lifting his cup to his mouth and taking a sip,

92

then lowering it again. 'OK. Are you…?' He stops and starts again, his voice harder, like he's annoyed with himself. 'You and Cole. Are you together?'

I shake my head cautiously. 'It's not like that.' I hesitate. 'We're… Well, to be honest, I don't know how to really describe… I mean, we're…' *Christ. You started this, Kayla.* I'm being incoherent, and I don't know how to end my sentence, but I see the tension in Ren's body tighten a little as I stutter. '*No.* The answer is no, we're not,' I finish definitively. It's the truth. That's what I want to tell myself, anyway.

The tension in Ren's body releases and then returns again as something even more magnetic. 'OK,' he says finally.

'What about you?' I bite the inside of my cheek. 'Are you with anyone?' It sounds foolish, because of course he is. He's with *me*, so intently, in this moment. His gaze agrees silently.

'No.'

'What if you're lying?' I ask, on the edge of a smile.

'What if I am?'

Because, really, it wouldn't make a difference. We both know it wouldn't. Not tonight. I close my eyes for a moment, thinking about it already: what he'll feel like…

I draw in a long breath, and he leans closer to me.

'I don't think you're that good at not telling the truth,' I whisper.

He blinks slowly. 'Yeah.' A pause. 'There… There was someone important a while ago. Didn't end well. There's no-one right now.'

I consider what he's said for a moment, and then pick

out a marshmallow as it floats on the foam of my hot chocolate and put it in my mouth, tasting its sweetness on my tongue as Ren watches me.

'What about that publicity lady…?'

He glances down finally at the Formica table with a small, guilty smile. 'OK. But only once. She and I fucked.'

I stiffen at the word, and he senses it. Not because I'm shocked, but because I know, again. He means that's not what we would do. We're barely inches apart across the table, but eventually I ease back in my chair, feeling heat from my body escaping around my collar. I take a moment to look around at the other people in the diner, as though they'd only just materialised in the room again. A Hispanic teenage boy on the cusp of handsomeness is feeding ice-cream to a young blonde girl who looks like she's wearing his shirt. She tugs the sleeves around her hands, pulls it tight around her slender body, surrounding herself. Maybe they've been together since last night. Maybe today is the day they made love for the first time, as the storm charged the sky. Maybe…

'Maybe the details don't matter,' I find myself saying quietly, turning back to find Ren still focussed on me. 'Who you've been with, who you'll be with, who *I've*—Does any of it matter right now? I mean, it's not like…' He scratches his neck, uncomfortable. I don't think he likes where I'm heading with this, but I say it anyway. 'I'll be in London for a few weeks, and soon you'll be on the other side of the world. And even after that, you… You don't even live in New York any more, do you?' I hate the hope in my voice. *It doesn't matter. You've committed to a plan. Ren's not part of it.*

He shakes his head. 'Los Angeles,' he says. 'Or nowhere. All over.' His features constrict.

'Maybe sometimes you just have to live in the moment, take what life gives you.' I roll my eyes at my platitudes, but Ren's still quiet, so I keep going—of course I do. 'Like, maybe there's a plan—' I regret my word choice. 'A blueprint for your life that you don't know about—certain things that are meant to happen, people you're supposed to meet. When you think about it, how much do we really need to know about another person to get their essence, anyway? To understand if they're… significant? No time at all, right?' I hear myself speaking, words avalanching, thoughts jumbling in my mind and out of my mouth. 'I'm only just starting to understand how important it is to not take things like that for granted. And to realise how lucky I am.' I draw another breath, shaky now, because maybe in spite of what I'm holding back from Ren, I'm being too truthful. I've never really admitted anything like that, even to myself. I'm lucky I've even got *this* far with everything I want to achieve. Look at what's happened with Christy…

Am I selfish, letting Cole do all of this for me? What if I ruin our friendship? What if I already *have* ruined things with my sister? It's a lot to face. Even more so when I think about the man sitting opposite me right now.

Because I don't want to ruin it with Ren.

'Those sorts of connections are powerful,' I continue

quietly, staring at him. 'They're more important to me than I ever thought.' Then I have to look away for a moment, because somehow, even not speaking, Ren is telling me he understands every word I've said. His eyebrows dance together and apart as he rests his chin on one hand, elbow propped on the table. His other arm is flat against its surface, his long fingers almost reaching me, almost touching me, but not quite.

Not yet.

Touch me...

I hear my voice again, reaching out to fill the silent space between us with honest thoughts that I feel like only he could elicit from me. 'If... if I type your name into a fucking box with a blinking cursor on the internet, I can find out facts about you, about your life,' I say tentatively. 'I *did*. Maybe you did the same for me too, I don't know. But doing that didn't tell me anything. It couldn't tell me if, say, you're lonely. And looking me up wouldn't have told you if, I don't know... If I've ever been in love.' He looks me dead in the eye at that—at the quiver in my voice that shows I never have. That I never thought it would even be possible. 'What I mean is, facts don't answer any of the questions I *really* want answers to.' My pulse keeps a loud, steady rhythm in my eardrums. 'You're telling me more now, here, just by looking at me in silence while I babble on incoherently because you probably... I don't know, find it funny to torture me.' My palms press against the edge of table, hot and anxious, and I let out a short, embarrassed laugh.

Ren moves his hand across the Formica slowly, until his fingertips finally reach mine, brushing them, feather-light. A smile breaks wide across his face, and I bathe in the relief of it.

'Kayla... I think you might be right,' he says at last, his voice deep and gentle.

'About which part?' I'm barely audible.

He blows out a long breath. 'Everything.'

We slowly move apart as I hear heavy footsteps behind me, and our waitress returns, balancing plates. We sit back and start to eat without saying anything more, but smiling down at our food like it's telling us a secret only we can hear. Something heavy has been lifted off us, but I'm worried it's still hovering, ready to drop again at any moment.

The pancakes are delicious, and since Ren quickly polishes off his eggs and all the sundries surrounding them, I reach over wordlessly and offer him a bite of my food. He hesitates, and I wonder if I'm mimicking the young couple too closely without the history to back it up, but then I watch his lips close around my fork, sliding the pancake piece off its fronds. Without a thought I quickly return the empty fork to my mouth to get the remnants of the syrup, and him. He watches as I lick my lips, his eyelids lowering slightly... I'm almost relieved when our waitress swoops by and fills his coffee mug again, distracting us. I finish my food and clatter my cutlery down, and she clears our plates.

'Definitely less intense than room service, though, yeah?' I murmur.

'Way, way less intense.'

I smile over the rim of my mug as I drain the last of my cold hot chocolate. Ren asks for the "check" and I pull my purse out of my bag and onto the table, rifling through it for some bills—but one warm, strong hand settles over mine and we both still for a moment.

'I insist,' he says eventually. Ren pays, leaving what I'd call a generous tip even for a New Yorker. We put our coats back on and head to the door. He holds it open for me, and I brush the tiniest points of connection between us as I pass, feeling his body in microscopic sparks. The rain has thankfully eased to nothing more than a drizzle, and the atmosphere outside feels heavy-limbed, almost spent. The opposite of how I'm feeling…

'Do you know this area much?' I ask, hearing myself sound almost shy now, but somehow not too self-conscious about all that stuff I said back in the restaurant. *Some* forms of truth sit well between us, I'm starting to realise. The essential truths.

'Not really. I grew up in the Village, and even when I moved out I stayed down there. My father taught at NYU.' Ren shoves his hands in his pockets, staring into the distance ahead of us. 'Since I lived with him after the divorce, that was just the part of the city I always knew, so…' He hesitates, pulling out a hand again to scratch his beard. 'Sorry—that counts as details, right?' He looks down at me now, deep brown eyes sparkling, but seeming almost relieved he has a reason to stop himself.

'Har har.' We're drifting vaguely in the direction of the hotel but not quite aiming for it. I slow down almost to a stop, and a middle-aged man in a flasher-trench huffs loudly as he has to walk around us. Ren slows too, turning to face me, and I take a breath. 'Look... You know I was talking about petty shit when I said that, right? Not, like, stuff you really felt like telling me, or...' *God, ease up, Kay.* I shake my head, trying to catch a light-hearted air. 'Listen, don't worry about it.' I start walking again, but Ren reaches out and grabs my hand, pulling me to a halt.

'Hey, come on. I know. Bad joke.' He doesn't let go of my hand, his expression beseeching, as if he'd need to persuade me to forgive him. I look up at him for too long, almost forgetting to blink, and Ren turns his head away from me for a moment then back, like a swimmer taking a breath. 'I do know this part of town a little, I guess. There's actually a pretty cool church over a couple of blocks that way.' His hand slips from mine and he gestures down and to the right, then he pushes his fist into his pocket again, curled tight like he's holding a part of me still gripped in it.

'Oh. A church?' I hear the tone of my voice, and worry I've got him completely wrong.

He chuckles. 'Yes. I'm not... That's not my bag, but it has all these remembrance ribbons tied outside it, and there's something kind of beautiful about it, I don't know. We don't have to go, I just thought maybe—'

'No, let's,' I say quickly. 'Lead the way.' I purse my lips because I already said it earlier at the hotel and I probably sound like a Girl Guide or something, but he smiles at me and starts walking. I fall in beside him.

The city stretches around us, and the breeze swirls, playing, opening the held-together coat of the Korean woman running to the 24-hour bodega up ahead of us, flipping construction tape off scaffolding to make it dance in the air. Ren and I are quiet, but after a while he looks over at me and I wait for him to speak.

'Do you ever think about that phrase, "throwing caution to the wind"?'

It's my turn to chuckle. 'Now, why would you possibly be thinking about that?'

'No reason.' One half of his mouth turns up. 'It's odd, though, isn't it? Caution, something delicate and tentative, and you ball it up and *throw* it, let it be carried off by some invisible force?' He looks up into the sky, like he can see his flying away. If I squint, I can see mine too. 'Actually, I guess it makes sense. If you're getting rid of caution, you might as well throw it, right? It wouldn't really work if you just gently cast it aside.'

I look at him. 'Might blow back on you.'

'Exactly.'

He glances ahead, and I see the church on the corner. We cross the road and walk over to it slowly. Ren's right—what must be hundreds of long satin ribbons hang from the iron railings outside the church, jostling in the breeze, their shine catching the streetlights, blue and green and gold.

'Wow,' I say, walking over and feeling one of the ribbons,

damp and slippery between my fingers. 'You're right, this is beautiful.'

Ren moves next to me, and we follow the railing around, finding a plaque explaining the significance of the colours. Each ribbon is a prayer: yellow for US soldiers, blue for the soldiers of the foreign armies, green, prayers for peace. I turn and look at all these hopes and wishes, their physical representation there for anyone to see. I wonder if mine are so obvious... I turn back and notice Ren staring towards the church's entrance. Light spills from inside it, although there's no service going on at this time of the night.

'I suppose God's open all hours,' I say, regretting the quip as soon as it leaves my lips. 'Do you fancy taking a look inside?'

Ren shakes his head. 'Nah.' He seems to be thinking for a moment. 'One of the last times I was in a church like that, it was for this kid from my class who died when I was in kindergarten. His funeral. He had a hole in his heart, and...' He trails off. I'm about to try and change the subject but he turns to me, leaning his shoulder against the railing and shoving his hands deeper into his pockets. His eyes are bright when he starts to speak. 'I remember after that, I asked my mother what praying meant, and she said it was making an invisible wish and hoping the universe hears you.'

I nod, brushing a hand slowly back and forth over the ribbons.

'It's funny, when I learned that, I would pray all the time, for any shit, you know? New sneakers, or for them to stop fighting.' His voice lowers a little at that. 'And then after a while, when I got older and started, I don't know, forming opinions? I stopped. Decided that wasn't my belief. But every now and then, whenever… There are times when life seems so overwhelming and I just want it to all be different, and for a second praying is all I can think to do. So it makes me wonder—what *do* I really believe?' He turns back towards the church and I follow his gaze. 'I mean I'm not sure it's ever worked before, so why even try?'

I listen to the wind for a moment, like it might have an answer to his question. 'Because maybe it helps,' I say finally. 'Because it allows you to acknowledge a desire inside yourself, and offer it out.'

He pulls both hands out of his pockets and runs them over his face, up through his hair, then steps closer to me, one eyebrow cocked, humour-crinkles back but sincerity in his eyes too.

'Oh good answer, Ms Joseph.'

Five

Ren.

We wander away from the church slowly, and as much as I don't want to right now, I'm remembering Evelyn: her head next to mine on our pillows, teasing me about how her Puerto Rican parents would never forgive us not having a church wedding. I hadn't popped that fateful question, but there was a strong air of expectation floating between us then. Who knew the notion of the rest of our lives together could be so swiftly swept away? But I don't want to think about my hurt pride right now. I want to just be in this moment, with *this* woman.

Kayla.

The more time I spend with her, the more I realise I haven't even thought about the cracks in my heart. I haven't felt the jagged humiliation of that rejection which usually haunts me. I haven't wanted to compare her to Eve. If only this feeling could continue…

Then I remember what Kayla said—*one night*. She's right. How *can* this work beyond tonight? My mind is churning, but the sound of singing—a deep, tuneful rumble—pulls me out of my thoughts and back to Kayla next to me, to that *now* I need to grip onto with both hands. The sound's not coming from her, of course: up ahead, two homeless guys are sitting on a bench eyeing us as we approach. One is leaning back, his arm stretched along the back of the wooden bench like he's relaxing watching TV on a Sunday night, and the other is sitting on the edge of the seat, his back straight, singing heartily and with a serious look on his face. I can't figure out the song, but he's actually pretty good. He finishes just as Kayla and I get near. I move closer to her and nod quickly at the guys on the bench.

'Good evening,' says the singer, his speaking voice surprisingly light given the depth of his singing.

'Evening,' Kayla replies, smiling at them both. 'Nice song.'

'Very kind, very kind,' the guy says. 'Say, either of you got a smoke?'

'Sorry.' I pat the front of my jacket stupidly, as though I'm tapped out. We're up in front of them now, and I almost feel like I'm trespassing. The singer's buddy has his legs stretched out in front of him, crossed at the ankles. I can sense the dark space of the grassy square behind them, and I feel bad about the tension in my body, but it's often when I think there's no harm that the worst things happen. I quicken my steps hoping Kayla will follow suit, but the relaxed guy calls out to us.

'Now you take care of that young woman,' he says, his voice garbled like he's struggling to hold his teeth inside his mouth. 'You take good care of her. A woman like that is *precious.'*

I hear Kayla laugh beside me. I want to tell him it's not her who needs to be taken care of; that she's not mine anyway.

'You're right,' I call over my shoulder.

The sky is beginning to clear, and there's suggestion of stars hovering above the blanket of artificial light covering the city. It's getting cooler, and I notice Kayla shiver in the thin material of her poncho. I'm about to move over, put my arm around her, hold her to my body the way I'm dying to—but then she comes to a halt and points up at a billboard looming over us.

'Look!' she exclaims, like I'd be excited. Like having this hanging over my city isn't borderline humiliating. *Detonate*: A film by João Ren Morgan. A film Ren Morgan can barely believe really has his name on it.

'Hard to miss,' I murmur.

'Ren...' Kayla begins, and I turn to her, but she's studying the sidewalk. 'Critically, it's been well-received so far, yeah? So, why... I feel like you don't—'

I sigh. 'Why did I make this, if I don't believe in it?'

'Well, yeah, if your heart wasn't in it? I mean you've already done so much, and you could do anything else. Why torture yourself? When you started out—'

'I *can't* do anything else, Kayla. When I started out I had no clue what I was doing. I needed—' I break off. *Dammit.* 'It's not always that easy, OK?' I stare up at the huge billboard, hating the tone of my voice, feeling her retreat from me. I force myself to look at her. 'I'm sorry.' I pull in air, so I

105

can force more words out. 'It's just… Lately I'm scared all my ideas are gone. Or I can't— Every time I try to write, to let something *real* out? I can't. It doesn't come. But this is how I earn a living, so when I had the chance to come on board a studio project and just direct, I… I almost felt like I didn't have a choice. I *didn't* have a sponsor, you know? Believe it or not, I'm still paying off my goddamn student loans. And I hate to admit it, but in a way I was relieved not to have to try so hard any more, when… When I'm not even sure I can now.'

Kayla's staring back up at the billboard again, her arms wrapped tightly around her. Some of her dreadlocks have come loose from her bun, and she's frowning like she's struggling to comprehend a lack of ideas. It wouldn't surprise me.

'But that's exactly what they're talking about, right?' I add quietly. 'That's why they're calling me a sell-out.'

'No, Ren,' she says immediately, still looking up. 'I don't buy it. It's all still there, inside you. It's just that not everything happens the way you want it to.' She pauses. 'I *saw* your films. Even with this one—maybe even *especially* with this one—there's something fresh, something really exciting. I don't think there's a limit to that kind of talent, I really don't. Look, if it's worth anything, *I* believe in—' She stops herself, shaking her head a little, but I'm glad she doesn't conclude her sentence. As it is, I'm embarrassed at the tight, emotional feeling it gives me in my chest. 'Well, anyway,' she finishes, inconclusively. She starts walking again, but ponderously, like her legs are a distraction from her thoughts. I follow her, and she draws in a long breath.

'You know, it's weird—at first, growing up, it never occurred to me that art might be something it would be hard to make a living at. My dad's a songwriter, my mum's a makeup artist, and me and my sister never wanted for anything, d'you know what I mean?' Kayla glances over at me and I nod, but she doesn't wait for me to reply. I don't care. I love the sound of her voice, the things she says.

'But they were lucky to make some success of it. I didn't realise how rare that was, and it's only when I got older that I understood what a struggle it's been for them. I thought creativity was what they valued, what they expected from me and my sister, too. As much as anything else, that could be why I try so hard all the time, like I'm trying desperately to live up to this imaginary—' She unfurls her arms suddenly and shakes them as though dismissing the thought, dropping it onto the ground. 'Anyway,' she mutters. 'I don't think art *is* what's important to them. It's more just *us*, our... our character. That in whatever we do, they taught us to try our hardest and not to accept "no" as a final answer.' She adds softly, 'Because so many of them were bound to come our way.'

I nod, transfixed by her. It makes sense, with the way she is, but her parents must have had to really drill it in to her not to perceive limitations, or at least not to accept them. I get the fact that it's a deliberate fight. Kayla's not unaware of what it takes to see herself and her art as valid. I've felt it too. Entitlement isn't something we assume.

'But at the end of the day, struggle wasn't their aim for us. They keep saying they want me to settle down, to take an easier route.' She smiles, but I see the determination laced in it. 'That's when I realised I was an adult, probably—when I could see my own path deviating from their expectations. That's why I'm having to work it out for myself. Why I do this, why I'm fighting so hard for it...' She swallows and glances up at me again. 'My point is—do what you have to do, and do it because you have to. Maybe you need time, money, whatever. But don't use that as an excuse.'

As with a lot of times after she speaks I'm not sure what to say. It sets my gears churning so much more than I expect.

'Here endeth the sermon,' Kayla says, gathering her arms back around her and adjusting the strap of her purse on her shoulder. 'Feel free to jump in with any personal advice you have for me, by the way,' she adds, her expression a mixture of irritated, self-deprecating and embarrassed.

'I wouldn't know where to start,' I reply, and she almost laughs.

'Cheers.'

'I'm kidding. From where I'm standing, I'd say you're doing pretty good.'

She does puff out a wry laugh now. 'Hmm. I think you might need to move a bit closer, then.'

I come to a halt, undo my jacket and pull it off. The wind's still strong, but I want to put my arms around her and this is the closest thing. She realizes I've stopped and comes back over to me. I step toward her, until we're close, face-to-face, and I slip my jacket around her shoulders. She pulls each side of it around her with opposite hands, staring up at me.

'You looked a little cold.'

'Thanks,' she whispers.

I zip my sweater up higher. 'What do you need advice on?'

We start to walk again.

'Oh, God. A lot. Sometimes I feel like I'm a stranger in my own body.'

I frown. 'How so?'

'Well, sometimes I feel kind of… impermanent. Maybe it's being over here, but sometimes I feel almost literally like an alien.' A husky chuckle escapes her. 'So much of the time I feel like I'm some kind of anthropologist just trying to understand how other people think or feel, or what they do, or how they manage to just *be*. They'll spill their guts or be emotional, or selfless, or vulnerable or whatever. They'll give of themselves. They'll… they'll *love*, so easily and I'll think, *how do they do that*? Do I even have that capacity? It's like I'm always trying desperately to understand other people—analyse them. Don't know if you've spotted that.' She smiles a little. 'But really it's because I'm worried that if they can just *feel*, without questioning themselves or each other and I can't, then maybe… Maybe there's something wrong with me.' She sucks in her lip.

'There's nothing wrong with you, Kayla.' It's insane how much I feel that's true right now. 'Why are you so sure you

109

don't feel the same way other people do, anyway? Maybe you're just… cautious.'

'Maybe I just don't know *how* to be vulnerable.' She doesn't look at me now, but she pulls my jacket tighter around her. 'So I face outwards, keep watching other people do all that, and hope nobody notices the giant question mark floating over my head.'

We're quiet for a moment, but I can't let that lie. 'Not vulnerable? If that was true, if you were that way I don't think you'd be here like this with me now,' I say, my voice low, just for her, not anything else around us. 'If that was true, this wouldn't feel the way it does.' It's a risk, but I've said it. And I want to feel it. I want to touch her, feel her against me. For once, it actually seems like she doesn't know what to say. Her eyes hold mine, wide, like she's surprised. Afraid, maybe.

'Yeah,' she whispers.

A bar up ahead spills music onto the street—slow, pulsing bass, piano, chucking guitar, a man's voice, sweet and pure. Reggae. Gregory Isaacs, I think. I sense Kayla's energy change—mine too. She hasn't spoken again, but she waits on the edge of the sound as we get nearer, and looks up at me. I reach over and grab her hand, fast, and pull her toward me. We hold our breath for a moment. The fingers of my right hand slip in between hers and I hold them up; my other hand finally smoothes into that perfect curve of her waist.

We start to dance.

After a little while, she sighs, moving in closer to me,

resting her head on my chest, and my heart beats into her…

She murmurs something.

'Huh?'

She lifts her head, and I'm pissed at myself for not just pretending to hear. 'My grandma used to listen to this all the time,' she says, her voice still soft, drifting in on a memory. Her face breaks into a smile, and it's dazzling, seeing it so close. 'She and I used to dance to it, too.'

'But not like this.' I move closer still, one foot in between hers. She can probably feel me through my jeans, but I think I want her to.

'No. Not like this,' she whispers, and lays her head back on my chest.

The song ends, replaced by something minimal and electronic. A bouncer wanders further onto the sidewalk from the doorway to the bar, smoking a cigarette and looking up and down the street, bored. He nods his head a moment when he sees me and Kayla. We've stopped moving, but I can't let go. Slowly, Kayla peels herself away from me. She lifts my jacket off her shoulders and hands it back.

'Um… I'm a bit warmer now. Thanks.' She smiles up at me again. If she hadn't, I might have been worried I'd overstepped a line.

But she smiles.

I put my jacket on, and we begin to walk again, close. My hand slips back into hers like it's found a brand new home, and her fingers tighten around mine, small but strong. Like her.

We walk the final blocks back to the hotel without saying anything, letting the breeze cool our skin, brush our ears and stir our thoughts. Before I can completely steel myself for being back up in the room alone with her, the bright lights of the Vincent are up ahead of us and the porter is holding open the heavy door, welcoming us back. The dark lobby is still bustling with people, and ambient music pulses low and womb-like. Maybe they're all in a trance. I think I might be.

The blonde lady at the desk calls over to me as we move past.

'Oh, excuse me, Mr Morgan, you have a couple messages here, sir.' I go over to the desk and grab them with a tight smile at the receptionist, remembering I'd put my cell on silent. I don't want to think about rescheduled meetings and deadlines and business. Not now. I glance at the messages— my manager, Ione, Nick. None of it seems urgent. Not when Kayla is waiting for me. I consider asking her if she wants to stay downstairs and have a drink, delay the nerve-jangling unknown waiting for us upstairs. But it's late—she's probably tired. I know I am. And I know that I'm anxious to be alone with her, all the same.

And Kayla's already headed toward the elevators.

'How 'bout that storm?' says the older guy who gets on with us, his beard impeccably shaped. He looks like a lumberjack-turned-retired-menswear-model. I'm simultaneously kind of glad and kind of pissed that he's here. He presses the button for the floor below ours.

'Mmmhmm, pretty bonkers,' Kayla says politely. I can

sense the tension in her body, too. We fall silent, waiting. He gets out. The elevator doors close again... but they're open again too fast. Kayla and I freeze a moment, then I step out finally, holding the doors. The elevator "bings" impatiently as she follows. As soon as I move my arm away the elevator doors slide shut again, as hurried as we are hesitant. We walk slowly down the hallway, the rapid sounds of our breathing muffled against the thick carpet and luxurious wallpaper.

'What time is it?' I ask, fumbling with the key card as we reach the door to the suite. Kayla stands close behind me.

'Just after half two,' she says.

'Damn.' I knew it was late, but the time still takes me by surprise.

I don't want to reach tomorrow too fast.

Just as the door unlocks with an electronic beep, I feel Kayla's hand on my back—cool against the skin just above the waistband of my jeans. She's slipped it up under my T-shirt, my sweater, my jacket... I hold still for a moment, my heartbeat gathering pace as she circles her hand slowly, her head resting on my shoulder. Fighting every impulse to turn around, press her up against the door and kiss her into next week, I instead push it open. Her hand slips away, and we enter. The door clicks shut behind us, and Kayla flips over the lock. The lights are low—somehow housekeeping must have been in to turn down the suite, despite the hour. Premium service. Kayla undoes her poncho and hangs it carefully by the door not saying anything else, but her eyes drifting back toward me every so often. I wait, but she's quiet

113

for the moment. Then I start to say something, but she beats me to it.

'Do you mind if I run a bath?' she asks, her voice a haze of smoke. I shake my head, mute now, my breaths coming shallow. She walks away from me into the bedroom, her purse dangling on her fingertips. I hear water start to run. Goddamn. I don't want to fuck this up. I'm not certain if she's going to bed, if I should say goodnight, if I should just go in there and—

No. Patience.

I take off my jacket, my sweater, my boots, and sit on the couch, waiting. For what, I'm not totally sure.

But I wait.

Six

Kayla.

The steam envelops me. I stare at the water swirling into the bathtub for a while, and then examine the bottles standing to attention on one side of its huge expanse. I open one, pouring the thick liquid under the stream until a cloud of bubbles begins to foam, the heady herbal scent imbuing the air. I pick one of the robes off the back of the bathroom door and head back into the bedroom. I can see Ren sitting on the sofa in the living room of the suite, leaning back and staring at the ceiling, his chest rising and falling fast. He feels my eyes on him and turns his head. The bedroom door is only slightly ajar, but it's enough. He can see me.

My nerve endings seem to be hovering outside my body, I'm so aware of my skin, my pulse. I don't know what's changed to make it almost unbearable now. Perhaps it's since he finally touched me, held me close to him... What's really scaring me is that it's not *only* physical. That would make more sense to me. That would be "allowed" in my twisted logic, I suppose. This? I have no idea what this is. I do not know this man. Do I? He's already deep under my surface, and I don't know how he got there. Am I already betraying this ring on my finger, even if the arrangement is a matter of convenience?

I don't want to think about it.

I'm not self-conscious as I start to unbutton my shirt, knowing Ren's watching me. I glance up at him and he's hovering on the point of a smile—controlled, but backed with undeniable desire. I hadn't really intended to tease, but I slow my movements down anyway, each one deliberate. Unbuttoning my shirt and pulling it off my shoulders, folding it, laying it over the back of a chair... My bra is black, semi-sheer, nothing special—but the concentration of Ren's gaze on me makes my nipples tighten against its seams. I push the button of my jeans through the hole, lower the zip, then I sit down at the foot of the bed to unlace my boots and pull them off, socks too. I stand back up. He's still looking at me, blinking slowly, quiet. Accommodating but coiled; ready if asked. I peel my jeans down my legs languorously, bending low to the ground to slip them off my feet, feeling the weight of my breasts shift. I straighten up slowly, dumping my jeans on the bed, not bothering to fold this time. Ren's leaning forwards now with his elbows on his knees, pushing both hands through his hair. When he turns his head back to me standing in just my bra and plain black cotton pants he opens his mouth like he wants to say something, but then just shakes his head. I go to where I left the robe on the plush chair in the corner and pull it on. It's warm, soft and thick, too big for me, but that just makes me more aware of my near-naked body beneath it.

I head out of the bedroom and pad over to Ren, stand right in front of him.

'Come and talk to me,' I say, looking down at him. He's still leaning on his elbows, and I lift one finger to trace the rise and fall of strands of his hair. He moves his hand suddenly, gripping mine as it hovers above his head, and weaves his fingers in between my own.

'Do you know it's my birthday today?' His voice is a low rumble.

I'm not sure if it's some kind of line. 'It's your birthday?'

He moves his fingers up and down between mine. 'Yeah.'

I reach my free hand up to sweep down his cheek and under his chin, my palm smoothing over the surprisingly soft hairs of his beard, and raise his face to look up at me. I brush my thumb over his lips, wide and smooth, then move my hand back up into his hair. He closes his eyes and exhales as I sweep through it in long strokes, back and back. It's so soft... I stare at his face and notice that the crease between his brows is gone, just for a moment.

After a while, I silently pull Ren to his feet and lead him through the bedroom and into the bathroom. In spite of how long it's been running, the huge tub is only now getting full. The room is filled with steam, the low lights under the mirrors making it just bright enough to see by, their illumination swirling in the droplets suspended in the air.

'Take off your socks,' I tell him. He sits down on the toilet seat to oblige. I wait, and he stands up again, deliberately close. I pull at his T-shirt, seeing his chest still rising and falling rapidly underneath it. 'This too,' I whisper.

He drags it over his head in that way men do, grabbing the back of the neck and pulling. It sends his hair into sexy disarray but I barely notice, because his body is right in front of me now; the dark hair dusting his chest, the golden brown shine of his skin visible even in the dim light. Before I can ask, he unbuttons his jeans and pulls them off. In the tight grey boxer briefs he wears underneath I can see the outline of him, hard, like I felt him against me when we danced.

I undo the belt of my robe, take it off and go to hang it behind the door. With my back turned to him, I undo my bra and hang it on another hook, then slip off my pants, leaving them crumpled where they lie on the floor. When I turn back to Ren, I see him thicken and grow a bit more, straining against the fabric of his underwear. I feel my pulse concentrating between my legs.

He clocks my gaze and gives me a half-smile. 'I can wait,' he murmurs, then lifts one eyebrow as I swallow. 'Can you?'

It takes everything I have to ignore him. He chuckles softly as I walk over, step into the tub, and sink down inside the warmth, the bubbles. 'Come on.'

I have to bite the inside of my cheek and flick my gaze away finally as he frees himself from his boxers and lets them fall. He steps into the water and lowers himself in with a sigh. The tub is big enough that I have to hold the sides to stay upright, but our legs tangle as we face each other, and Ren takes hold of my feet, letting me push against his hands, rubbing their arches slowly with his thumbs. I close my eyes for a moment, letting the heat and his hands melt the tension from my muscles. A groan slips from my throat and echoes around us, more erotic-sounding than I intended, but he only rubs my feet harder. I smile to myself: a good sign.

'Is it seriously your birthday?' I manage to ask at last.

He nods, his face slightly in shadow. 'From the stroke of midnight.'

The word *stroke* echoes in my mind. 'Oh… Shit. And is this usually how you celebrate? With a stranger?'

He frowns when I say that, and I know that I don't mean it.

'This is the best birthday I've had in a very long time, Kayla.' The water sloshes gently as he continues to massage my feet, edging up slowly to my ankles, my calves. 'Honestly, pretty often I do seem to be in an anonymous hotel when it comes around, yeah. But not often with anyone as… Mostly not with anyone at all, actually.'

The languid movement of his fingertips against my skin under the water is making it hard to form words, but I persevere. Nothing feels wrong tonight. 'Do you not enjoy getting older?'

'Who does?'

I splash one hand out of the water to gesture to myself.

He smiles. 'Of course.'

'Yeah. Seriously, I love my birthday. I love the focus of it. It's like a marker. Like, you're on a journey, but sometimes it's so slow you can't feel it. So you only know you're progressing because you pass that post, regular as clockwork.

It's a chance to assess, isn't it? Plus, I fucking love presents.'

Ren laughs, shifting the air and the bubbles. 'Oh yeah? Me too. Where's my gift, huh? I'm thinking as a journalist you should have known it was my birthday.' His hands leave me for a moment as he slicks his hair back. Bubbles settle in it, and drops of bathwater trickle down his face and into his beard. With his hair wet, his features seem more pronounced, even more beautiful. I restrain myself from pushing through the water and pouring my body over him. I want to let us talk. I want to let this build until it's unbearable…

His hands return to my feet, kneading slowly, testing my resolve. 'You know I'm not really a journalist,' I say, my voice huskier, giving me away. 'If I was, I'd have a hell of a story right now.' He presses my instep teasingly, and I wince. 'But you're right, I should have known that. I'll… I'll sort out something for a gift.' His face turns serious, because that's tomorrow-talk. 'Maybe I'll make you something,' I add in a whisper. This is all the epitome of wishful thinking, and we both know it.

'OK,' he replies softly after a while. 'I'd like that. Thanks.'

I sigh and lean back against the slope of the tub, and he supports my weight as he does the same. I reach over to turn the tap to run some more hot water. We fall quiet for a moment, with just the soothing slosh of water every now and then as we adjust our bodies slightly, and the muffled drip of the tap disappearing into soft bubbles.

'So how old are you now?' I ask eventually.

'Thirty-one.' He sounds almost surprised at the number.

I can hear him thinking in the silence that follows. 'You know how you said it's like going on a journey that's too slow to notice? It's funny, for a while in my life I actually felt like I was moving *really* fast—like, hurtling toward something. Maybe out of control, even. Then I got stopped in my tracks.' He takes a long breath. 'The people I loved most in my life... God, it seems so stupid now.'

'Tell me,' I whisper.

'I was with someone, like I told you. Evelyn. And she was everything I thought I wanted. Everything. But then she and Yannick, my best friend—'

'Yeah.' I nod, letting him know I know who he is, and what happened. 'That must have been hard.'

'Yeah.' He's silent for a while, and I let him be. 'It was. I guess in hindsight I could feel it growing between them, and slipping away between her and me. But I felt betrayed.' His jaw is tight. 'I still do.'

'Course you do,' I respond gently, but that seed of guilt—tiny but restless—begins to unfurl deep in my gut. Am I doing the same thing to him now, by not telling Ren the full story about Cole? Is that a betrayal of sorts, too?

Ren takes a breath. 'It hit me so much harder than I ever could have imagined,' he says. 'It was like being abandoned. As if none of it was ever real—our friendship, our love? I mean, they were my *family*, you know? It's not like I ever had a whole bunch of that before Yann and Eve. I'd known him since I was a kid scratching my balls in the schoolyard. And then meeting Eve at college... She was this beautiful

Puerto Rican Truffaut obsessive, and she just had this calm about her that I needed so badly... Man. I fell *hard*.' He shakes his head regretfully, embarrassed and wistful, glancing at me like I might know the feeling. I didn't think I did. 'It felt like they'd been there for every important thing in my life, creative or otherwise. We stumbled our way through to adulthood together. And it sounds fucking naïve now, but I always kind of thought of it as him and me, and her and me.' He gestures to either side of the tub to mark the delineation. 'I relied on both of them in one way or another, right? And then in what felt like a split second, it was all destroyed.' His face is stony, and I miss his hands on me. I'm beginning to wish we'd skipped this topic, and all this talking. But at the same time... *I want to know him.*

Ren laughs bitterly. 'You know what's fucked up, is even as angry as I was, to the point where I— Well, I know you saw the clip.' He looks at me wryly, and I have to shrug and nod. 'Even at *that* moment there was this super weird part of me that was actually almost *happy* for them.' He raises his eyebrows incredulously, and I can't help smiling. 'Can you believe that shit?'

'I can,' I murmur.

He looks at me for a moment. 'Anyway.' He closes his eyes, hiding from me, and shakes his head. 'Eve was... She was important.' The past tense resonates with me more than it should. 'But Yann was my oldest friend, my *best* friend. I know that sounds crazy immature, but he really was. And now it's all fucked up. We don't even speak.' Ren's voice grows lower. 'I just had no idea how much my sense of myself, my creativity, was tied up with *us*. With our collaboration. Now I guess I can really see myself, but who I'm left with is someone I'm not sure I want to be.'

'Come on, that's bollocks. Don't say that.' I lean forward again and find his hand under the water, entwine my fingers with his.

'It's true, Kayla. I mean, you asked "why do we create", and I honestly think I only started creating because he did. When we were in high school, I never thought ideas could become *things*. I just… *thought*, abstractly, you know? He *did*. He made us learn. We went to film school *together*. Honestly, he made both those first films what they were. And now I don't know if I can do it on my own.' He stares at me now, eyes wide, like he's finally admitted something out loud.

'Ren—'

'I know. You believe in me.' He pulls his hand away, and I try not to feel hurt. Obviously I've failed, because Ren sees my face and his expression softens. He reaches out and trails a fingertip down my arm. Warm trickles of water follow it and it feels so good I have to wait a moment before I speak.

'If… if all that's true, then why was it you that got the credit? Was that a lie, is that what your saying? What, you bulldozed your friend, stole his ideas, used him and took all the plaudits?' I'm being too harsh, but I do want to know. What if it's true? Would that affect how I feel towards Ren?

He shakes his head. 'No, I… No. But I know I couldn't have written or directed either of them without Yann's steer.

Obviously, because now I do bullshit for money. Apparently that is going to be my creative life now, because every time I try to do something else I just get…' He breaks off, running a hand over his face. I scoot my body closer to his, reaching out to rest my hands on his shoulders and bending my knees up so I can get in between his legs. He looks at me as I run my fingers up his jawline and cup it.

'You're just frustrated, Ren. That's what it is.'

He lets his eyes roam down over my body in the darkness and I know what he's thinking. I bite back a smile, but let it soften away. 'You're allowed to still be hurt.'

He exhales quietly. 'You have no idea,' he says.

I want to help him. His eyes say that I might be already, and I almost lean forward and kiss him right then, but I feel like somehow this means more—savouring just being here with him. The bathwater sloshes again as I slowly turn around, leaning back into him. Ren wraps his arms around my middle, his forearms underneath my breasts, his chin resting on my shoulder. He's still hard, and I can't help shuffling myself in closer. He twitches against me, and I take a breath.

'What are you thinking?' His words sigh against my damp skin.

'I don't know if I should answer that honestly,' I murmur, and his tongue sneaks onto the edge of my earlobe, brushing against the row of tiny hoop piercings there.

'OK…' His voice is so close. *Not yet.*

I think for a second. 'I know all about guilt,' I whisper.

'I know how to pretend to ignore it. I know it's a sneaky fucking bastard.'

I can feel him nodding. 'Oh yeah? What are you guilty about? Let's have a guilt party.'

I give a breathy, half-hearted laugh that fizzes out against the bubbles in the tub. 'If I really let myself admit it, I'm guilty about the way I seem to always get to do what I want.' I run my hands partway down his legs, feeling the coarse hairs on his skin under the water.

'I can imagine that…'

God. My nerve endings are singing. 'I feel guilty about…' I try to think how to express it. 'About how things seem to end up going my way, and maybe I don't always think about whether it might involve stepping on someone's feelings.'

Ren runs his nose up and down my shoulder. 'OK… Want to get a little more specific?'

'Oh, we're going full therapy session, eh?' I ask, shifting against him. I'm definitely scared to tell him the whole story with Cole—especially now. At the very least, surely he'd balk at the whole complicated affair. Would he see me differently? Is it stupid to even worry about it? There's no future here. That was the whole point of allowing myself to do this, wasn't it?

Ren doesn't need to know. *Just one night…*

There is at least one truth I can share, and it feels like a relief. 'Well, like with my older sister, Christy. We were close. Really close. And now we're not. When I admit to myself that I *had* a part in it, I feel pretty shit for it.'

'What happened?'

I chew on my lip for a while. 'I think we're just too alike. Too stubborn. And we both take things too personally when it comes to the other. We said some stupid things...' I feel my teeth clench. 'Thing is, I'd been jealous of her for so long. I *idolised* her. She's having to put her career on hold at the moment while she has a baby and I suppose I saw my chance to jump ahead, to be the one that reached that ultimate benchmark of artistic success. Even though that's pretty damn ironic at the moment, since I don't even know if—' I halt quickly and blow out air. 'Either way, we've reached what you might call an impasse.'

'So... What, you're not speaking because you don't agree with each other's decisions?'

'You make it sound irrational,' I say, and Ren chuckles, his breath tickling my neck. 'I suppose I just took it for granted that she'd be a constant. You know, someone who'd always have my back. And to find out that it's not true...' I swallow.

'It is true. I'm sure it is.'

'Why?'

'Well, because if it wasn't you wouldn't have felt that way in the first place. Remember you said I probably wasn't good at lying? I think when it comes to people you really connect with, it's just not that *easy* to mask your true self.' He pauses, and I feel his muscles tense. 'Um... Not to say that we're...'

'It's OK. I know what you mean.' *And it's freaking me out.* I'm naked with this beautiful man, fit to burst, but even just talking with him feels as good as I know he will when he—

Ren clears his throat. 'It'll all iron out. You were right, people really *aren't* that good at hiding the truth.'

I run my fingers along the veins in his hands, which are standing up because of the warmth of the bath water. 'I dread to think what other people make of the real me sometimes.'

'They think you're pretty incredible.'

Shit. I can feel my heart beating harder, and I close my eyes. When I open them again and turn my head to look at him, he's watching me through a veil of lashes.

I can't wait any longer.

'Ren?' I whisper.

'Yeah.'

'What do you want to happen right now?' I sit up, turning around to face him again and crossing my legs so that my knees press against the sides of the tub, stopping me from slipping down. The very tips of my nipples rise above the line of the bubbles, peaked almost to the point of pain. Ren's gaze drifts down.

'What do you mean?'

'Right now. What would you like to happen right now?' I think for a moment. 'I want you to describe it to me. Like you're directing a film.' My breathing punctuates each break in my words, and I feel the swell between my legs. 'Well, not all technical.' I emit a breathy laugh. 'I need to be able to understand it. What you would have us do, in the scene. Where the camera would go, what you'd let the audience see on the screen.'

His eyes burn into mine. For a second I think he won't do it, but—

'I'd open in close up, on your face. Your profile. The way the light is against your skin, like a silhouette picked out by fire. Hold on that for a few beats—just you. Still. Then I'd move myself into the frame, slowly. And… I'd press my lips against yours.' His eyes flick to my mouth for a moment, then back up.

'Yeah?'

'Cut to a wider angle, and show my hands skimming down your chest. Over your breasts, lightly. Brushing over your nipples. Then down, into the water.'

My heart is hammering. 'We can't see what they're doing under there.'

His smile is almost cruel. 'No.'

I swallow.

'You push me away and stand up. Camera changes angles, to capture the water cascading down your whole naked body.' He pauses. 'Then cut to wide, both of us in shot. Me still in the tub, gazing up at you.' He draws in a slow breath.

'Yes…'

'Then I'd stand, too. Wrap you in a towel, wrap my arms around you. Close up again on our faces as I lean in to kiss you. For real this time. Deep, so we feel it coming off the screen.'

'Mmm…' I close my eyes.

'And then…' He pauses. 'Kayla?'

'Yes?' My voice barely emerges. I open my eyes to his helpless stare.

'This is torture.'

I smile. 'The good kind.'

I do stand up, but I don't linger as he watches me. I splash out of the tub and onto the bathmat, facing away from him, letting water drip over my skin. I almost melt as I feel his fingertips reach over and smooth down the curve of my lower back. Exhaling loudly, I move away, picking the robe off hook on the back of the door again. I put it on but leave it hanging open and turn back to Ren, holding one of the enormous bath sheets in my hand. I walk over to pass it to him, but he pushes it away as he climbs out of the tub, still tantalisingly hard as he steps onto the bathmat in front of me. I take a step back and let the towel slip from my fingers to the floor unthinkingly.

He reaches both hands inside my robe, resting them on my waist and pulling me closer, running them up and down the sides of my body, slick with the damp of the bathwater. There's only a fraction of space between the jutting tip of him and the smooth span of my stomach. His gaze runs down the length of my body, slow. Mine follows, seeing what he sees. The dark gleam of my skin, the hard peaks of my nipples, the slight curve of my tummy, my curled fuzz of pubic hair.

My thighs, pressing together. My toes scrunching against the floor.

Ren's eyes travel back up and lock with mine. But then his hands retreat, and he closes the robe around me and does up the belt in a bow. He reaches up to my hair and unwinds the elastic that's now barely holding my locs up in a bun, letting them tumble down. And then he takes my face in his hands and moves closer to me—very, very close.

And kisses me...

And kisses me...

And kisses me.

His tongue sweeps into my mouth, tasting me, flicking against my teeth. He pulls my lips between his, kisses each of them separately, then together, over and over until I can hardly stand up.

We break apart for air, and he rests his forehead against mine.

'I am very naked right now.'

I wrap my arms around his neck and look into his eyes, so he understands when I whisper,

'Me too.'

Seven

Ren.

Why did I close her robe? That was supremely fucking stupid. But Jesus, it was because she's almost *too*—

I'm senseless. All I can do right now is feel.

I watch as Kayla grabs a bottle of body oil or something from the over-stocked counter and strides out of the bathroom. I lean down and pick up the towel where she'd dropped it on the floor, brushing some of the water droplets of my body. I'm so hard it aches, and it doesn't help when I wrap the towel around my waist and head into the bedroom to see her smoothing the lotion onto her legs slowly as she perches on the edge of the bed. She looks up at me, and I can't take it. I remove the bottle from her hands and place it resolutely on the side table. I crouch down between her legs, push away the sides of the robe then reach up and loosen the belt, but not all the way.

I lick my lips and she watches me as she leans back on the bed, resting on her hands and tilting her head to one side like a wordless challenge. *What you got?* I move closer, pushing her legs wider apart, slowly kissing the soft skin inside of her knees. She lets a tiny hum slip out, and I smirk a little.

Let me show you. I move inwards, still kissing. Eventually I reach my destination and run my nose against the soft hair between her legs. She smells like bubble bath and caramel and sex and *heaven*. I edge my fingertips up along her thighs, and she shuffles her ass toward the edge of the bed, closer to me—impatient. My fingers curve around her tight flesh and smooth up into the soft warm wet of her and she groans, her head thrown back. That sound... I feel myself spill a little when I finally move in to taste her: just the tip of my tongue against her small hard pearl, in tight, concentrated circles, then giving in and licking the whole length of her, bottom to top. Kayla moans again, loud... *Yes*. I close my eyes, making steady constant laps against her, not too fast, just until she starts to squirm enough, and then I suck hard—

'Oh fuck... Ren...'

Her body shifts as she fists one hand into my hair, and she's starting to drip against my lips, unbearably delicious, but I concentrate now, lifting one of her legs to hook over my shoulder, my tongue flicking faster over her in the spot that makes her emit that gorgeous moan again, louder and louder, and her bare foot is moving up and down my back, her heel digging into my spine, hand in my hair, pushing my face into her, my nose pressed right against her, my tongue flicking, my fingers helping now, pushing into her, curling inside her, until she's tight and so slick around them, until I feel her muscles seize... And then she comes, hot and wet, right there in my mouth, shouting my name so loud I really believe that one syllable is the very sound of her ecstasy—*my name*. And for that moment, kneeling between her legs, knowing I put that look on her face and that tremble in her body, I feel like a king. If I could do that every day? But…

Panting hard, Kayla curves her body forward, both her warm hands pressed against my ears, and she's kissing the top of my head then pulling my face up and kissing my mouth, the taste of her still on my lips.

'I want you inside me,' she breathes against them.

It takes everything I have not to stand and move her back and sink into her right then and there. 'I want that too, but we should—'

'There's probably some in the drawer.' Her voice is breathy with need. She moves, getting her balance by resting her hand on my shoulder, and I shuffle aside so she can stand. Then I get up too, walking behind her and pulling her robe off one shoulder, bending down to kiss it. She pauses, undoing the robe altogether and letting it fall to the floor, and I lift her hair so I can kiss her neck too. I can hear her breathing, loud and deep like mine. She steps away and walks the rest of the way around the bed to the other side, opening the drawer and roaming its fancy for-purchase contents furtively until she sighs in relief and produces the pack. I exhale too, and she climbs onto the bed and crawls back over to me. I ditch the towel, and she looks down and trails her fingers lightly along the length of my cock. My breathing hitches as she reaches the tip, but then her hands leave me and she opens one of the condoms. Usually I hate them, but I think it's just as well there's something to stop the overwhelming sensation of her, even a little.

Kayla's hands are shaking as she rolls the rubber over me, then she sits up and lets her hands move up my chest and around to the back of my neck, her eyes finding mine. I grab her, clambering onto the bed too, and we fall onto the overstuffed pillows kissing, her legs wrapping around me. We're on our sides, face-to-face, her fingers running up into my hair, which is still damp. I open my eyes for a moment and see hers squeezed shut. My heart constricts, and I have to wait a moment before I roll her onto her back, hold myself tight and seek her hot, slick center. I move inside her, finally, and as I do Kayla opens her eyes again and looks straight into my soul. Her lips part silently, her gaze not leaving mine. I can't help the low noises I make each time I move out and into her again, pulling her close, pressing away the space between us. Jesus, the amount of times I've fucked, I've never felt anything like this.

Like her.

After a while—or an eternity—like that, she moves back a little, letting me slide out. She turns over and drags one of the huge pillows low under her stomach, bending over it and looking back at me, her eyelids low, biting her lip. I can't move fast enough. I bend my body over hers and push inside her again from behind.

'Oh God, yes. Mmm, please...'

The words she's crying out, begging me, the sounds she's making, the sound of me moving in and out of her, the scent of her sweat and mine... It's almost too much. I move deeper and faster and harder as she urges me to go deep, fast, hard, more and more and more—until my name is on her lips again, muffled in the pillows as she buries her face and rides it out, and then hers is on mine, grunted tightly into her ear as our fingers twist and grip together.

Then whispered again softly.

Kayla.

I don't want to leave her, but eventually I pull out and slip the condom into a Kleenex from the box beside the bed. I drop it to the floor and flop back next to her. She curls her body into mine and I run my fingertips over the damp, smooth, beautiful length of her back, up to the tangle of thin gold chains at her neck. I watch goose bumps break out over her skin, and it makes me think of her questions. Even back when she asked them of me it felt like this moment was inevitable. Us, naked and together.

But—

'Was this a bad idea?' she whispers, and I tense.

'Really?'

'No. God. No, I'm just... That was...'

'Yeah. I know.' It felt too good. Too good for what has to happen soon.

I kiss her forehead, and she moves slowly to sit up, pushing the extraneous cushions and pillows off the side of the bed and manoeuvring awkwardly until she can pull the covers up and slip beneath them. She laughs softly, and I join her, standing and pulling back my side of the bedding. I get under the covers too, and she settles against me once more, her skin warm next to mine. I close my eyes, hating every moment I won't get to feel this with her again. A while passes, and I can tell she's not asleep. The lights are still on in the room, but she's quiet. I want to know what she's thinking, but at the same time...

'Kayla,' I begin, and she shifts a little. 'Are you OK?'

'Yeah.' Her voice is high, self-consciously affirming.

'Sorry, that wasn't what I wanted to ask.' But then I fall silent, because I'm not sure where to start, which question to ask and whether I really want to know the answers. 'I mean, you don't really regret it, do you? I'm just worried that you think this was, like, my *plan* or something, to just get you—'

'No.' She moves, propping a pillow against the headboard and sitting up, but she stays close to me. I sit up a little too. 'I suppose I'm not OK.' Her voice is quiet. My hand finds hers and squeezes. Fuck. 'But I'd rather have... Look this wasn't what I was expecting.' She plays with the comforter. 'That's a lie. I did expect this, sort of. Not the specifics, but when I met you there was just this—'

'Thing,' I finish.

She laughs quietly. 'Yeah. Some inexplicable *thing*. I don't know what that is, or what it means, but I also know that I just have to enjoy it while it lasts, right?'

'Right.' I don't know why that makes me so fucking depressed. My mind wanders to that idea of connection—especially that feeling of my body inside hers. That moment when there was nothing else to know. I could have stretched that experience to infinity and it wouldn't have been enough.

But it wouldn't have been the same without the feeling I have about *her*, as a person.

Nothing about this is the same as I've felt before.

God, what am I even thinking?

This can't be one-sided though. Kayla just might feel the same way, but I don't know if there's anything we can do about it. I guess at least if that's true, she won't have to learn the things about me that might make her feel differently, and neither will I. If this is it, then maybe it's perfect.

Screw perfect, though. Maybe for her, I'm willing to take a risk. I draw a breath. 'I don't want to ruin this, but—' I begin, then stop as Kayla shakes her head. She shuffles back down into the bed and turns toward me. Confounded, I lift my arm so that she can settle under it, her head against my chest.

'Then don't.'

Eight

Kayla.

I listen to Ren's heartbeat under my ear, feeling soothed and scared simultaneously. I open my eyes, realising that I might just be an utter failure at doing a one-night stand. What are all these feelings? This isn't supposed to happen. This *wasn't* supposed to happen.

I sit up a bit and reach over Ren to switch off the light by the bed. It's still not quite dark in here though—the low light from the living room and the bathroom cast a faint glow that settles over the room, and all of a sudden I feel how foreign this place is. But then as I rest back on his chest, it all seems to fall away into the familiar.

It feels right.

Ren's arms tighten around me. I trail my fingertips very lightly up and down his stomach and I hear his pulse quicken.

'That tickles,' he murmurs.

'Yeah?' I do it again, and I can sense him growing more aware of my naked body against his. I still ache with the memory of him inside me. 'I've always thought the stomach is one of the most sensitive parts of the body,' I whisper. 'There's something about the skin here.' My fingers rise and fall under the quickening of his breathing.

'Apparently,' he says, but then he catches my hand, holding it gently. 'But I'm not sure if...'

'Hmm?'

'Kayla, I want to, but I think if I... If we do that again, I'm not sure I'll be able to leave.'

He says it with an unconvincing chuckle, and in that moment I realise he means it. Finally, just for a second, I let myself think it: What if... What if we actually made love, just for this moment? Created it, with our minds and our bodies?

I want it again. I want more, while I still can.

I pull my hand free of his and move down his body, kissing the skin where my fingertips had been, brushing my lips against the dark trail of hair below his belly button but heading down no further, dropping tiny kisses all around his abdomen, then edging up to his chest and down again. I turn my head to look at him, and his hands sweep my locs away from my face as I rest my cheek against his stomach. I can't make out his expression in the semi-darkness.

'Maybe I don't want you to leave,' I whisper. It's the truth. I sit up slowly, and feel for the other condom abandoned somewhere in the bedclothes. My fingers find what they're looking for, and then I move to straddle Ren, my eyes adjusting until I can just about make out the wrinkles on his forehead as I look down at him, the frown between his knitted brows—his expression caught somewhere between pleasure and pain. I want to tell him it's OK, that I feel it too, but I can't find the words.

I reach down and push his cock gently against his stomach, then grind my hips, slowly slicking myself along his hard length, back and forth. We both moan at the sensation. Even just doing this, I think we could both... But eventually, I raise myself up and open the condom, rolling it on. I close one hand around him, feeling his hot pulse under my palm even through the latex. Then I kneel up and position him right where I need him.

I wait, just for a moment, anticipating... Then I sink down onto him, sighing into a groan. I lean forwards until my breasts are resting against Ren's chest, my face nestling into the crook of his neck, breathing into his ear, kissing his skin, and he moves his hips up to meet me. I shift so that my forehead is pressed against his, and Ren's breath is tickling my lips, until I'm breathing him and he's breathing me. I push down on him, rolling my hips now, and his low moans vibrate against my body, occasionally forming my name.

Eventually I sit up again, arching my back and moving my hips in a rhythm that overtakes me as Ren's hands sweep up over my hips to find my breasts, kneading, twisting at the peaks of my nipples. We make unconscious, primal sounds that surround us in the air. I begin to move faster, the burning ache building inside me, inside him. I almost can't tell which of us is which, where I end and he begins, and I sink all of myself over him as I feel his body tense and his fingers dig into my behind. A sudden, high sound emanates from my throat, and I realise I've been holding my breath—it bursts free and I cry out just as my orgasm clenches around him. Moments later he's coming too, sitting up and reaching one hand around the back of my head to grip my hair, the other still squeezing my bottom hard, his words a strangled incomprehensible strain in his throat.

His fingers slowly relax their press into my flesh as he sinks back onto the bed, but I stay on top of him, letting the tight feeling of him inside me gradually begin to slacken. Eventually, I raise up and off him. Ren makes a strange regretful sound as I leave him, and I feel the same. For a moment I turn on my side and curl away from him, pulling the covers around me. He shuffles, getting rid of the condom I suppose, and I try to breathe deep and ignore the sinking feeling in the pit of my stomach. Seconds stretch, my skin growing cold despite the warmth of the covers over my body, because he's not touching me. I try to convince myself that everything is going to be all right.

Because it's just one night, isn't it.

I'm on the very precipice of sleep when I feel Ren against my back, his body's shape mirroring mine, his arm reaching over me, drawing me in to him, his knees curving into the back of my own.

'Kayla… I don't know what to do with this feeling.'

His words are barely audible, but I still whisper back, 'No. Neither do I.'

We can't say anything else.

So we just drift…

When I open my eyes again, they're assaulted by bright

light flooding in through the open blinds. For a moment I'm not sure where I am, and I realise it's because Ren is not here with me. His absence feels recent; my skin still remembers his touch. I sit up, yawning, and notice the bedroom door is closed, but I can hear his voice low in the other room. As I move my limbs ache deliciously from the sex last night, but my heart begins to beat faster with apprehension. Today it will all be over.

I decide to leave him to his phone call—or perhaps I'm just delaying having to see Ren in the cold light of day. Instead, my eyes fall on the large notepad emblazoned with The Vincent Hotel's minimal logo, and the matching pencil next to it on the bedside table. Somehow a moment later the covers are tucked around me, the pad is balanced on my tented knees, and the pencil is sketching against the page like my hands are possessed. I smile to myself, somewhat sadly, as the drawing takes shape. It's only a rough, but probably the best thing I've done in months. Fitting, maybe.

Eventually I tear the paper off the pad and fold it carefully. I'll have to wait for my chance to give him my gift.

I grab some clean clothes and underwear from my suitcase, and go into the bathroom. The tub is still full of water, and faint evidence of what happened last night is evaporating on the tiled floor. I reach in and turn the dial to allow the plug to raise and begin to drain it. I stare mesmerised at the water starting to swirl, and then finally turn away, stepping into the vast separate shower cubicle and staring dumbly at the complicated controls. Eventually I manage to create a hard, pounding stream and step under it, washing myself slowly, but still feeling what's left imprinted on me.

This is ridiculous. Even if I *hadn't* accepted Cole's proposal and this crazy idea to allow me to keep the life I want... I'll be in London for now, and Ren doesn't live in New York any more. Even if he did, he'd never be here—he said as much himself. I *knew* all that already, and more, going in to this.

I'm the stupid idiot who did it anyway.

Not to mention that this wasn't the plan. This was the *opposite* of the plan. It was meant to be one night of letting myself throw caution to the wind with this stupidly unattainable guy, not some kind of inexplicable... weirdly meaningful... sexy as hell...

Shit.

I dress quickly, ignoring my reflection, and then take a deep breath as my hand rests on the door handle to the living room. I retreat for a moment, deciding I should probably check my own phone, see what's happening with my flights. It's heading towards midday, and my mate Sami's replied to my message from last night about my flight delay—I told her I'll get a cab from Heathrow to hers when I eventually get to London. There's also a couple of missed calls from Cole. I listen to his deep, familiar voice in my messages. He's heard about the problems at the airport because of the storm. I message him quickly to say that my flight was cancelled but I'm at a hotel, and within moments he replies with:

COLE:
For real? U should have come back home, Kay! Look, call if u need anything. Let me know when u back at JFK? xo

I feel a huge wave of more guilt. I'm too much on an emotional knife-edge this morning. I need to get it together before—

'Morning.'

Ren's standing at the door in his boxers and the T-shirt he had on last night, scratching his beard. Even though he's semi-clothed, it makes me want to strip off all over again. He walks over and sits down next to me on the bed, not quite close enough to touch.

'Hey,' I say, then cough to recover my voice.

'You hungry? I ordered some room service. Should be here soon.'

'Yeah.'

'Kayla—'

I stop him by closing the space between us, pressing my lips to his and angling my body towards him. He reaches around me, pulling me closer, his arms circling my waist. His lips grow still for a moment and he pulls back, staring into my eyes, searching them. He shakes his head and then moves to kiss me again. We're interrupted by his phone ringing.

'Shit. I'm sorry, I should…'

I nod quickly, and he stands, adjusting himself as he

walks out of the bedroom again to answer it, and I can't help smiling a little. The good feeling doesn't last though. Watching him walk away from me...

I need to start getting used to the reality of the situation. I wander out after him, and his call finishes fairly quickly.

'Do we need to check out?' I ask, trying to sound unaffected. Ren shakes his head.

'I, uh, had my assistant check on your flights while he was doing mine—he says they could get you on the six p.m., you just need to give this number a call.' He hands a piece of paper over to me.

'Oh, OK. Thanks.' I stare down at it. 'Eager to ship me out then?' I say, looking up at him with a terrible attempt at a smile.

Ren's hair is in glorious, ridiculously sexy chaos, and he ruffles his hands through it like he does, making it even worse. *Fuck's sake.*

'Trying desperately to get rid of you, yup.' He walks over to me, and without even thinking I reach out to wrap my arms around him. His tighten around my shoulders, and he exhales hard, kissing the top of my head as I tuck myself under his chin. 'They need me up in Toronto today. I'm on a three o'clock,' he murmurs. 'I've got to be out of here in like an hour.' He pulls away from me and looks down at my glum expression, then steps back, closing his eyes for a brief moment and turning towards the bedroom. 'I better get in the shower,' he says, his jaw tight. He grabs some stuff out of his case, then heads into the bathroom.

I sigh as I watch him go, and then remember my sketch. Pulling it from my back pocket I go over to Ren's leather holdall and unzip it, feeling a bit bad for getting in the midst of his things, but I want him to have this. I look at the '*Happy Belated. Don't forget me x*' written on the outside of the folded paper and kiss it, feeling like an idiot but meaning it all the same. I push it deep inside and close up the bag again just as there's a knock at the door to the suite. It makes me jump.

'Room service,' calls a woman's voice, and I go to let her in.

The dark-haired waitress enters and arranges a variety of plates on the table, then straightens her form-fitting beige waistcoat and discreetly hands me the receipt to sign. I'm not even sure if I'm really authorised to do so, given the suite's being paid for by Ren's studio, but I write on a $100 tip. Easy to be generous with other people's money, I suppose. I don't know why, but I think I see sympathy in her eyes as she tells me to have a nice day, like she knows it's unlikely. I'm starting to feel mopey already, like a stroppy kid. It's pathetic. I pick at the exotic array of chopped fruit, tearing pieces off a croissant half-heartedly, even though all the food is stupidly delicious. I pour out some coffee for both of us, adding sugar but no milk to Ren's with a sinking feeling. I know how he takes his coffee. I know what he sounds like when he comes. I know how well he listens. I know how he makes me feel.

I know nothing about him, and far too much.

He emerges out of the bedroom already dressed in black

jeans and a grey marl t-shirt, but with bare feet and wet hair and his overwhelmingly handsome general self. I hand him his coffee and he sips it, then nods.

'Thanks,' he says, then adds softly, 'Perfect.'

He looks away and sits down opposite me, pulls over a plate and lifts the silver lid. A flawless-looking egg white omelette nestles underneath, and he picks up a fork and starts to eat. I take my phone and dial the number he gave me, standing up to go and make the call in the other room. I close the door without saying anything to him. God, I really am in a weird sulk now, like this is all *his* fault; as if he's taking something away from me. My intestines feel like they've been crocheted. But I remind myself that I need to lie in this bed I've made.

It's easy to confirm my flight thanks to Ren's assistant's groundwork, and after I do, I drop my mobile on the unmade sheets and look around, gathering up the scattered clothes and bits and pieces I'd left around the suite, trying to stay busy and focus on what happens after, not what happens next. Let's face it—I'm hiding. I even pull my laptop out to check some emails, but then I realise I need the Wi-Fi password that's with the key cards in the other room.

When I open the door, Ren is setting his neatly zipped case by the door. He folds his jacket and places it on top. This really is all coming to an end. Maybe it already has.

'Kayla… Are you mad at me?' he asks as soon as I emerge.

I sigh hard. 'I'm just sort of a bit pissed off generally, I think. Maybe at you, I don't know. At myself. Just this whole fucking situation.'

He's quiet, and I stand in the doorway to the bedroom looking down at my hands, fiddling with my rings.

'Look, I still have twenty minutes before the car comes,' he says eventually. 'I mean, you can stay here if you—'

'No. I'll just leave when you leave. Maybe I'll grab a lift to the airport with you?'

He stands up straighter, like he's relieved. 'Oh. OK. Good. At least that gives us a little more time.'

I look over at him for a moment, his big brown eyes almost pleading with me, for what I'm not sure, but I wish I could give it to him. 'I'm not sure if it matters, does it?' I ask. I can actually feel tears hiding at the back of my eyes, and I breathe in long and slow. I turn away and head into the room, spotting my abandoned underwear from last night and squeezing it into an unzipped corner of my suitcase, and then I hear Ren come in behind me.

'Yes. It fucking matters,' he says gently. He's standing close, just his energy forcing me to turn around.

I try and sound calm and reasonable, which is pretty laughable. 'I think perhaps we're just letting this whole situation get inflated in our minds. Maybe we just need to take a step back.' *Kayla, are you serious?* I wish I was. I need to be. My breathing's coming in shallow gasps, each word threatening to let forth the tears I'm just about holding at bay. I need to listen to my own words. I can't be upset over *one night*. 'This is it, isn't it?' I force a smile, but it falls. 'So it *can't* matter, OK?' I add in whisper.

We stare at each other, seconds ticking by while we search each other's faces, as though it might somehow lead us to the miraculous answer we both want. Ren slumps down onto the bed, then reaches out and grabs my hand, pulling me to stand in between his legs. He wraps his arms around my waist and presses his face into my chest. I rub his back, my fingers working their way up his neck and into his hair, and I feel his body relax into me. We stay that way until the phone in the suite rings. I reach over to the handset on the bedside table and give it to him. Still holding onto me, he answers it and then mutters his thanks. I hang it up for him, and he finally moves away to stand up.

'Car's here.'

'Yeah. OK.' I gather my stuff, putting my hand luggage on the bed while I make sure everything is in my handbag. When I turn back to him, Ren has my Polaroid camera in his hands.

'Can I?' he asks. I nod, and he pops open the flash.

I pull my hair around my shoulders and adjust my mustard yellow T-shirt as he stoops a little and looks at me through the viewfinder.

'See, at least I let you get prepared,' he says with a smile.

'Amateur,' I say, ironically. He chuckles. I shuffle from foot to foot. 'I don't like having my picture taken.' *And I don't like how final this feels.*

Suddenly I want to confess—tell him everything, let the chips fall where they may. I try it out in my head: *Ren, I'm getting married. I'm engaged. Cole is my fiancé.*

But but but...

What would he do? What would Ren say if I just told him the truth? And more importantly, if I told him that I think I'm making a mistake. That *he's* the one I want. That going through with this will slam a roadblock in front of any possibility of us, because this is one situation where, even if we weren't going to be thousands of miles apart for the next few weeks, I won't be able to have my cake and eat it too.

I know the words won't come out of my mouth.

At last Ren presses the button on my camera, then carefully extracts the photograph and puts it back in its case and back on top of my hand luggage.

'We should go,' I murmur, though I stay almost rooted to the spot.

'Yeah.' He looks down at the picture, holding it carefully as it slowly begins to develop, then looks back up at me steadily. 'Kayla... In case I don't get a chance to tell you any other time, I just wanted say that you're the most beautiful woman I've ever met.'

Heat spreads across my whole body. 'Oh. Just that?'

He grins at me, and my heart squeezes. 'Yeah.'

'Well, your life's not over yet.'

He walks over and takes my hand. 'You're right.'

Nine

Ren.

Kayla's hand is gripped in mine, and her photograph is held between my free fingers. City blocks speed past in a grey blur, even with the bright glow of the sunshine. It's almost like the storm never happened, but faint memories of it hang in the trees, in the street signs now pointing fractionally away from their intended aim.

'Aren't you going to be bored, waiting for your flight?' I ask her, just to say something.

She shakes her head. 'I'll do what I was going to do before I bumped into you yesterday, I suppose. Fight over charging points, deal with rubbish Wi-Fi, read shit magazines, drink coffee…' She pauses. 'And daydream about you.' I lift her hand up to brush her knuckles against my lips just above her rings, and she clears her throat. 'Maybe I'll do some work, actually. I've got the *Detonate* interviews to write up, after all. And, um, the Polaroids to work on for the book.'

I look down at the picture I took of her, her expression caught between sadness and desire. I'm not sure it's how I want to remember her. But I also have to remember that she's not going to cease to exist. There's always the vaguest possibility that—

'Listen, Kayla, are we going to keep in touch?' I ask. I can't not-ask it any more. But just as I do, we pull up at the airport and she chooses to ignore my question, busying herself with checking she has her passport and allowing the driver to help her out of the car with her hand luggage. I shake my head at an approaching Skycap as we pile our bags on the kerbside. I can see my airline's check-in desk just inside the airport concourse.

'Let's go in,' Kayla says quietly. 'I'll meet you by the security bit and we'll go through together.'

For some reason, I suddenly feel a little panicked. 'You're not just going to bail, right? I mean, you'll... We'll be able to say goodbye?'

She smiles at me, though anguish is registering in her eyes too. 'Jesus, Ren, of course. Look, I'm sure you're going through the fancy premium super-fast-track check-in, but I've got to queue up. So just wait for me over there by security, OK? Don't worry.'

'I am worried.' She shakes her head. I take her hand again, rubbing the back of it with my thumb. 'Loitering in an airport is frowned upon,' I finish, smiling back at her to mask the sinking feeling in my words.

She laughs, and I'm both relieved and depressed at the sound of it. I let her walk away toward her airline's desk, and once I've checked my case I wait, watching young families and businessmen blow past me like they did last night and a world away. Finally, I see Kayla walking over to me. She slips her hand straight back into mine when she gets close.

'Managed to evade Homeland Security, then?' she says. I put my arm around her shoulders as we get in line for security, squeezing her tightly while we wait for our turn to take off our shoes and get patted down by a two-hundred-pound customs officer. I want to remember this feeling: Kayla's body, her… essence. I don't know, maybe she's right. Maybe I'm building this all up too much, so it was inevitable that when toppled it was going to be even harder. But I can't help it.

Once we're through, I hear the boarding announcement come over the intercom for my flight. *Dammit*. I try to pretend I haven't heard it.

'Ren—'

'Wait. Just… Come over here, please?' I take her hand and pull her over to a quieter spot that leads off toward the gates. I put down my bag and take hers too, putting them both on the floor bedside us. I stare at her face, brushing my fingers over her smooth dark skin, down the sharp angle of her cheekbones. Her eyes bore into mine, tears balanced in them. 'Why is this so…?' I begin in a whisper, and she shakes her head again.

'I honestly don't know.'

I lean down and kiss her, pressing my lips against hers too hard—a bruising kiss that betrays everything I'm feeling. Kayla whimpers a little and I relent, thinking it's too much, but she grabs the back of my neck and raises herself up on her tip-toes, kissing me harder, her tongue sweeping desperately against mine. We kiss until we can't breathe, and then we kiss some more. Finally we break apart, and her hands drop to her sides. She steps away and picks up her bag.

'Kayla—'

She cuts me off.

'Look, this was... I never thought in a million years... *Shit.*' Her voice is hoarse. 'I wish things were different, Ren.' She blinks, and tears fall silently down her cheeks. I reach over to brush them away but she gently moves my hand back. 'You've just turned up at the wrong time, you know?'

I look down at my watch. 'Hell, how about a couple hours' time then? I don't care, I'll miss another flight.'

She gives me a watery smile, but I'll take it. I reach for her tears again, and this time she lets me swipe them off her beautiful face. Her bag slips to the floor.

'OK, seriously,' I say gently, still stroking her cheeks. 'Three months. I can be back here in New York in three months. You'll be here then, right? Can I see you then?'

She takes a breath and sighs out shakily. 'God, Ren, if I am here then things will definitely be different. I don't know if—'

I interrupt her. 'Listen, no pressure. If in three month's time you feel differently, cool. Why don't we... We could just keep in touch, see what happens?' Jesus, desperation laces every single word I say.

Kayla swings her eyes skywards, almost like she's rolling her eyes, but I recognise it as frustration. She presses her lips together and backs away from me again. I push my hands into my pockets, trying to keep them from her, give her a second. 'Yeah.' She sounds doubtful. 'Where were you three months ago, though, d'you know what I mean? A lot can change in that time, let me tell you.' She lifts her locs off her neck, then lets them fall.

'Kayla, I don't want to throw this away.' I reach for her shoulders in spite of myself, and she lets me. 'Don't you want to try?'

She's studying the carpet tiles between our feet. 'I do... It's just... I've worked really bloody hard to get to a point where I feel like I'm in control of the direction of my life.' She pauses. 'You make me feel out of control, Ren. All these... feelings racing around in me? I-I've never had this before.' She's still not looking at me. My heart thunders. 'But I can't derail the plan. I have to stay focussed.' It's like she's convincing herself. 'Maybe it's better if we just leave this where it is.'

I crook one finger under her chin and lift it until her gaze meets mine. 'So you're saying you *can*? You'll just forget all about this? Live your life, ignore the feelings? You won't think about me? About us talking, about us walking around the city in the dark?' My voice drops lower, still touching her. 'You won't think about my mouth on you? About how it felt when our bodies connected?'

She reaches up for my wrist at that and rubs it slowly, her eyelids sinking lower. 'Of course I will. I'll think about it all.'

'Then give us a chance, Kayla. Three months. Let's just see where it takes us. We'll be apart, I know that, but there's these things called phones, there's this thing called email, there's—'

'All right, all right.' She takes my hand and plants a kiss in the centre of my palm. 'Let's see how it goes.' She avoids my eyes again, and I can see she means it when she says, 'No promises, though, OK?'

I want promises. But I smile anyway. 'Whatever you want.' I definitely mean that.

'You'd better go.' She looks up at me. 'Thank you, Ren,' she adds quietly. 'This was special.'

I nod mutely but I don't move, afraid at the thought of leaving her, at whether she could be right about what lies ahead of us. She still sounds so final. My flight call echoes around us again. It's only a matter of time before they start reading out my name impatiently over the PA with "passenger" in front of it.

'Well, how are we going to keep in touch?' I ask.

Kayla's lips curl slightly, that now-familiar challenge sparking in her eyes. 'You'll find me,' she says softly. I know I will. 'Seriously, Ren, you'll miss your flight.'

'Maybe I want to.'

'Ren—'

'OK, OK.' I don't move.

'Well, then *I'm* going to go.'

I take her hand and squeeze it tight, unable to speak. I lift it to my lips and kiss her fingertips.

'I'm going to go,' she repeats, and her breath catches. She takes a step back, and another, but then she rushes toward me again, wrapping her arms around my waist. I hold her tight against me one last time.

'Take care, Ren,' she mutters against my chest, then pulls herself clear of me, turns and walks away without looking back.

Life. Goddamn.

21st August 2016 – 7th October 2016

Ten

Kayla.

'Are you mad? I can barely walk *now*, Sam.'

Sami laughs at me, her tight brown abs clenching enviably between her sports bra and leggings as she lets us back into her flat. 'It's only Pilates, and it's not til tomorrow morning, you'll have time to recover.'

'Listen, I appreciate your efforts hun, but early morning exercise is not for me. I can't keep trying to gather speed before 10am.'

We spill over the threshold, and Sami bends down to pick up the post as she dumps her gym bag in the corner, then heads off to the bathroom. I hear the tone of a video call emanating from my phone, and I pull it from the pocket in my waistband. It's only just past six am in New York, but I'm not in the least bit surprised to see the familiar face on my screen.

I swipe to answer and head into the kitchen to run myself about a gallon of water. 'Hey, Coco.'

I smile at the bouncing image of him on my screen, Raybans on, white ear-buds in his ears with the mic dangling, already out on the streets—even if his eyebrows are scrunched together at hearing his least favourite nickname. He says it conjures either The Clown or Chanel. It's probably bad that I still use it anyway.

'Yo, anything yet? Miguel said the next set of papers should be coming through to you any day.' I can see the early morning New York sun glowing around him—he's walking to the subway from the apartment. Nostalgia and envy hit me hard, even though I'm technically in my home city. I'm itching to go back.

'Mmm, hang on, let me check today's post...' I lean over, still holding the screen up, then realise I might be giving a bit too much of an eyeful down my loose workout vest. I straighten up the camera, rifling through Sami's post—she'd let me direct all the visa stuff here to save questions at my parents' house.

Nothing looks especially official, but my heart stutters with a jolt of nerves when I see an A4 envelope, until I see Sami's name safely on there. God. I wish my reaction would be a sudden calm or a warm happiness that the gears were grinding into motion for the big Marriage Plan. But no— fear, eagerness and concern all rotate in a painful cycle of internal dialogue whenever I think about it. *Is this really all happening? OK, it's not just yet. Let's see how it goes. But is it bad we haven't heard anything more yet? What if there's a problem and I can't go back? It's only been a couple of weeks, Kayla, calm down.* Round and round.

'Nope, nothing,' I tell Cole, and I can see the disappointment etched on his face. He's so invested in this thing that will benefit *me*. Sure, he'll get his business partner and friend back too, but it's so strange to have him care this much about something that could complicate his own life, or at the very least inconvenience it. Then again, if he *doesn't* see marriage to me as getting in the way of anything…? I push the thought away again. 'Cole, don't worry. I'll let you know as soon as it comes through, yeah?' I exhale air and doubts. 'Anyway, what are you on today?' I balance the phone on the windowsill above the sink to wash my hands and get my pint of water.

'These fuckin' allergies got me up, but you know I can't sleep with the window closed. So I figured I'd head to the office,' he says.

'You're a nutter. Why not just work at the apartment til later?'

'Nutty or no, there's a shit-ton to do before the meeting with those ad guys next week, Kay,' he tells me, glancing up from the phone as he crosses the road. Maybe I shouldn't feel so bad about his motivations—maybe he really *does* just want his business partner back. 'You know I need the bigger screens for the layouts.'

'Right.' I turn away for a second to dry my hands, not wanting him to see the flash of irritation on my face at his tone. Doesn't he know this is hard for me, too? 'Listen, tonight I'm going to finish off those July reports and send them over to you. And actually I've got two columns nearly in the bag to send over to Una for subbing, too…' I feel better just imagining getting round to doing work later; a calm descends around me thinking about it. I pick up the phone again, my glass in my other hand. As I sit down at the kitchen table, suddenly something poking out amongst the letters catches my eye. I pull it out from the pile. A postcard. I stare at the image; a grainy black-and-white picture of a New York street from the 1940s, and my breath catches in my throat. A tiny hint of a neon sign deep in its background is circled in biro with a heart.

Our diner.

I flip it over to the other side. I have to squint to read his handwriting; he's packed a lot into the little space next to my current address, but as I glance at the return scrawled in the corner, I realise it's actually true. *Ren Morgan, The Hesseltine, Apt 2, N. Hollywood, Los Angeles, CA 91601.*

It's from him.

'Kay?'

Shit. *Shit.* 'S-Sorry?' I feel as though guilt must be radiating off my body, like Cole must be able to see that night, that morning, replaying in my head even as I speak.

'I'm gonna jump on the train. But yeah, send the reports and shit through when you can, and keep your eyes peeled on the mail, all right?'

'Uh, cool, yeah.' My mouth is dry. I drop the postcard and reach for my glass, glugging more water. ''Course.'

Cole halts suddenly, holding the phone up and pulling off his sunglasses. His green eyes glint as he squints into the camera. 'Ayy, I almost forgot. Today's D-day, right? You're telling your folks?'

I wait, swallowing. 'That's the plan.'

'Oof. Good luck. Maybe I should have officially asked for your hand or some shit, huh?' He chuckles and pushes his sunglasses back onto his face. 'I don't want your pops sending goons to my door.' Cole's image begins to break up as he jogs down into the subway.

I smile weakly. 'Don't worry about it. Your doorstep will be goon-free,' I mumble.

I only hear every other syllable of his reply as he waits for the train, but I know he concludes the way he always does. 'I'll get at you later, Kay. Miss you.' His face disappears.

I stare at the End Call screen for a moment, then put my mobile down and pick Ren's postcard back up. The sweat that had cooled on my body after the HIIT class Sami dragged me to blooms over my skin once again as I turn the card over, staring it. Words and phrases jump out at me as I try and delay reading it, to savour it.

Admit it, you're impressed, right? Come on. I know it takes a lot, but ...

He's correct, of course, on both counts. I am genuinely stunned. Not just that Ren managed to track down Sami's address, but that I'm feeling this level of unadulterated joy at the fact a man wrote words on a piece of card and sent it to me.

My lips move silently as I finally read Ren's note, a secret smile pressing them out wide. It's as if I had a crazy dream about winning the lottery and then woke up on a bed of cash. So often in the last couple of weeks I thought I might have made the whole thing up. Like I'd imagined him—the way I have every night since.

But there's evidence, here in my hands...

Kayla,

I got back to LA two days ago. I hadn't really had a chance to breathe since I went to Toronto, and somehow it was only when I got back here and dumped out all my stuff from my bags that I found your gift.

I didn't forget you. There's no way I could. All I do is remember.

I stare at that drawing every day (uncanny, by the way, and beautiful, even though it feels weird to say so). The mise-en-scene is great. Measuring out my life in coffee spoons like Prufrock, huh? And the signpost? Very funny. I should probably be mad, but I love the whole thing. Of course I do.

Admit it, you're impressed though, right? Come on. I know it takes a lot, but I went through genuine theatrics, risked total mortification, just to prove your words correct. Have I found you? I did once.

Now I can't let go.

Ren x

310-555-8719

I run a fingertip over his name, his kiss, and then walk in a daze through to Sami's spare room—my room, for the next few weeks—my eyes still trained on Ren's postcard, my phone absently in the other.

The number. He gave me his phone number. I can't call, can I? I do a brief calculation and realise it's just after 3am in Los Angeles, if he's even still there—who knows how long this took to arrive. Maybe I could just send a message for him to see when he wakes up, just to let him know I got it? My fingers tremble as I save Ren's number in my phone. It feels like such a normal thing to do, a *hey, let me get those digits* ordinary dating thing. If this was ordinary surely we would have just swapped numbers that night. It didn't feel *ordinary*. It still doesn't.

There's a reason for that, though, and it's because I shouldn't be doing *any* kind of dating things. It's too complicated, too fraught. I should never have even given Ren the notion that we could carry on with whatever this was. *Is…* But nearly two weeks had gone by, so I thought he'd realised it too, otherwise he could have direct messaged me on any of my social media accounts, or got my number from that PR chick, or—

But *he can't let go.*

I blow out a whoosh of air and open the messaging app on my phone. There he is, with the usual chirpy, generic status: *I'm available.* Oh the irony. I close my eyes, waiting, analysing. Suddenly the smell of pancakes begins drifting down the hallway to my room, and I'm transported to the diner in his postcard…

I jump as Sami shouts at my door. 'Babes, do you want

breakfast? I'm going over the road to get blueberries.'

'Uh… No thanks. I'm meant to be at Mum and Dad's by twelve. I should jump in the shower.'

''Kay. Back in a sec.' The door to the flat slams.

I look back at my phone, sit on the bed and flop back to lie down, lifting the screen above my face and letting my thumb hover over the keyboard… And I type.

KAYLA:
You found me. X

My breath burns in my lungs as I wait. Five minutes… Nothing. Seven. *Ren Morgan: Last seen today at 02.01am.*

'He's asleep. Obviously,' I tell myself. 'And it doesn't matter anyway. Have a fucking shower, Kayla.'

As I let the water pummel into me, I know that I'm standing on a cliff's edge. One night with Ren was something I could keep like a treasure, locked away. A tiny, special secret. But this? If I leap, there might be no going back. And it's been how long since I got back to London, and I still haven't had the guts to tell my parents about being engaged to Cole? He's right, the plan is to do it this afternoon while I'm helping them sort out their garden and downstairs for the party tomorrow, but…

No, this is stupid. I decide that as soon as I go back to my room, I'm going to erase that message, delete Ren's number, and just go back to pretending it was all some delicious dream. But I get out of the shower and practically run to hit the home button on my phone. The screen brightens. Nothing. I can't bring myself to erase what I wrote, and my phone continues to torture me with its silence as I get dressed. My three-word message sits there like an unexploded bomb.

'OK, just forget about it,' I whisper. Fat chance.

I nab one of Sami's pancakes from the kitchen to eat on my way to the tube, popping a couple of blueberries in my mouth and pushing the huge curls of her clip-ins aside to give her a quick peck on the cheek.

'See you later, hun.'

'Oh, Kay, let me know if you're coming tomorrow night, yeah?' she calls after me. 'I need to sort the list.' Damn. I forgot. I backtrack into the kitchen, and she puts her hands on her hips at my apologetic expression.

'I've got my parents' renewal thing tomorrow though.'

She rolls her eyes. 'The Space happens *once a year*,' she intones, a smile fighting to push through her irritation. 'Come after! Come on!'

I do feel bad—it's her biggest DJ set so far, in Room One at some enormous warehouse party. 'Well, my parents only renew their vows once every ten. Plus, you know today's going to be the big *reveal*.' I wiggle my ring finger. 'God knows how they're going to react. It's a lot. I don't know how late the party will go tomorrow or what time I'll finish there, then I'd have to come back and change, and…'

She waves her hands. 'All right, all right.' She does smile now, but I do feel slightly geriatric. When did I become sensible? I think about the message sitting unanswered on my phone. Maybe let's not speak too soon…

'You bloody well better hook up some bookings for me in New York to make up for missing it,' Sami tells me as I head for the door.

'Thousand per cent.'

If I don't fuck up my route back.

*

I descend the stairs from the flats and head out into the clammy streets of Brixton, marvelling in that tedious way people do about how much things have changed in the short time since I've been away. It's the same where my parents are in Peckham. Areas that even ten years ago might have caused raised eyebrows and warnings against straying into are now hipster havens packed with pop-ups that rub up against dying minority-owned local business. Gentrification: the same thing that's happening in the very Brooklyn neighbourhoods that my friends and I haunt—the thing we complain about and cause simultaneously.

I jump on the 37 bus and head upstairs to avoid the screeching toddler who seems too big anyway to be in the pushchair from which he's struggling to escape. Even as I pull my headphones up from around my neck over my ears, I do appreciate the sheer variety of people around me, gentrification or no. The hijabi mum trying to ignore her pushchair kid downstairs, the burly Polish builders clocking out for lunch, the group of black girls bunking off school with braids elaborately wound around their heads, the middle-aged white woman in a cheap polyester suit fiddling with the council ID around her neck. We all churn together somehow. Maybe it wouldn't be so bad if I had to stay in London? But when I try to imagine leaving everything I've worked for in New York behind and coming home, I honestly just can't. Some essential part of me is back there, rolling a boulder up a hill, desperate to reach the top.

But the plus side of being back here is that the final line isn't drawn under Ren and me. If he *can't let go* then I'll cling to this feeling for as long as I can, too. Until *"I Do"* means I can't. I pull out his postcard and re-read his words, almost memorising them and nearly missing the stop for my parents' house.

As soon as I turn on to their street, I feel my jaw clench, which is not a good sign. It's going to need to loosen the fuck up if I'm going to actually go through with telling them about Cole. The relative quiet of the road lined with terraced houses unnerves me by contrast with the bustling high street I've just left. I approach the house, noticing that the front door is open and there is a hive of activity as chairs are carried in from a white van parked outside. There's a figure in a stretch-jersey dress painted with what looks like a constellation of stars against a pink-purple sky leaning into the van's open side. Her own design, of course.

I can't help shouting her name. 'Christy! What d'you think you're doing?'

She emerges, holding a few folded chairs out in front of

her protruding belly. I rush over and take them from her as she rolls her eyes.

'They're light as a feather, Kay. Chill out.' We look at each other for a moment. I want to reach over and hug her, but I don't. I can see in her eyes she wants to, too. Stubborn, both of us. 'Time do you call this?'

I glance at my phone in my hand. 'I call it the bus took fucking ages. Are they inside?'

'Mum sent dad out to get ice. She's in there with Mike and Tina and the kids and Aunty P. You'll get a task the minute you walk in. She's—' Christy breaks off as a four-foot figure dashes past us. 'Oi! You just run out into the road, yeah? That's all we bloody need, you getting knocked down. Leave it!'

We both stare down our cousin Vernon, and the six-year-old is suitably intimidated. I jog after the football that's somehow sprung from the house and out into the street. I hand it to him and he legs it back inside. We smile at each other, and for that moment, it feels wonderful. *My sister.*

'I like your hair,' I tell her. She runs a hand over it, cut low all over her scalp. It makes her features—an exaggerated, more beautiful version of my own—stand out even more. It's weird not seeing a fuzz of golden-blonde on her head.

'Yeah, well the dye was growing out and it was annoying me. Couldn't re-do it until this one's out.' Her other hand goes to her belly, and my eyes follow. My niece or nephew is in there, and this is the most we've probably spoken in ages.

'Right. Course.'

Christy draws a breath, and I can feel it alter the energy between us before she even says anything. 'So you're back now, yeah?'

I've managed to avoid really chatting to her the two brief times I've seen her since I arrived; she's clearly been itching for this. 'Not quite.'

'What, are you going to be an illegal alien or something? How long can you pretend to be a student? Or, like a web entrepreneur or whatever—'

'I'm not. Listen, worry about your own shit OK, Christy?'

She turns away to pick up the large pack of frilly paper tablecloths that are about the only thing left lingering on the floor of the van, draping them over one arm. She has a smirk on her face as she turns back to me. 'Or maybe you've finally found yourself a man to hook up the Green Card, innit.' She chuckles to herself, edging past me to head up the short path into the house. The fact that she finds the notion so unlikely gets my goat, as it was intended to. But in that fraction of a second, I know my face has given something away, from the way Christy turns and looks at me, her smile dissolving away into curiosity. Her eyes drift down to the ring finger of my left hand, and she squints. Just then, our parents' voices call simultaneously from either side of us. My mum calls Chris inside for some kind of advice on aesthetics, and a familiar deep voice calls to me from the car that's pulling up across the road.

'What, it ain't safe to go in there?' my dad asks, switching off the engine and smiling at me. He unfolds himself from his beloved vintage Mini and begins lifting bags from the boot. His matching linen shirt and trousers should make him look like some kind of uncle drinking Guinness at a house party, but of course he flairs it with box-fresh trainers and his glinting, weird gold earrings.

'Is there even room in the freezer for this?' I ask as I lean the folding chairs against the tiny front garden's wall and go over to help, giving him a quick kiss on the cheek.

'Kayla, I don't ask, I just do,' he says, in the faux-exasperated voice he reserves especially for things to do with my mother. I know he loves it really—he's as fussy as mum is, he just likes to pretend he isn't. I can tell how excited he is about tomorrow. It gives me hope, the fact that they're still happy. But as I approach the threshold of the house my stomach starts to tie into knots. I have to just rip the plaster off and get this big reveal about me and Cole over with.

But of course, Christy does it for me.

As I head into the kitchen, a plastic bag clutched in one hand and the folding chairs under my other arm, she puts her hands on her hips and raises an already-arched eyebrow.

'So,' she says eagerly, 'you're getting married, aren't you?'

I have a few seconds' grace as her words dissipate around us—at first people probably think she's talking about mum and dad and their vow renewal. But slowly, as my sister's energy continues to focus on me, so does everyone else's, and she can hardly contain her mirth.

'*Aren't* you?'

*

It's weird, seeing your parents dance. Like bumping in to your teacher in the supermarket when you were a kid, it's a thing you kind of knew in the back of your mind that they probably did, but it's still bizarre to actually see it. I'm caught somewhere between hysterical laughter and a grimace as I watch my mum and dad get low to the ground while people shout 'ayyy' and throw money at them like they were newlyweds.

I haven't given much thought to what the actual wedding between Cole and me will be like, and an electric jolt of sadness hits me at the idea that the day won't be anything like the numerous West African weddings Christy and I were dragged to as kids, or even the kitsch/hip/romantic ones some of my mates are starting to have. Odds are it will just be me and Cole and a couple of witnesses, maybe a meal afterwards. My parents probably won't even be there. Why had I not thought about that? They know the situation now; I doubt they'll decide to come. I think I'd rather they didn't. I've never been the woman that fantasises about her nuptials—not even a bit—but I'm suddenly hit by just how wonderful it can be to show the world you're in love and you're committing to another human being. And what I'm doing isn't that. The kernel of upset that awakens deep inside me takes me by surprise.

'Look at all the cash you'll miss out on,' Christy says to me, walking over slowly with a glint in her eye. She folds one arm over her bump, a pungent home-made ginger beer clutched in her hand. I reach over to the table next to her and pour myself a splash of rum pointedly.

'Leave it, Chris. I'm not in the bloody mood.'

'I'm just say—'

'Why? Why do you have to make me feel so shit about my choices all the time?' I stop, sucking in a breath. I don't want to ruin what's actually been a pretty good day, and I don't want her to see any of my doubts. My mum's eyes drift over to us from the makeshift dance-floor in the middle of the back garden—it's lucky the neighbours are all pretty much invited otherwise the noise complaints would be something else. She can sense when her daughters are about to kick off. She straightens up to her full height, fanning herself with a white handkerchief, looking absolutely incredible in the creation Christy made her for the vow renewal. Purples and golds swirl in the traditional material, but the design somehow has that edge that makes me immediately know my sister's work. One look from our mother makes both me and Christy bite our lips but I sip my drink sullenly as mum comes over, palms up, reaching out to us.

'Come dance with your mother, Kay. Come on, Chris— you know you were practically peeking through my legs and I could still shake my bumper. No excuses. Come on!'

We can't help laughing as she pulls us into the middle of the circle. 'Ayyy's' start up again from the crowd surrounding us as somehow in perfect timing *Sweet Mother* starts up, and people lean in and rub Christy's belly for luck in time to the pounding music. My mum grabs my hand and presses it against my sister's stomach too, looking in both of our eyes. I look away.

But after the song my mum takes me to one side. I cross my arms and turn a sullen gaze towards the floor like muscle memory. I'm sixteen again—but now instead of curfews and cigarette-sneaking it's baby bumps and bride-to-be's.

'She loves you, you know that, right?'

I ignore her until she says my name in a manner that makes my eyes flick up instinctively. 'Yes, mum.'

'Listen, this is hard for her. She misses you.' Mum watches me as I try not to react, then kisses her teeth and chuckles a little, her expression amused and full of her own love for us. 'Kayla, honestly. Your sister's about to pop with no daddy in sight, you're off marrying some mate just so you can stay in that bloody country... I don't know.' She shakes her head, her long braids staying immaculately in place, pinned in a crown on her head. 'And you know what? I'm proud of both of you.'

'Really?' I'm not convinced.

'Look, I may not think what you're doing is the best idea, but let's see, eh? If you think it could work, you're a grown woman now. Your mistakes are your own.'

Great.

We're interrupted by a couple of my aunties coming to say goodbye, and I realise I'm not sure of the time. I've actually managed not to check my phone for just over an hour, I think. Well, at least twenty minutes. The party has been a distraction from the fact that I've heard nothing from Ren since my message yesterday. It should be for the best—what's the point in carrying on with something that can't go anywhere? But thinking about the idea *he* might have changed his mind makes a grey fog of rejection swirl in the centre of my chest. A cruel little voice inside me keeps chiming in to say that it makes sense; it was inevitable. I was kidding myself that someone like him would really want me...

Shit. I need to find some water before I get too morose on the rum in my system. At least all mum's cooking is soaking it up a bit. I wander to the kitchen, where her sister Patricia is already stuffing Tupperware with leftovers.

'Ah, Kay. You want to take some of this with you?' It's less of a question than a no-brainer. She starts stacking boxes of food into a spare corner-shop plastic bag and proffers it towards me, swinging heavily.

'Thanks, Aunty P.'

'Candy cooked enough to feed five hundred,' she says, wiping her hands on a dishcloth and surveying the kitchen despairingly, as if she didn't help her sister do it. My aunt is like a shorter, only-slightly-less-intimidatingly beautiful version of my mother, but they're looking almost identical tonight with their matching outfits and Patricia's extra-high wedge heels. How they've managed to command the dance floor for hours all dressed up like this is a marvel in itself. I'm already dreaming of the minute I can get home and take my shoes off. Seeing as it's Tupperware time, I'm guessing it might be OK to start making my exit—it's almost half-twelve I notice on the oven clock. I head off to locate my dreaded phone to call a cab.

I find my handbag wedged down the side of the sofa in the living room that's still stuffed with revellers. Mum and Dad's friends aren't the sort to sneak off early, but I think they'll allow me. I can already see Christy hugging people goodbye as well, car keys clutched in her hand. She's only five minutes away in the car, but it still seems weird that she's driving in her state. I remind myself she's pregnant, not an invalid.

She comes over to me just as I root my phone out.

'Well… bye.'

'Yeah, see you,' I manage.

'I'd offer you a lift, but—'

'Nah. Don't be stupid, you're only round the corner.' I glance at her as she reaches around to rub her lower back. 'Sure you're all right to drive?'

Christy smiles at me, knowing I can't help the *sister-ness* coming out of me. She ignores my question. 'Listen, sorry about before.' Mum's spoken to her, too, I reckon. But when I look in her eyes, I can see she means it. I take a deep shaky breath because sincerity, especially from her, gets to me sometimes.

'Me too.' I give in and reach over and hug her tight, her baby pressed between us. As I look over her shoulder, the screen of my phone in my hand illuminates with a message. I don't see it clearly, but I see one word that makes my heart leap.

REN

As Christy releases me, I resist the urge to read his message until I'm alone.

What if it's bad? What if it's... good?

I find my parents to say goodbye, overwhelmed again by the fact that the two people who made me are still so in love. Apparently word spreads fast because I endure a good deal of ribbing about my 'engagement' from random family members; less so from my parents' artsier friends who seem unfazed by the idea.

Finally I battle my way out into the muggy August air. I linger just outside my parents' house, taking out my phone and pressing the home button straight away to avoid looking at Ren's messages. I call a cab first, thankful that they're swarming around this area. I get in the car that turns up two minutes later, muttering one-syllable responses to the driver's attempts at small talk.

I can't wait any longer. I hit the icon on my phone, feeling queasy. The messages Ren sent appear on my screen, and I forget to breathe for a second.

REN:
Sorry. I'm terrible with this thing, plus it's taken me 24hrs+ to figure out what to type. Best I've come up with?

I miss you. All I do is think about you. I don't know what you did to me.

Basically that postcard should have said: "Wish you were here." Because damn Kayla.

Jesus. My heart is in my throat. I look at the timestamp. It's been thirty-three minutes since he sent the last one. I have no idea what to write back, but this is going to go nowhere if neither of us can send a message. This is already somewhere it shouldn't be, though. I glance out of the cab window as we turn towards Brixton, and then type the first thing that comes into my head.

KAYLA:
Sorry, who's this?

I regret it the second I send it, but then I see he's typing a message.

REN:
Ouch.

KAYLA:
Bad joke. Sorry.

REN:
  That's my domain, no?

KAYLA:
  I miss you too, Ren.

And that doesn't even cover it. I have no idea what he did to me, either, but it feels incredible and terrible at the same time. I can feel my pulse in my throat. I barely notice that we're pulling up to Sami's block of flats.

'Left side, right side?' the driver asks impatiently.

'Uh, right side, sorry. Thanks.'

He tells me to have a nice night with only the degree of sincerity necessary to get a decent rating on the app. I get out of the car and swipe the fob mechanically over the entrance pad at the door to the flats. Just as it squeals to indicate I can open it, I see another message come through from Ren.

REN:
  Can I call you?

I stand frozen for a second, then ignore the painfully slow lift and despite my high heels manage to run up the three flights to Sami's apartment, remembering suddenly that she'll be out all night. *Jesus, Kayla, what exactly are you planning to do?* Whatever it is, I don't want an audience. Maybe because it's embarrassing how much this is making my heart swell.

KAYLA:
Yes.

I'm barely inside the front door before my phone starts to buzz. Thank God, it's just a normal call not a video chat. I'm not sure I'm prepared for that yet. I dump my Tupperware bag in the kitchen then rush down the corridor towards my room, taking five deep breaths before I answer. My voice deserts me, and a dry croak that Ren obviously can't hear escapes my throat.

'Kayla?'

I cough. 'Hey.'

'Hey.'

'Hi.' I close my eyes. 'This is fucking weird.'

I can hear him laughing; his rich, deep voice that I can still feel from when I laid against his chest in the darkness of a hotel room. I sit down heavily on the bed.

'Yeah,' he says. 'But also kind of the only thing that hasn't felt weird in the last couple weeks.'

I nod but he can't tell, obviously. 'How did you get my address?'

He *hmmmms*, amused with himself, and I press my ear closer to the phone. 'Well it turns out they pay these actors too much, 'cause that shit is easier than it looks.'

'Oh yeah?'

'God I missed your voice,' he says and I lie backwards, kicking my shoes off my feet with greater relief than I'd ever imagined. 'Say more stuff.'

'Tell me how you found my address.' Why does just speaking now send a throbbing awareness between my legs? Maybe from the way he sighs into another chuckle. I close my eyes again.

'Well, first off I called your office at To Murder and Create—'

I sit up, my eyelids flying open. 'Oh.'

'Yeah, pretending to be *Kyle from the Vincent Hotel...*' He adopts a faux-efficient service industry voice.

'Right...' I'm still worried.

'And the kid who answered the phone must have been an intern or some shit, or you're working with some dubious child labour laws.'

I frown, confused, then I remember Cole agreed to let his nephew Shawn do some nonsense paperwork and stuff to put on his resume. He's all of fifteen and has an awkwardly intermittent baritone. Ren carries on. I can hear the smile in his voice and, in spite of myself, it makes me smile too.

'I told him that you'd been staying at the hotel and left your journal behind in your room, and we wanted to send it back. So, give the kid his due, at first he said I should just send it to your office or whatever, but I insisted you'd already called the hotel and said you wanted it sent to you in London, but another guy was on shift at the time and lost the address...'

I start to relax at last. '*Kyle* is nothing if not efficient,' I interject.

'Absolutely.'

'I thought you might just, like, hit me up on Twitter or something.'

He laughs. 'Damn, why didn't I think of that?'

'That card was pretty much the best thing I've ever had in the post, though.' I say it before I really think about it. Ren's quiet for a second.

'I'm glad,' he says at last. His voice is low. 'I thought maybe I came on too strong. I have a tendency to do that.'

I don't really know how to respond. It's true—this is more intense than I can really handle right now. Is this an opportunity to bring us back to earth again? To come to my senses and stop it once and for all?

'Kayla?'

'Yeah,' I whisper. *I don't want to ruin it…*

'I love my picture, by the way.'

'You said.'

'But I can *say it* say it now. You're really fucking good at that, you know? I feel like I should have it appraised.'

I laugh even as I flush with the compliment. 'Yeah, good luck with that. I doubt you'd get much for it.'

'It's worth a lot to me,' he says.

I bite my lip, scared to tell him just *how much* I miss him. Scared in general. Even now, with all the things he's saying to me, I can hear that tiny cruel voice again telling me that it's not real, that this doesn't happen—not to me. I fall silent, trying to block it out.

'Kayla… are you there?'

Eleven

Ren.

I wait, pacing back and forth in front of the window at the back of my apartment next to my desk, watching the light as the sun starts to sink lower. Coming up for Magic Hour. Every time I see light this good it makes me wonder why I'm not shouting 'action'...

The only reason I paid the extra for this place was to get the view of the basketball court across the street: watching kids shooting hoops somehow calms me, even if they are kind of over-privileged. It's not really helping right now, though, from the way Kayla's still silent on the other end of the line. I fucking hate the phone anyway; I knew there was a reason.

'Kayla?'

'Sorry, yeah,' she says at last. I can hear her smile, but also a hesitation. Her voice sounds higher, more vulnerable without my being able to see her. I *want* to see her. 'I... I'm just not used to anyone saying stuff like this to me, Ren.' I wish I could reach down the line to touch her. Guess it's best not to tell her that.

'Well, I haven't said anything but the truth.'

She's quiet again for a moment. 'I suppose I had all these plans for how this next part of my life was going to go,' she says eventually. 'Everything was going to be simple—as simple as it could be, anyway. I was going to focus on my work, on getting where I need to be. I didn't expect anything like… you. Like what happened that night.'

I lean my forearm against the windowpane, and my forehead against my arm. 'You can still do that. I'd never want to stop you doing that, Kayla.'

She sighs, and the sound is cold against my ears. 'That's easy for you to say.' She doesn't sound angry, more resigned. 'You've already achieved something.'

'I don't know about that.'

'Well, it's true,' she says flatly. Something in her voice makes me not want to argue.

'OK. Tell me what your afraid of.' I close my eyes, a little afraid myself.

I can hardly hear her. 'I'm afraid of…' She exhales hard again. 'I don't want to think about it tonight, Ren. I just want to talk to you. OK?'

I don't know what's going on, but I'll take any scrap she's willing to give me. 'All right,' I tell her. 'What have you been up to? How's London?'

I hear a feathery laugh against my ear and my muscles soften in relief. I sit down on my office chair, wincing at its increasingly bad creak as I swing my feet onto the desk. 'It's been hectic,' Kayla says. 'I actually just got back from my parents' wedding vow renewal tonight.'

'Oh yeah? Cool. How long they been married?'

'Thirty years to the day.'

'That's great.'

A pause. 'Yeah. It is.'

'Only about fifteen years longer than mine have been divorced,' I add wryly, and she laughs. 'How are things with your sister?'

'Ugh,' she says.

'That good, huh?'

'Well… to be fair, I think we might be on the way to getting better. At first I wasn't sure, especially since she found out—' Kayla cuts off mid-sentence, but then she carries on swiftly. I feel like I missed something. 'I mean she's still being spoilt and stubborn, but maybe we'll just get to a point where we can move on.'

'Yeah,' I say, still a little confused. 'Well, I hope so.'

'Mmm. Me too.'

'Hey, I saw your piece on the *Detonate* junket. It was great. And I loved what you did with the Polaroids too.'

'Thanks.'

I haul my legs off the desk and lean forward on my knees. 'I could feel the parts that were missing though—the stuff you kept to yourself.' My voice lowers. 'Or between us.' I run a palm down my thigh as it starts to clam a little just thinking about it.

'Yeah.' The change in her voice tells me she's thinking about it too.

I let the memories sit for a moment, then draw a breath.

'Honestly? I've been looking at your website every day like a crazy person. Looking for stuff you've written. Like, clues about you. How you are, what you're thinking. What fucking movies you've been watching, even.'

She laughs again softly, but I can hear her breathing a fraction faster still.

'It's kind of pathetic,' I add. 'But I've got to say, your "Cynical Wednesdays" column is now my favourite thing on the internet ever.'

I'm not even kidding, but she still chuckles. 'Given it sounds as if there are probably only, like, five websites in your bookmarks, I'm not sure I should take that as a compliment.'

'Oh, you should. I'm very discerning.'

'Mmhmmm. Well, I'm glad you like it.' She adds self-deprecatingly, 'You know how I love to opine.'

'I do.'

Kayla sighs. 'To be honest, it's been hard keeping up with posting stuff on the site while I'm over here.' She pauses. 'I keep getting distracted.'

I rest an elbow on my desk so I can press the phone to my ear. 'Yeah? What distracts you?' I know what, from the tone of her voice.

'Memories.' I murmur an agreement and hear her take a slow breath and continue. 'Like, my mind will be busy, I'll be trying to focus on the things I need to do and then—boom. I end up thinking about you.' Her voice is dreamy now, and I close my eyes again. 'The other morning, my friend was making pancakes and the smell... I was back in that diner, with your fingertips barely touching mine across the table. Or even just the sound of a plane flying low and I'm back in your fancy free-coffee airport lounge, telling you I thought you looked sexy just like the embarrassing groupie I clearly am.'

I laugh, but I'm affected by her words. 'I'm the same with thunderstorms,' I tell her softly.

'Yeah,' she says. 'General nostalgia fest. And sometimes… Sometimes I'll just stare at the bathtub here in Sami's flat and…' She blows out air, but God, I want her to finish that sentence. 'How is it possible to feel this empty ache for someone I only knew for one night?' He words are so faint, I almost wonder if she's talking to me or herself, until she adds, 'Maybe you're the wrong person to ask.'

I rub between my brows. This is killing me. 'I don't have the answer, Kayla. But I feel it. Believe me.'

She's quiet for a moment. 'What time is it there?' she asks.

I move my mouse to wake up my computer screen, nudging the Polaroid I took of her that's perched next to it. 'Just coming up to five p.m.' I turn toward the glowing late afternoon light coming through the window. 'Shit, so it's almost one in the morning there, right?' My mind conjures an image of Kayla lying in the dark…

'Yeah. It's late.'

I hear shuffling on the other end. 'What are you doing?'

'Trying to hold the phone and undo my skirt.'

I sit up straighter. 'Is that so?'

'Yeah,' she says breathily, then she chuckles. 'So I can put my jogging bottoms on.'

The phrase coming out of her mouth is one of the most British-sounding things ever. 'You mean sweatpants?'

'Whatever.'

'Either way, I'm enjoying imagining this visual.'

She sighs. 'Hold on, I'm gonna put you on speaker...'

I pause, only for a second, as I hear rustling on the other end change. Then I find myself saying, 'Just leave your skirt off. Don't put anything else on.'

Everything goes quiet for a moment. 'OK,' she whispers.

'Where are you?'

I hear shuffling. 'On the bed.'

My jaw clenches for a second, every muscle in my body tensed. Kayla feels like a magnet; if I let go, who's to say I wouldn't be sent flying across the Atlantic to her? I stare at her photograph in front of me, then let my eyes drift shut. 'Lie back, but keep your feet on the floor.'

I can hear her breathing. 'I can only reach my tiptoes.'

'Even better.' I picture her, feeling myself getting hard. 'What have you got on up top?'

'A... A T-shirt.'

'Push it up. Over your stomach. Up over your breasts.'

I hear more rustling. My hand presses the phone into my ear, the other clutching my knee to keep it away from my cock. This is for her.

'I've done it,' she says, her voice low.

'Good. Now, take one fingertip...'

'Ren—' There's need in her voice already. I'm almost *mad* at her, I want to be there so bad.

'Take one fingertip,' I repeat, not wanting to stop, 'and trail it down to your abdomen then up over your stomach. Up and down over that sensitive skin there.' I swallow, remembering her lips against my own stomach…

'Y-yeah?'

'Now up, in between your breasts. Then over them, over your nipples… circle around them.'

'O-over my bra?'

'Yes.'

'Mmmhmm.'

'Now pull the straps down and do it again.'

I hear her breathing louder, and it's agony just imagining her face. After a while she says my name again, her voice begging for something I can't quite give her. 'Ren…?'

'I want you to touch yourself,' I command, matching her ragged breaths. 'Imagine your fingers are my tongue.' I hear her groan. She doesn't say anything for what feels like forever. I hear her panting louder and louder.

'I can feel you,' she whimpers at last.

I squeeze my eyes shut tighter. 'Where?'

She doesn't reply. I hear her breathing getting faster.

'Kayla?'

'I can feel you…' she moans again, louder now, almost desperate.

'*Yes.*' *Fuck.*

'Ren!'

192

I break in half hearing her say my name that way. Knowing why. I wait, and suddenly her voice is closer, the phone next to her mouth now. *Her mouth…*

'But you're not here.'

Twelve

Kayla.

I sit up on the edge of the bed, pressing my thighs together, electricity still pulsing right through the centre of me. Through the fog, I'm relieved Sami wasn't here. She'd have... questions. Probably starting with *who the hell is Ren*?

He's the man whose voice alone just made me—

'Kayla?' I can hear him faintly still on the other end of the line. After I grabbed the phone and took it off speaker, I somehow managed to drop it again as more sensation overwhelmed me. The emptiness of wanting him here, now, to hold me... Tears prickle my eyelids, and I blink them away, embarrassed. I hear Ren repeat my name again and I scoop my phone off the floor.

'Sorry.' My voice is hoarse. Now he's quiet. I don't really know what to say either. How is it like this? How do we end up so overwhelmed? 'That wasn't fair.'

He half-laughs. 'Are you saying it's my turn now?'

I lean forward and let my locs envelop my face. 'If you like,' I tell him. I start getting hot again just thinking about him stroking his—

'Goddamn. I definitely like. But I... *Damn it.*' He clears

his throat. 'I have a meeting.'

I'm caught somewhere between devastation and relief. 'OK.'

'I don't want to go.'

From the tone of his voice, I believe him. I don't want him to, either. I want to go to sleep with him saying beautiful things to me. I shuffle back and lie down, curled up with my phone pressed between the pillow and my ear. 'What *do* you want?'

He hums, low. 'I want a lot of things. Mainly you.'

It's working. I smile a little and let my eyes drift shut.

'Kayla, when are you back in New York? I… God, I don't know. I leave for New Zealand in just over a week, but maybe I could—'

Reality slaps me awake again. Why won't it leave me alone to enjoy this, just for a second? I sit up again. 'I'm not sure yet, Ren.'

'Why did three months sound so *possible* before?' He chuckles mirthlessly. It sounded impossible to me then, and it does even more now. I try and hold an image of Cole in my mind. I try to remember what it is I'm doing this all for. Maybe once everything is settled with the wedding and I'm getting somewhere with all these plans and ideas I have crashing into each other in my mind, *then* I'll be free to be with Ren?

But that's insane—if three months seems impossible, some vague time in the future is inconceivable. I don't even know what the end point of my *getting somewhere* would truly be.

Maybe that's the problem.

'I don't know if it ever did,' I tell Ren. Why can't I just be honest? Why can't I just explain all of this to him?

Because he whispers, 'We can do this.'

And I want to believe him.

*

I wake up to the sound of my phone ringing. My eyes spring open and blearily adjust to the bright light streaking into the room, searching out the clock on my bedside. Thoughts of Ren bloom in my mind, and I flush with heat. It's twenty to eleven in the morning. Maths has never been my strong suit but it must be the middle of the night in LA, so it's extremely unlikely it's him again. Still, I grab at my phone greedily, but pause when I see the caller ID. It's not even Cole, though that would be unlikely, too.

She never rings me…

I hear hard breathing as I pick up.

'Christy?'

'Hi Kay. Um, I can't get hold of Mum or Dad, they must still be asleep after—'

'Are you OK?'

'I think my waters have broken, so—' She breaks off and I hear her breathe even harder. Contractions. She's having contractions.

'How far apart are they?' I struggle to think of what

would be bad. Five minutes? God, why haven't I been more involved?

'I'm in a cab,' she pants. I know the sound of my sister in pain and worried, and I know how she'd try to mask it because I'd be the same way. I want to comfort her, but I also know that would dissolve her resolve and I can't let her do that right now.

'Cool. Good. You're going to King's, yeah?'

'Yeah.' Her voice is high and helpless, and my stomach tightens.

'Listen, Chris, do me a favour, take a deep breath with me, all right?' I wait as I hear her inhale raggedly, and I do the same. We blow out simultaneously. 'I'm going to be there in twenty minutes.' It might be a lie, but I'm already pulling on jeans as I speak, then moving the handset away for a moment to pull a jumper over my T-shirt. I'll run there if I have to. 'Don't worry about Mum and Dad, I'm going to ring them now. You just concentrate on deep breaths. OK?'

I hear her groan, and it cuts through me.

'Christy.' I deepen my voice demandingly, trying to channel Mum.

'OK, I will. Th-thanks babe.'

Phone still in my hand I grab my keys and bag, and rush to the front door, wincing only slightly as I slam it behind me—though through Sami's slightly-open bedroom door I could see her snoring face down on the mattress fully clothed, so it must have been a good night. As soon as I get down-stairs I see an empty black cab at the traffic lights and I'm in it before he has much choice, shouting instructions about where to avoid as he makes his way towards Kings College Hospital—the place where both my sister and I were born and now *her* child will be too. *God, please let everything be all right...* I suddenly remember Ren's thoughts about praying, our talk that night, and it sort of calms me down. I try the landline at my parents' house since both their phones still seem to be off, and after eleven rings I finally hear my dad's groggy voice on the other end of the line. I take a breath so as not to sound too panicky.

'Hi, Dad. Listen, Christy's gone into labour...' I glance up to see the hospital ahead of us and sigh with relief. 'I'm just getting to Kings now, so I'll let you know what room she's in and—'

'She's all right, yeah?'

I don't know. 'Yeah, yeah, she's fine. I'm just jumping out of the cab now, so I'll message you in a sec, OK?'

'Uh, all right sweetheart. We'll be there as soon as we can.' I can hear mum's sleepy, concerned voice in the background now. It's weird to hear my dad so out of sorts. Usually he'd be the one reassuring *us*, taking charge. I really do feel like an adult all of a sudden.

I shove cash at the driver and then jog inside the hospital, searching the signage for the maternity ward. When I reach the reception, I hear a familiar voice down the hallway shout 'I *am* pushing!' and my heart swells, because it's then that I know Christy's OK.

Ignoring the receptionist calling me back to the desk, I

head towards my sister's voice, and as I enter the small suite her eyes lock with mine. 'Kay,' she breathes, and I rush over to her side and grip her hand in mine.

'Hiya. All right?'

She nods as another contraction overwhelms her, and I let her crush my hand as the midwife quietly encourages her to push. I feel Christy's body tense hard, then relax, and the sound of screeching baby-cries fills the room. While everyone's eyes are trained on the little squirming mess that the midwife holds up, my gaze is fixed on my big sister.

'Oh my God,' I whisper. 'You just pushed a fucking human out of your body.'

*

A couple of hours later, I'm sitting in the only-slightly-comfortable chair in the corner of the room while Mum and Dad fuss around Christy and coo over my niece—*my niece*. I'm an *aunty*. My phone buzzes with a push of emails and I realise I haven't even checked my inbox at all today, so I hit the icon on my phone with trepidation. There's at least seven work-related messages that I scan and decide can wait until later, but my scroll halts when I see an address ending in @edenstreetproductions…

Ren.

Hey
August 27 2016 9:27 PM (GMT-7)

To: **Kayla Joseph** <kaykay@murdercreation.com>
From: **Ren Morgan** <ren@edenstreetproductions.com>

I wanted to put something super-smart as a subject heading, but my head is full of cotton wool after that god-damn production meeting. Remind me never to schedule meetings for late night, London time? I'm still mad I couldn't stay with you. In a lot of ways I guess…

Anyway. "Kyle" got your email address too, by the way, as you can (hopefully) see. I didn't want to message you in case you don't switch your phone off or don't keep it on silent when you're asleep. But I hope you slept well.

And I meant what I said. We can do this.

X

It's awkward to read his email and allow the feeling it brings to settle within me while my whole family is in the room, especially given that they've only just found out about my plan with *Cole*. Even with the flood of warmth that Ren's handful of words give me, I know this is a complete and utter fantasy, but there's no way I can stop it right now. I'm clinging to all of it—to the memory of him, to every word.

So I hit reply.

RE: Hey
August 28 2016 2:17 PM (BST)

To: **Ren Morgan** <ren@edenstreetproductions.com>
From: **Kayla Joseph** <kaykay@murdercreation.com>

That Kyle, eh? Someone give him a raise.

Hey, guess what? I'm looking at my new niece. My sister had the baby this morning. She's doing really well, and the baby is too. Well, she's a bit just-born-squidgy at the moment, but it's all good. She'll be cute soon. Hah.

I slept very well…

And actually, I've been thinking about something—you never answered my questionnaire. So first, Ren:

"Do your dreams feel real?"

Mine do. When I dream of you.

X

As I look up, I see Christy watching my face. She raises one eyebrow, like she's reading my mind, but I doubt even she could imagine the emotional pickle I'm in.

'All right?' she mouths, and I nod, getting up to come and join them in looking down at the baby. Who am I kidding?

She's extremely cute already. 'Any closer to a name?' I ask my sister quietly, and to my surprise she nods.

'Yeah. I'm going to call her… Joy.'

Thirteen

Ren.

'Are you even listening to me?'

I glance up from my phone. Damn, when did I become *that* guy? Somewhere around the time I discovered Kayla's Instagram feed… and her Twitter… not to mention her website, and her email, and her messages, and—

'*Ren?*' Neela sounds even more exasperated with me than usual. She's a diamond, and could be running any production company anywhere. Lord knows why she stuck with mine.

'Yeah. You said that Nick sent me the latest itineraries to go through. I'll do that tonight, I promise.'

She leans back in the chair pushed up to our tiny glass-walled meeting room's table and massages the back of her neck with one hand. I only just noticed she's wound her crazy-long hair into a bun using two of my favourite pens. It's a sauna in here, but I had to move the fan out because it was like being in a Mariah Carey video. There's basically only room for the chairs, the table, and the coffee machine that we usually have parked in between our computers to keep the unhealthy number of refills going on our espressos.

Desperate times and long-ass final prep meetings have made us move it in here with us.

'Ugh, you're so annoying,' Neela tells me, pulling one of the pens out of her hair and flipping it at me. I deflect. She takes a breath, leans forward and types something rapidly, then nods at her screen. 'Cool, OK. So I think we're about set for the meeting with Galaxy tomorrow for the final budget.'

'Hooray,' I mutter, eyes back on my phone screen. I hate numbers-talk—they always act like there's some reason to be careful. They seem to have forgotten that I looked at shoe-strings with envy on my first films. I almost want to openly *weep* at the kind of money they're letting me spend now.

I sense Neela's patience has reached its limit, and she shuts her laptop with an air of finality. 'Great. Well, I'm going to get out of here while there's still a glimmer of daylight in the sky for once. I suggest you do the same.' She re-tucks the sleeves of her *Bad Feminist* T-shirt into the tops of her bra straps, where she's crafted it into sleeveless-ness.

'*You* have a person to get back to,' I tell her, and she chuckles. I wish my person was close enough to get back to. *Is she my person…?*

'Mo's in Boston for the rest of the week, which is why I want to get into my hammock, take at least thirty minutes to get in any kind of comfortable position, and then watch my shows on this—' She gestures with the laptop now under her arm, '—and smoke my herb without feeling judged.'

I laugh. 'That's company property,' I tell her, pointing at the computer.

Neela makes a talking-puppet hand. '*I am* this company,' she retorts with a laugh. I have to agree though, especially after the void left by Yann… 'Besides,' she adds, nodding toward my phone. 'Seems like you've got something bubbling away there, am I right?'

I shrug, but I may be actually blushing to some degree, which is catnip to her.

'Oh my God. Ren! Who is she?'

'I… She's…' There's no point trying to deny it. 'You don't know her, Neels.'

She leans in closer, like she needs to examine my face for clues. 'You are *sprung*!' She straightens up. 'Wow. That's great, Ren.' She fixes me with a look. 'Seriously. I mean, I thought after…'

I purse my lips. 'You can say their names.'

Neela sets the laptop down on the table again for a second and tilts her head to one side. I've known her since our final year of film school, and I can feel when she's about to get earnest. I brace myself, but it gives me a rush of affection for her, too. 'Ren, I can't front. You know I was as shocked as you were about what happened between Yann and Eve. But more than anything, I guess I've been a little afraid that… that you had your relationship with Evelyn up on some impossibly high pedestal. That nobody else would ever come close to her for you.'

It's nothing I haven't already thought myself. I guess even the particular, spectacular way Evelyn broke my heart made her special.

'I'm happy for you,' Neela tells me, squeezing my shoulder. 'Really happy, Ren.' Then she picks up her computer again. 'Don't fuck it up.' She winks and heads out of the room.

Great pep talk. I'm about to head too, but as I go to close Instagram down on my phone, a picture catches my eye. It's not Eve's account, and it sure as hell isn't Yann's—I don't follow either of them any more. But some half-remembered friend of Evelyn's is somehow in my feed, and so suddenly they both are too. Yann is standing behind Eve, leaning down to rest his chin on her shoulder. They're both grinning at the camera, and the tight, striped dress Eve's wearing doesn't hide it. Neither does the way Yann's hand is resting on her stomach.

She's pregnant?

Very pregnant, from the roundness that protrudes out from her painfully familiar tall, slim frame. They both look obliviously happy, and for that moment, in spite of everything with Kayla, a pure anger ignites every ounce of blood in my body.

That could—*should?*—have been me. I've never even thought of wanting a family before—mine barely qualified as one, so I guess I had no real example to aspire to—but seeing the two of them like that? Their smiles seem to be directly mocking everything we all used to be. It was all a lie. There was never any future there.

I close the screen and stare into space, barely registering Neela calling goodbye. I don't want this to ruin my day, but...

Too late.

*

'Yeah, hey, could I get a—'

'Number fifteen, to go, yes?' The Cantonese woman looks at me expectantly, impatient. *I am a predictable sad sack single dude, yes. You're entirely right.*

'Yeah. And some egg rolls, please.'

She flicks me an imperceptible nod. 'Ten, twelve minutes. We're busy. Sit please.' She's already looking over my shoulder to the couple behind me, who are sandwiched together and giggle-whispering to one another intimately as they study the menu in their hands. I take a seat in the window and pull out my phone again. It's two hours since Yann and Eve's baby bump photo-bombed me. Something's bothering me about it besides the obvious, though. The *timing* just doesn't seem right. I mean, unless she's having twins— Woah. What if they're having twins? Unlikely. So how can she be almost ready to pop when it's only been eight months or so since… But I guess, who knows how long they were…

Goddamnmit. I don't want to be thinking about any of this again. I'd been doing pretty well. I blame Neela for bringing them up, setting off some Ren's-relationship-nightmares Baader-Meinhoff reaction. Thing is, right before it all imploded—when Evelyn must have felt guilty or conflicted or who the fuck knows what—she and I fell into our bed. We made love one last time, the way we always did:

to make ourselves feel better. We tried to pretend that things were OK. So…

I start to sweat.

No. *No.*

I can't even entertain it. I just want to sit on my couch, pound beers and eat my Chinese food, listen to records too loud and—

Wait. I know how I can distract myself. I was too busy trying to stay focussed in my meeting with Neela this afternoon to actually reply to the email that Kayla sent me about her sister, and her questionnaire. Maybe I could call? Hmm: seven PM here… three AM there. I curse time zones again. This is going to be even worse in a week or so when I'm halfway across the world. Still, I open her email and a smile slowly spreads across my face. *Kayla.* She's what I need to focus on. When nothing else can, she helps me forget I was ever betrayed. She makes it damn near irrelevant…

I open up my email and start to type.

RE: Hey
August 28 2016 7:07 PM (PDT)

To: **Kayla Joseph** <kaykay@murdercreation.com>
From: **Ren Morgan** < ren@edenstreetproductions.com>

So it sounds like you've patched things up with Christy then, huh? I'm glad. Life's too short, and now she's brought one into the world…? Congrats. I knew you could get past what you've got between you. Climb over it, see around it. I had faith you would. You already have the answers anyway; you always do. That baby's pretty lucky.

I stop typing for a second as Eve and Yann's grins try to push into my mind again, but I force them away, along with the guilt over what might make me be wanting Kayla more than ever right now. I continue, trying to concentrate on her. On *her*.

I was thinking about your questions just this morning in the shower, actually. Among other things... I mean, you totally stole my answer to the 'dreams' question, but whatever. I'll get over it. Honestly? I guess my dreams do feel real. Way too real. That's the problem—I feel like I often don't get past that layer, the dream layer, into forget-sleep. I wish I did. Well, not when I genuinely do manage to dream about you. But a lot of the time they're about the past. All that stuff with Evelyn and Yannick. Probably even more now that I've just found out something so crazy that I'm trying not to really think about it.

Shit. I don't know why I wrote that. I'm not sure I want Kayla to see this bitter, insecure part of me—not all of it, anyway. I consider deleting it, but I guess I also want her to magically help with the solution without even knowing the problem...

If I Don't Have You

It's probably nothing anyway. I'm letting my imagination get ahead of me. Hey, you know what sucks? That I'm sitting on my own, waiting for takeout which will probably be cold by the time I get back to my apartment, thinking about you like I do every spare moment that I'm not thinking about work, and I can't come see you. I can't even call you because it's the middle of the night there. One of us may need to start working on becoming a night owl, vampire, whatever suits. Any day now I'll be getting on a plane that I wish was heading to you, but will actually be headed halfway across the world, in an even *crazier* time zone, not to mention the fact that I'll be on an insane shooting schedule... But don't worry, we'll figure it out, I promise. Heh.

Did I tell you the studio is super-stuck on calling this thing **Revolution World**? Ugh. Here I was thinking *Detonate* was on the nose. They've been pissing their pants over how good the returns have been on that, though. Apparently I'm edging into *wunderkind* territory rather than *bratty indie upstart*. I've always wanted to be a wunderkind... And I guess the critical reception's been way better than I expected. It feels a little unearned. Maybe I'm guilty over how down I was on the movie. Perspective is giving me more appreciation for it. That, and the fact it brought me to you.

It's also meant that I've had a little more freedom to work

on RW—I'm even doing a pass on the screenplay re-write, so I guess that's a start, right? Thank you for encouraging me. I have a couple tiny germs of new ideas maybe, possibly, starting to form, too. We'll see. Maybe you should come help motivate me at my buddy's place in upstate NY after RW is wrapped, and I'll knock out some award-winning shit while you write brilliantly witty internet prose and take photographs and do incredible art? Or maybe that's a bad idea—we'd never get anything done, because I'd be too busy wanting to taste that incredible caramel taste of you again, and trying to find new and better ways to make you scream my name that way you did... that way I can still hear if I concentrate... that way that even hearing it in my imagination is about to make things real awkward for me in this Chinese take-out if I'm not careful...

I'm gonna get the jump on your questionnaire while I'm waiting. So, after the dreams one it was 'What is it you admire about the person you admire most?' am I right? I'll resist being corny as hell and saying something about you again, even if it would probably be true. It hurts to be honest on this one, but the fact is that the person I admire most would be Yann, in spite of everything. And the thing I used to admire the most about him? His alchemic ability to turn ideas into beauty. I fucking miss that.

Damn it...

If I Don't Have You

Anyway. I'm going to get ahead of you. So, next was 'How often do you look up?' right? Again, I'm feigning a lack of knowledge about every moment of our interactions. Well it's funny—living in the city, surrounded by towering buildings, I almost never did look up, because I sort of knew what would be above me, but in LA all there is above is blue sky, unending. It should make me happy, but I like light and shade.

I look up suddenly as I hear the lady shout '*Number Fifteen with egg rolls!*' like she's been repeating herself.
    'Yeah, that's me.'

Gotta go. My takeout's ready and I think she's going to throw it at me if I don't get my ass up to the counter.

Hey Kayla? This 'missing you' thing won't go away.

X

Fourteen

Kayla.

I sit up in bed and pile the pillows around me, closing the email on my phone and opening my laptop to go over Ren's note again on a bigger screen. I'm flooded with the same warmth as I re-read his words. I can almost hear him speaking…

There's so much else there I wish I could focus on, but I can't help it; the warmth is punctuated with slivers of ice as I read her name. My eyes snag on it every time. *Evelyn*. Why is he worried about her—about them? What could he have found out that's *so crazy he doesn't want to think about it*? I frown, and it deepens as I turn inwards. Is this jealousy? If it is, it's fucking pathetic. But it also makes me so aware—too aware—of the fact that I'm not the first person that Ren might have said honey-coated words to. I'm not the first person he's had any deeper feelings for. I'm… some woman he met a couple of weeks ago, who lives on the other side of the ocean. This might not be the same thing at all for him that it is for me.

'Jesus, Kayla,' I murmur to myself. Why did I even look at my phone so early? Because it's always the first thing I do when I open my eyes now—search for him. 'He said it's nothing.' And that's definitely always the case when people say it, right?

Now that I'm awake I need to wee, so I head to the bathroom, use the loo and wash my hands. Then, since I'm standing over the sink anyway, I splash some water on my face and brush my teeth, trying to start afresh. I don't want to be the kind of woman who lets one sentence fan giant flames of insecurity. I'm a bit disappointed that the embers are so hot inside me, to be honest. Ren's ex pretty much ripped his heart out and stepped on it—it seems unlikely he's secretly still harbouring something for her. *Although*… I think about what would happen if Ren ended things now. Would I just shrug, lower the shutters and reset my heart? I spit toothpaste into the sink. Every element of that scenario freaks me out, especially the two parts I've been trying to ignore: that he has got so deep under my skin—and that at some point soon this really will have to end.

I head back to bed and settle into the cocoon I'd created, sitting up cross-legged against the pillows. My silk head-scarf must have slipped off and burrowed itself among the bedclothes over night, but I leave my locs twisted up in their bun, adjust my vest top to make sure nothing is hanging out where it shouldn't, and then take a deep breath. It's probably stupid, because it's going to be late there, of course; when is it *not* too late or too early? But somewhere between the bathroom sink and this bed, I've decided I need to see Ren's face. I open the video messaging on my phone and study the image of myself projected back at me that blinks a moment after I do. I see the excitement in her eyes—a look I never see when I call Cole, the person I'm *engaged* to. I hear that voice in my head again that tells me it's crazy to be falling for a man I don't even really know. A man who can't be in my life. A man who—

—*Is video-calling* me *right now.*

Shit. He must have seen the *Online* notification thingy next to my picture. My heart leaps at the static picture of Ren with the word 'calling' underneath it, and my finger trembles as I hit the answer button. He scrambles out of the pixels and into a gorgeous real moving image in the confines of my phone screen.

'Ren,' I say, my voice embarrassingly shaky. He leans closer to the camera and smiles breathtakingly.

'God damn.'

'What?'

'You're really there.' He laughs softly. 'Hi.'

'Hi. I… I was just going to try you, but you beat me to it.'

I see his eyes roaming around his screen, looking as strangely surprised as I do. 'I'm glad I did. How do you look this good at… What, seven in the morning?'

'Twenty five past,' I murmur, and he chuckles.

'Ahh, OK. That twenty-five minutes is what makes the difference.'

I just want to stare at him, but I force myself to speak. 'I… I got your email,' I tell him. 'How was your take-away?'

Ren flips the camera on his phone and I see some of his apartment—spacious and pale, tiled and wooden. He zooms towards some left-over white boxes with Chinese symbols on them, chopsticks still poking out of one and a couple of beer bottles beside them. Low light comes from a large designer floor lamp in the corner. He flips the camera back around to his face, and I sigh in relief.

'It was a sad reminder of the fact that I should cook more,' he says with a smile. 'I feel like I've hardly lived in this place since I've been here.' He glances away, looking around, then back at me. 'And I'll be gone again in a couple days.'

'Revolution World, here you come,' I say, and he grimaces.

'Right? They might as well have called it Generic Movie Title.'

'It's not *that* bad. Anyway, whatever they call it, you're going to make it good. And New Zealand will be beautiful, too.'

'*You're* beautiful.'

I swallow. Ren just stays blinking at me, and I draw in a breath. 'Um… I'm glad to hear you're doing a bit more writing. I'm not sure I can take any credit though.'

He leans back on the low cream sofa he's sitting on. 'Well, it's true,' he says.

I smile, remembering. 'You've definitely been getting creative with your upstate retreat fantasy, I suppose…' He arches an eyebrow at me, making his forehead wrinkle irresistibly. 'That sounded pretty good to me.' I'm distracted from everything else in my head as I watch his face, completely overwhelmed with the desire to kiss him. 'I can't stop missing you either, Ren,' I add softly. He sighs and ruffles his free hand through his hair, and it kills me how familiar the gesture is for having spent only one night with him. Before I know it, I hear myself saying, 'And… I have fantasies as well.'

His eyelids lower. 'Yeah?'

'Mmhmm.'

He shifts. I sense his muscles tighten. 'Tell me.'

Every inch of my skin heats at Ren's command. I lean back on the pillows stacked up behind my back and let the camera on my phone drift lower so he can see the loose, low-cut black vest that I know doesn't leave all that much to the imagination. It was hot last night; I'd usually have been in a T-shirt at least. 'Well… one is… You're in the shower. We're in a hotel room, because, well, we have a good track record in those so far.'

He smiles. 'Agreed.'

I'm not sure how much to really confess, but the way he looks at me I can't resist. 'You've been all stressed out, because you're a big shot movie director and that's stressful.' Ren chuckles, but stops when I say, 'And I want to help you relax.'

He closes his eyes for a second, and I know his free hand has slipped lower…

'So, while you're in the shower, I've gone to the vending machine in one of those white hotel robes, disposable slippers and nothing else and fetched a cup of ice chips, because it's so hot everywhere, even with the air conditioning. And I make sure I'm back sitting on the sofa in the suite, sucking on one of them when I hear the shower turn off.'

He exhales, then breathes in long and slow.

'Show me what you're doing,' I whisper, my own hand snaking inside my pants. I lower the camera for a moment to show him, then lift it back up to my face with a teasing smirk.

'Goddamn.' He lowers his camera to his grey sweatpants, and I see the outline of his hard-on, tenting them. It's ridiculous and dirty, and I start to move my fingers in a lazy circle. Ren's hand moves under his waistband and he starts to stroke slowly too. 'Tell me more,' he says.

'You come out of the bathroom with steam following you into the suite. You have a robe on too. It's open, and I can see your boxer briefs, your stomach, your chest...' I close my eyes for a second to picture it. 'You're all distracted, looking for your phone. You have a meeting, you're worried you're going to be late.'

Ren chuckles again. 'This is a little too real,' he says, but I can hear the strain in his voice, and I laugh softly too but it hitches because I know where this goes next.

'I'm sucking ice chips on the sofa, but you don't seem to notice. I say *come here*.' I pause, change my voice to exactly how I'd say it: forceful, so he can't ignore me. '*Come here.*'

I hear Ren's breathing getting louder, the phone camera less steady.

'I beckon you closer, in between my legs so you're standing right in front of me.' I gesture at the camera lens with one finger, crooking it towards me. *God, if only...* 'Closer...' I lick my lips slowly and watch his eyes as he focuses on my tongue. 'I run my hands up over the muscles of your stomach. Your skin's hot to the touch from the shower.' I stop for a moment, my fingers still working inside my pants. There's a whimper in my voice that I can't hide as I continue. 'But my mouth is cold.'

'Jesus, Kayla...'

'I pull your boxers down. You're getting hard. I stroke my fingertips very lightly over you until you're where I want you to be.'

I hear him grunt, watch his face, his eyes locked onto mine.

'I take another sliver of ice in my mouth and then I move my tongue over your cock...' I'm rubbing myself harder now, too into it to even be shocked at myself, at how easily I'm telling him this. 'You try to jolt away from the cold, but then you start to like it. The ice melts against your skin and I take you all the way to the back of my throat...'

'*Fuck*...'

Ren's camera only captures part of his face now as he starts to lose control, and I do too. My voice sounds loud and high and foreign as I continue.

'I suck harder, and you slip one hand inside my robe and cup my breast, run the pad of your thumb over my nipple, circling it slowly until it's so hard I can't stand it—' I break

219

off, suddenly distracted by hearing Sami's bedroom door open next door to mine, my hand frozen inside my pants. I'm jolted back to reality. *Shit.* How loud was I talking? Ren is breathing hard and loud, oblivious, and I quickly turn down the volume on my phone just as I hear him groan my name. He finished without me…

All at once, I find myself bereft and angry and worried, like I'm about to be caught exposed in more ways than one. I hear the bathroom door shut as Ren's image on my phone screen rights itself, and I take in his bewildered expression.

He draws a few deep breaths. 'Kayla… You are way too good at that.' He smiles at me and readjusts himself, but in that moment I feel something so much more than sexual attraction or lust. Something I don't think I'm equipped to define. *How have I got myself into this?*

Ren's smile fades a bit as I watch him. 'I think I get it now though,' he says. 'What you said the other night. The feeling of you not being here is…'

We're both quiet for a moment, just looking at each other. I keep one ear tuned to the door, just in case.

'Hey,' I whisper.

'Hey.'

'I have other fantasies, too, you know.'

A wry smile spreads across his lips. 'I'm not sure I could handle another one yet.'

I shake my head. 'No, just… Just ones where we can talk, face-to-face.' I raise my eyebrows. 'I mean really face-to-face. And just talking.' I sigh and lean back on the pillows again.

'Or you're just holding me, stroking the back of my neck. Where we're just *together*, spending time.'

He looks down. 'Kayla… Soon, OK?' His gaze returns to me, sincerity all over his beautiful face. How can he be so certain? Because he doesn't know the whole story, of course. My mind catapults back to Evelyn's name in his email, and the certainty he must have had about them before it was all smashed to pieces. But they at least had a foundation of time, of shared experience. What do we have? I shake my head again more vigorously and draw my knees up to my chest.

'I wish I could just be completely honest with you, Ren,' I whisper, and the frown between his brows deepens.

'You *can*—'

'No.' I stop and draw in a breath. 'Sorry. I'm bad at this,' I tell him softly. 'I know before, that night in New York I said that maybe the details didn't matter and that's true, but… Maybe I just have an overactive imagination—'

He interjects. 'Absolutely not. It's a *great* level of active.' His mouth quirks, and I flush.

'Ren…'

'My bad.' He holds up his hand and gestures for me to continue with that earnest look on his face that frustrates me and melts my heart in equal measure.

I sit up straighter. 'I'm just very aware that you have a romantic past. That you've had someone in your life before me, someone really important to you. And I feel pathetic and naïve to say it, but I really haven't.'

'That's OK,' Ren whispers.

'But it isn't. I… I'm suppose I'm jealous.' I roll my eyes at myself, and he smiles, reaching towards his screen as though he wants to touch my cheek. I wish he could. 'How do you ever get over someone when you've felt anything even close to this?'

And I see it—his eyes dart away from mine, for a fraction of a moment, but they do. I think I have my answer. *You don't.*

'Kayla, forget about that. Since you came along… None of what's happened in my past matters, OK?'

I try to slow down my pin-balling thoughts, but I fail miserably. 'But we don't really… We're not in each other's lives, Ren. Do we really even *know* each other? There's all sorts of shit going on with me that I can't…' I stop myself, even though I know he must be confused. 'And what about you? It sounded in your email like you've got stuff you're dealing with, too. Stuff about *her*, and—'

'It's nothing.' He rubs that space between his brows, but searches for my eyes through the screen. My stomach knots. 'Really, Kayla. It's nothing that matters for *us*.'

I swallow hard, because the thing I'm hiding is something that matters a lot for us, and I still can't bring myself to say it. 'OK.' We stay on the phone but silent, our thoughts pulling us back away across the very real distance between us.

After a while, Ren takes a breath. 'Kayla, maybe we don't know each other, but—'

'You know what scares me the most?' I interject in a

whisper. 'It's that I don't fucking care. I just... I *want* you. And that scares me half to death, because I've never felt like this, Ren, and the timing is extra-specially shit.'

I expect him to question me, or tell me "we can do this" again but he doesn't. He has that capacity to sometimes just take things in, and it makes me fall for him even harder.

'Kayla.' He says my name like it's a complete sentence, packed with meaning.

I need to get off this call. 'Let's talk later, all right?'

Ren nods at me. I watch him for a moment longer, and then hit the 'end' button.

But as I close my eyes and push back down under my covers, I hear the beep of a message come through on my phone.

It's him.

REN:
How well do you need to know
someone to know you've fallen in
love?

Fifteen

Ren.

I've felt every single one of the seventeen hours it's been since I sent Kayla that message with the damn 'L' word it in. I must have been delirious from the phone sex. I try to avoid thinking about it, because the mingling of the crazily erotic with the heartache-inducing little talk we had afterward is fucking with my mind. Instead, I've been keeping my head down and finally typed THE END on our shooting script, which is just as well seeing as it's now two days until I'll be on a plane to New Zealand with our crew.

I sense Nick as he pokes his neatly-quaffed head through the crack in the office door behind me, ever the efficient assistant. 'Do you need me for anything else, Ren? If not I'm going to head out.'

I hold my laptop over my head so he can see the screen, and turn, pointing to those final few letters. 'Oh, awesome!' he says. 'Just in time. You want me to take the USB over to the GS offices tonight on my way—?'

'No, no,' I tell him. Though maybe it wouldn't be a bad idea—if I hang on to it, I'll probably end up messing with sentences for the rest of the night. 'Don't worry about it. I'll leave it here at the office,' I resolve. 'The morning's fine. As long as the copies are with Jen on the plane, it's all good.' Jennifer, our script supervisor, has been patient almost to a fault, but even she has been starting to get itchy about the final draft. I'm happy with it now though. I think.

'If you're sure...' He watches my face. 'Uh, how about I watch you save it, and lock it in my drawer until tomorrow?'

I sag in relief. 'What would I do without you, Nicholas?'

He smiles, folds his arms and waits, and a minute later I tentatively press the USB into his hand. 'This is final,' he intones. 'It's going straight to their offices first thing. I'm Teflon to any bribery, regardless of if you stay here tinkering.'

'You think I *tinker* at my desk when you guys aren't here? What kind of a man do you think I am?'

Nick sighs at my childishness and turns to head out. 'See you in the morning,' he calls over his shoulder. He already knows me pretty well, apparently. But just thinking that catapults my thoughts to Kayla, and remembering what she said last night, and to what I, Señor Dumbass, typed, and to her silence since—

My thoughts halt as I glance back at my screen and see an email has appeared in my inbox. The subject heading is one of her questions:

Why is that song your favourite?

I click 'open' immediately and sit back hard in my chair. The message contains a link to a video, with a few sentences underneath…

This one is my favourite now. Because when it plays, we're outside that bar, and your arms are around me, and I feel your need for me, and nothing else matters. And because its lyrics are starting to feel true.

Kx

I click the link, and the suddenly-familiar piano and bass begin to emerge from my speakers, followed by the sweet, yearning voice of Mr Gregory Isaacs. *If I Don't Have You.* I listen to the sweeping, romantic declarations in the lyrics, absorbing the idea that for Kayla there'll be nobody else.

*

'Hey Benji, can you switch seats with me? I need an aisle. I don't want to have to climb over Watts and Neela every time I need to pee. Do you have any idea how long this flight is going to be?'

'You're actually giving up a window seat?'

'You know, you'd have thought Galaxy would spring for us to turn left, huh?'

'Poor, innocent little Brian…'

'What? My buddy spent a month on *Attack the Desert* last year and he made out like it was deluxe accommodation all the way.'

'They shot that shit-pile in Dubai, there's nothing *but* luxury—'

'When did you graduate sound school anyway, lil bud?'

'When your mom stopped paying my tuition…'

I tune out as the conversation descends into a play-fight, trying to pretend that I'm not with the crew guys scrambling over one another in the departure lounge. Neela is already Zen-ed out with her travel pillow, eyes closed and headphones firmly planted over her ears. I follow suit, glad I sprang for these fancy noise-cancelling cans. I look at my phone, opening Kayla's last message again with a sigh.

KAYLA:
Sorry I missed your call—again… I
miss you, and I miss you, all the time.
Please make sure you let me know
when you land safe in NZ. X

I replied, but it's 4am in London of course, so she won't see it until she wakes up. I close my eyes for a second, picturing Kayla in those few, unaware moments before sleep ends… It calms me, but I'm doing OK considering the task ahead. I'm definitely feeling ready for this shoot to get going. Principle photography starts in ten days, and I'm itching to get the final locations confirmed, get the actors acclimatised, get everything ready. Shooting is my favourite part. It's the only time I really feel like a Director, this thing everyone keeps telling me I am… *God,* I can genuinely hear Kayla calling bullshit on those kind of pseudo-self-effacing thoughts, even in my mind. I crack open my laptop and find her last email, the one with the Gregory Isaacs link that I haven't gotten around to replying to with all the last minute prep for this trip. I hit 'reply' and start to type.

RE: Why is that song your favourite?
September 3 2016 8:19pm (PDT)

To: **Kayla Joseph** <kaykay@murdercreation.com>
From: **Ren Morgan** <ren@edenstreetproductions.com>

Hey again.

I'm at LAX still. Airports should come with a trigger warning for thoughts of you, by the way. I think I'm ready for this shoot, though. Kinda excited, even. I'd feel *more* ready if I could have gotten to kiss (etc.) you goodbye, though. But I'm keeping in mind that sometime soon-ish I'll be kissing (etc.) you hello…

So: 'Why is that song your favorite?' Here goes. I mean, obviously now that I know the name of that Gregory Isaacs song (I tried and failed to find it before), it's way up there, for the same reasons. But—and this is weird, because I haven't thought about it in a long time—but I guess other than that, the song that's my favorite is *We've Only*

Just Begun by the Carpenters. Yeah, my cool points just skyrocketed, I know. It reminds me of my mother. She loves the Carpenters insanely, or at least she used to, and I remember her playing that record over and over when I was a little kid. Before the divorce, before she went back to Brazil and pretty much checked out of my whole situation. I guess that song makes me happy, but at the same time totally resentful, because it's all fucking hopeful and optimistic, and that's how I felt as a kid, but then it all got slowly stripped away. I don't know. That's what came into my head the minute you asked the question at the junket. It's actually a pretty cool song—the harmonies, and Karen Carpenter's voice is just so fucking clear and soulful, you know? My mom sounded just like her when she sang along, in my mind anyway. Maybe the stereo was just up real loud... Hey, those lyrics kinda feel right for us, too. Is that corny? (I know the answer, thanks).

You should feel privileged, by the way, because I don't really like to talk about my mom. But I even thought this back at the junket, when I started spouting off about my heritage: you are some kind of magician who will elicit all sorts of things out of me. And that's why my answer to the next question of yours, "When did you last get goose bumps?", would have to be August 10th, the moment I saw you walk through that door. I hope you haven't had any since I ran my fingertips over the gorgeous curve of your back after the first time we...

I want to type "made love".

We're at the end of your set of questions, I guess, since I kind of answered "Why Do We Create?" that night—but I maybe it was more of an "I" than a "We". I think as creative people, you, me, any of us, create because it's inside and needs to come out. Because we're human beings, and making art is what defines us as such. Like making love, without necessarily the intention of making life. I've been thinking about that idea a lot lately... But as much as I think creating is a need, I also think sometimes we create for the hell of it. Because we can, you know? What do you think? I await your answer, and you.

Ren x

I sigh as I hit send, then look up just as a pair of balled-up socks that my Second Assistant Director has—I hope—removed from his carry-on luggage is hurled in my direction and hits me in the face. I can't hear what they're saying, but my headphones give the crew's escapades an Al Green soundtrack. I laugh, giving them all the finger. Al cuts off mid-croon, though, as my phone starts to ring and my heart quickens embarrassingly, but it's not Kayla—why would it be?

It *is* a number I recognise, though.

'Evie?' In my shock, I revert to her pet name without thinking.

'Ren. Hey. How's it going?' Her voice sounds calm, unhurried, familiar.

'Is everything OK?'

I hear her swallow and know instantly the calm is a front. My mind goes to Yann. Could something have happened to him? She'd know, even after all that's happened, that I would want—need—to know.

'Yeah, everything's good. Great, actually. Um, I guess… I saw that you'd come across our… the news. About the baby.'

I get up, moving away from the others, and stand staring at the Starbucks across the way unseeingly. Did I actually hit the '*like*' button under that picture? Guess so. Jesus, it must have been some kind of reflex, some desperate need to show them I didn't care. 'Yeah, I heard. Um, congratulations.'

'Thanks. I, uh… Well, we just brought her home. I had her three days ago.'

'Wow.' I'm not sure what else to say. I don't get why she's calling.

And then suddenly, I do. Of course I do.

'Listen, Ren, we need to talk. Can you—?' A loud boarding announcement comes over the speakers, bringing her to a halt. 'Oh. Are you at the airport?'

'Yes. I can't talk now, Evelyn. I'm about to head to New Zealand for a shoot, so—'

'New Zealand?' I hear her take a breath. 'But Ren, I need to… The baby… We think…' I wait, callously, as she struggles to find the words to tell me the child she's just given birth to is mine. *They* think?

'God dammit. *God dammit*, I don't want to hear this, Eve.' My voice is almost unrecognizable. 'I don't want to—'

'Ren.' She silences me. 'We have to be sure.'

I fight the urge to explode. 'Sure?' I hiss into the handset. 'Why the hell aren't you *sure*, Evelyn?' I struggle to keep my voice low. 'Is it because you were screwing us both?' I squeeze my eyes shut, trying not to let cruelty take over. 'Look, this is a bad time. OK? I cannot hear this right now.'

'I know this is a shock, all right? But... Jesus, Ren, she might be your daughter.'

The words hit me like darts. 'Goodbye, Evelyn.' I end the call before she can say anything else. *Daughter. Daughter. Daughter.* The word echoes in my mind. 'Fuck,' I utter in a whisper.

I push my headphones back over my ears, go back to my seat, and try to pretend my world didn't just get shaken to the ground.

Sixteen

Kayla.

'Oh, just chuck that stuff on the floor,' Christy tells me, nodding to the sofa occupied by bags of new nappies. To be honest, I'm still distracted by the perfection of the tiny human in the bassinette on the floor. Baby Joy is already more stylish than most of my friends. Christy has her decked out in a minimal-chic onesie whose oatmeal colour offsets the perfect smooth brown of my niece's skin. I'm mesmerised by stroking the soft soles of her feet as I crouch down to stare at her. She stares back, looking every bit as fascinated. What a madness just discovering life must be. I feel like I'm still getting used to it myself.

'Joy, why are you so adorable, eh? Sorry, it's actually not legal to be this cute. What's your mum playing at, eh? Eh?' I lean in and coo more, listening to myself and marvelling at how I can be relatively cool one second, and melt into a squeaky puddle the next when a baby is wafted near me. Eventually I manage to peel myself away and stand up to see through to the kitchen, where Christy is clattering about.

'I can do that,' I call to her. It feels weird, being in her place, seeing all this baby-related stuff around her still-somehow-also-chic small flat. It feels weird that this is the first time we've been together alone for so long.

'S'cool. Do you want sugar in your tea?'

'Nah.'

A few moments later she returns to the living room and puts two mugs on the table, then goes back to the kitchen to grab another plate. 'Aunty P brought me a metric tonne of rice bread the other day,' Christy says, setting down some slices. 'There's more in the freezer if you want to take some?'

I break off a piece of the dense, banana-y loaf and cram it in my mouth. 'Mmm. I would, but I'm not sure how long I'll be here now.'

Christy nods, but I feel her eyeing me sideways. She has questions. 'So you've got all the stuff from the Embassy then?'

I blow on my tea a bit and then sip it. 'Well, I have one more appointment tomorrow, and then I'm basically good to go back.' I put my mug back down and pull my laptop out of my bag. 'Sami's internet is buggered, so I thought maybe I could start looking at flights—'

'So, but then... You're just going to go back to New York and get *married*?' There's less judgment in it than when she first found out, more just incredulity—and if I'm not mistaken, a bit of admiration too. It encourages me, because that's the same question running through my mind every other moment as well. It's unbelievable how fast things have started moving. Less than a week ago, I hadn't heard shit about my Visa application, and Ren was still in LA, and thoughts of him and his 'L' word had almost forced my engagement to Cole out of my mind. Now it's hard to think of anything else.

'I know it sounds mad but this is what I want, Chris. I think I'm on the verge of something. Do you know what I mean?'

She looks at me, then glances wistfully down at Joy— but her face is soon overtaken by a loving smile that I can practically see radiating towards her sleeping baby. 'I know, babe,' she says softly. 'You're lucky, you know. I can't wait to meet this Cole—I wish half *my* mates were that dedicated.' She chuckles, but then her face turns serious. 'You're sure it's not going to end up bogged down in some complicated shit, though? I mean, you don't have feelings for him or anything that could end up making things awkward?'

I open my laptop to avoid looking my sister in the eyes, debating whether to confess everything. 'I don't have feelings for him,' I tell her, with the certainty of a woman who is emphatically mired in some *other* complicated, awkward shit.

'OK.' She's still regarding me like my feelings are an epic novel written all over my face. 'I just… You also shouldn't let all of this get in the way of finding someone you *do* have feelings for, though. I mean, you're a catch, Kay.'

I smile and try to look away again, but she touches my knee. 'I mean it. Just because so far the right person hasn't come along doesn't mean—'

Hah. 'Chris, honestly. Don't worry.' *Open your mouth. Tell her. Tell someone.* But I don't want Christy sowing any more seeds of doubt in my mind about the plan with Cole than I already have. It was always going to be difficult, but we've come so far—I'm not turning back now. When I think about seeing him and all of my friends again, of getting back to our little dilapidated *To Murder and Create* offices, to my half-abandoned sketches and my ideas for bigger pieces, my Polaroid book... The rest will work itself out. I have to believe that is still true.

I can remember the feeling that morning six days ago when Sami excitedly bounded into my room—thankfully or disappointingly devoid of me and Ren engaging in phone sex, given I haven't even had a chance to speak to him properly since—and dropped a big fat envelope on my bedspread. She'd raised her eyebrows as I tore it open, and then I nodded, both of us suddenly grinning. That reaction was genuine, and ringing Cole to tell him had felt like a huge reward. At last the finishing line was in sight.

'*Finally!*' he'd shouted down the line. I could hear live music pounding in the background. 'Kay, this is fucking awesome. It's a *go*. I told you. Didn't I tell you? This is going to be *wild!*' His laughter and sincere happiness was infectious. 'You need to get your ass back to New York, pronto. We got work to do. We got *nuptials* to figure out!'

I laughed too, but then an image of Ren's face popped into my mind, along with the realisation that I'd finally have to tell him the truth. I ended the call with a confusing blitz of excitement and devastation whirling within me.

But I just need to book these flights and face the reality

of what I've been planning to do all this time, despite the gorgeous Ren Morgan-shaped spanner that got thrown in the works...

Joy snuffles and then starts to cry. I know how she feels. Christy picks the baby up and cradles her, then begins breastfeeding. I watch them for a moment: that beautiful connection between the two of them, how they don't need anyone else.

I don't want my ambitions to overtake the meaning of other parts of my life, but I want to see them through. They're the part of me that I believe in.

*

'One more,' I murmur from behind my camera as the low glowing light in the sky illuminates Sami irresistibly. She lies back on the red and white striped sun lounger, the white frames of her now-slightly-unnecessary sunglasses making the perfect image. I hit the button, and the Polaroid churns out.

I stand up from where I've been straddling her to get the best angle, and Shane fakes a disappointed groan. 'Aw, I was enjoying that.'

I bat the peak of his cap so that it lowers almost over his eyes. Sami sits up and leans over to give him an appeasing peck on the lips. They've been together for as long as I can remember, but lately I've wondered if having her boyfriend as her booking agent has ever complicated things. Probably because mixing business and relationships has been at the forefront of my mind. But whatever else, Cole's my best mate and I'm really looking forward to seeing him. It feels almost surreal that I'll be on a plane in the morning, that in twenty-four hours I'll be back in New York and a few weeks away from finally sealing this deal and getting hitched...

I try to think calm thoughts as I return to my own lounger, marvelling again at the late summer London heat and grateful that my friends are bougie enough to have membership at a private club with an actual rooftop pool, for the week or two of the year that it's actually useable. Media wankers are everywhere we look, but they're probably thinking the same about us to be fair. Being a poseur is all part of the programme at places like this. I drain the last of my cocktail, glad I've restrained myself to just two over the course of the afternoon. Being on a plane with a hangover is definitely not my idea of fun.

It was weird, saying bye to my parents and Christy and Joy last night—the fact that my family's grown in number in what feels like the blink of an eye, and that me and my sister are somewhere better than we were. It's not perfection, but it's better. I was even getting sort of sad that none of my family would be at the wedding—though it's true that if they were, it really would feel too much like something it was never supposed to be.

I glance at the time on my phone screen, or more like I check my phone for anything from Ren, and notice the time. 'I should probably be heading back to the flat soon, you know. I still haven't packed and the cab's coming at nine a.m.'

Sami sits up, taking off her sunglasses at last to study the poolside menu. 'Babe, let me get you a goodbye dinner before you jet off, though, yeah? What do you fancy?' She Frisbees the menu over to my lounger as I shrug into an oversized pink hoodie, pulling it down a bit to cover my bare thighs and rearranging my locs. I notice a vaguely recognisable actor eyeing me from the other side of the pool and glance over at Sami because it's way more likely she'd be drawing his gaze—but no, he's smirking in my direction. Maybe it's true that you're more attractive when you're not available? Not that I've ever been strong on signals. It is definitely a fact that I've never been *less* on the market, which is a turn up for the books. I can barely deal with the men I've already got. Still, I know I must be ready to go back to work when my next thought is whether I could get away with asking him for a photo and the answers to my questionnaire. I smile to myself, then let it fall quickly, in case the guy thinks his staring tactic is working. I turn my attention to the menu, not feeling all that hungry. 'Thanks, hon,' I tell Sami. 'Maybe just the seared tuna salad?'

'Bor-ing!' she intones, but she signals the waiter over and orders us all some food, then goes back to canoodling with Shane. I cross my legs up on the lounger and pick up the next of the newspaper supplements I've been working my way through—but then I notice my phone screen illuminate next to my knee as it starts to ring. My mouth goes dry at the caller ID. We've emailed a bit, a couple of messages, but Ren's been so busy with starting the shoot and I've been making excuses to avoid telling him what's happening with me, of course, so we haven't been in touch properly for a week or so.

Still, the rush of being able to even just hear Ren's voice outweighs everything else.

'Hello?' I quickly unfurl myself, slip my feet into my pool sliders and head over to a quieter part of the rooftop, staring down at the city below.

'Kayla.' I hear the smile as he says my name, the relief. I try to slow my breathing.

'Hi.' I'm smiling too.

'How's it going?'

I laugh, I don't even know why. 'Good, good. Um, what time is it there?'

'Coming up for six thirty a.m. I'm in the future.' He laughs, but my face starts to fall. God I wish he *was* in my future. It's almost time for that dream to die. I just have to work out how I'm going to let it while I still feel like *this* just at the idea of him ringing me, let alone kissing me, let alone... Loving me.

'Yeah,' I say softly.

'We're setting up, but I had a second spare, so... I've been trying to find time to get to talk to you.' He exhales. 'I wish you could see it here, Kayla. It's incredible.'

I lean on the railing and gaze down at the traffic below. 'If only.'

'Well, hey, maybe… I mean, I could grab you a ticket? I know it's a long way to come, but…'

The way he tries to make it sound casual when I can tell he's been thinking about it every day, just like I have, makes me flush warm with feeling. 'I would have loved that, Ren, but actually—' I take a deep breath, '—I'm off back to New York tomorrow.'

'Tomorrow? Wow.'

'Yeah… I haven't really had a chance to—'

I stop, willingly, as I hear his name being called in the background and he moves the phone away from his mouth to shout out a reply.

'Sorry. Uh, so you're done in London for now?'

For now, for who knows how long? 'Yeah. Got to get back to work.'

'Sure.' He goes quiet. Something seems off and not just with me, but the pull I feel towards Ren is unrelenting.

'You all right?' I ask. I hear the sounds of the hustle and bustle around him growing more faint, and his sigh is louder in my earpiece.

'Kayla… I… This is fucking weird, and I guess I don't know how to explain it, but I've wanted to tell you about it since I found out.'

I swallow, unsure what this could be about. 'Tell me what?' Is the severing of what we have between us going to be done *for* me, before I even have a chance to explain my situation to Ren? Is the thing I thought I controlled actually completely out of my hands?

It wouldn't surprise me.

'My, uh, my ex called me when I was on my way out here,' Ren begins.

I frown reflexively. 'Evelyn?' My jaw clenches.

'Yeah. She... Turns out she'd been pregnant pretty much since we ended things.' I press my lips together hard, suddenly unable to see the cars on the street below as Ren continues, 'And now she's had the baby.'

'Um... OK?'

I can feel where this is heading, and a sense of inevitability swamps me. Heaviness thuds into the pit of my stomach as he finally says it. 'Eve thinks the baby might be mine. I... I might have a daughter.' I hear him swallow. 'God, that feels weird to actually say out loud,' he adds in a murmur.

I know I should say something but I'm not sure what to say, and the silence stretches on.

'Kayla?'

'Oh,' I manage. 'So... Wow.'

He laughs softly. 'Exactly.' But I can hear it in there, lurking—the excitement in his voice. He might *want* this. And why shouldn't he?

Why do I feel so bereft? Because them having a baby together is the *ultimate* connection. If there's even a grain of love left between them, it can only grow by sharing a gift like that, surely. And because it makes me feel more strongly what I've already been scared to confront: that I couldn't be the one for him.

Which is obviously ridiculous, given I'm about to fly

back to New York and marry another man.

'We haven't… I mean obviously this is all really fucking complex, and we'll need to do a paternity test and whatever,' Ren says. 'And it's tough, you know, with her and Yann—'

'Are you glad?' It bursts out. 'I mean, are you happy? This is… Bloody hell.' I stop for a moment, doing everything I can to sound unaffected. 'It's kind of a head fuck, isn't it?'

'Yeah.' He lets out a breathy, incredulous laugh. 'Yeah. I haven't even started letting myself *think* about whether I'm happy, Kayla. Lord knows I didn't plan for this. A goddamn *kid*? I didn't exactly have the greatest examples of how to be an outstanding parent. I don't know what the fuck to think.'

I grip the railing, trying to steady myself. 'You'd be a great dad, Ren,' I affirm, unable to help myself. It's true. I blink rapidly to hold back tears, feeling like we're finally drawing a line under something. I want to get off the phone. 'H-how involved would she want you to be, do you know?' *Why am I even asking?*

Ren sighs. 'I don't know. If this little girl is mine, I don't want to just be *some guy* to her, you know?'

'Yeah. So you and Evelyn… You'll have to put all the stuff from the past aside—'

'Kayla,' Ren interjects softly. 'I don't have answers yet. The only thing I do know is that you're the only person I wanted to talk to about this. You're the only person I really want to talk to about anything. You're the only one I think about before I fall asleep, before I—'

'Don't right now, Ren,' I whisper, closing my eyes. He

stops, and I hear him swallow. He waits, because he knows me, I can feel that he does, and he knows to be patient. A tear falls away onto the ground by my feet as I open my eyes again. It's all piling onto me suddenly, overwhelming me: that I really might lose him. 'Listen, you have a lot on your plate there, and I'm heading back to New York… It might be a good idea for us to just take a bit of time and—'

'I don't want to do that.' He says it simply, frankly, and my heart pounds.

'This is a big deal, Ren. The future could be something different to the way you're imagining it.' *God, you coward. Spit it out.* I can't. 'Right now you think one way, but things could change. Things between you and Evelyn… Th-things between us…' I trail off, and he doesn't say anything this time; he doesn't jump in again with more romantic declarations. I can't tell if it's because I asked him not to or because he can hear the truth in my words.

'Yes, I don't know for sure what's going to happen, Kayla,' he says eventually. 'I just want to take each thing as it comes, OK? Please, I don't want you to worry. I didn't want this to…' He sucks in a breath. 'Just let me know when you're back in New York, OK?'

The wind picks up suddenly, and I pull up my hood, goosebumps prickling my bare legs. 'OK.'

'Promise?'

'I promise, Ren.' I hear them calling him again.

'Dammit. I'm sorry, I gotta go. Speak soon, OK, Kayla?'

I nod, but a moment later, the line goes dead.

Seventeen

Ren.

'Playback…'

I lean toward the monitor, stuffing the earbuds back into my ears, feeling everyone's eyes on me. I nod once. But—

'Let's go one more,' I say, looking up to seek out my DP. 'Greta, can we sharpen it just a little more?' She nods wordlessly and heads back to the cameras. I wait for the reset, then call for us to go again. We're close—it's the last set-up of a long-ass day, and I can feel the crew and cast are long past *starting to dip*. I watch closely, and that one feels right.

'OK. Hold there. Perfect. Thanks guys. That's it for today.' I grin at the smattering of applause that breaks out on the set, and a couple of the guys clap me on the back. If only this was a wrap on production, but we're just heading into a six-day break that the producers managed to build in seeing as we're going longer than we first planned—and also so the studio can take a look at what we've got so far. Given the happy noises the couple of suits who flew out here were making a couple weeks ago it should be OK, but it's not exactly helping the flow of the process. Still, I definitely need this break. I need to get home, even for a little while, and figure out the mess that is my life.

I keep expecting a veil of calm to suddenly descend on me, to prepare me for the idea that thousands of miles away there is a child that might be biologically half me. I asked if they couldn't just test Yann, see if the baby is his and if it isn't then... process of elimination. But apparently for the legal shit and the birth certificate they need all the parties involved. Eve wants it all to be official so that things don't get complicated down the line. You gotta laugh at that. I don't even really know where this is leaving her and Yannick, but I can't deny that a petty, fucked up part of me can't help seeing it as karma—that their perfect little picture is not quite so perfect now. That I might be part of the reason why gives me some kind of pathetic vindication that I'm not proud of, but there it is.

I stay back to watch more rushes and debrief with my key crew over a couple of beers, then we all jump in the Jeeps back down to civilization at the apartments the studio's booked out for us. I'm bone tired and have to be up at eight for my flight to Los Angeles, but I still find time to stare at my phone, wondering why Kayla has still hardly called, messaged, emailed. She let me know when she got back to New York, but her message wasn't exactly verbose. I guess she really does need to take a little time, but it's making me nervous. It's hard to give her space when I'm feeling like I need her the most. I don't want to feel like I'm relying on her to make me feel calm, to help me feel certain. I don't want her to be a prop. But—

Set it aside for now, Ren…

I'm not exactly excited to be heading back to California, especially. It's fucking crazy that all three of us—me, Eve and Yann, born and bread East Coast diehards—have ended up on the goddamn Left Coast for the sake of this business. I know they had settled on Santa Monica for their little love nest, probably in the hope of avoiding bumping into me too often, and other than one or two prearranged meetings with Yann when we were monosyllabically extricating ourselves from one another in terms of the company, it kind of worked. He's starting to be a big shot with his latest producing gigs now anyway, and Eve's been making a name in the set design. They've been getting on fine without me until now.

We've got ourselves a pretty significant meeting coming up in a couple days though, and I'm dreading it. They haven't scheduled the precise date for the test and seeing the lawyer and what not, and it's not like I have a lot of days to play with before I have to get back out here. If only we were doing this all back home in New York, I could at least have something positive to cling to: that I could see Kayla and iron out any doubts that either of us—mainly she—might have about how right this thing between us is.

Back at the apartment I finally crash into bed, but as I reach for my phone to set multiple alarms, I decide to try one more time to send Kayla a message to let her know I'm thinking about her. That it's my natural resting state.

REN:
> Hey beautiful. Prufrock was right on
> some things, you know. "There will be
> time, there will be time... Time for you
> and time for me." Time for us. I still
> believe that. X

*

Los Angeles

I know it's him immediately, even from way across the street. His tall, lean gait is practically as familiar as my own—and I sure as shit can tell when Yannick Roy is stressed. I take a breath and head toward the front of the building, watching Yann's shoulders hunch as he draws hard on the cigarette pinched between his thumb and forefinger. He's scrolling his phone, probably trying to distract himself with work. He seems to sense me approaching and turns around, eyeing me warily.

'Hey man,' he says, blowing out a white cloud of genuine smoke. I'm so used to seeing vape pens everywhere now that it almost seems novel.

'Back on 'em, huh?' I ask, kind of a dig but mainly empathetic. I think he gave up for a while, but I knew the guy who used to be my best friend would never fall *too* far down that green living California rabbit hole.

Yan smiles wryly. 'Can you blame me?'

I shake my head. 'Uh… So she's in there?' I haven't seen the baby yet. It feels like a lot of pressure to have that big reveal as well as the result of the swab that we all pretty much know was a formality. It's been an expedited one-day turn around, and part of me had half-hoped the result wouldn't come through until after I'd gone back to New Zealand and that I could just run away from it all again. But I've had a lot of time to think, to reassess. To maybe—just maybe—even start to forgive and move on, start to get excited about this little life we've all somehow ushered into the world instead. It would sure as shit be easier if I had heard a decent-sized peep out of Kayla. The vague responses and general limbo is killing me.

'Yeah, they're both inside,' Yann tells me. I take a step closer as he stubs the end of his cigarette into the ashtray outside the main doors to the office building. Neither of us makes a move to go in though. Yann stares at me for a moment, then blinks and looks away. He's buzzed his hair again like he had it in college, and it's taking me back just looking at him, all dense, dark intensity and needling blue eyes. Back to when he was my closest buddy, my ally, my co-conspirator. The guy I thought would be the best man at my wedding to a girl who's just, more than likely, given birth to a kid that's biologically mine but meant to be his.

'I'm sorry, man.' The words are out of my mouth before I can stop them, and I wonder just who the fuck I am. I shouldn't be the one apologizing.

'Ren, I—'

'I am.' It's true, in spite of it all. 'You thought this was going to go down one way with Evie and the baby... and...' I run out of empathy juice. 'I don't know. Life, huh? Goddamn.' *Nice. Real fucking articulate.* I leave it there for a second and watch Yannick as he rubs the back of his neck, then runs his hand over the stubble on his chin and cheeks that always seemed to appear five seconds after he shaved.

'You're right,' he says, then pauses for a few moments. 'Ren, are you... I mean, how is this going to work out? If she's yours...' Our eyes communicate that the *if* is not all that uncertain. 'I'd spent all that time thinking of her as my little girl, you know? Shit.' He turns and paces away a few steps, but I catch up to him.

'I didn't ask for this, Yann. You think I planned to have a kid with a woman who broke my heart into pieces with the aid of my best fucking friend? To get sucked back into all this shit with the two of you? Let me tell you, this was not on my wish list. Nowhere fucking near.' I take a breath, trying to calm down. 'But it is what it is. I'm not trying to get in the way of anything, but if that's my daughter, I... I just want to be in her life.' Suddenly, I think even if this little girl *isn't* mine, it feels wrong to abandon us all back to the animosity that I've been holding on to all this time. That all forgiveness takes is to open up your fist and let it go.

Yann's processing—the expression on his face now is familiar, too. He glances up at me, and the smile in his eyes tells me this might just be OK. 'Remember Glenn Benson?'

I know immediately what he means. Beginning of senior

year of high school, the douchebag who inexplicably seemed able to get young women to fall for his shtick every time ended up getting the sweetest girl in class pregnant. We all thought it would end up as some disaster that would highlight just what an asshole the guy was, but it didn't turn out that way. Dude stepped up, straightened out and was Dad of the Year while we were still popping zits and fretting over what college to go to. Yann and I bumped into him in the bodega buying diapers one time while we were arguing over who would risk trying to buy the beers that night. People are surprising—especially when it comes to being a parent, the ultimate test of selflessness. *Jeez. A parent.*

'To tell the truth,' Yann says, 'my plan was to have no plan. I've been taking this whole fatherhood gig as it comes. None of us know what the fuck we're doing, so I guess… what's one more little thing to navigate? We can work this out, right?'

'Yeah.' I give a half-smile. 'Well, you're nothing if not a pragmatist, man.' I pause, and then add in a mumble, 'I don't really know how the fuck I'm functioning without that.'

Yannick gives me the look that I get a lot from people who know me—the *shut the fuck up Ren, and take the win.* 'Uh huh. That's why Galaxy are on their second feature with you. Because you don't have your shit together.' His voice lowers. 'Because you're not one of the best out there.' I regard him for a second, and then shrug. He reaches over and punches my arm. 'Come on. Eve and Olivia are waiting on us.'

Olivia. Our daughter. The name is one I know Evelyn always loved. Even though I didn't get a say in it, the idea of us all—of the three of us, working this out—suddenly feels like it's always been on the cards.

Like I said: *Life. Goddamn.*

Eighteen

Kayla.

I look over the documents spread out on the breakfast counter again, and the printed page of info on how the day will go. *City Hall.* I've never felt closer to being an actual Yank than the idea of getting hitched at *New York City Hall.* Though I suppose soon I'll be even closer to being an American, seeing as I'll be married to one. Less than twenty-four hours from filling out the final bits of paperwork, Cole and I have an honest-to-God marriage licence. We're all ready to go. Tomorrow morning we'll head off to City Hall, quite literally take a number, and a short while later we'll be husband and wife. Wife and husband. Married. Legally wed.

I swallow. It's *finally* sinking in. This is real.

'All right. I'm out,' Cole says, hitching his backpack on as he comes out of his room. He holds a suit-carrier aloft to keep it from dragging, then flips it over one arm, grinning at me.

I look at him. 'You know this is ridiculous, right?'

'What?'

'All of it,' I say, and we both laugh nervously. 'But mainly the idea that you're going to Marcel's.'

'Yo, I'm not taking any risks with this, Kay. It's bad luck for me to see you the night before the wedding.'

I roll my eyes for the fiftieth time. 'I'm gonna go out on a limb and say tradition has taken a back seat here, CoCo.' I raise an eyebrow. 'There's sure as shit not going to be a *wedding night*-wedding night, so what does it matter what happens the night before?'

He leans down at me with his eyelids lowered. 'Sure about that, girl? You might all of a sudden find yourself overwhelmed, you never know.' He's teasing, but there's a hint of an edge to it that makes me even more nervous, if that's possible.

'I think I'll be able to control myself.'

Cole laughs, and I try to relax. 'OK, so don't forget your ID and the documents from Miguel…' He looks around, patting his pockets to check he's got his own stuff.

'Yup, it's all here.' He nods, but I reach over and take the suit from his hands, putting it down on the stool next to the breakfast counter. Cole's face turns serious as he sees my expression. 'I just have to ask one more—' I start, but he cuts me off.

'Kayla, I swear to God. Stop. I promise you, I want to do this.' He takes my shoulders, and I look up into earnest pools of familiar moss-green. 'I'm not some sucker, you know what I'm saying? I'm going into this with my peepers open.' He widens his eyes even more, and I can't help smiling. 'You're my best bud. There's nothing…' He pauses, quirking one corner of his mouth wryly. 'There's *almost* nothing I wouldn't do to help you out, all right? This is light work. It's cool. OK? Do you get it? I. Am. Down. No regrets.' He stares at me, eyebrows raised. 'Can't hear you.'

'Yes. Yes. I get it. I promise that's the last time I'll ask.' I draw in a breath, because what I really want to say is on the tip of my tongue. If he knew about Ren? If he knew all my hypotheticals had some real basis behind them, would Cole be singing a different tune? 'But—'

He makes an exasperated noise and lets go of my shoulders, still smiling, but I can tell he's starting to get pissed off. Who wouldn't? The man is doing me the biggest favour of my entire life and I'm here questioning him. 'I just want us to acknowledge that this is complicated. The next time you catch a fever for... I don't know, some undergrad who shows you the college enrolment essay she wrote on Blue Note cover art or whatever—'

'Kayla—'

'I'm just saying, don't feel like you owe me some kind of special loyalty now. You're the best friend I've ever had, CoCo.' He pulls a face at me. 'It's true, you know it. And this is the best thing anyone's ever done for me. So I'm just acknowledging that, out loud. And, like, making sure, just one last time, that we both understand the parameters of this whole arrangement.'

'Acknowledged,' he says gently. 'Understood. I can bone undergrads and you won't feel a way. I get it.' He looks at me a moment too long, and my heart sinks again. But he means it, he'll let us stay the way we are, if that's what I want. And it is. And I love him even more for that.

'Cole?' He reaches for his suit with a sigh, but I catch him and squeeze him into a hug. 'Thank you.'

'You're welcome, Kayla.'

*

'Babe, is it weird to say you look fucking great?'

I smile at my reflection then look back at my laptop screen to see Christy and Joy beaming back at me. Well, Joy might just be filling her nappy. 'I always look fucking great,' I quip.

'OK, I take it back,' my sister says, then I see her go out of range as she puts the baby down in her cot for a post-feeding nap. I smooth down the voluminous fabric of my vintage palazzo trousers. I decided I might as well treat myself to something new—any excuse to shop. And my *wedding day* seemed as good a reason as any.

'So who's going to be your witness then?' Christy asks as she pops back onto the screen. 'It's so mad that you just rock up to a building and they'll marry you off.'

'Yeah, there's hardly been any hassle at all to get to this point. Piss easy.'

She purses her lips. 'Sarcasm is not becoming of a bride, love.'

'Apparently it's pretty standard for other couples who are going after you to just stand as witnesses, so I reckon that's what we're going to do.'

Christy nods, and then shakes her head, and it's how I'm feeling too. Yes and no. 'Well… Good luck, Kay. I really hope this is the start of something amazing for you, for this… branch of your life, I suppose.' She means it. I reach for the bottle of water on the side table and glug before answering her.

'Me too, believe me.' I grab my binder stuffed with all the documents, and my little handbag, and then I turn back to my sister one last time. 'I think it will.'

But as I pull on my jacket and start my walk to the subway, as much as I've tried every conceivable way to avoid it, I finally let my thoughts drift to Ren. I've avoided any notion of calling or emailing him, even as it felt like a wrench to my heart not to respond with anything more than the briefest of replies to his messages. Thankfully he must be flat out, because it's not like he's inundated me. He's giving me the space I asked for—or he's moved on, I'm not sure which. He must be going through a lot with this baby stuff…

I can't help worrying that he's realised who's really important to him. Who knows what might have happened with all that now? Maybe he's reconciled with Evelyn, maybe this has made them reassess everything that happened between them in the past. She was practically his childhood sweetheart, for crying out loud, and frankly I don't understand how she could ever have wanted anyone else but Ren. *These are the wrong thoughts to be having on the way to my own wedding.* Thing is, the depth of his feelings over that whole affair, for good or very ill, practically radiated off him when he spoke about it. The levels of betrayal Ren felt were understandable, but maybe telling. He wasn't over it—or her. Or maybe I'm just paranoid. Or jealous. Or insecure. Or all of the above.

Does it even really matter now? It's not like I can marry Cole this morning and then gleefully carry on with the idea of me and Ren in the afternoon or any time afterwards. Nobody else in my life even knows about him, about what's happening—or happened—between us. I realise, suddenly, how mental that is. It's really all just been between us.

While the uncertainty over my decision to marry Cole is pretty much gone, the guilt of not at least letting Ren know what I'm about to do is too much for me to ignore. It's time for me to finally be honest. It's last minute, but I still have a chance, even if it's a slim one, to put it right—to tell him the truth. Even if it will kill me to do so.

I do a now-familiar calculation in my head. We're heading to City Hall as early as possible, so it's only just after eight in the morning; a clear, crisp, perfect New York city day. Almost as perfect as that one night Ren and I spent here... So I work out that it's just after midnight in New Zealand, already edging into tomorrow, but there's every possibility Ren will still be up. I'm not sure I want him to be, but I can't hedge any longer. I pause on the corner across from the subway entrance and pull out my phone. Blood pounds in my ears and I hold my breath as I scroll to his number and hit dial. I expect the weird, long international ring tone, wondering exactly how much this call might cost—and not just in money—but it goes straight to his voicemail. My body heats just at the sound of his message saying his name and number, but I freeze up as the beep sounds. Agonising moments go by before I finally speak.

'Ren… Hi. I, um, I was hoping I'd catch you. I wanted to…' *Shit shit shit.* I can't say this on a voicemail. 'I wanted to let you know that, um… That I miss you. And… I'm sorry. Look, I'll try you another time, OK?' Could that have been any more of a car crash? I hang up, but a second later my phone buzzes, and I actually jump, almost dropping it. It's just a message from Cole.

> COLE:
> OMW. You're not going to leave me at the altar, right? See you real soon. If you beat me to it—grab a number! Heh x

I wait for my heartbeat to slow as I message him back. I need to focus on one thing at a time. No matter whether Ren knows about it or not, I'm going through with this, so I better get on with it and let the rest of the chips fall where they may. Ultimately, this is what I need to do, what I *want* to do. It's so close it makes my nerve-endings sing, and that's why I still know that I'm doing the right thing, in spite of everything.

My brain is certain. My heart?

It's going to have to wait its turn.

Nineteen

Ren.

Maybe one day we'll all have to live on airplanes in order to survive once we fuck up the Earth for good. Right now, it already seems like that's my life. A five-hour flight to New York feels like a breeze by comparison with the epics I've flown back and forth to New Zealand so far, but I'll still be grateful when we land. Mainly because the degree of anticipation and trepidation I'm feeling for actually seeing Kayla is taking me to the edge of distraction. Spontaneity is not really my thing, so I'm not really sure what's gotten into me, other than obviously this driving, insatiable need to be in her orbit. I was too close not to just go for it, and the fact that the paternity stuff is all over and done with already... It's been a lot to process, and the only thing that seemed to keep me sane was just the idea of Kayla. No, not the idea. The actuality of her.

The captain announces our descent, and my heart swells as I look out the window and see my city looking like a model of itself below us. It feels so much more like home just knowing she's down there somewhere. Well, I hope she's at her place or there's going to be a pretty long wait on her stoop or whatever. I guess worst case I'll just call her, even if that'll kind of ruin the corny surprise.

I should be through with surprises after the baby revelation and all the stuff with Eve and Yann. That whole situation with little Olivia and the two of them feels a little more solid now though, I guess. One look at the kid pretty much affirmed what we eventually found out to be a hundred per cent true. She's my daughter. And she's beautiful and perfectly small, and for sure I was surprised at how immediately I felt an overwhelming need to protect her from the world, to keep her as innocent as that moment when I had her cradled in my arms and saw her looking up at me with my own eyes.

They're drawing up some formal custody agreements and shit to cement Yann's stepdad status, but she'll live with Eve full-time, so with him, too, obviously. That's still a little tough to deal with, but I'll see her whenever I can. I'm already feeling bad about not being there all the time for this tiny person I didn't know I'd created. I'm also trying to get used to the fact that Eve and Yann say they're getting married at Christmas. They want me to come apparently, but there's only so far my acceptance will stretch and watching Evelyn walking down the aisle and into his arms is definitely somewhere past my line.

But even remembering what led us to all of this, and expecting to find that well of anger inside me that was just below the surface before, I find it's sunk somewhere deeper now. It's still there, don't get me wrong, but it's way further out of reach. I don't know if that's maturity or confirmation of the fact that my heart is with someone else for real. Given that I still definitely think it's acceptable to have cereal for dinner, I'm pretty certain it's the latter.

I open up the email that Nick sent me, thankful again for his efficiency, tenacity, and the fact that "discreet" is basically his middle name. I was ready to create some feeble excuse for why I was asking him to find out the home address of a chick who interviewed me almost three months ago, but I decided honesty was quicker. The guy is nothing if not a romantic— but who am I kidding? So am I. Less than an hour after my request, he had what I needed.

It's only now, as I sweep through the airport toward the line for the cabs, blissfully luggage-free apart from my holdall, that I'm starting to think of the many ways that this could go horribly wrong. I mean, we've hardly spoken since I told Kayla about the baby. I guess I've been telling myself it's not a bad sign, just her needing a little space and the usual near-miss time zone issue, coupled with the fact that we both have demanding work shit to deal with. She's running a damn business, and in a way so am I—there's barely time to squeeze anything else into a twelve-hour day of shooting, plus debrief and maybe if I'm lucky a second to eat before I crash out. In spite of how stressful coming back to the States has been these past few days, it's actually been a pretty welcome break—and this should be the cherry on the cake.

Kayla.

My excitement to get going means it's only when I

actually hop into a cab and give the guy the address that it occurs to me to check anything else on my phone, and it gives me an extra spike of adrenalized excitement mixed with fear to hear her voice in my messages. I hit play again as the cab edges through NoLita toward the Williamsburg Bridge in the dying sunlight. *She misses me…* I'm practically crawling out of my skin to get to her. 'Please be home,' I mutter to myself. I wonder again whether I should call, but I want to see the look on her face, to see if she feels the way I do. Because if she does…? My whole body hums with thoughts: dirty ones, corny as hell ones, embarrassingly mushy ones.

I expect to feel a little more panic when the cab finally pulls up across the street from her place, but it's all I can do not to just throw my cash at the guy and run to her door. I hoist my bag onto my shoulder and jog across the street, taking a breath as I start up the steps behind a couple so profoundly dishevelled and stylish that I know I'm in the right place. Kayla would fit right into this neighbourhood— and she'd also stand out.

But I pause as I see them press the buzzer for the apartment I'm pretty sure is hers. I hang back, not wanting to seem weird, but I see the woman shake back her short dark hair and take a swig from a bottle of beer, and as I watch the couples' bodies sway a little I can see they're clearly not all that aware of their surroundings anyway. They must have, at the very least, pre-gamed a few more of those beers before they got here.

The woman presses the buzzer again several times

impatiently, and then take a couple of steps down to stare up at the building. It's warm, and a lot of the windows are open in the apartments. A couple of floors up, I notice music is pulsing out of one of them.

'Fucking...' the woman begins. 'Hey!' she calls up ineffectually, still not seeming to notice I'm there. The guy hits the buzzer again as the woman starts to rummage unsteadily in her bag and pulls out a cell phone. 'I'm gonna call them,' she tells her companion, but he points to the door as it buzzes open.

'Magic,' he says to her with a grin, and then nods down at me. 'Hey man, you here for the wedding party?'

I frown, confusion starting to build. 'Uh... wedding?' But he ignores me. I must have this wrong, it can't be that they were buzzing her apartment after all. Still, he holds the door open for me, and I figure I should just take the opportunity to find the right place. The couple ignores me, giggling and whispering to themselves as they walk a little ahead of me up the stairs to the second floor. I check my phone again—42 Bethel Street. Apartment 7.

We're definitely headed to the same place.

Warm light and pulsing music spills out of the open door of the apartment. The guy and girl push inside, and are greeted by a handful of cheers as I stand back, scared to go any further. If nothing else, this is a bad time. There's obviously some kind of celebration going on—maybe Kayla's friends are using her apartment after their wedding? It seems weird, but the full awkwardness of the idea of walking into that situation makes me freeze up. This is why I don't do surprises.

'Shit,' I whisper to myself. But then I hear her voice cut through all the noise. I don't know if it's her accent or if I'm just somehow more attuned to her, but hearing her call out '*You made it*,' to the newcomers, my legs move of their own accord. I take a step further to stand in the doorway, and as Kayla pulls away from hugging her friends, she looks up, and we lock eyes. Everything seems to fall away, and my heart shocks into a pounding rhythm. She looks incredible. Her locs are half pulled back from her face, and some kind of huge flowing pants frame her lower half, with a simple white wife-beater tucked into them that shows off the beautiful glow of her skin. The very sight of her makes everything OK for a second.

She frowns and mouths my name, still staring at me. Nobody else seems to have noticed. I kind of sense a crowd inside the apartment—people sitting on the floor and sofas, swigging from tiny champagne bottles; the window open to the fire escape, weed and cigarette smoke drifting gently in; people crowded around the breakfast bar laughing and fixing cocktails. As she stands staring at me, the woman who walked in before me grabs Kayla's hand and pulls it right up to her face.

'Holy shit,' she exclaims. 'You guys *really did it*!' Kayla's still watching me, her arm dropping back down by her side as the woman lets go. 'Where's Cole? I gotta kick his ass for this!' She and her boyfriend stagger away. Kayla's still frozen to the spot.

'What…?' I hear issue from my lips. I'm still standing in the doorway, and a smaller guy with glasses has to practically push me to get past as he heads out.

'Sorry man,' he says. He sounds a thousand miles away.

'What…?' I say it again, but I can't finish a thought. I'm trying to get her to hear me. Kayla takes a step toward the door, but someone intercepts her.

'I need a picture of you guys!' says a tall woman with braids down to her waist wearing a man's suit. 'Cole! Get in this shot with your *wife*!'

'Wife?' I whisper. I can feel Kayla still staring at me, like we're locked inside some kind of nightmare where we can't get to one another. Where people are saying things that cannot be true. Her eyes drift away from me for a second as a guy slips his hand around her waist. Cole. I recognize him. He's in a button-down and blue flat-front dress pants. A white rose is tucked behind his ear.

'Kiss! Kiss!' A couple of people take up the chant as Kayla and Cole pose. My bag slips from my fingers to the floor. I'm still rooted to the spot. Everything seems to be happening in slow motion, but I can only have been here for a couple minutes. The voices sound like they're reaching me through molasses. *Kiss… Kiss…*

Kayla's eyes finally flick back to mine, then away again as Cole's mouth finds hers. It's just a peck, and as they break apart he's grinning and laughing, stepping away from her, his arm slipping away from her body easily, in a way I could never understand because up until a moment ago all I could think about was holding Kayla and never letting go. But now…

'Heeyyyy!' goes an enthusiastic chorus as a new song starts, and dancing begins to break out.

I have no idea what in the hell is happening. This can't be what it looks like. It can't—

'Ren.' Suddenly, she's in front of me. 'Wh-what are you doing here?' I stare down at her, still unable to comprehend. I look over her shoulder at the party going on behind her.

'I wanted to surprise you,' I mumble automatically, still gazing past her to the glinting gold band I can see on Cole's finger as he dances in the centre of the room. The guy I thought was just her friend. The guy who they're saying is her— 'Guess the surprise is kind of on me.' I turn, almost stumbling over the bag by my feet. I pick it up, and Kayla grabs my arm.

'Ren, I can explain…'

I shake my arm free and start down the stairs. I only realize how hard I was finding it to breathe once I pull the door below open and get out onto the street. I take a deep, shaking breath. Her voice follows me, and I turn slowly, looking up at her standing at the top of her stoop as the door slams behind her. Strains of music still float above us, but it's just her and me now.

'Ren! Wait!' She doesn't need to say it—I'm not moving. She runs down the steps to the sidewalk to stand in front of me again. Nothing makes sense. All I want to do is sweep her up in my arms like I'd been imagining for days, weeks. To spin her around and kiss her with everything I have.

'You don't have shoes on,' I find myself saying. She ignores me.

'I… I wanted to tell you.' There's panic in her eyes, tears glistening in them. God, she's so beautiful. 'I, um…'

'Kayla, are you *married* to him?' Even as I say the words, I know she is.

I see her searching for the words, but eventually she just settles on one that emerges on a tiny breath and slices me in half.

'Yes.'

Twenty

Kayla.

In my wildest dreams—nightmares—I never imagined quite how awful this moment could be. *He's here. He came to see me. He wanted to surprise me...* I reach for him, but he flinches away. My voice is breathless, faint. 'Ren, I wanted to tell you.'

'But you didn't.'

'I didn't know how to.'

His jaw clenches. 'I'm guessing it wasn't a spur of the moment decision, though, right?' I stare dumbly, tears beginning to spill down my face. He looks away, shaking his head. 'I can't believe this. I swore I'd never let anyone else do this to me.'

'Ren, please... I'm so sorry.' I only have one chance at this. I draw in a long, trembling breath, but before I can start, he speaks again.

'Do you love him?'

I can see how much my answer hangs in the balance for him, and for the first time I can really see his wounds. I truly comprehend just how badly he's had his heart broken before, and how reckless I've been. All I'd taken the time to worry about was that there would be a reason *he* wouldn't want *me*.

'No. No. I don't. Not like— Please, Ren. This was just a means to an end. Everything's here. My whole life. Everything I want to achieve. Cole is my friend, and he offered me a way to hold on to it all, to stay here in the States. When I met you I never expected… I never expected to…' I can't say it.

'To *what*, Kayla?'

He almost shouts it, and the strength of his hurt makes me take a step back, but I force myself forwards again. I'm scared to tell him that I've fallen in love with him, because there's no going back from what I've done. So I stay silent, tears tumbling. Telling him wouldn't be fair. The finality of that knowledge sends a sob up into my chest.

'Why couldn't you just fucking be honest with me?' I can hardly stand to look at him, the deep grooves between his brows, the uncomprehending betrayal etched on his handsome face. He drives two hands through his hair, his bag abandoned on the pavement between us like a referee. 'God, if this is just a fucking Green Card thing then why the hell couldn't you just tell me about it? Unless it's *not* just "a means to an end", a goddamn business arrangement?'

I open and close my mouth like the floundering fish that I am. 'Ren, if… if I told you… I was scared of making that choice. If I told you, I'm not sure I could have gone through with it. And I need this. It's so important to me—'

'More important than us?'

'You don't understand, Ren.' I search his eyes through the blur of my tears. 'I-I had an opportunity to keep climbing, not to have to start again from the bottom of this unbelievably steep bloody mountain, and I took it.'

'And you couldn't do that with me?'

I wrap my arms around myself, suddenly cold despite the warm summer air. The hard concrete pushes against the soles of my feet. 'Ren, I'd known you one night. This was a real chance—'

'*This* was real, Kayla,' he says sharply, gesturing in the air between us. The word "was" hits me in the gut and I want to crumple to the floor.

'I didn't know it would be,' I whisper.

'Fuck this,' he says, taking one stride to bend down for his bag, leaning forwards like he doesn't want to get too close to me. 'Kayla, one night, fifteen thousand nights, *I* knew. But apparently I'm a fool.' He pierces me with his eyes. 'I can't do this again. I cannot do anything in this fucking ball park.' He shakes his head. 'How could you—?'

'Because… I'm not used to this, Ren!' I shout. I barely register how insane this must seem to anyone who might be taking any notice from upstairs; me having a screaming match with someone they think is a stranger. How confused Cole must be—if he's even noticed I'm gone? But I don't care. 'Christ! I've never been in love, OK? The only thing I'm sure of is *me*. What I know I can do as… as an artist. You have no fucking idea how hard I've worked to even believe in that. So don't tell me I've done something wrong. I didn't know, OK? I've never felt like this before!' I can sense just how crazy I must look and sound, but we're locked in some kind of reckoning that feels freeing and terrible all at once. 'And then you tell me you've got a kid with a woman who was the fucking love of your life. *She's* the one who betrayed you, Ren, not me. How was I supposed to know I wasn't just going to turn out to be some kind of fall-back, some distraction for you until you decided she's the one you really wanted all along?' Saying it out loud makes it all the worse.

Ren pulls a hand down his face, breathing hard, and looks at me for what I can feel is the last time. Really *looks at me*, the pain on his face surely echoing my own. I want to see past this, like he told me I could with my sister, but I don't see anything but darkness, and no him.

He takes another step, until I can almost feel the heat of his body in front of me. 'Kayla.' He says my name with a soft finality. 'If you really believe that, then this was a mistake. At least we know, now, right?' We stare at one another, and he shakes his head again. I try to drink him in, whatever I can, before the inevitable comes.

He turns away and I stand shivering on the pavement on my wedding night. I close my eyes as Ren reaches the corner, and when I dare to open them again, he's gone.

How it Feels in the Moment

10th July 2019 –

Twenty-One

Ren.

He had to go in summer, of course. Somehow it feels like one last little test.

I can feel damp blooms of sweat soaking into my suit jacket as I stand at the exit to the church, feeling the clammy hands of strangers pressing into my own. I try to maintain a neutrally bereaved expression as his former and current students file past me saying '*Your dad was…*', the reverent and devastated tone of their voice making me feel like he was their father and not my own. Probably in some ways that's true.

'*Meu filho…*' Luiza's slim, fragrant hands are already cupping my cheeks before I have time to prepare. They are, of course, smooth and dry. 'What is this on your face, by the way, huh? I thought you shave it? And this hair…? Life of an artist, huh?' She tuts and then smiles, the edges of her immaculately painted mouth wrinkling minimally as she pats the wisps of my beard before taking a step back, her eyes wide with love and concern that I'm not totally sure I buy. It could be real, but it's three years since I last saw her—it's hard to calibrate. 'Oh, your father,' she sighs, like she's remembered all over again why we're here. She grips my hand tightly now. 'You are all right, Joãozinho? You're OK? We're heading back to the apartment now. That will be better.' She exhales again shakily. 'It's finished, he's resting.' She hasn't been to the apartment in God knows how long, and technically it's mine now, but she still manages to make it sound like she never left. 'You want me to wait with you?'

'No. Thanks, Luiza. I'll see you back there.'

She stiffens briefly at my continued refusal to call her mãe or mom, or any other term of affection, then heads off. I'm feeling selfish. And fuck, I'm not sure how much longer I can pretend I don't want to scream about it all. About this day. About how much I didn't expect it to hurt. I'm still not sure I wasn't a disappointment to my father. I look down at his stern face in the photograph on the order of service still clutched in my other hand.

Dr Maurice Earl Morgan. 1946-2019.

The End. My fingers twist and curl the program in my hands, but they relax a little as I hear a high voice behind me, and a small hand tug the pant leg of my suit. I look down, a smile already breaking through my clouds.

'Ren!'

I crouch down to her level. 'Hey there, Livvy.'

A tiny-toothed grin spreads across her face. 'I did a picture.'

She thrusts a crayoned abstract into my hands.

'For me?'

'Yah!'

Something catches in my throat out of nowhere, and I cough. 'Thank you,' I whisper, then stand again as I see Evelyn catch up to Olivia, tucking smooth lengths of hair behind her ears with a weary sigh.

'Hey,' she says to me, her eyes conveying everything else they need to. She reaches over and pulls me into one of the only hugs so far today that hasn't felt forced. 'Sorry,' she says softly into my shoulder. She pulls back. 'I was going to leave her with my sister and pick her up after, but it didn't make sense to go up there then back downtown—'

'No, no, of course. I'm glad you're both here. Was she OK with it all?' I ask, my voice lowered, but I can see Liv's small face peering up at us. She works her hand into mine, and I squeeze it, so close to letting everything go that I have to swallow hard, twice.

'*She's* fine, Ren,' Eve says, her eyes blazing with sympathy. She takes a breath. 'I don't know how much she understands what it means, you know?'

I nod. 'Right.'

'Listen, Yann was going to change his flight and come, but their shooting schedule was, like, carved in rock, so he really sends his…' She tails off, shaking her head with a sigh, and I wonder if it was apologies or love or just regards he was going to send.

'I know. He called me. I understand, of course. Thanks, Evie.' I wince at the way that version of her name still trips off my tongue.

'He really wishes he could have been here.'

I glance at her and I think she means it. I try to push back memories of when she and Yann would have been the exact people to hold me up. But then I feel Olivia's little hand fluttering in mine, and I wonder how it is that a tiny almost-three-year-old girl is feeling like my rock in this moment.

'Yeah.' In spite of everything, I suddenly feel lucky. Even if we haven't explained to Olivia exactly who I am to her—we decided it would be too confusing for now—I'm so glad to have her in my life. A faint emptiness chases up the happy thought; the might-have-beens still hurt, just a little. 'I'll finish up here,' I say to Evelyn. 'You gonna come to the apartment for a little while?'

'Of course.' She places a hand on Liv's head. 'She has Theo and Willow from Tots and Toddlers coming for a play-date later though, so we'll have to get back.'

Olivia's eyes light up at the mention of this, and then she begins to chatter happily if a little nonsensically to her mother about ice cream. Eve leans over and pecks my cheek lightly.

'I'll see you back there.' I look down. 'OK, Livvy? You can make me another picture.' I smooth her dark hair as she nods enthusiastically.

I wave off a couple of my college buddies who offer to hang back with me as well. I want to be by myself for a little while. The church is finally empty, and I thank the pastor again for his help, then sit down heavily on one of the hard wooden pews for a moment, taking several deep breaths. I don't know why I feel like I shouldn't cry. Maybe because I don't think my father would have liked it.

As I wander back out into the sun, I decide to walk the few blocks back to his apartment, feeling the heat rise off the sidewalk. I watch a bunch of teenagers on the corner chug beer they probably had to beg to be bought just like we used to, the bottles sweating out their cold contents as the kids flirt with each other in barely-there clothes. I'm jealous, wishing I had no fucks to give, too. That was me, right in this neighbourhood not all that long ago. Actually, who am I kidding? A *lifetime* has passed since that was me. Who have I become since then? People know my name now. Well, some: the people who acknowledge credits beyond whose name is above the movie's title. But suddenly it makes sense to me, what Kayla said that night, feeling like a stranger in your own body...

Shit. Sometimes it still amazes me, how much I remember the details. How much I remember her, and that whole experience—how close it feels. How much regret I still have, just remembering. Days like today, especially.

I find myself outside the apartment building, with people still filing in: Tanya, Dad's long-time assistant, shepherding people, and my Aunt Nina handing out drinks up in the apartment, shakily pointing out the hors d'oeuvres. I see my mother half-heartedly engaging with Olivia on the couch. I only recently told her, and her reaction was about what I thought it would be—mild surprise and a faintly puzzled attempt to sound happy. I almost felt like she didn't deserve to know she has a grandchild after she checked out of my adolescence. But I know that's bullshit. The main reason was because it took me so long to *face* telling her, to deal with explaining it all over again. I guess I'm still a little caught up in the complications, no matter how much I love the tiny human result.

It hurts that my dad won't get to see Liv grow up, though.

I look around at his books still lining the shelves on every wall, the groups of people squeezing in between his dark, worn leather furniture. Jesus, it still doesn't seem real, the lawyer telling me my father had left his place to me. I don't know who else would have stood to inherit it, obviously, but somehow it took me by surprise. Even though I've been leasing a place in the city for the last couple months, the fact of him leaving me this apartment—the place we lived together until he told me it was time for me to stand on my own, the place where it seemed like he damn near ignored me as I was growing up, but now I realise he was kind of invisibly nurturing me, too? It makes me feel like I'm home again. Finally.

A tear slips out, but I wipe it away.

*

'Hey. It's me. You at your place?'

Her voice on the phone is breathy, sexy and soft, as always. Yesterday she'd offered to come over and help me feel better, and much as that sounded really good, something forced me to have dinner with Luiza before her flight back to Rio. I know my mother would have loved me to bring a date—especially Brigit—but I'm not sure it's like that. If anything, in the back of my mind I wonder if it's Bridge who wouldn't want me dragging her currency down. I can't see her looking to hit the red carpet with me on her arm, even if she was into me directing her on that god-awful perfume ad. They paid a grip to have a Best Supporting Actress nominee do three days' work pouting and spouting nonsense. The idea that they wanted a "name" director to shoot it and thought *I* fit that bill was pretty goddamn hilarious. Brigit's definitely happy to have me direct her away from the lens too, when the mood is right...

'No,' I tell her. 'I'm still down in the East Village. I'm... I wanted to get the jump on clearing some stuff out of the apartment. Nick's sending a decorator to start getting some ideas together while I'm in LA, so I thought—'

'Sure, sure, I understand. Well, you know what, I'm actually right in the area, why don't I pick you up?' she says. 'Or... I don't know, I guess I could help?' Her voice is different now, and it warms something inside me a little, unexpectedly. Besides, it's kind of amusing to think of Brigit Curtis weeding through my father's old sweaters and dusty books on philosophy with me.

'Uh, OK...' I hear myself saying, before I can talk myself of it.

'Great. Message me the address. I'll get dropped off and I'll have Philippe pick us up later, then we can head to your place, or mine. Or, I guess that sort of *is* your place now, too, if—'

'Yeah.' I cut her off. I can't imagine doing anything like that with her here, not yet anyway. It's still too much like my father would be watching, like I'd be a kid again. Guess I should start getting used to it though, if I'm going to move in here in a few weeks. 'Call when you're here, I'll come down and get you—the buzzer isn't working.'

'OK. See you soon, *JR*,' she purrs teasingly. She knows that little nickname irritates me, but it does sort of make me smile too, for no real reason. This thing with Brigit has taken me by surprise, but I guess it's funny what a little on-set power does to the way people see you. I'm still getting used to it—or maybe I should just trust in things a little more. That's always a tough one, of course...

The payday from shooting the commercial really helped while we were finalizing the financing on *The Memory of Moments*, though. Man, I'm still nervous about finally doing something of my own, even with it all wrapped and in the can now. I can't wait to get into that editing suite and start working on it once the last of this promo on *Revolution World* is over. Flying back to Los Angeles for a three-day whirlwind at the tail end of the press tour seems kind of pointless after them letting me have a week and a half off to deal with everything here, but again, apparently people are a little interested in me now.

Still, it's a relief to be based back in New York again, finally. Los Angeles felt like an obligation, but now that I am a little more established, it feels good to just be able to say 'fuck it'. It's only a plane ride away when I do have to wade back into that sea of plastic, and since Livvy's here now with Eve and Yann moving back too, it all just made sense to come back. I'm glad she's getting to grow up in our city.

I just hope people won't be disappointed with my next project. *Moments* is back to my "indie roots" I guess, but now that I've got these big-budget studio flicks under my belt people might have forgotten that. Compared to *Revolution World*, the shoot on *Moments* was such a blur, writing, directing, producing, thinking on my feet every day just to make sure we didn't go over budget. I don't even want to think about what they're spending just on the *promo* for RW. If I thought what they did on *Detonate* was over the top…? At least promoting that one had its benefits.

For a little while, at least.

Anyway, I can't wait to get into the guts of building the new picture up in the edit, seeing if I really have something—

The sound of my cell phone ringing again makes me jump, pulling me back from my usual path towards self-doubt. Guess she really was close.

'Be down in a sec,' I tell Brigit, then straighten myself up a little before I head downstairs, and see the dark sedan lingering on the kerbside. Out of habit when I'm around her I check up and down the street for photographers—but it's dark and it's the Village, and to be honest if those assholes really want a shot, you probably wouldn't even know it's happening. I nod toward the tinted back passenger window and push my hands into my jeans pockets as her door opens.

Brigit strides over to me fast, smiling a million dollars, her long legs clad in leather, a loose tan-colored jacket thing swirling around her, tossing back her choppy blond hair. Casual chic that probably cost more than my entire wardrobe put together, but she looks fucking great, of course. The car lingers a moment before pulling away.

'Hey.'

'Hey, yourself,' she says with a wink.

I step aside and point her up the stoop and into the building. We're quiet as we head up to the apartment, but as soon as the door is closed she turns toward me, placing one long, manicured hand against my chest.

'Hi, handsome.' She presses her lips to mine, only lingering slightly. 'Nice place your father had here. Thanks for letting me come.'

I return her kiss, holding her waist a moment, breathing her in. Then I let her go and wander away, picking up another empty box and taking it over to the shelves now half-devoid of his books. It still feels wrong to be moving them—it's taken me days to get up the nerve. I glance back over to see Brigit slipping off her jacket and resting it over the brown leather Eames chair that I can still picture my dad sitting in, frowning at an article in the New Yorker or underlining passages in some huge hardcover I didn't understand as a fourteen year old, and probably still wouldn't now.

She draws in a breath. 'Boxing up books?' she asks, stating the obvious. I smile at her and nod without saying anything. She walks over to me again, pressing her body in closer to mine. 'How are you doing, JR? All up in your head tonight, huh?' she murmurs, then kisses me softly again, running her hands up to smooth her fingers over my hair, smiling against my lips. 'I told you yesterday, I can help you feel better without talking...' One hand drifts down to my zipper, but I gently pull it away.

'I'm just... You know when you've been by yourself all day?' I say. She stares into my eyes, hers like warm pools. I draw in another breath of her and shrug apologetically. 'Just need to readjust to speaking to people, I guess.'

She frowns a little, though she's still smiling. 'You're an odd bird, Ren.' She presses her lips to my cheek, then walks over to the bookshelves and begins to scan them. She pulls down an anthology on the Situationist International and starts flicking through the pages, seeming interested. 'In the box?' she asks, turning to me and holding the book up.

'Yeah,' I say, and she places it in carefully. 'Listen, I can do this another time. Maybe we should—'

She shakes her head, and I stop. 'It's fine,' she says. 'I'm here now. And... it's actually kind of nice.' She looks around the warmly lit space. 'I don't really see what you'd need to change in here, honestly.'

She's right. Maurice Morgan had pretty impeccable taste. But I at least need to adjust it so it's not quite so... I don't know. Nostalgic isn't quite the word. 'I grew up here,' I volunteer. 'So it just feels a little weird to leave it as is. I need to...' I sigh. 'I don't know, maybe I should just sell it.'

'Too many memories?' she enquires, and I shrug again,

pulling the elastic band loosening out of my hair and re-catching half of it back from my face again.

'Something like that.'

Brigit folds her arms. 'Listen, bucko,' she says, waggling her eyebrows at me. 'I get that this is hard. But if not-talking's off the cards, while we're here at least, then maybe you could give me a little more than grunts?'

I manage a smile at that, and go over to her and slip my arms around her slim waist. She puts her arms around me too and looks up at me, resting her chin on my chest. It really feels like we could be something, and it's been a long time since I felt that way.

'You're right,' I tell Brigit. 'I'm sorry. Yeah, I guess there are a few too many memories here. It was... Dad moved in here before it was totally decided—the custody—and it never quite felt like this was a place he expected me to be, even when my mom moved back to Brazil.' Her eyes turn even more sympathetic. 'But he had me stay with him, full time,' I add quickly. 'No arguments. It was just... He wasn't the most demonstrative guy. There was a lot of being left to my own devices.' My jaw tightens. I think I'm still too emotional. I probably shouldn't have suggested Bridge come here tonight. I should have just gone to her place later.

'My parents handed me over to a nanny before I could walk,' Brigit says, relaxing her grip a little and shaking her head. '"They fuck you up", right?' She lets her hands drop to her sides and looks back at the shelf full of books.

'It's character-building,' I say, smiling at her, and she

laughs. 'At least feeling like my father was never totally satisfied with me means I'm always trying that extra bit harder at whatever I do.'

Brigit nods, pulling out another hardcover, one missing a slip-jacket, that's tucked next to a selection of different editions of my father's published academic work. As she picks it up, a few loose pieces of paper fall out. Magazine cuttings...

'Hey, look!' she says. She crouches down to gather them as I stare at the paper that's drifted to my feet. 'Maybe your father was a little prouder of you than you're giving him credit for, huh?'

They're all articles about me, reviews of my work, carefully cut out of magazines and newspapers, printed off from the internet. I bend down and pick up the stapled-together pages nearest to me, swallowing hard. Of course it would be that article. I stare at the pictures, remembering suddenly. *Her telling me I was sexy... her getting so adorably pissed about the way they write these things. The pull I felt toward her getting stronger with every word she said...*

'Maybe he was,' I murmur in reply to Brigit, but I'm years back from now, memory making my heart race. *Shake it off, Ren.*

'It's really beautiful,' I hear Brigit saying. 'Him keeping all of these.'

She's right. I actually can't believe he did. Sadness begins to shroud me again, for the loss of him, for neither of us having the courage to really express our love, father to son and back again, while we still could. And I look over at Brigit, and she takes my hand and squeezes it, bringing me back.

'Let's get out of here,' I tell her. 'Let's go to your place.'

Twenty-Two

Kayla.

From the reflection in the tiny window, I see Cole come in—he's smiling, I can tell even in the candlelight. I reach up high to put some final flecks of white into the irises, the peak of her hairline, and then clamber down off the ladder and raise an eyebrow at him.

'Always did like watching you stretch, Kay,' he says, his voice laced with humour.

I tiptoe over in my bare feet and peck his cheek. 'Oh, I bet you did.'

'And *I* bet you're going to ruin your eyes in this hidey-hole. What's up with the overheads?'

'Wrong kind of light for my mood,' I say, swiping the excess wax chalk on my hands down my dungarees.

'You shouldn't work so late,' he tells me.

'Full of advice tonight, yeah? You know I don't have that long now.'

We both stand in front of the picture, staring around the montage of images and portraiture I've built up for this piece.

'Do you think—?' I begin, but Cole cuts me off.

'C'mon. She's going to love it, Kayla. Damn. Put your *foot* in this one.'

I hope she will. More than any, I need to get this portrait right. Penny Diaz has been more than just a broker to me. She's become like my New York art mother. She let me really believe I could make something of my art, after I'd started feeling like it was never going to pan out, when I'd resigned myself to pretty much just focussing on the website. She's stuck with that belief for years and kicked me up the arse to just do it, and it's finally starting to pay off. I want to do her justice, and to make her proud.

The piece is good. Objectively, I can see that. I think? Hopefully I didn't make it too big, but for some reason I'm just really drawn to larger scales now. I can already picture Penny's sly, appraising smile when I show this to her, even though the thought makes my palms sweat a bit. And when I think about the *rest* of the show? Jesus. It's been a long time since I've been this nervous about my work. But a solo at the bloody Font Gallery, on this scale? I'm shitting myself. I put my hands on my hips, still seeing things I'd like to adjust. My expression obviously says as much, because Cole playfully stands in front of me blocking my view and pulls my hands away from their critical stance.

'Tweaks live on eternally, Kay, you know that. Come on, Shaline and them are waiting at Tivoli's already, and I want to get there before they go too crazy with the M&C tab. We got to lead by example, right?'

'Mm, you mean you want to order that overpriced

tequila and get pissed off when people slam and don't sip.' He chuckles, and I sigh and turn away from the picture, unhooking one strap of my overalls. I feel Cole's gaze drift towards me, watching—I only have a plain black sports bra on underneath, but I get too hot when I work. He's seen it all before, anyway. 'Eyes to the right, mate,' I say, but his laugh is more self-conscious now. It's *still* a bit awkward sometimes, I'll admit, but we definitely know where we stand now. It was weird there for a while, when I didn't know where to turn after what happened with… I harboured a cruel notion of sweeping it all away by considering really being with Cole. We were married, after all; we had to live together anyway, and I suppose part of me wanted to tie things up in a neat little bow, wanted all the stuff with Ren to have been worth the pain if it clarified my life somehow, led me to the place I'd been all along or something.

But it was ridiculous. Obviously I was kidding myself, and it wasn't fair at all to even think about playing with Cole's feelings like that. We're somewhere outside of romance, but maybe we're more than mere friendship could describe. He and I are some kind of *other* that has no definition, but it works. And very soon Cole and I will be able to make it official—the divorce. We'd skirted around discussing it while all the wedding stuff was being organised, as if it was getting ahead of ourselves, but it's felt like a countdown ever since. It'll be weird being free of our arrangement, especially after all the sacrifice it took to get to this point, to be indefinitely allowed to remain in this bonkers-fest of a country.

One sacrifice in particular still lingers with me, even all this time later…

Whatever, it's been two and a half years. It took a lot of fucking effort, more than I ever could have imagined I'd need, but I've moved on. Soon I'll just be a flirty new divorcee, looking for… fun? I don't know. Now that we're so close to being done with the husband and wife thing, Cole and I have been more open about looking for new relationships. I wasn't ready or even interested before, but now I'm trying to get my eye back in. Of course, having made that decision nothing much has come along in the last couple of months, even with my friend Shaline's best efforts and trials on various apps that made me retreat in haste. In spite of myself I still felt a kernel of jealousy when Cole hooked up with his newish girlfriend Chou. She's a trainee optometrist but looks like a supermodel with her impossibly long hair, six-foot frame and Japanese intellectual hipster air. Apparently she was giving Cole an eye test and told him his eyes were beautiful. I had to bite my tongue from telling her that I said something similar when I met him, and he replied "yeah, if you enjoy the fruit of the sexual violation of your ancestors". But I'm guessing that's not the route he went with her. Now he's pretty near obsessed with the woman. You wouldn't necessarily know it from the expression that's still on his face as I get changed, though—but like I said, sometimes old habits die hard.

'You got my message about bringing the books from the office, yeah?' I ask him, and he reaches around behind him to tap his backpack.

'Yup, got 'em.'

'Nice one, thanks Co. I said I'd give Dave and Keema copies, and I won't see them again before they go.'

Even seven months after publication, it's *still* a bit weird seeing the Polaroids all in print with my artwork and the answers to my questionnaire. Some of them, anyway… But holding the small, chunky book in my hands, seeing my name on the cover—it feels pretty incredible, despite all my stuff on M&C, obviously, and (almost) even in comparison to showing my work in galleries. The book is something that people can buy and keep and walk around with. I'm finding it kind of mental that Kamal's already thinking about a second print run.

I slip a loose, loud printed cotton dress over my head, shimmy my dungarees down the rest of the way and off my legs, then push my feet into my high tops.

'Right, ready,' I tell Cole, who is now wandering in vague circles around my studio, tapping away at the screen of his phone with focussed intent. It's really handy having this space only a couple of blocks from M&C's new offices, and I'm still finding it hard to wrap my head around the fact that we're doing well enough I can afford to lease this place *and* the rent on my new place in Brooklyn.

We're keeping things under the radar in case there are any last-minute interviews before my official permanent status is confirmed, so quite a lot of my stuff is still at Cole's place, but it's a nice feeling to have these spaces of my own. 'Come on—let's head,' I say emphatically, sighing as Cole trails behind me, and I wait impatiently for him to step through the door so I can lock up. I can see on his phone screen that he's back on work emails, and I nudge him with my shoulder as we walk in the direction of the bar where the others are waiting. He looks over at me absently.

'Ease up, yeah? It's Friday night.'

'Uh huh…' He reluctantly retires his phone, but I can tell his mind's still churning. 'Yo, before I forget though, Kay— you're going to go show Paul and Rene the new features list on Wednesday, right? You're cool with going through it all with them?'

I roll my eyes. '*Yes*. I've already set up the meeting, don't worry about it. Shit's not going to fall apart without you, all right?' I soften my tone, remembering how hard I find it to relinquish control myself. He deserves time off. I just hope he'll unclench enough to enjoy it. 'Focus on how amazing it's going to be swishing down Mount Hood—'

'Swishing?'

'Whatever. Swooshing?'

Cole laughs and shakes his head in exasperation. 'This is why I could never get you to come snowboarding with me and Benny.'

'No, you know it's because I hate being crap at stuff, and I didn't want to have to deal with you and Ben lording it over me while you *swooped* past me on the slopes. God knows the two of you together are competitive enough.'

Cole's smile now is inward and affectionate at the

mention of his brother. They hardly get to see each other with Ben living over in Hong Kong, so I know it means a lot to him that they finally got this trip planned. I know how he feels—I'm practically bursting at the seams that Christy's going to be coming over to visit in a couple of weeks so she can see my show, and to meet with a few ateliers over here in New York. I know she's just flirting with them. There's no way she'd be leaving London, not after how well her debut showcase went down at LFW back in February. It's unbelievable how quickly she's got back on track after the baby. And it feels really surreal to think that we could even have had a period of time where anything got in the way of us. I know it will be hard for her to leave little Joy behind for a week, and I am gutted I won't get to see my niece, but I can't wait to get some sister time in. I'm *really* gutted that my mum and dad can't come either, but Mum managed to break her leg a few weeks ago, and she and Dad will be looking after Joy anyway. We've promised to take copious videos and pictures.

'Timberline's going to be dope,' Cole's saying. 'It's just I'm kind of bummed to be leaving Chou, you know? I'm… I'm really digging her.'

I chuckle. 'Yeah, but it's not that long you'll be away, though?'

'Right,' Cole says, but he comes to a halt and turns to me with a slightly worried look on his face. 'Listen, Kayla… uh… Me and Chou have been talking about moving in together. We'll wait til after the final confirmation for your paperwork and everything, obviously, but her lease is up pretty soon. I know it's fast, but we feel like it's right. I just thought you should know.'

I take a breath, expecting to feel envy, or regret, something like that. I can tell that's what Cole is prepared for, but as I think about it, I realise that all I feel is happy for him. Glad that someone is making *him* that happy, after everything he's done for me.

'I appreciate you telling me, Co, but honestly that's great. Seriously, it is.' I fix him with a look. 'I mean, if she fucks with you, that's another story.'

He laughs. 'No doubt,' he says, then rubs my shoulder. 'Thanks.'

I reach up and squeeze his hand. 'Course. Now, can we get to Tivoli's or what? I'm going to drop dead if I don't get a G&T in the next five minutes.'

Cole grabs the straps of his bag and begins a comical run up the street, dodging people and shouting that a Tanqueray and tonic will be on the bar before I get there. I smile as I watch him go, and it's only then that a feeling really does hit me. He's moving on—but maybe I still haven't.

And maybe he's not the one I haven't moved on from.

*

Shaline lays her forearm on the table, ignoring the puddles of beer, and I lean in closer to look at it in the gloom.

'Oh, riiiight,' I shout over the pounding bass line, nodding and grabbing her arm to examine the new ink more closely. A vivid Mexican flag is now flying proudly on her wrist, nestling in amongst all the other tattoos—some of which I even had the privilege of drawing. 'Wicked!' I smile at her, taking another sip of my drink.

'*Innit*,' Shay replies, trying for her best South London accent. It is, as ever, piss poor. 'Oh hey,' she continues, abandoning it swiftly. 'Remember my cousin Jorge, who moved to LA…?'

I nod, even though my recollection is vague.

'Guess what? He got cast in some HBO movie and I just read on Deadline that they're trying to get that fucking hot director guy you interviewed a couple years ago…' She snaps her fingers in the air, squeezing her eyes shut, trying to recollect. 'Jow…'

'João Ren Morgan,' I murmur.

'Yeah. They're trying to get him to direct it. Man, that guy's too sexy to be behind a camera. Anyway, I kind of thought the whole acting thing was a pipe dream for my cousin, but kid is really doing well, it's dope…'

I lose focus on what she's saying for a second, and take a breath. 'Mm, yeah. Good for him,' I muster, knocking back the last of my third gin and tonic quickly. 'Same again?' I ask, pointing at her rum. I can feel the night teetering on the brink of getting messy, but I'm just drunk enough not to mind.

'Oh no wait, Kay, don't go too far. I've got a gift for you.' I'm curious, but then she winks at me, shaking a hand through her short bowl cut with a satisfied sigh. Shit.

Another set-up.

'Shay…'

'No seriously, this is a good one. I promise you.' She bats her eyelids at me earnestly. 'Would I steer you wrong?'

'When have you ever steered me right?'

Shaline purses her lips. She's not having it. The woman is a match-making machine. I don't really understand why she gets such pleasure from it, when everyone *she* dates she finds a flaw with in about five minutes. 'Come on, girl. He just messaged, he's going to be here any minute.' She's already glancing towards the door, past Cole and Chou huddled together in a corner. She holds a loose fist in front of my face, clearly planning to count off attributes on her fingers. 'OK, so, he's arty—I met him back when he was a goddamn *jazz drummer*, though he had the good fucking sense to give that up.' She raises her thumb. 'But either way good rhythm, right?' she adds, smirking, and her index finger flies up. 'Also—employed, full time. He's the manager at Jean Jacques, which has got, I don't know, a whole bunch of Michelin stars or whatever. So he's got the sick meal hook-ups.' Middle finger joins the other two. 'Dude could play for the Giants, he's so stacked. Aaaand? I have it on good authority that he's not afraid to go…' Her ring finger raises and makes a swooping arc downwards, but I grab her hand before she can get any further. 'What?' she protests, raising her eyebrows. 'Important criteria, you know this.'

'All right, all right,' I say. She's not going to relent. 'All I know is, this authority better not be yours. I'm not taking your sloppy seconds.'

She shakes her head, snickering. 'But sloppy ain't the way to do it, know what I'm saying?' She raises her five splayed fingers triumphantly for the final bullet point. 'Anyways, last but not least, he's really smart, because— Oh shit, you know what? There he is.' I'm left in semi-suspense as Shay waves her outstretched hand in the air, looking up over my shoulder, and I hold my breath, waiting for the ensuing embarrassment.

'Shaline,' I hear a deep, amused voice say behind me. 'Got that "I've been talking about you" look on your face.'

'That's because I've been talking about you, Marcus,' she says, smiling at me. 'This is Kayla.' She gestures at me, and I resist the urge to turn my head, waiting for him to walk around. When he does, I know I'm sitting down, but I have to crane my neck to get to the top of him, he's so tall. And, as Shaline said, "stacked". He pulls his hands out of his pockets and folds his arms, making his biceps bulge in the sleeves of his black polo as he shakes his head in mock-chastisement, then smiles down at me. He's clean shaven with low-cut afro, edges sharp, and strong eyebrows dominating his handsome face. Preppy, but definitely sexy, to be fair.

'She's been saying bad things, I hope,' Marcus says, extending a large hand towards me. 'That way at least there's a chance I might end up being a pleasant surprise?'

I laugh and shake his hand, pleased that his grip is strong—I hate weak handshakes. It makes sense, I suppose, if he used to be a drummer, but he doesn't exactly fit my image of a jazz musician. I sweep my locs over one shoulder, suddenly feeling a little hot. He already is a pleasant surprise.

'Oh, what, you mean this is a set-up?' I reply, flirtatious almost involuntarily. Damn gin. He's still holding my hand, but he lets go slowly and laughs a low, rumbling laugh.

'No, no, I'm just… conducting a survey,' he says.

'Yeah? On what? I love a questionnaire.'

'On… Shit—I've got nothing. On how to speak to beautiful women? I guess I need to up my witty repartee game.'

I chuckle, and he leans down to give Shaline a kiss on the cheek.

'Nice,' she says, gesturing between Marcus and me. 'You two are cute already.'

'Uh huh,' I say sarcastically, widening my eyes at Shay in the hopes that she'll dial it down, but Marcus seems unfazed.

'Can I get you both a drink?' he asks.

'Um, yeah could I—'

Shaline cuts me off. 'Didn't you just say you were headed to the bar, Kay? Maybe you could help him with our beverages?'

I give her another look, but Marcus helps move my chair back as I stand up next to him, still barely making it past his shoulder. She mouths "you're welcome" as he leads the way to the crowd at the bar, and I give her the finger subtly, even though I have to admit the prospects are promising. Marcus guides me in front of him a bit so that I'm not crushed by the hordes anxious to get more alcohol into their bodies as soon as possible. The wait is five people deep to get served, and I remember again why I rarely bother with Tivoli's on a Friday night.

'So you're Shaline's boss?' he asks, leaning down a little so I can hear him.

I smile. 'Is that what she told you?' He shrugs. 'Well, yeah I suppose it's true. She's the music editor at the website I co-founded—*To Murder and Create?*'

'Yeah, I know it. And you're an artist,' he states, his deep brown eyes lingering on mine. It's sort of unnerving.

'Yeah, I suppose I am.'

Marcus's lips tilt. 'Well, I'm happy to say I can confirm it. I saw the portrait book. It's really great. Shay said you have a new show soon?'

'Yeah, next month.' I shuffle forward as the crowd at the bar shifts. 'Was that part of her pitch?'

He laughs that rumble again, and it buzzes through me, the way he's standing so close because of the crowd. 'I didn't need selling on the idea, Kayla. I actually met you a few years back, for all of about ten minutes, at Five and Dime. I think it was, uh, someone's birthday?'

Cole's. I vaguely remember now. The champagne might have had something to do with my limited memory. 'Shit. Yeah, I think I sort of recall—'

'Don't worry about it. I'm just saying I remembered you, that's all.' Again, I expect to get some sense of awkwardness coming from him, but Marcus just looks down at me with an amused expression. 'Timing's everything, huh?' he adds, his voice lower this time, raising an eyebrow.

'Well, Shay said you used to be a drummer, so I'll take your word on that,' I say, meeting his lingering stare with my own. It's cheesy as fuck, but whatever. He opens his mouth to reply, but then his gaze flicks over my head to the bar—he's obviously caught the eye of the woman behind it, perhaps unsurprisingly, given he towers over most of the people here. Not to mention the way *her* eyes seem to be stripping him out of that T-shirt.

'What'll you have?' Marcus asks.

I tell him what Shay and I were drinking, and he orders a Jameson on the rocks for himself, handing me my G&T. I turn around to fight my way back out of the crowd, feeling Marcus's heft behind me, clearing a path despite me being in front. I don't know if it's the drinks, but I'm suddenly feeling very aware of all my senses. Bloody Shaline. I suppose even a broken clock's right twice a day, as my grandma would say. We make it back to the table, where Shay is busy chatting up a beautiful Chrissy Tiegen look-alike, and barely acknowledges our return though she takes her drink pretty sharpish. Maybe there's something in the air tonight. Something lucky.

'So, Marcus…' I take a sip of my drink, my head starting to swim. My filters starting to falter. 'What is it about you that's going to make me regret wanting to take you home tonight?' I blink up at him, but the man is unshakeable. He takes a slug of his whiskey, the ice in the glass clinking together, then waits for a moment, as if he's considering his answer.

'I can't read the future,' he says, moving closer. 'But if you want to take me home tonight, I don't think you'd have any regrets.' A fingertip reaches out and traces my jaw. He leans back a little again, and I exhale. I think he's right on that. My skin still tingles where he touched me. 'I'm a straight arrow, Kayla. I'm not into games—or regrets, to be honest. What can I say? I'd like to get to know you better. That's it.'

That *is* it. The thing that's always missing. Having to *get* to know—not just knowing instinctively—

No. I've decided I'm ready to give this a chance.

Marcus is still watching me closely, and I turn on a smile. 'Hmm. No games, no regrets? I'll hold you to that,' I tell him.

And I hope he's right.

Twenty-Three

Ren.

'Sweetie, please don't touch that, it's still wet, OK? I said *don't*, Olivia!' Her voice drops below her breath. 'I swear to God...'

I know I still have a ways to go with this parent gig, because all I can do is smile. Even with Evelyn at the end of her rope and Livvy obliviously stumbling around causing havoc to my new interiors, the smile won't leave my face. See, I know it was probably just from hearing other little kids say it, and maybe she says it to Yann too, I don't know, but even that idea doesn't bother me. Her mother didn't notice, she was on the phone.

Daddy.

It slipped out of Olivia's mouth a few minutes ago, but it felt better than I ever could have imagined to hear her say that word to me.

Evelyn gathers Livvy up and turns to me with a sigh. 'We'd better get going. This one's due at her grandmother's by four. It was great though, Ren. You've got to give me that salmon recipe.' I nod and hold out my arms to take Olivia while Eve finishes picking up their stuff, chuckling to herself.

'Listen to me. Salmon recipe? Jesus. I think we're finally grown ups.'

'Speak for yourself.'

'Hah. But you know, the place is looking great. It's... It's really cool us all being back in the city together,' Evelyn says, pausing and looking over at me with a smile that turns complicated as she looks at Livvy clinging around my neck for a piggy-back. 'Ren... I know I've already said it, but it means a lot. You being closer, moving back here so that—'

'I wanted to,' I tell her, cutting her off. The coward in me still not really able to talk about it.

'Yes. But I'm still grateful,' she says. 'It's all just so... I just wish—' Her gaze drops to the ground as she searches for her words. Instead, she sighs. 'You know. That things could have been easier.'

'Yeah.' Regret and pain and remnants of love drift back and forth between us, until her phone beeps with another message. I exhale in relief as she checks it. 'So,' I nod to her cell. 'Yann's shoot going OK?'

Eve looks a little awkward. 'Yeah, it's just... Hard with him away.' She smiles again, and I recognize that feeling—missing someone. It's still tough, knowing the space next to her that used to be filled by me is now his, but it doesn't feel wrong any more. And I want happiness for myself, too. Times like now, with Olivia's little arms practically choking me out, I have a true glimpse of that happiness. I want to cling to it as hard as she does to me.

'Uh, by the way, Mister Page Six...' Evelyn says, changing

the subject as she walks around me to grab the little monkey off my back. 'Let's get your shoes on, honey,' she interjects quickly, then turns back to me. 'I nearly spat out my coffee yesterday when I was messing around online. Brigit Curtis? Damn. Even I'm jealous.' Maybe she wants to alleviate some guilt, but it's OK. 'How long have you been…?' She wags her eyebrows at me, and we both glance down at Olivia, tongue clamped between her teeth as she attempts to pull on her tiny sneakers determinedly.

'Oh, what, it's got to be purely physical?' I retort as I bend down to help the kid.

'*I'll* put them on!' Livvy protests, and I chuckle.

'Isn't it?' Eve asks, her tone almost upsetting in its level of surprise. But I guess I'm surprised too, because these last couple weeks it really has started to feel like the thing with Brigit could be more.

'I'm not sure,' I reply slowly.

Eve slips her purse onto her shoulder. 'Well, be careful. I don't want to see you get hurt,' she says. *Ironic.* Still, I want to gripe, but I know she's right. It would more than likely be me, not Brigit, who'd end up the wounded party in this scenario, regardless of how things go down. Am I that fucking sensitive? The fact *that* seems obvious hurts a little, too.

I scoop Olivia back up into a hug, which she returns with a giddy little yelp, then I set her down. Evelyn takes Liv's hand as I lean over to peck her on the cheek. 'Say hi to Yann,' I say quietly but earnestly, and she nods.

My mind drifts back to Brigit, and I wonder what might be there with her. It feels weird to entertain the idea of having an emotional connection with someone again. But there it is. For now, I push it all to the back of my mind, crammed back there along with all the other shit, and instead focus on seeing Eve and Livvy out.

*

'Are you *kidding* me? Uh, no. The guy was constantly "napping" like he was a goddamn five-year-old at kindergarten. I swear to God, I have no idea what the hell was happening in that trailer, but I wasn't about to find out...'

Brigit's tongue trails against my ear as I struggle to concentrate on the conversation her friends are having around us. 'I'm going to miss you,' she whispers, and I turn to look into those sea-green eyes. 'Three weeks seems like kind of a long time.'

'Yeah,' I begin, knowing exactly what she means, but then I hear my name being called.

'Hell-o? You worked with him, right Ren?'

I glance at Brigit for help, and she leans away, looking back at her friend Heather with a hint of irritation before rolling her eyes and saying to me. 'Bolt.'

'Oh... Yeah, on *Detonate*.' I shrug. 'You're right. Big on, uh, nap time. But hey, it's tiring work being that mediocre.'

Heather hoots loudly, and I can't help glancing around the bar to see how the regular folks are dealing with the cacophony coming from our booth. All three of the friends Brigit decided to invite tonight are aspiring actresses who didn't seem to get the memo about bringing a date. I think at least one of them even auditioned for *Revolution World*, and to be honest I'm kind of surprised that these are Brigit's people. Alone, she seems so much more engaged with reality, and even now she doesn't seem to be paying them all that much attention. It could be because of the way my hand keeps getting drawn to her inner thigh, though.

I take advantage of the others going for a simultaneous bathroom break to return my full attention to that spot she likes just behind her knee. 'Three weeks *is* long,' I murmur, kissing her neck, then suddenly wondering if we're making too much of a display. Every asshole in here has a camera on their phone, and probably a hotline to TMZ or whatever. Or maybe I'm just paranoid, or letting my ego get to me. Most of the people in here are too cool to care what we're up to, or feign it well enough at least. 'Reshoots are a bitch,' I add, leaning back to take a sip of my beer.

Bridge runs her hands through her hair. 'Heather's a bitch, too. Sorry, I don't know why I invited them. We should be making the most of this week. We're still good for dinner tomorrow, though, right?'

I swallow another mouthful of beer. 'For sure. But Tommy's out of town day after, so we might need a late one with the edit…'

She sighs but nods her head, and selfish gratitude swarms my chest. 'I get it. I'll check in after the *W* mag shoot and see how it's going. You guys are super close to first cut though, right?'

'Yeah, I think so. That's the thing, if we can just get that done, then we'll *be* somewhere, you know?'

She smiles knowingly at me and winds a long strand of my hair around her finger. 'OK,' she says. 'How's it going? Are you happy with it so far?'

I rub the back of my neck and shrug. 'Yeah, I think so. It's looking... I think this one feels good. I don't know, maybe I'm too close to it right now.'

Brigit takes a breath, raising her eyebrows and looking down at the table like she's trying to seem nonchalant. My jaw tightens a little, knowing what she wants to ask, and that something is holding me back from wanting to say yes.

'Well maybe I could stop by the edit suite in the next day or two, come and take a—' She's interrupted by the return of her friends, giggling and sniffing, and her face turns annoyed again as they settle back into the booth, but I'm relieved. I'm a little too particular about who offers their opinion on the *Moments* first cut maybe, but it is what it is. 'You guys, you know what?' Brigit says. 'I think we're going to take off.' It's news to me, but I'm definitely more than happy to go. 'You don't mind, do you? I know we didn't get long to catch up, but—'

'Do your thing, B,' says her other friend—Kelli, I think it was—checking her lipstick in the camera on her phone. Guess she didn't have time to do it back in the bathroom in between coke rails. 'I don't blame you.' She winks at me, and I'm half-complimented, half-unnerved. Brigit's already sliding out of the leather-clad booth, grabbing her purse. And I thought *I* was anxious to get out of here.

'I'll call you, OK,' she says to her friends quickly, glancing around nervously now. I think I missed something. I tell them goodbye and follow Brigit, who's already headed to the back exit where a huge man-mountain allows her through, looking me over suspiciously before realizing I'm with her. She's tapping rapidly into her phone, not looking back at me.

'Bridge. Slow down. What's up?'

'Goddamn Heather. Guess her new leaf got flipped back over,' she mutters, holding her phone to her ear, and then glancing up at me. 'Our old dealer just showed up eyeballing me, and I couldn't handle having to talk to him.' Her expression softens. 'To be honest, I just want to hang with you and… relax. That's not my scene right now.'

I kind of hope "right now" means "any more". I haven't clocked her getting into any blow—or anything else—since we've been together, but it's not much of a surprise if she's been into it in the past. I'm not usually judgmental about these things, but I don't want anything to complicate what might be starting between us.

We head out into the side alley next to the bar. 'Philippe? Yes, we're just waiting outside. Oh, you know what, it's not so easy to pull in here, we'll come up to the corner. Thanks, sweetie.' She hangs up and reaches over to slide her arm around my waist. 'He'll be here in a minute.'

I've got to say, now that the Galaxy Studios gravy train is paused on the tracks, I miss being able to get Nick to call me a car service on their dime. It did come in handy from time to time. One time in particular. I shake away the memory of the storm, the airport... Luckily, Bridge has Philippe on speed dial. I wonder if he gets time to do anything else? I'm not complaining though—getting a cab is a pain in the ass on a Saturday night.

I'm surprised when Brigit doesn't hesitate to head up to the corner where there are bound to be at least a couple of photographers loitering, to wait for the car. The cynic in me thinks the opening weekend on *Revolution World* probably hasn't hurt in terms of her being happy to be seen with me. But the romantic in me wants to believe it's because this is going somewhere good. Anyway, I rest my arm around Brigit's shoulders, which are now also balancing her jacket—I never understood what she has against putting her arms through the sleeves—and while she slips on her dark glasses and begins to tap into her phone again, I glance up the street to see the gleeful expression on the photogs' faces as they realize their long, tedious wait to take a mundane picture of people going about their business is over.

'Ms. Curtis, over here! Who's the guy?'

'João, this way, this way.'

'Brigit!'

I can't help but laugh to myself that I'm actually pleased one of them knew my name, even if he did butcher the pronunciation. Shutters click rapidly and I reach up and shield my eyes as I see Brigit's car making its way slowly to the kerbside. The door guys at the front of the bar begin to clear the handful of paparazzi off to the side. Meanwhile, I try, but I can't stop it—the flashes of their cameras in front of my eyes only make me think of one thing, again. One person.

Flash. Flash. Flash…

And then, suddenly.

She's here.

In front of me. Out of nowhere. How—?

My heart lurches, and then begins to beat at a pace I didn't think humanly possible. She's come to a sudden halt on the sidewalk, squinting up at me, a confused frown on that beautiful face.

'*Kayla?*'

'It's… It's you,' she seems to whisper. I can hear it though; it's like every other sound has fallen away. Jesus, the number of times I thought I saw her, that around every corner in this city I knew there could be the possibility… But I wasn't prepared. She's so much more her, so much more here, than I could *ever* have been prepared for. I'm only slightly aware of Brigit pulling away from the arm I still have draped over her shoulders, and reaching over for the handle of the car door.

'Sorry sweetie, we're just heading out. I can't sign anything right now,' Brigit's saying. Kayla's expression turns stony. Fuck. She thinks this is an autograph hunter? It would almost be funny, if I could even understand the concept of funny right now. 'Ren?' Bridge says, her voice edged with impatience as she opens the door and climbs into the back of the car.

'One… one second,' I manage, still staring at Kayla. Her dreadlocks are even longer now, swept over one shoulder, which is smooth and bare like the day we met. Thin straps are holding up a royal blue silk dress that skims the perfect curves of her body. She still has all the rings and necklaces, and… I can hardly process how incredible she looks. I swallow, trying to find some words. And then I notice her hand is in someone else's.

'Um… How are you?' she asks, her voice still barely audible, but that husk, that swirl of smoke remains in it. She looks over at the car. 'Sorry, you're trying to get into your—'

'I'm good.' Jesus. 'How are you?' I glance over at the guy she's with, who's looking between us with a bemused look on his face. 'Hi,' I say to him, my jaw tight. In my head it sounds like "Who the fuck are you?" and from his expression now, he's thinking the same thing.

'Yeah. I'm fine. I'll… I'll let you get on, anyway. Nice to see you,' Kayla says, shaking her head slightly, like she's contradicting herself. 'Are you visiting, or…?'

'No. No, I'm back in New York.'

'Oh.' She takes a breath. 'Right. Cool. Well, um, good to see you.'

'Yeah. Yeah. Maybe—?'

'Ren?' I hear Brigit's voice again.

'I better go.' I try not to let them, but my eyes lock on to Kayla's, and goddamnmit I wish they hadn't. Everything is there, swimming in them. Bewilderment, hurt, embarrassment. And memories. And—

'Ren?'

Then I'm in the car, and it's driving away, and Brigit's questioning gaze is on me, but I feel like I'm still standing on the sidewalk.

Like I'd never left her.

Twenty-Four

Kayla.

I'm focussed with every fibre of my being on chewing, on swallowing, on listening to what Marcus is saying, on making a point of laughing dismissively about what just happened outside the bar. Because if I lapse in concentration for one second I'm going to have a heart attack or something.

I can't believe it.

Just like that. *Ren.* Poof, out of nowhere, like a magic trick. I'm still not completely certain I didn't just imagine it. I smile stiffly at Marcus as he asks me how the scallops are. At any other point I would have been able to honestly tell him how delicious they are, but all my senses feel dulled at the moment.

'Mm. Tasty,' I say, feeling the rigor in my face. Bloody hell. This isn't such a massive deal, is it? It was bound to happen some time. Apparently, anyway, since he's back in New York. *He's back in fucking New York.*

If I'd had the self-control to just look him up once in a while without it sending me into a spiral, then maybe I could have avoided this shock. I can't stop thinking about how good he looked. His hair longer like that, with some of it pulled back from his face? God. His *face*. His skin. His voice, his eyes… I cannot believe he was with *Brigit fucking Curtis*. But I mean, why should I be surprised? It's not like she's out of his league, especially not now he's in the bloody Premiership. Did I make a fool of myself back there?

'Kayla?'

'Hmm?' *Shit*.

Marcus chuckles at me, shaking his head. I look over and see the waiter standing beside our table.

'Are you done, ma'am?'

I realise my fork has been hovering over my empty plate, and I put it down with a clatter. 'Oh, yes. Sorry!'

'Thanks, David,' Marcus says to the waiter, who clears our table swiftly. Then he leans over and gestures for my hand. I place it in his tentatively, feeling awful for being so distracted. Every single thing is flooding my head with memories. *Ren's hand on mine, at the table in the diner…*

'So. From the look on your face, I'm guessing it wasn't a tidy breakup,' Marcus says, his eyebrows cresting in an amused expression that's shadowed with worry. 'Was it, uh, recent, or…?'

I swallow, feeling my palm begin to tingle with sweat. I still have no idea how to explain what happened with Ren and me. I don't think there really *is* an explanation, at least not one that won't sound childish and ridiculous to anyone who didn't experience it first hand. Or perhaps it's childish and ridiculous whichever way you slice it, no matter how it felt at the time.

Or still feels now.

'No, it was a couple of years ago, and it wasn't even… Sorry, it was just a bit surreal seeing him after so long.'

He exhales a little. 'It's OK, I get it. An ex left me for a guy I used to work with, and I once hid inside a Dean and Deluca for close to forty-five minutes trying to avoid having to run into them.' He smiles that charming smile at me, and I feel even worse. 'Brigit Curtis isn't, like, your former bestie or anything though, is she?'

I can't help smiling too. 'Oh yeah, me and Brigit are old chums. 'Til she stabbed me in the back, obviously.'

Marcus nods, pretending to frown in concern. 'Yeah, I could feel the tension. Boy.' But his frown seems to turn a little more genuine than I'm comfortable with. I squeeze his fingers as my hand clasps his.

'Listen, it was just a bit weird, and I'm really sorry to have let the weird seep into our evening. I promise you, it's all good.' I lean forward and he meets me across the table for a quick kiss. I pull back as I see the waiter hovering in my peripheral vision, and then feel guilty for the fact that my eyes were still open.

This is stupid. Ren was with someone else, and so am I— someone who's really good for me. Stable, sexy, clever. Not jealous or irrational. Someone who lets that slightly domi- neering part of me take over just enough, but not too much. Marcus makes me feel calm. He makes me feel good. He takes his time with me, he's strong, he's not…

He's not…

Shit. I shouldn't have to try and convince myself. I'm being an idiot. But why can't I stop thinking about Ren being back in town? Why did I even fucking *ask*? And what was he going to suggest when he said "Maybe—" and then got interrupted by that stupid blonde—?

Ugh. *Stop it, Kayla.* I need to focus.

Marcus nods at the waiter, who comes over and hands us the dessert menus.

'You should try the caramel pecan sponge. It's almost as sexy as you,' Marcus says under his breath as the waiter walks away, and I blush. Then I blush harder, hotter, suddenly remembering Ren telling me how I tasted, and then remembering his mouth on me... God. Panic twists in my stomach, because it's like a *floodgate* of memories has opened now. I cannot believe how pathetic I'm being.

'Well,' I say, my voice quavering slightly. 'Yeah, better get that, then! Um, I'm a bit full, though. Are you happy to share?' That sounds awkward even as the words leave my lips. I can tell the faintest flicker of the same thought passes through Marcus' mind too, but he says nothing. 'I'm just going to pop to the loo.' I stand up and walk around the table, bending to kiss Marcus slowly on the cheek as I pass him, breathing in his scent, trying to get something to bury the memory of the way *Ren* smelled. The way faint wisps of him sparked off recollections as we stood gawping at each other on the pavement—

Stop it, stop it, stop it.

I move through the chic interiors of the restaurant

towards the Ladies. Once I'm finally inside, I shut the door of a cubicle and lean against it, taking several deep breaths and trying to remind myself how fucking hard it was to move on from what happened with Ren. How there's no way I'd invite that gut-twisting barrage of pain and embarrassment and "what-ifs" to take over again. The past is the past. It's not like anything has changed. He walked away from me, and I let him. And it *was* only one night and a handful of exchanges when we were miles apart. We were swept up in a moment that was just that—a moment.

So why does seeing him again feel like I'm about to lose control all over again?

*

The match flares suddenly, like it wasn't sure if it was going to burst into flame or peter out. I hold it against the wick of a fresh candle, then shake it out and breathe in the smell, watching the smoke spiral away into the darkness above the light shed by the other candles dotted around my studio. There's something so comforting about that struck-match smell.

It's late. Too late. Cole's right, this probably isn't the healthiest thing to be doing, and it's possible that after a full day at the office my mind might not be as focussed as it could be, but I just like being in here. Once I get here, it's hard to leave. And I suppose it's good that the pieces I'm working on have become so real to me, so visceral. Sometimes I look around, and it's like they're not my own. But then I look closer, and see the flaws, the things that still need work. I roll a chalk up and down my thigh absently.

It's no use. The minute I stop, even for a moment, I'm thinking about it all over again. About Ren. About *that* night, and the other night…

And the message he sent me a couple of days ago.

I had deleted his number a good while back, which took a frankly rather mortifying amount of effort on my part, but I recognised it straight away when it came up.

Ren's message didn't come that first night we bumped into each other, after Marcus and I had sex so thoroughly that I almost did convince myself it was no big deal running into Ren. Marcus was certainly doing his (very considerable) damndest to *make* me forget… But then I'd lain awake, wondering, replaying, fretting, my hands itching to rifle through my bedside drawer and find that first postcard Ren sent, and his emails that I had pathetically printed off all that time ago before deleting them from my inbox. Even with Marcus breathing softly beside me.

Ren's message didn't come the following night when I lay in bed alone with the postcard and pages spread over my duvet now, guilt and desire and anger and longing and regret all prickling hotly over my skin.

But the night after that, as I tiptoed to the bathroom in Marcus's tastefully minimal loft space, my phone on silent but its screen suddenly glowing in the darkness like he knew I'd be awake—there it was.

REN:
   Hey.

One fucking word. One word, waiting for me to open a door that I just couldn't, as much as I was absolutely dying to. So I left it there and there it has sat, waiting for me to decide what to do with it.

My chalk rolls down my leg to the floor as I reach into the back pocket of my dungarees and pull out my mobile, its screen smudged from my dirty fingers. I unlock it and look at his word again. My fingers tremble, hover, indecisive.

But this time, I type back.

KAYLA:
   Hi.

I can hear myself breathing. I shove the phone back into my pocket. 'OK. Done now, Kayla. Concentrate,' I say to myself. God, this is ridiculous. Exchanging one-word bloody messages has me breaking out in a sweat? I severely need to get a grip. Why did I even send it? I head over to my ancient, paint-spattered stereo and press play again on the Coltrane CD that's already in there.

My phone vibrates in my pocket, and I swallow.

It doesn't stop. It's not just a message back.

It's *ringing*.

I wipe my palm down my thigh again and pull out my phone, half-thinking it's probably just Christy up early with the baby and wanting to confirm something about her trip. Or Cole having a late-night brainwave, or—

But no. It's him.

I swipe, and wait.

'Hey.'

'Hi,' I say.

He laughs, low and soft, and my pulse goes into overdrive. 'I think we covered that before.'

I chuckle a little too. 'Yeah.'

'Are you… I didn't wake you, did I?'

'No, no. Well, I just messaged you. Plus, it's only…' I lift my phone away from my cheek to check the time, and frown. 'Shit. Half one. Er, no. I'm just in my studio.'

He's quiet for a moment. 'Your studio,' he repeats, and he sounds like he's smiling a bit. I'm smiling too, and I don't even know why, other than just the sound of his voice in my ear again.

'Yes.' I wait, trying not to let him hear my shallow breaths.

'I'm working too.'

'What are you working on?'

'Cutting together a new picture. Something I… Well, actually I started to write it right around…' He clears his throat, trailing off.

'Yeah. I think I remember you mentioning—'

'Kayla,' he says, on an exhale, and I stop talking. 'Listen, can I… Would it be OK if…'

'What?' My voice is somewhere between anger and

complete desperation.

'Could I see you?'

I'm silent, knowing that I should one hundred per cent immediately say no. Why is he asking me this? How could this even vaguely seem like a good—

'All right.' Words, falling from my lips on their own.

I hear Ren blow out hard. 'Where's your studio?'

Now? But of course, I reply straight away. 'Dumbo.' And then I'm giving him the address, and he's telling me he's only over in Tribeca so he'll be here soon, and I'm telling him to call me when he's outside. A voice inside my head is ready to tear me in two, telling me I'm self-destructive and ridiculous and incredibly stupid. But I don't care.

All I can think about is having Ren in front of me again.

I stand stock still for what feels like twenty minutes after we end the call. Then I walk a slow circle around the studio, looking at my work with blank eyes, trying to sort out exactly what the fuck I'm doing. My phone is still in my hand when it starts to vibrate again. I lift it to my ear.

'I'm outside.'

He hangs up, the urgency in his voice suddenly making me hyper-aware of my body, my breathing, my skin, my…

I head to the outer door, my hands trembling as I unbolt it and see Ren standing there under the streetlight as a cab pulls away, his face in shadow but the direction of his gaze unmistakeable. He takes a step, hesitates for a split second, then quickens his stride. He moves through the door, forcing me to take a step back, and I shuffle around him in the entry space trying to get my hands steady so I can re-bolt the door. Just as I manage to, I feel his body press against my back, and my hands splay against the cool metal of the outer door. His hands hold me somewhere between my waist and my ribcage, and he turns me around. The space here is so small we barely fit. I feel the cold door behind me, and Ren's hands still holding onto my sides. There's next to no light, but somehow I can still perceive the slight frown between his brows, and I can definitely feel the rapid pant of his breathing, matching my own. He leans down at the exact moment I raise up onto my tiptoes and our mouths crash together, desperate, his tongue diving into my open mouth, my hands rushing up, my fingers feeling the slight damp at the nape of his neck, his arms circling me completely, pulling me up and in towards his body. His jeans do nothing to conceal that he's growing hard, and I whimper against his mouth as he moans into mine. His lips slow, falling into a steadier rhythm, and he moves one hand up to support the back of my head as he tilts it, savouring the taste of me. I feel tears trying to infiltrate past the tight press of my eyelids. He exhales and breathes in again through his nose, his mouth never leaving mine, and I copy him, my fingers tangling into his hair...

Finally I break away, dizzy, and Ren leans the flat of one hand beside my head against the door, both of us still breathing hard. I duck under his arm and stumble through into the small main space of my studio. The warm, low candlelight swirls and flickers, and I wonder if this is going to be any better. I feel him follow behind me and I force myself to turn around and look at him, keeping my distance. He's gazing around the space, rubbing his lower lip absently, and I get a chance to properly look at him. Even in this low light, he takes my breath away all over again. I suppose because it's summer, his skin shines darker, deep brown and gold, and his long hair is half-caught back from his face like it was the other night, making his features stand out. His beard is a bit thicker now. The slim, taut muscles of his arms are prominent against his white T-shirt. He's still wearing brown leather boots, even in this warm weather. I take in a long breath and exhale it slowly, trying to make my head stop spinning.

'This is... Wow,' Ren says, wandering over to some of my pieces to inspect them more closely. He turns back to me, lowering his voice. 'Sorry about before.' He gestures back towards the door. 'I... I couldn't help...' He glances down at the floor, shoving his hands into the pockets of his jeans.

'Yeah,' I whisper. 'I know.'

Trane solos in the silence between us, peaking climactically.

'Kayla—'

'I'm not sure if this was a good idea,' I say, interrupting, and then I can't help letting out a small laugh at the absurdity of the statement.

'It's a terrible fucking idea,' Ren replies, smiling at me, and it's so overwhelming I almost need to sit down. Then his expression grows more serious. 'But I haven't been able to stop thinking about seeing you since the other night. It was like a… a…'

'Burst-dam sort of situation?' I finish for him. 'Know the feeling.'

'Yeah. Stuff… *Memories*—' he glances at me again, '—coming flooding back. Guess we need to hire better engineers.' He seems to roll his eyes at himself, then slumps down hard onto the small, battered, spring-less sofa in one corner of the space. He grimaces slightly, like he expected it to have more give. I wander a bit closer, bending down to pick up some charcoals I left scattered on the rug on the floor, and sit down on it cross-legged in front of him. He leans forwards a bit, looking at me and shaking his head, and I give him a quizzical look.

'Goddamnmit, you're beautiful,' he whispers, and I have to turn my eyes back to the ground. 'It's not that I forgot, it's just… I forgot how much.'

'Yeah, you said something like that before,' I murmur, embarrassed at the egotism coming out of me but flushing hot with the memory. That morning, when we were leaving the hotel… 'I would have thought dating one of *Esquire's* Sexiest Women Alive or whatever would have changed your views though?' I fiddle with the charcoal in my hands, coating my fingertips. 'Sorry. God, I sound jealous, don't I?'

'Takes jealous to know jealous,' he says quietly.

I wave my hands, trying to wave it away. 'Ignore me. It was just weird seeing you with—' I pause again and attempt to regroup. 'I suppose these days I've been trying not to know

328

what you've been up to, and, like… who with. It probably shouldn't have taken me by surprise.' *Ugh, great work.*

Ren draws in a breath, then shuffles forwards and slips off the sofa onto the floor in front of me, leaning his back against it and mirroring my crossed legs. 'This whole thing has taken me by surprise, Kayla. Seeing you, so suddenly, after all this time?' He laughs a bit. 'But then it was like…'

'Like it was no time at all,' I finish quietly.

Ren nods. 'And yeah, Brigit is…' He tails off. 'You're with someone, too,' he says instead, his eyes trained on mine.

'I am.' I don't sound sure, because I'm not. How could I be, with Ren sitting in front of me, making my pulse pound like my heart's tripping down a fucking staircase? 'And now you're back in New York.'

We stare at each other for a while. 'Too much time had passed,' Ren says finally, his eyebrows knitting together in that way that just kills me. 'Like, moving-on kind of time, you know? And… I thought I had.'

We're quiet again for a while, but his eyes stay on me.

'H-how have you been?' I ask at last.

'Good. Good. And shitty. My dad died a few weeks ago.'

'Oh. Ren…'

Without thinking, I reach for his hand and scoot closer, weaving my fingers in between his as they rest on his leg. He squeezes them. I don't say anything more, but he nods at me, understanding the meaning.

'I got his apartment. And it's funny—' He pauses. 'It's not funny. But I found a bunch of articles he'd kept about me, and that fucking Hauteur-Auteur article fell out right at my feet.' He chuckles anyway. 'Kayla… It is *insane* how I can barely remember what I had for breakfast yesterday, but almost every moment of that night is still etched in my brain.'

I swallow, and we're both silent, remembering. Eventually, I manage to pull my fingers away from his.

'How are you?' Ren asks. But really asking.

'I'm OK. I'm… nearly divorced.' I look at him pointedly, and he presses his lips together for a second. 'It's like I'm on the edge of happy. I can see it down below, if I really had the guts to jump. I think I'm close.' I swallow, because again, now I'm not so certain. I fiddle with the rug. 'I have a show. A pretty big one, in a couple of weeks' time at the Font Gallery. Maybe you—?' I stop myself, and I know my face has fallen now, because I see it reflected in his eyes. I don't know if I could bear the idea of him there, on that night, with someone else.

'I'd love to,' he says quietly.

'Well, if you're not busy.' The silence turns more tense, and I bite the inside of my cheek. 'So… You're working on something new now that *Revolution World* is done and dusted?' I smile, adding before he can answer, 'I tried my hardest not to, but I did end up checking out some of the press and whatnot around it.' I swirl my fingers around the pattern on the worn carpet, frowning now. 'And—' God, it's painful how impossible I find it to edit myself around him, '—I saw the film, too. Alone. A late show. And then all I could dream about was...' I finally manage to stop myself, knowing it's a terrible idea to verbalise any of that. I bring my eyes up to meet his. 'Pretty bonkers movie,' I say, to change direction. 'Um... Congratulations?'

Ren laughs. 'Right,' he says wryly. 'Jesus, *bonkers* is the word.'

I shrug. 'I really liked it, though. You always manage to make... I don't know. Something that just always really connects for me.' My voice gets quieter as I finish, and my cheeks heat. *What are you doing? Tell him to leave.*

'Man,' Ren says softly. 'Those press junkets on *RW* were pure hell.' He smiles a little, and I smile back. His fades away. 'The number of times I looked up, fucking dying for you to walk through the door.' He shakes his head. 'Stupid, I know.' I watch his long, brown fingers reach up to scratch the scruff of his beard. 'Anyway,' he sighs. 'I'm done with all that kind of stuff for a while.'

I think he must mean the big budget shoot-'em-ups, but his words still cause a jolt in my chest, because in spite of all the shit that's happened—all the shit I thought I was completely over—I don't want it to mean he's done with *me* kind of stuff.

'Tell me about this new project, then,' I say. He hesitates, getting a bashful, proud look on his face, and I can't help laughing softly. 'OK, wow.'

'I *think* it's good. I mean, I'm fucking scared of it, like, in a good way, so yeah.' He clears his throat. 'It's called *The Memory of Moments.* And... Yeah, it may not sound like it, but I've actually embraced a little more of the BSU mentality at last,' he says with a chuckle, glancing at me to check I remember. I do. Of course I do. 'But it's much more story-focussed too, I guess. It's, uh, it's a personal one.' He watches me. 'Don't worry, it's not about us,' he says quietly, reading my face. I'm almost disappointed, but then I register the "us", and my entire soul squeezes. 'Well, not... not *directly*. I think, for whatever it's worth—and personally I think it's worth a lot – you helped to free me up to actually do it, Kayla. And to make it honest.'

I want to be angry. Part of me is, but only a small part. I want to tell him that's bollocks; that what happened wasn't just some unblocking process. But that's not what comes out.

'I'm really glad, Ren.'

Jesus Christ. The thing is, it's true.

He shrugs and shakes his head again, his voice even softer now. 'I still have moments of doubt, you know. Doing this totally on my own? No Yann to bounce off, nobody else's script, no studio breathing down my neck? It was weird. I felt like I heard *you* in my head a lot, though.' He looks down with a smile. 'Angry cheerleading. I needed it.'

'Oi!' I reach over to smack his knee without thinking. 'Anyway, you don't need anyone else.' My hand rests where it lands. 'If it feels right, then you just have to trust that. Trust *yourself*. It's all you can go on, isn't it?'

'Yeah, you're right.' He takes a breath, his eyes trained on my hand, and then they dive back into mine. 'You know, I almost forgot...' he whispers.

'What?' I move my hand away again, swallowing.

'The way just talking to you makes me really believe…' He closes his eyes for a second, then opens them again. 'I think I've changed, too, though. Maybe I *do* trust myself a little more. Even the whole thing with Olivia…'

I frown. 'Olivia?' And then I remember. 'God. Your… She's definitely yours, then?'

It's like something soft, something light, drifts over Ren when he replies, 'Yeah. She's my daughter.'

I raise my eyebrows. 'Gosh.'

'I know.' He shakes his head. 'I spent a long time feeling shock and worry, and nothing else. But now, don't get me wrong, the shock and the worry are still kind of there, believe me, but there's also just pure *love*.' His expression is almost awestruck, and it draws me to him even more. 'I didn't know that's what it would be like.'

I smile slowly. 'That's lovely, Ren. My sister said something similar when she had Joy. I suppose until you're really in that position, you can't know.'

He nods. 'I just… I just wish I'd chosen it, had a little more chance to prepare. I wish that getting here hadn't been so *messy.*'

I'm not sure if there's anything to say to that. We're quiet for a moment.

'So you and Christy are good now, huh?'

'Yeah. It was… Sometimes with family, you just revert to being a child again. Well, I do anyway, and it just got out of hand. But that's all behind us.' I hesitate. 'I suppose a lot of it was all the stuff tied up with the reasons I married Cole, with doing all of that to stay here. My ambitions. The fact that I was so caught up in pursuing them.' I look Ren in the eye. 'But you should know, I don't regret it.' I can't hold his gaze, because it's not entirely true. 'Not... Not the actuality of it.'

'Kayla—'

I shake my head. 'I shouldn't have brought it up. Water under the bridge.' I can still hear the lack of honesty in my voice.

'Is it?'

I don't answer. Eventually I take a breath and try and think of something unrelated to say. 'So anyway, what's—?'

'Kayla.'

I come to a halt. The way he says my name is different now.

'Yes?'

'I... I want to talk. Chat. Catch up, like it was all just... Like we could pretend we're just friends now. I really do. I want to tell you more about Olivia, and my new project, and I *really* fucking want to know everything about every minute of what's been going on with you. And I know I should just try and figure out what the fuck this is to just show up here, and whether it's fair—on you, on... on other people. Or even if we really *could* try to just be friends—'

'Ren—' I don't think I ever heard him speak in such a rush.

'But more than anything?' he continues, ignoring me. 'I want—'

'What?' My breathing catches.

Ren shakes his head. 'Not want. I *need* to kiss you again.'

Twenty-Five

Ren.

Goddamn honesty getting the better of me.

But my whole body feels like it's being pulled toward Kayla, and I couldn't take another second of talking with her, being near to her with her eyes on me, seeing those lips and the little cropped bra thing she has on barely showing underneath her overalls, and the beautiful dark glow of her skin in this fucking candlelight.

I should leave, I know I should, before…

Kayla stares at me, her jaw tense. It feels like minutes tick by without her saying a word. I've fucked up, again. But she doesn't give me permission. Instead, suddenly, she raises up onto her knees and shuffles closer to me. I unfold my legs instinctively. It's like we can anticipate each other's movements. She lifts one leg over mine, then the other, straddling me, sitting in my lap, and I bend my knees up slightly, my hands sitting low on her waist. She looks down at me, her dreadlocks falling around us, shielding us as her hands cup my face. God she smells incredible; chalk and charcoal and her achingly familiar amber perfume, and the faintest hit of sweat… She leans down, her lips parted only a little, and kisses my mouth gently, barely brushing against it. But she's straddled over me, and the soft tease of her breath against my lips makes my cock stir immediately. I pull her closer to me, and her thighs clench against my sides, and she squeezes her arms around me, and I crush my face into her neck, sucking at her skin. I can't help it—I rock up against her, wishing too much that we had nothing in between us, that I could be inside her. She moans even from that, raising up and adjusting her position a little. I rock my hips again and she tilts her head back. 'Mmm...' she hums, and then looks down at me. How far can we go? It's the question in her eyes, and I know it's in mine, but the question should probably be *how strong am I?* I'm weak, so weak, because she's finally in my arms again. I rock my hips once, twice more. Her breath hitches audibly, and I hear myself give a low, helpless response of my own. *Idiot idiot stop, haven't you learned anything? What about—?*

But my hands are reaching for the straps of her overalls, my fingers undoing the buckles, and hers are curling against the bottom of my T-shirt, pulling it up and over my head. The straps are falling down now, and the bra thing underneath is white, but smudged with the black of her charcoals where she's rubbed her fingers against it, against herself, without thinking, while she's working, and for some reason that's just *the sexiest thought*... I lean down, pressing my lips against the burning skin of her chest, her fingers digging into my bare back as I rock faster now, and she's moving too, helping herself to whatever I can give her. Her nipples push against

337

the thin fabric containing them and I lean down further and bite at them, the noises she's making getting louder as I do.

Suddenly they're muffled as her mouth finds mine once more, our tongues slipping and sliding against each other, then our lips breaking apart wetly as she throws her head back again, her fists pulling at my hair as her breathing gets louder and shallower, her hips moving, grinding faster and faster, and I know she's close, and I know I am, and Jesus Christ *I'm* going to—

I come, hot and hard, with nowhere to go. Her body against mine, so close and so far away, it's like sorrow mixed with ecstasy. I'm still breathing hard, riding down the wave as she tenses, her thighs squeezing into me again, then she breaks apart, gasping for air, and I cradle her as she trembles in my arms, our hot damp skin pressed together, our bodies entwined. She holds on to me like she never wants to let go, and neither do I. I cradle her as she starts to calm, her face nestled into the crook of my neck.

I don't know how long we stay that way, but it's not what I want.

It's not forever.

Eventually she raises up and climbs off me, sighing hard and not looking my way. She flops back against the couch beside me, sweeping her locs away from her face.

'Ren, I... I can't...' she begins, and I think she feels me tense up because she seems to soften, changes tack. 'I did though, didn't I?' she says, shaking her head. 'God.' She's quiet for a while. 'Nothing like what happened when I met you has ever happened to me before,' she murmurs. 'And then afterwards? It was all so… *intense*. I know that's a rubbish word for it, but it's the only way I can think of to describe it. Everything just seemed so extreme. Admitting all those things, writing them down, *feeling* things that made so much sense but also no sense at all? Because how could they? I hardly even knew you. Why did— Why do you mean so much to me?' She turns and looks at me, tears in her eyes. I reach for her but she pulls away a little, and my hands fall back down, my fingers scratching at the quick of my thumbnails like I want to pull them out. *Goddamnit.* I open my mouth to say something, I don't know what—but it doesn't matter because she's not done.

'Ren, I… I *sobbed* through half the night after you came to the apartment, trying to hide from people, trying to get you to answer me, to let me explain it properly. I sat there in the early hours of that morning trying to figure out what to write in that bloody email. I wrote and deleted fuck knows how many drafts. I don't even know if you *got* it.'

'I got it,' I whisper.

She looks at me. 'But you didn't reply.' Shaking her head, she draws in a trembling breath. 'I moved like a zombie through work for weeks afterwards, when I was meant to be happy because my fucking plan was finally in motion, I was finally doing all this stuff I'd been building towards for all that time. But there I was just wandering through it all in a fog. I read your old messages over and over again. I deleted your emails and then I actually panicked, like I was going to have a fucking heart attack and retrieved them, *printed them out* so I wouldn't lose them.' She laughs exasperatedly, and a couple of tears do fall now. 'So that I wouldn't lose words that pretty much broke my heart every time I looked at them.'

I refuse not to hold her. I grab my shirt and carefully wipe Kayla's face with it, and she laughs a little more between soft sobs, the combination of sounds reaching into me and twisting my guts. I move my arm around her shoulders, and she finally gives in and lets me start to pull her towards me, but then she stiffens again.

'You'd better put that on first,' she says, sniffing, as she nods toward my shirt. I pull it on, seeing it already marked, like her bra top was. Like my fucking soul is, I guess—with her. Finally she rests her head against my shoulder, and I wrap one arm around her, holding her to me tightly.

'I know,' I say softly. 'I get it, Kayla.'

'No, Ren, I'm not sure if you do. It's pretty bloody ironic to say at the moment, after…' She presses her eyelids shut for a second. 'But it can't be like this anymore.'

'OK.' It's not OK, and the tone of my voice shows it.

'It can't just be about how it feels in the moment,' she says. 'Because we *know* it feels good.' She shifts a little against me, and I close my own eyes like it might stop me hearing her. '*Really* good,' she continues, her voice a whisper now. 'But I'm scared to death that there would be some reason, even if it's a good reason, that would make it all grind to a halt again. It was like… zero to sixty, and then suddenly it was zero again. So fast. And that was just… I don't know if I can do that again. We have to *think*, not just feel. I mean—'

'Bullshit.'

She straightens up, incredulous. 'What?'

'You've just said it yourself, Kayla. You're scared. I get it, OK? Maybe it wasn't right then. But now?' She stares at me, but I can't stop myself. 'Zero…? *You* pushed *me* away, Kayla. I flew across the country to find you on what turned out to be your fucking *wedding night*. You dictated everything that happened between us. You kept your… your plan or whatever a total secret from me. I had no *chance* to understand until the shit was right under my nose. How did you think it was going to pan out?'

She exhales hard, shaking her head, avoiding my eyes. 'I don't know, Ren.' She studies her hands. 'I don't know how I was going to deal with it, but it's something I had to—'

'And you told me you wanted to "draw a line under it", remember?' I continue, interrupting her, hearing the escalating emotions in my voice. 'You're not the only one whose heart got broken. *Fuck*,' I utter the last word under my breath, feeling my muscles tense as she stands, pulling up the straps of her overalls. I suck in a long breath and try again. 'Look…'

'No, no, fine,' Kayla says. 'This is my fault. But if I'd told you I was marrying him, would it have made a difference? We weren't… tangible.' She flutters her fingers in the air, like everything we had is slipping through them. 'All I had was this fucking *feeling*, which I didn't know was love until it was too late.'

Love. The word reverberates around my brain. 'Kayla, I didn't mean—'

'I can't just keep going on gut with you, Ren. Look where it gets me!'

I scramble to my feet too, holding my hands out to her, trying to think of the words to appease her. More tears are already on Kayla's cheeks, but anger is in her eyes. It's like a pent up pain, a pain I didn't know I had caused being finally and fully unleashed.

'Jesus Christ, this was the stupidest…' she mutters, then turns back to me. 'You didn't give me a *chance*. You didn't even try to understand—' She breaks off, breathing shakily. I can't get to her, she won't let me. She folds her arms around herself, a barricade. 'Why was it so easy for you to walk away, Ren?'

'It was *not* easy,' I say. 'Walking away from you was the hardest thing I've ever done.' I can barely hear myself. I'm in a daze. 'Kayla, I felt betrayed all over again. I was hurting. You have no idea how much. *I'd* never felt anything like what I felt for you, not even after losing my girl and my best friend in one fell swoop.'

She wipes her eyes with the backs of her hands. 'I-I should have been more careful with your feelings, your past. I'm sorry. But you should have been gentler with me, too. I know I front it out like I'm tough…' She pauses to let out an ironic sigh of a laugh. 'But I'm not. I just found it hard to believe that this was real… Th-that *you* could really love—'

She breaks down into tears again, and I'm on the verge now myself. I try moving a fraction closer to her, and she backs away.

'Kayla…' I swallow, scrubbing a hand over my face. 'You're right, I shouldn't have shut you out like that, but you shouldn't have kept secrets from me. It wasn't fair.'

She presses her lips together for a moment. 'You know what's not fair, Ren? This. Why now?' Her eyes shine in the dim light as they bore into me. 'You've been back living in the city again for how long? You knew where to look for me. Why now, when you're with someone else, when I'm with someone else? Why did you have to wait for me to just *fall* back into your life to suddenly give a shit again?'

'I told you—'

'Oh right, too much time had passed,' she repeats sarcastically, and I find myself getting angry too.

'I was trying to leave you alone, like you asked me to. As far as I knew, you were fucking *married*, Kayla.' I take a breath and try to lower my voice. 'And… And I tried to stop believing in fate after you.' I move a step closer to her again, feeling the desperation rising in my chest. 'But dammit, there you were. This feels right. Doesn't this feel right to you?'

She walks away from me, as far as she can in this space, then whirls around to face me again. 'Ren, I'm not an *idea*, OK? I can't just be something that occurs to you, and then you're like a train that changes track. I'm going to get run over.'

I step closer. 'That's not what happened,' I say quietly.

'I never *stopped*... Kayla, please don't push me away. Let's just—'

'No.' Tears spill down her face and onto her chest again. I feel like I'm breaking in half. She swipes at her cheeks but the tears won't stop, and she seems almost startled at the fact. 'How do I know this won't fall apart again? If I meant so much to you, why did you walk away? Why didn't you listen, why didn't you try, why didn't you *fight* for me?' Her eyes are wide, firing more questions, but before I can speak she says, 'Maybe I wasn't worth it.'

'Kayla—'

'You know what? You're passive, Ren. You just wait for these things to just *happen* to you. You turn up before I'd figured out how to explain the marriage thing? Bam, that's it. You're the victim, you're the blameless one. Your best friend and your girlfriend were merrily carrying on, you could feel it, and you did nothing about it. Victim. You can't make your own films? It's Yann's fault. Even with your own bloody *child*, no doubt you buried your head in the sand about her until the last minute playing the hurt victim, once again.'

What she says runs through me like a sword, and her eyes widen suddenly with regret as she looks at me. Silence ricochets between us.

'Jesus Christ, Kayla,' I murmur eventually, and she starts to shake her head. 'I knew you were critical, guess I never knew quite how much.'

'I-I'm sorry,' she says, her voice interrupted like she's struggling to catch her breath. 'Ren, I'm sorry. I didn't mean that. I'm just…' She stops, a burst of sobs taking over.

How the fuck has this happened? Everything has just crashed down on us like an avalanche.

'I can't do this, Ren,' Kayla whispers. She sets her jaw. 'It's late. You should go.' She looks up at me, regretful tears still glistening in her eyes, but they're also marked with resolve. I stare at her a moment longer, then I start to back away toward the door, hardly able to turn away from her in spite of everything. I feel like I've been punched hard in the gut.

Eventually I make it to the outer door space, pulling back the bolt hard. But just before I do, I see the piece she's been working on hanging on the wall nearby. Abstract and beautiful, it's a huge drawing of a hand—her hand, I know it is—nestled against the cheek of a face I know is mine.

We hadn't moved on.

But now?

The metal door clangs loudly as it slams shut behind me.

Twenty-Six

Kayla.

'I swear she must have been, like, twelve—'

'Twelve?! That is *actual* bollocks, Christy,' I shout, waving my hands in the air to try and stop her, but Shaline grabs them, sputtering with laughter.

'Let her finish!' she says loudly, and I know the tables next to us are starting to get annoyed but it's hard to care. God it feels so good to have my sister here right now, helping me forget—even if I haven't had the strength to tell her about what. Well, it would be if she weren't intent on completely over-embellishing every bloody story.

'Are you having a laugh? I can't just let her *lie* about—' I start, but Christy ignores me.

'So Kay jumps out of bed, comes into my room—'

'I was, like, five years old maximum, OK?'

Cole holds a hand over my mouth and nods to Christy, who leans into her story, elbows on the table, as we finally grow quieter. I push his hand away, shaking my head. '*So* glad you aren't still up a mountain,' I mutter at him. He grins.

Christy starts up again. 'So, my little sister nestles onto

my bed, with this contemplative look on her face, and she's like "Chriiiisss… Y'know poos?"—' She starts chuckling again, pitching her voice even higher to mimic mini-me. '"Y'know how babies come from when mums do a poo that's special?"'

They're all howling now, and I hold my head in my hands. 'Is this appropriate brunch chat, I mean, really?'

'She's like, "Well, I just did a massive poo, and I flushed it away, but what if… What if…?" And she actually starts to fucking *cry*!' Christy bursts out laughing and the others join in again. '*Mate!* It was too, too much, I'm telling you.'

'Yeah, 'cause you were the height of sophistication at that age, Chris.' A flash of real irritation shoots through me, but it's gone just as fast. Doesn't she know I idolised her then, and I do now? I take a breath. 'Bloody hell, anyway—enough. Let's get the bill.'

Christy uses her napkin to blot tears from her eyes, using a knife's reflection to check her eye make-up; the expertly-applied false lashes make her eyes look huge. Her bone structure is even more pronounced now with her septum piercing and her close-cropped hair, what's left of it dyed back to its usual honey-blonde. It almost makes me want to revisit my plan of shaving off the sides of my locs, but I'll keep thinking about it. Just seeing my sister do something always makes it seem so much cooler. She notices me looking at her and winks. 'Sorry, babe, too good to resist telling that one,' she says, still smiling to herself.

Typical Christy. I think it's sort of inherent to her

big-sisterness, but weirdly I feel a pang of emptiness about it since most of the time we're so far away from each other, even if it means we can't piss each other off as much. I just need to try and enjoy having her while she's here, as long as she doesn't keep delving into her archive of humiliating anecdotes.

The waitress brings over the bill and Cole snatches it off the table. 'I got this. My treat. Well, actually, Shaline, you still owe me twenty bucks from the other night, but—'

'Bull*shit* I do,' Shay begins, but Cole laughs.

'Don't make me tell them why you lost that bet. I mean, Kay's familiar with your nasty ass but Christy doesn't know you like that, so all I'm saying is—'

'All right, all right,' Shay says, throwing up her hands and then reaching for her purse.

Cole waves her away. 'I'm playing, it's cool.' He slaps his credit card down and leans back on the rear legs of his chair with a self-satisfied air that's one of the few things I sometimes find grating about him, and even that is tinged with a certain amount of affection too, I suppose. I see Christy studying him, then sliding her gaze over to me. I can practically see thought bubbles above her head—wondering how our "marriage" worked, if we ever contemplated making it real. If only she knew. I haven't had the guts yet to confess the *half* of the conflict going on in the romantic entanglement department of my over-stuffed brain. She has no idea about Ren, and I've been trying to compartmentalise all that for now. If I let my mind drift to it for even a fraction too long, I can't get anything done. The tangle of emotions gets caught in my chest again and I feel like I can't breathe. It's been a week and a half since what happened at my studio, and I still have to actively combat my mind from straying to it and replaying it what feels like every moment of the day. To keep it from asking the same question over and over again: *why did I push him away?*

We say goodbye to Shay and Cole, and Christy links her arm through mine as we walk slowly towards the Strand bookstore, trying not to over-exert ourselves in the heat. The streets are busy with tourists and people who don't have work because of too much money or not enough. Lately I've been finding myself on edge every time I'm in this part of town— scanning faces and looking away, worried that somehow like a magnet I'll be drawn back to Ren. That, like before, I'll just be walking along and *wham!*

The thing is, I want it to happen… and I don't. He hasn't tried to call, no texts, no messages, no emails. God, why did I open my big fucking mouth? Because I was still scared of how I feel about him. He was right. *Why did I—*

'So how comes you don't have to go back to the office with them?' Christy asks, interrupting my thoughts, thank God.

'Well, it's quite flexible. Cole's got a couple of meetings this morning about some advertising stuff, but he takes care of most of that side of things. I reckon Shay's probably about to miss our reviews deadline, so she'll probably be doing some last minute frantic stuff for that, but I'm fine til this afternoon when we've got the pitch meeting, and then I'll have a few articles to edit and stuff. I thought the bookshop was always the plan for after we ate? Are you trying to ditch me already?'

'No, not at all. I'm just really… I hate to admit it—' she pulls down her cats-eye sunglasses pointedly to look at me over them, and I laugh '—but I'm impressed, babe. Seriously. I know I don't say it much, but I am. You're really, like, bossing it up. It's wicked.'

'Thanks, Chris,' I say dubiously. We reach the bookshop and give the rows of stalls outside heaving with second-hand books a quick glance over before heading towards the entrance. It is the family tradition not to be too free with a compliment, so I can't help feeling a bit suspicious. As we head inside, we both sigh at the air conditioning and inhale deeply at the scent of all these glorious books.

'OK, so is it in photography, or…?'

'This way,' I say, not even vaguely pretending I don't know where they have a few copies of my Polaroid book. We reach the table display of local stuff, and Christy whistles as she sees it sitting in a small pile. She grabs a copy and stares at the cover.

'Blimey. Look at it.'

'You've seen it millions of times, Chris.'

'But… not in context.'

I laugh at that, but she's still looking through the pages. She pauses on the one of Dad, and smiles down at it. 'I'm still surprised his answer to "Why do we create?" wasn't

"Because I said so.'"

'Innit.'

Christy chuckles. 'Between this and the show at the Font Gallery?' she continues, still absently flicking through the pages. I look away as Ren's face appears briefly. 'Jesus, Kay,' she continues, shaking her head. 'Look where you are, man. I'm so proud of you, you know,' she says quietly. 'You did it. What you set out to do.'

I start to chew my lip to fight the swirling emotions her unexpected words bring up in me.

'Oh, come on, you'll set me off in a minute. I'm already without my baby right now, let's not overdo it.'

I swallow. 'All right.' We start to look around, and she examines a fashion photography book nearby. 'It's going to be your work in there soon too, you know,' I tell her, since we're on the compliment train. 'Well, I mean, *after* everyone sees renowned artist and internet doyenne Kayla Joseph in one of your creations at my show next week, obvious—Oi!'

I scrabble away from her as she tries one of the knee-buckle moves we used to do to each other as kids—knocking your own knee into the back of your victim's in a sudden assault. She's fully gone back to childish-and-annoying again already.

'Truce?' she says, grinning.

'Truce.'

Still, I keep her in my eye line, but I really do want to get this out there. 'I'm being honest, though. You're... you're my benchmark.'

She shrugs. 'Not sure about that, babe.' I can see the uncomfortable but proud smile on her face too, now. Shoe-on-the-other-foot time.

'It's not like I was surprised at how well you've bounced back,' I carry on, 'but it really just made me realise how stupid I was before, to think that it had to be one of us or the other, you or me…' I trail off, spinning a display of feminist greeting cards to avoid looking at her. 'I had no idea what I was talking about when I said that you having Joy would finally give me a chance to be the one that achieved something. *So* stupid. I was just—'

'When did you say that?'

I look up at her, and her eyes are narrowed, one hand on her hip. I know she's only fucking with me, that we've been over this already, made our accusations to one another in the heat of the moment all that time ago. But it's effective. Guilt ricochets in my chest all over again.

'Christy…'

She exhales hard and relaxes her stance. 'All right, all right. Look, I know.' She steps closer to me. 'I've never really admitted how much I admire you, Kay—I was a glory hog for a long fucking time, and it wasn't really fair to you. You've done a lot, babe. Jeez.' She chuckles. 'But as for having my baby?'

I shake my head vigorously, dismissing any of the petty, negative bullshit—I can't have that anywhere near thoughts of Joy. I reach up quickly to hold the sides of the headwrap my locs are poking out of so it doesn't unravel. Christy smiles as she reaches over to adjust it for me. 'I know,' I say, looking into her eyes. 'I'm sorry. I was a dickhead.'

She chuckles again, softer now. 'Well, so was I. I mean, I get it now. The marriage, the whole thing. Why you stayed by any means necessary to work on your art and your business, the website—'

'Getting married to Cole wasn't some Malcolm X shit,' I interject. 'Honestly,' I say over my shoulder as I begin to wander away up the stairs. I head over to the coffee table art tomes. Christy purses her lips as she follows me, but doesn't say anything to counter me. 'Marriage isn't something to take lightly, but like I told you then—it *wasn't* a light decision.'

Christy holds up her hands. 'I can see that now. And Cole is a sweetheart.' She takes a breath, and I see a twinkle in her eyes. 'Jesus, I can't believe you're going to be bloody *divorced* and barely thirty, though…'

I roll my eyes. 'Uh huh.'

She laughs, and I join in, relieved that the intensity of the conversation has dissipated a bit.

'So, what about this Marcus guy, the one Shaline was talking about?' Christy asks. 'When am I meeting him?'

Shit.

I've been a massive coward as far as Marcus is concerned, using Christy's visit as an excuse for not seeing him properly, other than a quick lunch before she arrived at the beginning of the week. Even that was basically just a series of forced smiles and "fines" on my part. I feel awful. Marcus is a good man, and not in a "you'll do" kind of way. He's even offered to take Chris and me to dinner tomorrow night at a new Japanese place that's just opened, and I want to say yes, but I've been delaying because I'm worried about seeing him. As if I think he'll see my disloyalty draped over me like dirty sheets. And for what? The whole thing with Ren the other night was a complete shambles of blame and bundled emotions.

But the things he said to me, the way he *felt*…

'Tomorrow,' I say suddenly to Christy. The best way to deal with all of this might be to just ignore it, move on again. Before all this stuff with Ren turning back up, Marcus and I were on a good path. Or we seemed to be… 'He's, um, invited us to have dinner tomorrow. You know he's in the restaurant business?'

Christy nods, eyeing me closely. 'Yeah, I think you vaguely mentioned.' She's suspicious already.

'Yeah. Let's get a coffee in and, um, I'll tell you all about him. In fact, I'll just give him a call now and confirm tomorrow night.' Suddenly I'm eager to hear Marcus' voice, to try and justify what happened with Ren as just a terrible blip.

I'm delusional, obviously. But it might work if I try.

Twenty-Seven

Ren.

I stare at the screen again, then reach up and rub my eyes like it might make things clearer. 'Maybe half a second faster on that last cut?' I say, and Tom nods and tries it again.

'Better?' He runs it a few times, his already-wrinkled forehead furrowing more in concentration, and then he smiles crookedly as he sees me nod in satisfaction. 'Great,' he says. 'Listen, I might grab another coffee if—'

'No, no, let's call it a night. Thanks, T.'

'Almost there, huh?' His grin is wry now, and I roll my eyes. We both know there's no such thing as *there*.

'Night.'

He finishes up, grabs his worn leather knapsack and gives me a quick pat on the back as he heads out. I can practically sense relief lifting off him like a vapour. I sometimes forget that this is just a job, even for someone as dedicated to his craft as Tom. He has a wife to get to, though I'm sure after thirty-some years in this business she's used to him going late.

I think I've been letting myself get completely drawn in to the edit on *The Memory of Moments* because it's allowing me to block out my *actual* memories, and any other thoughts, for good solid chunks of time. Sometimes I forget where I am and what day it is when I'm working in here. It feels like the womb or something. It's a little indulgent, but it's the only place I get to take our footage and make the story I've been seeing all this time in my head real—or as close as I can get, at least. I'm glad to know I can still focus when I have to. When I don't have this to concentrate on, I don't like where my mind goes. Well, I love it, then I hate it.

I stare around the dark, state-of-the-art editing suite, all plasma screens and computers and wood grain and leather. It's so quiet now everyone's gone home. My folder of scrappy notes is half-stuffed into my bag along with my sweater and jacket, all bundled in a pile on the expensive and insanely comfortable couch. I look down at it. I've slept overnight on that bad boy before, and I'm strongly considering it again now, seeing as I'll just be back here again first thing in the morning. But maybe I could use some air. A shower. Living some of my actual life, such as it is, even just for a few hours.

I gather up my shit, and reluctantly take out my phone to see the messages and voicemails and emails piled up on it. Nothing from the one person I'm still dying to hear from, even in spite of the way we left things. Either way, if Kayla doesn't get in touch then I know it's not a good idea to go blazing in again myself, as much as I want to. There's only so much rejection I can stomach. And I guess it's pride too. I can't pretend what she said to me didn't really fucking hurt, whether I deserved it or not. Thing is, I know in some ways she wasn't wrong, and I know she was just being defensive, fighting against this thing between us. Trying to protect her heart. The heart I broke.

Dammit.

In any case, the messages are mainly business stuff, and one from Evelyn sending a photo of another drawing Livvy made of the turtle I got her—that one makes me smile. I send a quick message back telling Eve to kiss the kid good-night for me, though thinking about it, it's after midnight and she'll long be in bed.

And there's a voicemail from Brigit, too. I think I need to be home before I deal with that. She's been as crazy busy with her re-shoots over in Ireland as I have been with the edit, and I think that's been a good thing. Well, it's been good for me, because I feel guilt-ridden every time I think her name. She tells me she misses me, but she sounds less convinced every time. Distance seems to be unpicking what had started to knit together between us. Deep down she probably knows I can't give her what she needs or deserves. Could be vice versa, too. I mean, I do miss her, but not with that ache. I know what *really* missing someone feels like. Now more than ever. I know that what I feel for Kayla is the real fucking deal, otherwise I wouldn't feel sick to my stomach at the mere thought that we might not work it out. I miss *her* and we're in the same goddamn city. And I know that's unfair to Brigit.

I exhale hard and head out to the lobby and nod to Dawit, the night security guy behind the desk. His slim frame is hunched forward as he stares intently at a screen in front of him, its light reflecting against his smooth dark skin. I know better than to think he's studying the surveillance cameras—as I walk by, I clock the Malick film he's watching so absorbedly, and I smile. He straightens up and hits "pause".

'Goodnight, Mr Mor—Ren. Sorry,' he says, his wide smile showing his small, white teeth. I'm glad he's finally dropping the formalities. There have been more than a couple nights we've sat together going through the archives here when he should be guarding or whatever, and I should be sleeping elsewhere. If someone actually tried to rob this place we'd be screwed, but Dawit knows more about cinema than pretty much anyone I know. Even though it felt completely weird to be seen as any kind of mentor type, I helped him out with some film school application stuff and funding, and I have no doubt he's going to do something awesome—determination just comes off him in waves. It reminds me of Kayla, which is probably why I like the guy so much.

'Goodnight, man. That's one of my favourites,' I say, nodding to the screen.

He nods. 'Yes, mine too.'

'Next time you're on, I'll show you the latest cut on *Moments*,' I say as I head out the door and he nods again more vigorously, his smile growing wider. I feel a little better as I walk down the street. There's something invigorating about enthusiasm, I've realized—and Lord knows I could use *something* to stop me sliding further into this emotional slump.

The air outside is still warm, but it feels like rain's coming. I'm glad it's only a few blocks back to dad's apartment—I'm still struggling after all these weeks to think of it as mine. But being out in the city in the dark makes me feel lonelier somehow, makes the space beside me that for one night was occupied by Kayla feel more acutely empty. I jealously watch cabs flashing by with figures huddled together in the back-seat and couples walking hand in hand, sort of late to be out but lost in each other's company.

I get to the apartment building and head up, sighing with relief when I finally let myself in, grab a beer from the nearly-empty refrigerator, and sink into my father's old chair, turning the TV on and muting it right away. I just like the flicker.

This chair is the one thing I kept from before, and it still smells of him. Leather and judgement and his aftershave. I breathe in, trying to remember if he'd ever have given me romantic advice. Even if it was just a weary look, I feel like I could use it now. I wish I'd been around him more as an adult, when maybe there was more we could relate to about one another. Who knows, maybe he had torrid affairs I never knew about after Luiza, or during their relationship even. He never *seemed* interested in having a partner again once she'd left, and I was glad about that. I wasn't in the market for a stepmother. And my father never seemed to care about what girls I brought home, or whether I'd had my heart broken—a regular occurrence when I was in high school, even before college and Evie, and... Guess some things don't change.

Still, my father feels so cemented in my mind from that time, I genuinely can almost imagine the look on his face when it would come to this kind of thing. Dismissive, but in a sort of caring way, like he felt this wasn't what I should be expending so much of my energy on. Maybe he's right.

I wonder what advice I'll have for Olivia on shit like this. I don't think it's going to be sterling stuff, given my track record. It feels weird thinking about her as a grown up person with romantic feelings.

More than anything, I miss having a fucking buddy, a best friend. Yann would know what to tell me to do. I even consider calling him… but that's not for tonight. Soon, maybe. I chug at the bottle of beer, thinking. Oddly I see Yann in Livvy, even in spite of all the realities. Nature/nurture, I guess. I can't help still feeling a little angry about it sometimes, jealous even, but if I had to share my kid with anyone I'm glad it's him. Yann knew me and my issues, better than pretty much anyone. And he forgave them. I think it's finally time to try and forgive his.

I swig my beer, considering if anywhere is open to order some takeout… but as I stare at the silent television screen, my mind drifts back to what Kayla said to me the other night. Do I really play the victim? As painful as what she said was, I think she was right. I *used* to be that way. Passive, letting things happen to me. But now I know what I want, professionally… personally. And if I *am* so resolved about how I feel, then there's something else I need to do right now, regardless of the outcome with me and Kayla.

I sit forward and grab my laptop out of my bag, opening

it and balancing it on my knees. I click on Skype and dial, waiting and half-hoping she's not going to answer.

'JR…' The image transforms from abstract pixels into Brigit's beautiful, dewy-skinned face. 'You're lucky you caught me, I was just about to jump into bed.' Her voice sounds tired, and I realize I didn't even think about the time over there.

'I'm glad, then,' I say.

'You got my message about the night shoot wrapping early?'

Man, I hate seeing myself in that little box in the corner of the screen. I pull my hair back behind my ears. 'You know what, I actually just got in,' I tell her. 'I haven't really checked my messages yet. I just thought I'd try you.'

'Aw, that's sweet.' Her voice sounds distant, a little insincere, and I don't think it's just because we're on a video call. She takes a breath. 'Um, listen…'

I blank out momentarily, and I have to acknowledge that some part of me is kind of reprehensible, because just hearing that "listen" makes my muscles slacken with relief. I've said that "listen". Hell, I think I was seconds away from saying it myself. I guess I'm a little surprised it's Brigit who got there first, but maybe I was right about absence actually making the heart see perspective. I settle back in my father's chair, and we play out our conversation like we'd learned our sides.

Then I put my computer away, and go to bed still feeling downcast.

Because I'm going there alone.

Twenty-Eight

Kayla.

I stare down at my untouched plate of bruschetta and then reach a faintly trembling hand over to my wine glass, bringing it to my lips and taking a long sip. Christy's turned away from me, chatting what may as well be a foreign language to Taye, our fashion editor, and I can't help a small smile as I look down at the sleeveless tailored jumpsuit my sister has made for me. The vibrant mustard yellow colour shouldn't work but it completely does, and the way she's cut it is perfection; the fit is so good. I try to focus on how lucky I am, and how if my sister is this talented then maybe it really does run in the family, but try as I might—and unfamiliar as it feels—I'm gripped with what can only be described as *crushing doubt*. In an hour's time people are going to be wandering around the Font Gallery, scrutinising the pieces that I've spent months working on with what could well be an entirely dismissive air, before they head off to the next party. This is New York City, for fuck's sake. You walk outside and trip over an artist. What the hell was I thinking?

Marcus reaches over and squeezes my hand. 'Not hungry?'

'There's no room for food with all these butterflies in my stomach,' I reply, looking up into his warm, reassuring brown eyes. I lace my fingers in between his, willing his touch to really make me feel better. 'Thanks, though,' I say.

He leans down and pecks my cheek. 'It's totally normal to be nervous, Kayla.' Something about the way he says it makes my heart sink, just a little, at the fact that he doesn't understand this is different—that nervous isn't normal for me. I hate myself for being so unfair, even if it's only in my head, because I'm thinking about the person who *would* understand, who isn't here.

I'm relieved when the ting of a fork hitting glass draws my attention away and makes everyone on our table settle, but then I cringe as I see Cole standing up.

'Really? We haven't even had our mains yet.'

'Yes, really,' he says with a grin, 'this shit is happening. I want to make a toast to my almost-ex-wife!' He glances down at Chou, like he's a little worried about us interacting in front of her, but she just smiles back up at him adoringly. An odd mixture of jealousy and smugness rises in me. I really need to get my emotions in check tonight.

Cole's face grows more serious as he turns back to me. 'Kay…' He clears his throat, and I'm moved to see that he's a little emotional himself. 'OK, don't worry, I'll keep it short, all right? I just want to say that I'm proud of you. I mean, I knew this was where you were headed, but you're on some next level shit now. I'm just glad to know you and be around your talent all day long, and to… to call you my friend.' He swallows a little as he looks at me, and tears bubble in my eyes.

'Aw, CoCo,' I say, my voice barely making it past the lump in my throat. 'Thank you. I owe you so much. *So* much. I mean, you know I wouldn't even *be* here if you hadn't made the kind of sacrifices that make me wonder what I've done to deserve—' I stop, because the tears spill. I resign to it, and smile as Christy reaches around me and squeezes my shoulders.

'Eye makeup, babes,' she says to me, and I laugh through the tears. 'Yeah, don't worry, you can fix it.' I see tears in her eyes too.

I stand as Cole pushes out his chair to walk around the table to me, and we hug tightly. I whisper my thanks to him again. 'But not so much for making me a blubbering mess before we've even eaten. That's enough of that, OK?'

'Cool, cool, I promise,' he says, holding me at arms length and looking at me. 'I mean it, though, you know that.'

'I know. I do, too.'

Finally we sit down to eat our main course, and I can't help feeling the distance between me and Marcus growing even as we sit beside one another. He's a new passenger on this journey, and tonight more than ever, it shows.

After we rush through dessert, realising 9pm is rapidly approaching, I head to the Ladies to fix my face and take some alone time. I sort out my makeup and stare at my reflection in the mirror. Suddenly, the idea of *pride* overtakes my thoughts: having it for other people is a good feeling, but too much pride is not necessarily seen as a good thing to have for yourself... I remember Ren and I talking about Prufrock, and about self-doubt, and his suggestion that I'm not one to agonise over much. I think most of the time it's true, especially when it comes to knowing the path I wanted to take. How did he know me straight away, the very essence of so many things about me? Because he was right about more than just my determination: he trusted in that intangible feeling between us, when I was too busy being a coward about the possibility of love.

That's the thing—in one respect I might be more like Prufrock than I thought. I let doubt become an insecurity when it came to Ren. But I miss him. I miss every word we've ever said to one another. He forced me to think about my feelings, about things I'd never really wanted to question... but if I'd just let him, maybe he could have shown me some answers, too.

I stare at my reflection a moment longer, then shake my head, sighing. Whatever has happened in my emotional life, this show tonight is the culmination of what I've been working towards so far as an *artist*.

'Well done, Kayla.' I whisper it to myself out loud, sincerely, just to hear it.

I worked really hard. I worried I wouldn't ever get here but I have, even in the face of so much potential for failure. I poured out my soul into my work, and even if I'll never be fully happy with it, for each and every piece, I got from a blank space to what I'm happy to call Art. Something I *created.*

'I'm proud of you,' I tell my reflection.

Because I need to hear it, in spite of everything.

*

'... I'm sure you'll agree that being amongst these pieces is a privilege indeed. Please help me in congratulating once again, the incredible Ms Kayla Valerie Joseph. Kayla, ladies and gentlemen!'

I flush, the champagne bubbles already starting to tickle my brain as applause echoes around the gallery. Penny raises her voice again over the noise.

'And don't dawdle—an orange dot means it's already gone, I don't need to tell you that. So move fast. Speak to Yelena over here to discuss purchases, or myself. OK? Thank you. Kayla? Enjoy this night, darling...'

I blow her a kiss from across the floor, and smile at chic strangers I'm sure I'm probably meant to know as they congratulate me. Then they begin to fold their arms and drift away to study the walls. I can't believe how many people are here. I glance around for Marcus, but I lost track of him after he saw one of his business partners on the way in. Christy's popped out to take a call from home—Dad's up with Joy because she has a cold, bless her, and Cole's with Chou while she finishes a cigarette outside. Everyone's chatting to someone, and it feels weird to be all alone at my own show. I start to circulate around the gallery space with a fixed smile, trying to project an air of confidence, rather than what I'm actually feeling, which is manifesting as a "*pleasepleasebuy-buylikelikelikesomethinganything*" internal monologue. I'm conscious of getting too much in anyone's face, in case they feel pressured to say something positive, which seems amusingly English of me. I move off to the side for a moment, swapping out my champagne glass as a waitress brings more past on a tray, and I notice that I'm standing near my sole sort-of-self-portrait.

I stare up at it: my hand against his cheek, the rings on my fingers—including the engagement ring hiding in plain sight—my fingernails pressing into his skin ever so slightly, cupping his jawline... I turn my head away but look back almost immediately, trying so hard not to feel too emotional as my eyes scan the huge canvas. Blowing out a sigh, I attempt to focus on the fact that I'm pleased with the lighting and mounting we decided on. I'm even almost satisfied with the way it came out as a piece. I just about nailed the scale I was going for, and the zoomed in hyper-reality of—

Forget it. It's no use. As I look at the picture, all I can feel is the soft hair of his beard under my palm, the way our eyes would be connected just out of the frame...

Quite a few people are gathering around it, actually; it seems to be one of the most popular pieces, and I'm not sure how that makes me feel. Maybe it's too raw. Maybe they can sense what went in to it. What it means to me.

'It's beautiful.'

My hand freezes as I lift my glass to my lips. The voice

behind me is low, next to my ear, under the pulse of the music and the echoing gaggle of voices.

'I wanted to do a thing where I buy it anonymously, and then you find out later it was me and it would be all… romantic.' He's quiet for a moment. 'Guess that ship has sailed, though.'

I turn around slowly. He's alone.

'Sorry,' Ren says to me. 'I know we're not… But I was walking past the gallery a couple days ago and saw the date, and I just… I couldn't miss this.'

I gawp at him. He's wearing a suit. A really nice, expensive-looking one. I mean, it's very Ren: an unfussy plain black, jacket unbuttoned with just a simple, un-tucked white T-shirt underneath it, his hair half-pulled back again, neatly. He looks Too. Damn. Good. I drink him in, and exhale. Somehow, in spite of the shock of seeing him, I feel myself relax. It's wrong, but now everything feels right.

'Nice whistle,' I say hoarsely, briefly tugging at his jacket lapel to indicate what I mean with the hand that isn't still shakily holding a champagne flute.

The corners of Ren's mouth turn up a bit, and my heart judders. 'That's London-speak, right?' His eyes heat my skin as he takes me in. 'You don't look so bad yourself, Kayla,' he says, his voice cushioning my name as he speaks it.

'I'm… Thanks for coming, Ren,' I whisper.

His expression changes, like he's remembering the last time we spoke. It hits me too. *Shit.* I want to take it all back. God, I want to take it all back.

Ren shakes his head. 'Like I said.' He glances at the floor, then looks over at our picture again, drawing in a long breath.

But then I realise—I finally have a chance to say something. 'Look, a-about the other night... I'm so sorry about what I said. It was completely out of order to—'

He holds up a hand to stop me. 'I understand,' he says.

'No, it was a horrible thing to say. The stuff about your daughter, especially.' I study the bubbles in my glass.

'Yeah, it was.'

My heart is tethered to lead balloons, and I can't look at him.

Ren clears his throat. 'You were sort of right, though. I wait for things to be easy, or until they're unavoidable.' I open my mouth to speak again, but he stops me. 'Thing is, I think you were always unavoidable. From the moment I met you.' He clenches his jaw. 'It hurts sometimes, when people tell you the truth. Some more than others. But if nothing else, I don't want you to think I'm not aware of my faults.'

'Ren, please... I've felt fucking awful about saying all of that since the words left my mouth. I don't want *you* to think that I reckon I'm flawless. Far from it. Jesus. I'm... I'm a dickhead. It's me who—'

He laughs softly, grinding me to a halt again. 'You're not a *dickhead*, Kayla.' He scratches his beard, looking over at the picture again like he can feel my hand there.

I want to touch him. Badly.

Ren sucks in a breath, palpably trying to lighten the

mood. 'To be honest, the main reason I didn't buy this is because I already have one picture of myself framed on the wall. Two would definitely be ego overkill, I think.'

He knows it's us... 'Yeah,' I say softly, relieved for even a hint of forgiveness, relieved that he's stopped me from melting down right now and throwing myself into his arms. It's still only a thought away. He framed the picture I gave him? It's on his wall?

'Speaking of which—didn't you say something about the drawing you made for me not being worth anything? I thought I saw twenty-five hundred on one of those tags.' He leans towards me and knits his eyebrows together in that unbelievably sexy James Dean way that I can hardly endure. 'So I think you might be wrong...' I chuckle tentatively, but his smile fades. His eyes drill into mine, and he adds, his voice a low rumble, '... About everything.'

We're lost, our gazes fixed on one another, so I jump when I feel a large warm hand on my back. Another moves out into the space between us.

'Hey. I'm Marcus,' he says, nodding at Ren. 'You're the movie director, right? We ran into you outside the bar a couple weeks ago?'

I turn and look up at Marcus. His jaw is tight, though his tone is perfectly friendly. Ren shakes his outstretched hand. 'That's right. Hey, man. Ren. Good to meet you.' He withdraws, shoving both his hands into his pockets.

Well this is fucking uncomfortable.

'How are you doing?' Marcus asks, lowering his head to

talk to me, his hand still on my back, rubbing a circle. 'Sorry I got held up. Still nervous? You can't be, right? I mean, look at this place.' His eyes crinkle at the corners as he smiles down at me, but I'm still too aware of Ren, standing in front of us having procured a glass of champagne as a waiter carried another tray past. He drinks it down to the middle quickly.

'No, it's… It's amazing. I'm fine. Err, actually, I should probably…' I gesticulate with "walking fingers" pathetically to indicate that I should circulate a bit more. I step away from Marcus's hand, just a bit, but I can sense that he notices.

'Well, I guess I should get going,' Ren murmurs.

'Yeah, thanks for keeping her company,' Marcus says pointedly. Testosterone is starting to seep into the atmosphere around us, and I purse my lips.

'I just wanted to stop by and see the work.' Ren takes a step forwards. 'It's incredible, Kayla. Congratulations,' he says quietly. His hand skims over one of my bare shoulders, pulling me gently towards him, and he slowly presses a kiss against the soft skin of my temple. He steps back, and I don't know where to look. He nods at Marcus. 'Good to meet you, man.' He turns back to me, and something in his eyes makes this seem far too final. Maybe it is.

I want to stop him. I want to go *with* him. Tears prickle in the corners of my eyes as Ren takes a breath, then says, 'Bye, Kayla.' He sets his glass down on a nearby table as he walks towards the door, hands in his pockets, and my heart wrenches as I watch him retreat.

Then I turn to Marcus, and my heart twists again,

because the look in *his* eyes shows a world of comprehension.

'Marcus—' I begin quietly, but he shakes his head.

'No, I… I don't want to ruin your night, OK? We'll talk later.'

'I'm sorry.' My voice is barely a whisper.

He shakes his head, then draws in a breath. 'I will say this, Kayla. You have a choice here. With me. It might not be the same as… As that.' He nods towards the door, and I swallow. 'But it's a choice.'

He's right. There's a choice to be made. I just have to make it, once and for all.

Twenty-Nine

Ren.

...And so I've been thinking lately about the idea of pride. It's an unexpected feeling, not one you plan out—it tends to hit you out of the blue, like an opportunistic mugger. And I'm the mug this time, it seems. In any case, thank you a thousand times to the people who came out to the Font Gallery to look at my scratches and etches and scribbles and such. To those of you who didn't, as a wise playground philosopher once said, "suck your mum". Though in this digital age, perhaps I'll forgive you for the restrictions of distance. So just "suck your mum" to those of you in the New York State area.

Yes, you haven't read this wrong. It is Wednesday, but for once I'm only semi-cynical.
Until next time.

—Kayla Joseph

I barely conceal the involuntary smile that comes to my lips as I finish reading. I scroll back to the top of the screen on *To Murder and Create*, considering starting her column all over again, but my stop is coming up soon so I grudgingly put my phone away, still trying to read between her words for anything that might be about me. Is she saying she's glad *I* turned up? Maybe? Jesus, my goddamn ego. Ironic I guess, given what she's written about in *Cynical Wednesdays* this week—but ego and pride are two different things. I should know.

It's been almost two weeks since I saw her, and I still can't shake the memory of being near Kayla and seeing her surrounded by her work—like that night in her studio but so refined now, so brilliant. And the way she looked with her dreadlocks hanging down her back in that incredible yellow outfit like some kind of insanely beautiful superhero, standing so close to me—the smell of her, and that smooth gorgeous dark skin where that jumpsuit thing buttoned together at her cleavage...

But. But then there was everything else.

I can't ignore it. Walking away from her this time felt like the end.

I shouldn't let my mind go there again right now. Not when I have to focus on work. I blink, trying to bring myself back to the present, here on the subway: the hard seat under me, the people around me. I think I notice a petite brunette surreptitiously snap a picture of me while pretending to look at something on her phone. I glare at her and she turns beet red. It's sort of satisfying because I need an outlet, pathetic as it is, but even at that I feel bad.

I stand when we reach 77th Street and head off the train,

making my way up and out onto the street toward the Pointe Hotel, steadily concentrating on getting my head in the game. I'm used to most fancy places now, but the Upper East Side still makes me break out in hives from time to time. Whatever, though. I'll endure it if it means Belinda Sherman will sit down with me about more independent financing, and bringing her considerable sway to bear on the potential distributors for *The Memory of Moments*.

At least I have this. Filmmaking is a sanctuary, even the business side of it. I'd never really thought about that until now: that I create to feel *safe*. To feel like myself, somewhere on this fucking Earth. *Man*. Kayla's questions, coming at me all over again. But I guess I am just about ready to accept now that this is really what I do, and that I'm happy with it. That I really can make art and make it accessible. That I can make it truthful, not trite. That I'm allowed to believe in myself.

She taught me that.

Now I just have to convince someone else. I draw in a breath, prepare to adopt my most charming demeanour, and hope Ms Sherman doesn't laugh in my face, or notice the fragmented heart I've got hidden just below my surface.

*

'So, how did it go?' Neela asks, grinning knowingly at me over her shoulder, and shuffling through a handful of mail as she heads further into our new office space. 'Right call to go see her solo, or should you have taken some backup?'

'Hey, I thought that kid—what was his name… Henry? Weren't you going to ask him to move these boxes?' I stall.

She stops in the cramped space between our desks and leans on one of the stacks of cardboard boxes stuffed with paperwork. 'Little Hank's internship finished on Friday, which was not a moment too fucking soon, Ren. Dude was like a thumb-less toddler for all the use he's been. I'll get Nick to help me when he gets back from Cabo.'

'Cabo? The trip was to Cabo? I'm paying that guy too much…'

She rolls her eyes. 'You're definitely not paying enough *attention*. Evan wanted to take him on a late birthday thing, remember? I think he's going to propose, but you didn't hear it from me.'

At least someone's romantic life is getting the happy ending. 'Yeah, because there are so many other sources in a three-person office,' I retort. I secretly thank my lucky stars again that she and Nick were so loyal as to not balk at the idea of a move East for Eden Street.

Neela frisbees an ancient screener disc at me. 'Anyway, don't dodge my question.'

I fail to stifle a grin. 'I think it's safe to say that after today, Ms. Sherman's going to be making our TIFF experience about fifty times easier.' I shuffle around the mess and slump into the chair by my desk.

Neela applauds theatrically, and then drops a bunch of mail in front of me. 'Great! Toronto, here we come! Roll on September. Hell, *I* might even endure the woman if she bumps our slot to Saturday night and gets us a bidding war...' She's interrupted as the phone rings loudly, and mutters about needing another intern ASAP, lurching over to her own desk with her black hair swinging down her back. 'Eden Street Productions...'

I start to look through the mail, kind of amazed we still get so much these days. It's mostly bullshit—but I stop suddenly as I recognize the handwriting on one of the envelopes. Why would she—? It doesn't matter. I'm tearing it open, my hands trembling like a fucking school kid.

If I Don't Have You

Kayla Joseph
173 Kenware Street, Apt 3
New York
NY 11222

8th August 2019

Dear Ren,

This is weird, I know. And I had to dig out
this old typewriter I bought at what you guys
call a yard sale, that I would call a jumble
sale, but potato potato. Hmm—that doesn't
really work typed out. The point is, my handwriting is pretty shit, but I remembered how
much I loved getting that postcard from you
and so I hoped that getting something in the
mail might bring a smile to your face like
you did to mine. But I had a bit too much to
say to fit on the back of a card. Too much to
say in a letter, even.

Sorry for writing to you at your office, but I
don't have the address for your dad's place.
We move about a lot, don't we? Hopefully soon
we'll stay in one place for a while. Either

way, I hope this gets to you.

Ren, I wanted to say thank you so much for coming to the show. I wasn't prepared for how much it would mean to me, having you there. I should have known though, given how it felt when I saw you standing in the street after all that time. And the night you came to see me at the studio. And before that, shocked at the door to my apartment. And before that looking down at me at the airport departure gates, and before that looking up at me from that bathtub, and before that sitting in a press junket with lights trained on you like a spotlight... It doesn't matter when it is, or what's happening. Seeing you makes me feel complete.

It's been hard knowing you're here in the city, so close. And yes, it hurt knowing that you'd been back and not come to find me, but I do understand. I fought SO hard to get back to being in control after you. Then being around you again, touching you, talking to you? It was like being back on some drug I thought I'd kicked.

Anyway. I mainly want you to know again that

I'm sorry, and that I was never judging you, in spite of what I said to you that night. I'm not even vaguely in a position to judge.

I suppose I'm writing this because I don't like how we left things. If you'd rather leave them there regardless, well, then I accept that too. Honestly, this time.

But if not...

Jesus.
If not—write.
If not—call.
If not—email.
If not—message me.
Anything. I don't care. Just tell me.

Because I'm willing to give up that control.

I must be addicted.

Kayla x

'Ren? Ren!'

I flinch as I finally register Neela calling my name. 'Huh?'

'Wow, what is that a blackmail letter? You totally spaced!

I'm going on a coffee run since we still haven't got the goddamn machine fixed. You want?'

I shake my head, staring down at the pages. Holy shit. I guess… Is that Marcus guy out of the picture? Why is *that* the fucking question in my mind? I know why. Even after all this time, it takes a lot to trust that I won't be betrayed. My hands are shaking. It seems crazy to be so amped over something like this. But it's her. Since the day we met, it's been her.

'Back in five, Sir Drift-a-Lot,' Neela calls, and I hear the door close. I pull out my phone and stare at it as if it's a completely unfamiliar device. Should I call her? I don't know what to say.

My thumb taps the keyboard, and I hit send.

REN:
   I got your letter.

I wait, the heat of my hand fogging the screen. Shit. I should say… I should have called. I should—

KAYLA:
   Good.

Good? That's it? Maybe she's changed her mind. Maybe this is fucking stupid.

But then I see the dots. She's typing more.

KAYLA:
Sorry, stuck in an endless meeting.

The smile on my face is almost embarrassing. I reply.

REN:
No problem.

I wait, seeing that she's typing again.

KAYLA:
Ren, pls can you message me your home address? Something for you. Best it not come to your work.

Hmm. I send it to her, bursting with curiosity, but I don't want to seem over-eager. Even though I'm overly eager as fuck. She types back 'Thanks', with a kiss that I literally stare at like her lips might come through the screen and really do it. I don't know what this means, but at least I know one thing now.

It's not over.

Thirty

Kayla.

I push through the warm damp air, feeling it coat my skin as the rain evaporates off the pavement and hangs in the darkness. I check Ren's message again, making sure I have his address right. Should I have just couriered the package, like I was going to? No, this is going to be OK... Hopefully. I'm trying not to worry. Trying to remember what Christy said to me when we flopped onto my sofa and kicked off our heels after my show a couple of weeks ago.

"*So who was that beautiful man in the suit I saw you talking to with all that intensity?*" she'd asked. And suddenly that was it: my floodgates were flung wide. She was actually quite shocked, and that takes a lot. I told her all about Ren, that night and everything afterwards. How I feel about him. How unexpected and fucked up it's all been. It was such a relief to tell someone, and sort of right that it was her. My sister drank it in and pulled me close, then told me to stop crying and just take that leap. The rest, I'd have to leave up to fate. It's had some funny ideas so far, but I think Christy was right as she so often, so infuriatingly is. But now I'm left with only hope in my corner. I don't want to live with regrets; maybe I'm not quite Prufrock, but I think I understand him now.

I juggle the cardboard tube that's tucked awkwardly under my arm, look at my phone again and notice it's heading towards eleven PM. I had no intention of getting here so late but by the time I got home, showered, agonised over what to wear and what to say and whether this was all going to end up a huge, heart-obliterating disaster, it was late. Then I decided to walk because it's not too far and I needed the air, but the air is about as refreshing as a steam bath.

And yet, it seems right. The suspended droplets calm me down, take me back to that night during the storm, when it all started to make sense even if I didn't realise it at the time. It reminds me why I'm doing this.

Finally I'm outside Ren's building, and I look up at the steep stairs leading to the outer door, my heart struggling to beat its way out of my mouth. I look up at the few illuminated windows above me. He's up there. Well, I think he is. Shit. What if he's out? Buzz the neighbours, leave it outside his flat. Or is that a bad idea? A thought suddenly grips me. What if he's not alone? What if *she's* there with him? What if...

Fuck this. I've come this far. Fate, do your worst.

I climb the steps slowly and squint at the buzzers before pressing his.

'Hello?' he says, his voice fuzzy with electronics.

'Hi,' I reply. Silence. Should I say something else?

'Kayla?'

'Yeah. Sorry, is now a bad time?'

'Uh… no. No.' A moment later, there's a loud buzz and the door clicks open. My sliders clack on the tiled linoleum interior, and I head up a good few flights of stairs before noticing his shadow cast from the light spilling out of his doorway. He takes a few steps down to meet me, and we both come to a halt. I rest the cardboard tube on the step next to me. The smell of something delicious is wafting out of his flat.

'Lucky for me they just fixed that buzzer,' he says, then rubs the back of his neck as he looks at me.

'Were you making dinner?' I ask. God, is that the first thing I should say? He looks at me for what feels like a lifetime, and I adjust the loose, roll-sleeved white cotton shirt I'm wearing, the one I'd screen-printed "YES/NO" onto the front of in black capitals on an impulse a few months ago. Was this a stupid choice of clothing? I only just realised it's more than a little bit ironic. Is it unbuttoned too low? I pull at the hem of my denim shorts self-consciously, and Ren finally seems to remember himself.

'Uh, yeah. I got in late.' He points at the tube. 'Need some help with that?'

'No, no, it's fine. Sorry, I shouldn't have just turned up like this. I could have just had it sent, actually. I… I should have asked if you had company.' My voice echoes down the stairwell, amplifying my awkwardness. 'I can just—'

'No! I mean, no. I don't. Have company. I wouldn't. Any more.' He frowns and shakes his head, embarrassed, but I have to stop myself from doing a jig. 'Uh, come up,' Ren says. 'I don't know why I'm making you stand out here, I guess I just sort of had to see you as soon as I could, like a chump,' he finishes his sentence in a murmur, and I chew my lip like it's spearmint Wrigley's. I follow him up the final few stairs and into his apartment. Ren lingers behind me at the doorway as I move inside.

'Oh,' I breathe. The light is low and soft, under-cupboard lighting in the kitchen, lamplight from a desk and a couple of floor lamps making it warm. A single tea light burns in a holder on a small dining table, flickering gently. 'This is… really lovely, Ren.' I hear him close the door behind me as I look around. Lovely is a completely inadequate word. Somehow it's so *him*, and I'm sort of taken aback to feel like I'm home. I take in the vintage movie posters and photographs, the dark wood furniture, the crammed bookshelves, the vinyl records, a small purple toy box, the sofa and the woven rug, the leather chair, the open-plan kitchen. The corridor beyond that must lead to his bedroom…

I turn around to face him, and Ren still hovers by the door like he's afraid to get too close to me. I'm kind of afraid to let him. He walks over towards the kitchen and I follow, watching his bare brown feet, his long toes. I usually *hate* feet but somehow, of course, I find his sexy. He's wearing flat-front khakis and another of his plain t-shirts, this one navy blue. His hair's all back in a messy knot, which should seem completely passé, but on him it's perfect. I'm not sure how much longer I can bear not to touch him. I'm still holding the cardboard tube, but I prop it against the counter and move over to the stove.

'What are you making?' I ask, lifting the lid off a pot. Fragrant steam rises to meet me. God, what am I doing? But I'm some bizarre combination of relaxed and unbelievably nervous, so it's making me behave strangely.

'Uh, it's *galinhada*. Chicken and rice. My mom's friend Ana Maria used to make it when we went to her place in New Jersey. My mom's a terrible cook, but she'd drag me to Ana's so I could have something Brazilian every now and then when I was a kid. I learned to make it so that I didn't feel too culturally disenfranchised or whatever.' He laughs a bit. *He's nervous, too.* 'Are you hungry? We can... Actually it's crazy I don't even know, you might not eat meat, or... or carbs or whatever.'

He takes in a breath as I turn and walk closer to where he's leaning against the fridge. 'I do eat meat,' I say, locking eyes with him, a small smirk on my lips, then I look away, horrified with myself. 'Sorry, that was weird.'

He laughs, and I'm relieved. 'Sounded good to me. Are you hungry?' I raise an eyebrow, and he shakes his head. 'That's not what I meant,' he says, still smiling, but something else behind his eyes. 'You started it.' He draws in another audible breath, shifting his weight. 'So what is that?' he asks, pointing at the tube.

I go over and pick it up. 'Oh. Like I said, I was going to send it, but then I just thought... Well anyway, you probably have an idea what it is, at least.' I look around. 'Then again, for all your claims about having my other picture up, I don't see it anywhere in here.'

'It's in my bedroom.'

The way he says it sends a warm jolt right through the centre of me. 'Oh.'

He looks at me for a moment. 'So, can I see it? The suspense is killing me.'

I nod, take a breath and prise off the plastic lid. I lay the cardboard tube down on the linoleum floor of the kitchen and nod to the other end.

'Would you mind holding it?' I ask, hearing my voice sound almost shy now.

Ren pushes away from the fridge and squats down to hold it while I start to pull out the large roll of parchment paper. I pause. He's not that close, but he's close enough I can smell him, clean and masculine and Ren-like. It almost makes my mouth water more than the food. I pull the picture out the rest of the way, still rolled, and stand up again. He follows suit. I take a deep breath, more nervous about showing this piece than I've ever been about any other, ever. I unroll it slowly, reaching my trembling arms wide to accommodate its span. I close my eyes, not sure I want to see his reaction right away. 'I... I'm sorry, I know it's not the one you liked at the show. Um, but I just wanted to make you something. Um, like, specifically for you. S-so I started to draw and this is what came out. It's a bit... I haven't... I don't usually work this fast so it's probably a bit rough still, I don't know.' My rambling rolls to a halt, but Ren is still quiet, and I risk opening my eyes. He's studying the picture I'm holding out in front of me. I count to twenty, to fifty. He's still looking at it. 'My arms are getting tired,' I whisper, and he finally looks at me.

'Sorry. I… Kayla, it's beautiful.'

I start to roll it back up, but he takes it from my hands and moves into the living room space, unfurling it on the rug and weighing down each side with book from the table next to the leather chair. He's still looking down at the picture, with that slight furrow between his brows. I stand next to him and look at it too.

I stare back at myself from the charcoal drawing: one bare shoulder slightly turned towards the viewer, resting my chin on my palm, one breast peeking out from behind my arm, the other hidden beneath my dreadlocks as they hang in front of me. My eyes are vulnerable, quizzical, maybe a bit argumentative too. It's unnervingly *me*.

'How did you do this?' Ren asks quietly.

I'm not really sure myself. It's almost too real. I walk away from it, hanging back by the bookshelves, remembering again why I avoided looking at it once I was finished. 'I used a mirror, and just sort of… I thought about things I wanted to say to you, things I have said, things you've said to me, things we've done. I just summoned it all into my mind and looked at the expression on my face, and that's what came out. A… a half-naked selfie drawing.' I let out a half-hearted laugh, but Ren just pushes his hands into his pockets and stares down at it. He won't stop.

'I think I'll be moving the picture you made of me out of the bedroom,' he says eventually, turning around to smile slowly at me, but his face falls as he sees the agonised expression on my face. 'Kayla?'

'Sorry, it's just weird seeing it again, I forgot how... It's just... It scared me a bit, the way it came out.'

Ren comes over to me, my breathing increasing in pace with every footstep he takes. My arms are tightly crossed over my chest, as if I'm naked in front of him right now, and he reaches for me and slowly unfurls them. He pulls my arms around his waist, and finally I sink in towards his chest. His own arms encircle my shoulders, and he sighs deeply.

'So, um, happy birthday,' I murmur against him.

He chuckles, the vibration against my ear, and I nestle in closer.

'Thank you. Jesus, I'm surprised you remember. I almost forgot myself.'

'Of course I remember. It's our anniversary,' I say, and lean back a little to look up at him. I'm only half-joking, and panic trickles through me as the words leave my mouth.

'Yeah. It is,' he says quietly, and pulls my head back onto his chest. His hand rubs up and down my back slowly, and I want to melt into him and be one. I inhale his scent. 'I'm starving. You want to eat?' he asks me eventually, his voice clouded with some emotion I can't place.

'Uh, yeah, OK.' He lets go of me, and I follow him as he starts towards the kitchen again, but he waves me away.

'No, no, go sit down. I'll bring it over.'

I settle at the dining table, feeling nerves churning in my stomach again. All he told me in his messages was that he got my letter, not really anything more. There's every possibility that at some point soon, the words "let's just be friends" are about to be uttered, and soul-breaking mortification will follow me out of this flat and onto the street and into my life forever. Jesus, and I thought I felt out-of-character-anxious at my show. Maybe I'm not who I thought I was at all.

I should just fucking *say* something—

I look up, startled out of my thoughts as Ren brings over cutlery and glasses, then a bowl of the chicken and rice he's made. The delicious smell wafts up at me. He hovers, and I notice he's proffering a bottle of red wine. I nod emphatically, and he fills my glass. I pick it up quickly, taking a long sip. Finally, he sits down opposite me, and I pick up my fork. 'This looks amazing.' I take a bite. It's… actually not that great. Ren grimaces a bit himself, and reaches for the salt cellar.

'It's a little under-seasoned,' he says. 'Sorry. It's usually really good, I promise. I got distracted,' he says pointedly. *Whoops.*

'It's nice.' I can hear the over-earnest tone of my own voice, and he pulls a face at me as he hands me the salt and reaches for the pepper grinder and hot sauce.

'I mean, yeah, maybe it could use a little kick, but it's really nice. To be honest, Ren, I didn't really see you as the cooking type.'

'Oh yeah?' He smiles at me. 'Cool, I'll try not to be

offended...'

'No, I just—'

He laughs. 'No, I can't front, I don't get to do it much. The kitchen was kind of surprised to see me.'

We're quiet for a moment, and I push some rice back and forth in my bowl. It's taken so long to finally reach a place of possibility with Ren, I can't help feeling like the rug is going to be snatched out from under me any minute. I want to hang on to this feeling between us a moment longer, where we can pretend there's not a huge undercurrent of emotion threatening to pull us below the surface. But no. *This is why you came here, Kayla. Stop being pathetic.* I draw in a long breath. 'Ren?'

He looks at me. 'Yeah?' His voice is wary.

I clear my throat. 'I'm worried you're trying to let me down gently, soften the blow, or whatever.'

The achingly *Ren* furrow between his brows appears. 'What do you mean?'

'Well, my letter was maybe a bit full on.' I close my eyes briefly and draw in a breath, trying to steady myself. 'I'm not used to really talking about shit like this. I'm not used to not being able to control how I'm feeling.' I reach up and rub my forehead reflexively, heat creeping up my body. 'If I'm honest, when I said I was scared before, that didn't really even begin to cover it. I was *terrified*. Because when this all started, I had this stupid plan for my life, and I didn't think that love could be a part of it. That... that *you* could be a part of it. I didn't think I could have you and still get everything

I wanted. And really?' I blow out a breath as Ren watches me, listening, because he does. 'Deep down I had this stupid doubt that someone as amazing as you could really *want* to be with me that much, and I thought I was proved right when you walked away from me.'

'Kayla…' He begins, then pauses, formulating what he wants to say. I take advantage of his thoughtfulness to keep spilling my guts, my soul. I can't stop now.

'The thing I didn't realise was that you're the answer to the question I'd been asking all along. It didn't matter how fleeting our time together was. I mean, that in itself is fucking scary. But… Being with you is the most real thing I've ever felt.' I reach for my wine and gulp some more quickly. My throat is sandpaper. 'And losing you was the worst,' I add in a whisper. 'I don't even know if you even *want* this anymore, if you still don't trust me, or… Tell me, Ren. If after all of this you'd rather—'

'Kayla. Wait. Stop.' He puts down his cutlery suddenly. 'You… You think I don't want this?' He pushes his seat away and stands up, then moves around the table to me. My fork clatters down too as he pulls my seat back. He takes my elbow and I let him guide me up to standing in front of him. I open my mouth to speak again, but he cradles my face in his hands, resting his thumbs on my lips, and I stop. He brushes them slowly back and forth. 'Kayla,' he begins, his voice low. 'I trust you. I was a *fool* to ever let you think any different. And now? I was trying to take it slow. Dammit, I'm just so fucking worried about messing everything up again.'

'D-don't be,' I murmur, barely able to form words.

'OK.' His hands sweep around my neck, up under the weight of my locs, down into the back of my collar, his fingertips tracing slow, sensuous circles against my skin. 'Because being cautious hasn't worked. Neither has staying away, or lying to ourselves. I don't *want* to be cautious with the way I feel about you. I don't want to wait another second.' His grip tightens at the nape of my neck. '*I want you.*'

Before I can react, Ren tilts my head and my mouth gasps open. He plants his mouth, hot and urgent, over mine and kisses me deeply, like he wants me to feel the words he's just spoken—and I do. God, I do. His kiss slows and he pulls away reluctantly, his face still so close to mine I can taste his breath. 'Kayla, I lo—'

'No,' I say suddenly, goosebumps prickling over my skin. 'Wait.'

We fall silent, just the sound of our breathing passing back and forth between us, and I can even hear the clock on the shelf ticking. I see worry in Ren's eyes, but it melts away as I smile up at him. Slowly I take a step back, and unbutton my shirt as he watches me, sucking in his lower lip. His eyelids grow heavy. I leave my shirt hanging open and undo my shorts, sliding them down my legs. I step out of them, and over to Ren, slipping my hands underneath his T-shirt and onto the hot skin of his abdomen. I raise them higher, up to his chest, feeling his body, dragging his shirt up a bit as I do. My hand rests over his heart, then retreats as I pull the T-shirt up over his head. His face is hidden a moment, and I miss it, even for that second. Miss his eyes on me, anticipating… I lean forward and kiss his chest, to feel the pounding of his heart underneath my lips this time. Ren pulls me closer, his hands inside my shirt as it hangs open, drawing my body against his, and I tilt my head up to receive his kiss again.

We stumble backwards, stopping as my back hits the exposed brick wall beside the dining table. My arms circle Ren's neck and I hop a little, wrapping my legs around his waist as he supports my weight, squeezing my behind, a glint in his eyes as he presses me against the rough brick. A laugh leaves me, feather light and breathless as he buries his face in my neck and begins to kiss and suck; the laugh turns into a moan. His hands are working underneath me, his long fingers edging towards the gathering wetness between my thighs, feeling their way, finding my wanting.

I drop my legs to the ground, just for a moment, and remove the thin cotton barrier, my knickers crumpling on the hardwood floor. I twist the button of Ren's khakis free, lowering his zip slowly, and he helps, pushing his trousers down and away, and his tight black boxers too. His erection is freed, and the breath rushes from my lungs. A moment more and my legs are back around his waist. He presses tantalisingly against my stomach, pushing up between us, his hips pumping fractionally against me, eager to find his home.

'Kayla, we should…'

'Like this.'

His eyes question me silently, cautious after what's happened before, but eager too.

'It's OK,' I say. 'I'm on the pi—'

His tongue sweeps in to my mouth again, and I can't speak. I reach down between us, and Ren grunts in the back of his throat as I guide him to my entrance, about to let him in. My breathing is coming in needy pants, a slight whimper at the end of each one. My legs tighten around him, and my hand moves away now, he's there, so close...

He sinks into me, pressing a word out of me, high and desperate.

'*Now.*'

'I love you,' he tells me. He slides out and in again, harder, deeper. 'I love you.' Again. 'I love you.' My hand finds his mouth, fingers slipping inside it, tangling with his speech. Tears hold, ready to drop in our locked gazes.

'I... love you... too.'

Then, just for now, we give up on words altogether.

Thirty-One

Ren.

'Are you still hungry? We can call for take-out.'

Kayla shifts against me, and I pull the blanket closer around us. After a moment, though, she lowers her feet to the floor, careful not to step on her drawing on the rug beside the couch. 'I really do think you're selling your... *gally*—'

I laugh. '*Galinhada.*'

'Exactly. I think you're selling it short.'

'It's gone cold.'

I can see corny thoughts forming in her mind just from her expression. 'But other things got hot,' she says, grinning ironically, and I groan and roll my eyes, flipping her onto her back and resting my weight on her again. It feels too good, I can't stop being as close to her as I possibly can. As I lean down to kiss her, something suddenly occurs to me.

'You know what?' I murmur against her mouth.

'Hmm?' Her response is muffled as she reaches up to continue the kiss.

I wrest myself away and sit up, pulling her up again too and then resting my arm over the warm skin of her bare shoulders.

'This place really feels like mine now.'

Kayla chuckles. 'You didn't shag in the living room when you lived here with your dad?'

'Well, only on the weekends.'

'Hah.'

She stands up, and I can hardly keep from staring at her beautiful body in this light. She looks over her shoulder and half-smiles at me knowingly, then bends over to pick up my T-shirt. She slips it over her head and rearranges her locs. God, I'm not sure if that's not even sexier, her wearing my shirt...

She returns to her chair at the table, where our bowls of food still sit, picks up her fork and starts to eat. 'It's pretty tasty cold,' she says through a mouthful, with a smile. I join her, picking up the box of matches on the counter to light another candle.

I can't believe this is real. I chuckle a little, incredulous, and she shakes her head.

'Have you gone a bit mental?' she asks, though the goofy grin on her face makes me think she's caught the same bug. I eat a mouthful of cold rice, and she's right, it is kind of good.

'No,' I say, swallowing. I think for a moment. 'Maybe. It's just hard to comprehend that I won't have to imagine now. What you're doing, where you are, how your work is, what you're thinking about. Fuck, I don't know, even... whether you like the sandwich place they opened on the corner down the street, or whether you'll think my buddy Mackie's really a elitist snob or just acts that way, or your specific views on our shit-show government. Or where I should put that jump cut, or whether that sentence works. I just… I won't have to imagine any of it. That's going to take some getting used to. That I won't have to wonder. That you might be in my life every day.'

Kayla smiles that beautiful smile, reaching over to weave her fingers in between mine. 'Yeah. I know.' She looks down at her bowl. 'When we first met, there *was* no obvious next. I suppose I felt like I could be open because I'd never see you again.'

I put down my cutlery and beckon her over to sit on my lap. I have to focus, since I'm only wearing my pants and she's not wearing any underwear…

'I get it,' I tell her. 'Being that way with each other was easier when it seemed like there was nothing to lose. But Kayla, I can't tell you how much it means to me to know I can see you, and talk to you, and be with you tomorrow, and the next day, and however many days we can be together. There's fucking *everything* to lose, and I plan to do everything in my power not to lose you again.'

She cups my face, kisses me between my eyebrows, then leans back and looks into my eyes. Way, way into me. 'Having tomorrows with you is everything I want too, Ren.' She brushes her lips against mine. 'So that's it now, yeah? We're in this. You can't complain if you don't like the coffee I buy when you stay at my place—What if you *hate* my place? What if I have some crazy collection of creepy porcelain dolls that you know nothing about?'

'Do you?'

'Well, no. But, there's other stuff. Like, you can't go getting jealous if I'm seeing… my friends.'

I nod. 'OK.' I know who she means. It'll take some work, but I'll try.

She smiles. 'And… What else? Well, you can't start getting sick of me not keeping my opinions to myself, or being a bit too—'

I stop her speaking with another kiss, and she shifts her weight in my lap, not playing fair. I fight to stop myself getting hard, because I want her to understand. 'I *love* your opinions, Kayla.' I kiss her again. 'And I will try not to be jealous or… insecure. If I am, it will be my shit to deal with. I won't take it out on you.'

'OK,' she whispers. 'And I promise to be open, and not to dig or nit-pick, or any other shitty behaviour. I'll trust you to believe enough for the both of us when I have doubts. I'll be better. I'll try, anyway.' She smiles, and I reach up and push her dreadlocks back from her face. 'Who knows?'

'Yeah. Well, I'm willing to take a few unknowns. You?'

She's quiet for a moment. 'Yes. Definitely.' She reaches down and unbuttons my pants, then pulls my T-shirt slowly up her body and over her head. She leans me back on the chair as she straddles her legs over me and settles back down into my lap. 'Unknowns sound good.'

*

'Are you going to give me a cuddle, then?'

Liv giggles, like she does every time she hears Kayla say that. 'Cuh-dool,' she repeats, obliviously mimicking her accent, then breaks out into another fit of laughter. Kayla leans down and tickles her mercilessly, then gives Olivia little choice but to comply as she drops onto both knees and squeezes her into an embrace.

'See you later, Olivia.'

Livvy ignores her and tugs at my leg. 'Let's do dancing again!' The kid starts to do some kind of shuffle and wiggle that makes me laugh pretty hard myself. Kayla holds up her hand and I help her off the floor, then pull her toward me and kiss her a little longer than I meant to. Seeing her with my daughter does something crazy to me.

'Hey! Watch me!' Livvy shouts, still shuffling.

Kayla smiles at me. 'Cole was playing some new guy from Houston's mixtape in the office, some unbelievably repetitive post-trap thing. It's already driving me up the wall, but clearly he knows his sh— stuff, given how mental this one's gone over it.' She holds a hand over Olivia's bobbing head. 'Start 'em young, eh?'

My mouth still goes a little tight over the mention of Cole, but I'm getting used to it. I know I'm hers and she's mine now. I know it's gooey as hell, but I can never not feel it, even when we're apart.

'Thanks for watching her today,' I murmur. 'I'm sorry it took so long.'

Kayla brushes off her shoulder like it was no big deal,

even though I had seen the look of fear in her eyes when I asked if she could look after Olivia for a couple hours during my meeting this afternoon.

'No worries. It was fun. Wasn't it, Livvy?'

Olivia's gone off to the corner to start unpacking her toys. 'No honey, I've got to take you back to Mommy and Yann's, we don't have time—' Too late. Still, at least it keeps her occupied for a second. When her back's turned, I kiss Kayla again, slipping my tongue in because I can't help it.

'Easy, cowboy,' she whispers. 'Come over to mine once you've dropped her home?'

My hands slide over the curve of her ass in response. 'Absolutely.'

She steps emphatically away and picks up her bag, shrugging on the embroidered denim jacket that she wore that night at the airport when we first met. That does things to me, too.

'Oh, so, shit!' Kayla exclaims suddenly, forgetting her attempts to curb her language. The kid's heard way worse from me anyway. 'Can I see it? Did you finalise the one-sheet?'

Damn. I was going to save it until tonight, but since she's asked…

I grab my bag and pull out the folder, opening it slowly. 'It's only a print-out for now, obviously.'

'Ren,' she breathes out. 'Oh my God. I thought they'd tweak it more. I mean, I-I didn't think you guys would go for the whole image—'

'Everyone freaking *loved* it, Kayla. Look at it, how could

they not?' I swallow a little. 'It's perfect.'

She reaches for the poster, running her fingers over the wording. 'Blimey, it looks so official with title and the actors and everything on here,' she whispers, smiling at her work—our work. A picture she made, on the one-sheet for my film. The first film that's finally felt like mine since... Well, since my life changed. Since all that pain, and gaining her.

The Memory of Moments.

In three weeks it'll be out there in the world, on a screen at Toronto International Film Festival, and out of my hands. I try not to think about that part too hard, try to concentrate on the light in Kayla's eyes.

'I'd better get going,' she says softly. She heads over to kiss Olivia on the head, then returns to me and presses her lips to mine. 'See you in a bit.'

'Yeah.'

I open the door for her and watch her head down the staircase. It's hard watching her go, but now I know—it can be a long time or a little, but we have it.

We have time.

Acknowledgments

This novel was a long time in the making, and I'm so grateful to Valerie Brandes and the whole Jacaranda Books team for believing in me, and bringing *If I Don't Have You* into the world. Cherise Lopes-Baker, thank you so much for your editorial insights. I'm thrilled to be part of the Jacaranda family for their incredible Twenty in 2020 initiative.

My gratitude and thanks to my agent, Sara Keane of Keane Kataria Literary Agency for all her efforts and support.

All my love and eternal thankfulness to my husband, Will, and my family—Larry and Valda, my brother Lawrence, to all my extended family of aunts, uncles and cousins, and particularly to my Aunty Laura for letting me know that I'm one of her favourite authors!

Thank you to my sister-in-law Deirdre for your huge encouragement with my drafts of this book, and to all my early readers for their feedback. Thank you to my wonderful friends, especially Cicelia, Micallar and Laura for your unwavering support. Thank you to Melissa and Natalie of Black Girls Book Club for providing an essential space for Black women—you're queens, as are all the incredible women I've met through BGBC.

Thank you, as ever to sweet inspiration, and to everything that is keeping me here—most especially, love.

About the Author

Sareeta Domingo is the author of The Nearness of You [Piatkus/Little,Brown, 2016], and the editor and contributing writer of upcoming romantic fiction anthology Who's Loving You [Trapeze, 2021]. She has also written numerous erotic short stories and an erotic novella with Pavilion Books. Her books for Young Adults are published under S.A. Domingo, including Love, Secret Santa [Hachette Children's, 2019]. She has contributed to publications including gal-dem, Stylist and Token Magazine, and has taken part in events for Hachette Books, Winchester Writers' Festival, Black Girls Book Club and Bare Lit Festival among others. She lives in South East London.

sareetadomingo.com // @SareetaDomingo

Photo Rosie Matheson